Gh of Redemption

B J MEARS

The Dream Loft

First published in Great Britain in 2015 by The Dream Loft
www.thedreamloft.co.uk

Cover photographic images provided by Winternetmedia. Image of
Prague's astronomical clock courtesy of Charles Sibthorpe. Graphic
design by The Dream Loft. Featured models: Oriana Weids, Dainelle
Grant and Joyy Tamsett.

ISBN 13: 978-0-9574124-8-4
ISBN 10: 0957412487

Dedicated to Ed.

*

Special thanks:
To Joy for your support and encouragement,
to my ever-diligent editor, Edward Field,
to Charles, Pete, Kate, Paul, Elliot, Ann,
Dainelle, Joyy, Oriana, and to all the friends
who have helped along the way.

'When a cloud vanishes, it is gone, so he who goes down to Sheol does not come up.'

Job 7:9 (ESV)

'Success is not final, failure is not fatal; it is the courage to continue that counts.'

Winston Churchill

Contents

Glossary of Terms

Brimstone Chasm: a setting and specific power of the contrap (a portal into a Hell-like realm).

contrap: a ghost machine with ten settings, each corresponding to an individual power or ability, powered by ghosts trapped within its realms.

contrapassi: jackal-headed, armoured giants (singular: contrapasso) of the *Brimstone Chasm*.

cloak/cloaked/cloaking: the ability of ghosts to become invisible upon demand (this uses energy and cannot be sustained for extended periods).

Flight: a setting and specific power of the contrap (giving one the power of flight).

Future Eye: a setting and specific power of the contrap (through which one can view the ghosts' conclusions about the future).

gallows iron: iron nails drawn from gallows or from coffins, or any other iron associated with death. Gallows iron has the ability to send ghosts on to another place.

GAUNT machine: (Guided Analytic Utility Necro Transducer) a machine that retrieves ghosts from the under realms and inserts them into the living bodies of selected victims to create *gloved* ghosts (gloves). During the process the victim's body takes on the dominant form of the ghost and is left with a faint blue glow to the skin.

GCHQ: the UK Government Communications Headquarters.

Ghost Portal: a setting and specific power of the contrap (a portal into a ghostly realm).

Ghost Squad: Tyler's selected team of ghost spies.

gloves: ghosts paired and joined (gloved) with living people.

GPS: Global Positioning System

Heart: a setting and specific power of the contrap (switching to the heart symbol turns the contrap into its ghost form).

Hell birds: huge, dangerous birds of the *Brimstone*

Chasm.

liliths: winged she-demons of the *Brimstone Chasm.*

JIC: Joint Intelligence Committee

NVF: originally revealed as *New Vision Frontiers*, the NVF is an underground neo-Nazi organisation, the Nazi Victorious Federation.

Past Eye: a setting and specific power of the contrap (through which the past can be viewed).

Present Eye: a setting and specific power of the contrap (through which the present can be viewed).

reveries: ghosts who have hung around their grave sites for so long they have become zombie-like. Prolonged proximity to reveries results in a zombie-like condition for the living, and ultimately leads to suicide.

Safeguarding Skull: a setting and specific power of the contrap (prolonging life, promoting healing and preventing death).

SOCO: Scene Of Crime Officers (UK's forensics police).

TAAN: The Activists Against Nazism.

Tower of Doom: a setting and specific power of the contrap, and the tower within the *Brimstone Chasm* (a device measuring one's progress and a means of locational guidance).

the oppressor: an ancient evil spirit/fallen angel who has appeared throughout history in the guise of men (Hitler amongst them).

Tree of Knowledge: a setting and specific power of the contrap (ghosts within the contrap answer questions).

wilco: military call sign meaning 'received' and 'I will comply'.

Agents & Code Names

Freddy Carter:	*Pratt*
Lucy Denby (Mojo):	*Pointer*
Melissa Watts:	*Cog*
Tyler May:	*Ghost*

(*Weaver, Klaus* and *Chapman* are only known by their code names)

Tyler's Notes

Rules of the Contrap

1. *Never use the contrap for too long. The ghosts within only have so much power and it could shut down when you need it the most.*
2. *Always use the balancing spell after releasing or collecting ghosts. Failure to do so may have catastrophic consequences!*

THE CONTRAP

BACK

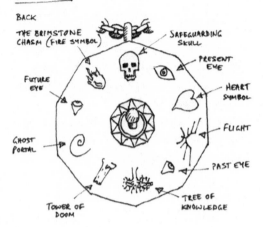

THE BRIMSTONE
CHASM (FIRE SYMBOL)

SAFEGUARDING
SKULL

PRESENT
EYE

FUTURE
EYE

HEART
SYMBOL

FLIGHT

GHOST
PORTAL

PAST EYE

TREE OF
KNOWLEDGE

TOWER OF
DOOM

SYMBOLS

- SAFEGUARDING SKULL — SAVES FROM DEATH
- PRESENT EYE — LOOK THROUGH WALLS, ETC (TELESCOPIC).
- HEART SYMBOL
- FLIGHT — MAKES YOU FLY!
- PAST EYE — LOOK INTO THE PAST!
- TREE OF KNOWLEDGE — ASK IT A QUESTION & IT ANSWERS
- TOWER OF DOOM — ACHIEVEMENT INDICATOR
- GHOST PORTAL — IT'S A GHOST PORTAL!
- FUTURE EYE — LOOK INTO THE FUTURE
- FIRE SYMBOL — ?   THE BRIMSTONE CHASM

FRONT

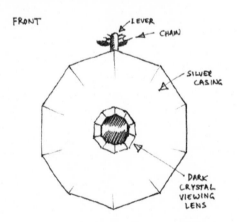

LEVER

CHAIN

SILVER
CASING

DARK
CRYSTAL
VIEWING
LENS

Prologue

Cold flagstones and barren walls enclosed the claustrophobic cell. A naked bulb hung blinking as quick footsteps approached.

The prisoner listened intently at the solid, iron door. He dragged himself away from its cold, rust-incrusted surface as it rattled. A guard opened it. The warden, clean-shaven and wearing a pristine, grey suit, strode in to place his satchel on the worn table, one of three basic furnishings in the dank cell. He eyed the grimy prisoner with weary tolerance, taking in the unkempt beard, the haunted eyes and gaunt complexion.

"You *will* tell me its location, one way or another." The warden's Austrian accent was heavy, his speech staccato. "It's only a matter of time and, perhaps, a good deal of pain. That is *your* choice."

The prisoner turned away to peer from his miniscule, barred window at the forest sloping away beneath his incarcerating tower, the middle of nowhere, Austria.

"Speak! Why do you not speak? Do you grow fond of pain?"

The prisoner faced the warden and met his imploring gaze.

"I will not tell of its whereabouts. By all means torture me until I die. Do what you will. I came to terms with my fate long ago. I will never tell you." He hobbled to his stool to sit as a guard blustered in.

"Sir, a word if I may?"

"Yes, yes. Not here. Step outside," said the warden, following the guard out. Leaving the door ajar they whispered.

The prisoner rose and limped to the table. He opened

the warden's bag to swiftly riffle its contents, pilfering a single page of blank paper and a pen. He pocketed his finds, re-buckled the bag, and resumed his seat with an air of innocence as the warden returned.

"I must leave but will be back in a matter of hours. I urge you to reconsider." The warden glanced at the prisoner's bare, damaged feet. "Your fingers are next and then it will be your knees. I do not enjoy witnessing these mutilations but, truly, it is your choice. Farewell, for now." He grabbed his satchel and left.

The jangle of keys accompanied the prisoner's pained smile as the guard locked the door.

Alone again.

He drew out the hastily folded sheet and the pen, straightening the paper. He knew a certain easily-bribed guard. He had tried and tested the man and, every time, the bribe had worked. He felt sure the guard would deliver his message in secrecy in exchange for the last of the gold sovereigns. The prisoner had managed to secrete the coins behind the brick air vent of his cell wall before his captors had strip-searched him and begun their long, gruelling treatments, all designed to loosen his tongue.

But what to write? If he were to give coordinates, his message could be easily understood should it be intercepted. If he used code, his brother might never decipher it. It was just as well, he thought, that he had predicted his capture. He considered words that only his brother, born and bred in Prague, would fully comprehend. He would need to use the path he had prepared for this exact eventuality; the three houses of the skull.

The Gates of Sheol

Deep fog stifled the air across All Saints' sloping grounds. It clung to trees and gravestones like reveries drawn to gallows iron. The gothic spire rose high, piercing the night sky, guarding the interred with stoic patience.

The ghost of Edwina Newton floated in shadow, the skirts of her midnight-blue bustle dress billowing. To her side, three girls huddled in Edwina's exposed grave, before them, an iron jewellery casket barely thirty centimetres long. Tyler May, an athletic agent aged eighteen, opened the casket's lid and peered inside at an overturned candle that perched on a layer of dry, dusty soil. The blonde intellectual, Melissa Watts and the no-nonsense Goth, Lucy Denby, also known as Mojo, watched over her shoulder expectantly.

"Hello? Is there anybody there?"

As if in answer, the dirt in the iron box crumbled in on itself, falling into an expanding hole. The candle rolled and dropped, vanishing into the void. Tyler leaned closer as the unearthly darkness spread across the base of the old casket. Beyond the liquid, shimmering fringes of the void, huge stone gates loomed like the monoliths of ancient and sacred places.

"What is it? What's happening?" asked Lucy.

Tyler stared into the hole, trying to discern details. It remained irritatingly vague and shadowy.

"It's another portal. I see a dark path leading to some kind of entrance, but it's closed."

"The Gates of Sheol," said Edwina, drifting closer. "It's the doorway into the underworld. Only the dead may enter."

Tyler called the names of her lost ghost friends. "Zebedee? Izabella? Kylie?"

No answer came from the gloom on the other side of the portal.

"What do we do?" Melissa asked, turning to Edwina. "We can't go in there."

Aloof, Edwina drifted towards her grave. "I must go now," she said before sinking to the casket, her essence morphing into ectoplasmic light as it smouldered and streamed into the portal.

Lucy lurched after her. "Wait! Don't go. You could help us find the others. Help us!"

"The others are here," said Edwina, her voice strangely disembodied. A blinding light burst fleetingly from the portal as it consumed her. Tyler peered after Edwina, straining to see into the pitch of the otherworld beyond.

Inside, Edwina approached the stone gates and the white light blazed again. When the light died a moment later, Edwina had gone.

"What was that? Where are they, then?" asked Lucy.

"I thought she said the others were here."

"I don't know," said Melissa. "Did she mean the Ghost Squad?"

"What else *could* she mean?" asked Lucy.

"She's gone. I guess she didn't feel like helping," said Tyler. "She's gone into Sheol. Fetch Albert."

Lucy left the graveside, returning shortly with Albert drifting alongside. He hovered over the portal and, feeling it tug at his essence, peered into the casket.

"Can you do it, Albert? Can you go into Sheol and bring out the Ghost Squad?"

"I'll try, Missy."

"Then do it. We'll wait here for you. Be quick."

He nodded, watching her pensively. "When you need me, seek me out. Goodbye, Missy." The bright light shimmered again from the portal as he morphed and entered as a stream of electric-blue plasma.

"Wait! What do you mean?" asked Tyler, fear registering on her face as Albert left her. The portal light dimmed and died. She turned to the two girls, now her only companions in the forbidding graveyard. "What did he mean: *When you need me, seek me out*?"

"I don't know," said Melissa, her frown intensifying. "I *really* don't know."

*

Albert stood beneath the towering stone gates. He reached out to touch one, feeling its rough, cold surface and was surprised to find it resisted his touch. The ground, too, was solid to him and he understood that the substance of this realm was confining for ghosts. Spirits within these boundaries were trapped and could not pass through walls or doors, or any solid object.

"Well, I'll be... I ain't never seen the likes!" He

stepped closer, consumed by an unwelcome compulsion to enter. He felt an unseen presence drawing him on and walked to the looming gates as, all around, a shifting darkness of living shadow lurked. Glancing back he glimpsed Tyler squinting at him as though through a puddle of murky fluid, mouthing unheard words, and knew she was beyond earshot. "So these are the Gates of Sheol," he muttered to himself.

Quiet voices shook him from the encroaching stillness.

"Speak your name, you who wish to enter."

"Who are you, spirit?"

Albert spun, seeking those who spoke.

"Where are you? Show yourselves!" He had not meant to sound so afraid. Lights birthed from the surrounding murk either side of the gates, growing until their brightness dazzled. Albert gazed in amazement.

"The *others*!" he said, taking in the solidifying beings and marvelling at their powerful, white-feathered wings, bronzed physiques and swords of flame. Albert squinted at the brightness of their eyes and had to look away. "My name's Albert Goodwin."

"Do not be afraid, Albert Goodwin." The *others* regarded him with curiosity. The one on the right dropped to one knee to meet Albert face to face and study him more closely.

"Do you wish to join the sleepers in the dust?" He examined Albert, head to toe. "There is something different about you, spirit." The seraph's voice boomed.

"I 'ave to go in to get my friends out."

"Your request is unusual," said the kneeling seraph. "On whose authority do you undertake such a doomed goal?"

*

The girls waited. Tyler climbed out of the grave and paced to warm herself while her mind spun.

"What if he never comes back out? What if he's gone? What if they're all gone for good?"

"Edwina said only the dead can enter," said Lucy. "She didn't say anything about them not being allowed to leave."

"I don't think she was interested in returning."

"Maybe not."

"Sheol is the domain of the shades, the disembodied spirits of the dead," Melissa explained. "The ancient Hebrew texts say there is no return from Sheol."

"We could... *You* could call up another ghost from the *Ghost Portal*," suggested Lucy. "Ask them about it. Maybe there's a way."

Tyler swore. "I should have asked Albert. I shouldn't have just let him go in like that. He could be gone for months, years even. Who knows? He might not know anything about Sheol. What I wouldn't give to have Izabella here right now."

Lucy checked her watch and kicked at a long tuft of grass. "If I ever get my hands on that Edwina it'll be the world's first recorded instance of a ghost being punched in the eye." Lip curling, she zipped her black leather jacket against the cold. "We'd better tell Chapman. Have a guard set around the grave. We can leave it open and have them report in if..." She caught Tyler's gaze. "...*when*, Albert returns."

Tyler peered up at the mist-occluded stars. "Okay. Call it in, but I'm staying here, at least until the relief shift arrives. You guys may as well go home. This is a dead end. No pun intended."

Melissa glanced at the casket and then at Tyler.

"Don't worry. Nobody's laughing."

*

Albert stepped back. The mighty gates swung slowly open and groaned to a halt. The two *others* inclined their heads as an ominous wind escaped from the way ahead, billowing through Albert.

"You understand you will not be able to call us from the other side? We shall not be able to open the gates. You shall be confined forever in the lightless and silent hollows within, the realm of the rephaim."

Albert looked over his shoulder before nodding grimly. "I got to try anyway."

"Then, Albert Goodwin, you may pass."

Albert stepped tentatively through the passage into a deeper darkness. The last groan of the closing gate at his back brought silence. The faint light of the grave's portal entrance and the glow of the *others* died with the sealing of the gates. Albert stood in quiet solitude. He tried to call Zebedee but the thickness of the air deadened his voice.

Then came the black mist.

*

The General watched. Of all the secret operations he had endured, his mission to stakeout the grave of Edwina Newton had been the most tedious.

Until tonight.

He spied from his hiding place behind the graveyard wall, peering through a rut in the top where two sloping stones formed a deep V. The lookout, the ghost they called Albert, had not seen him. He was quite sure the Victorian ghost with the flouncy dress was also oblivious, likewise the three girls who dug the grave, but things became interesting when Flouncy disappeared into the grave, followed by the boy. The General had been warned about the athletic girl with the dark skin named Tyler. She was to be avoided if possible, unless she began freeing ghosts from the box. *So far, so good. Not happening.* A ghost *entering* the grave portal was perfectly permissible.

He watched the three girls as they talked, and smiled wryly to himself when two of them left. Now there was only the dangerous one remaining on guard at the graveside. The General brushed a hand across the swastika on his sleeve and toyed with the gallows blade in his hand, eager for action.

*

Increasingly tired and hungry, Tyler stopped pacing. A loneliness she had not felt for a long time settled over her. She perched on a cold gravestone, missing Albert and the sense of protection his presence conveyed. In her hand she grasped a large, silver medallion with ten incised symbols and a central switch on one side. On the other, a dark, smoky crystal was mounted at the centre: the viewing glass of the contrap.

For a while she peered into the contrap's *Ghost Portal* wondering if someone of help might come to her, but the crystal lens offered only a mesmerising swirl of memory mist. She switched to the *Tower of Doom* and scrutinised the ruined tower to see it if was building or crumbling. It did neither but remained static, half-built.

What does that mean? I'm neither going forward nor backward in my quest?

She rose and paced to warm herself, fingers stone cold, and her clothes damp and chilled with dew.

What did he mean, 'When you need me, seek me out'? Does he not plan to return to me through the open casket? She knelt over the pit and called softly, her voice a megaphone in the quiet of the night.

11

"Albert? Albert, if you hear me, come back to me."

She spent an hour texting Klaus and felt guilty for disturbing him in the middle of the night. When he eventually told her he had to go she was left alone again in the eddying fog of the graveyard, shivering and trying to stay awake. Feeling wretched she allowed her mind to wander, recalling better times.

At the age of nine she had spent an unforgettable two-week beach holiday in France with her family. She closed her eyes and tried to recall the sensation of hot sand beneath her feet and the taste of fresh chocolate crêpes, bought from a wandering beach vendor. She pictured the smiling faces of her parents as they reclined in the sun on colourful towels, the scent of coconut oil tanning lotion mixing in the salty air.

None of it worked but her memories triggered a shadow in her mind.

Her relationship with her parents had soured when she had joined Chapman's crew at the age of fourteen. Their smiles were now rare when she visited. It was the same for Melissa and Lucy. Their parents' ferocious arguments and debates had persisted until burnout, and all six parents caved to the inevitable. It was an unusual and remarkable opportunity, and the girls were signing up to the secret services together or family relationships were going to be irrevocably damaged.

Tyler conceded. Her efforts to bolster her mood failed. She called Chapman and apologetically explained her situation at the graveyard.

"Don't worry. The girls filled me in. I've already dispatched agents to relieve you. I want you to leave the guarding to them, at least for a while. If Albert and the others return, our people will be there. I promise you'll be one of the first to hear as soon as they arrive. Go home. Get some rest."

"Yes, Sir."

*

The graveyard appeared very different in the light of morning. The school across the road bustled noisily with children and teachers. The street beyond the stone wall, crammed with cars, offered no parking for Tyler. She negotiated the narrow, sloping roads around the block until she found a place to leave her VW Beetle, a shade of Tic Tac green and complete with bulletproof glass. From there she walked back to the church.

All appeared well as she approached the gates into the grounds but rounding the church she noticed a small gathering out in the graveyard and knew something was wrong.

An unsmiling, dog-collared minister accosted her as she dashed between gravestones to the forensics tent.

"Hello. Can I help you?"

Two policemen guarding the tent greeted her wearily.

"Miss, do you know something about this?"

She pushed past to enter the canopy.

"Wait! You can't go in there! There's been a double homicide." They grabbed her by the arms, yanking her out of the tent, but not before she saw the two dead agents sprawled at the graveside, their bodies peppered with narrow blade wounds. Not before she saw Edwina's iron casket was missing, along with any chance of Albert's return.

A Very
Different War

Monday

Melissa collected her laptop case and left the apartment.

Lucy had the morning off and intended to be as lazy as possible. Looking forward to some time alone, she watched Melissa go. She dressed and put on makeup while listening to *Burn It* by Filter. Lucy never felt complete until her black eyeliner and mascara were on.

She made fresh coffee and toast, and was about to take the first bite when the doorbell rang. She reluctantly killed the music to check the live feed from the downstairs door monitor. The feed showed only a craze of static. She stared at the fuzzing lines with suspicion.

The bell sang again. Lucy returned to her bedroom, opened a drawer from her bedside cabinet and grabbed her P99. She snapped a full clip into the grip and took the stairs down to the outer block entrance. Closing one eye she peered through the door's spy hole. On the other side Melissa waved apologetically.

Lucy's mobile rang. She pulled it from her pocket.

"Hi, Klaus."

"Hi, Lucy. I just thought I'd check in with you and the Melissa. Everything all right there?"

"Yeah. Fine. Why?"

"Oh, no reason."

"Okay."

"Lucy, you would let me know if you had any... problems, wouldn't you?"

"Yeah, of course."

"Okay. Make sure you do."

"Okay."

"Okay, bye."

"Okay."

Lucy slipped her phone into her back pocket, unlocked and opened the door, scowling. Melissa forced a smile and shrugged.

"Sorry. Forgot my keys. Only realised when I reached the car."

"The live feed is down," growled Lucy.

"Yeah, I meant to tell you. I noticed yesterday. Can you fix it?"

*

Tuesday

Tyler dumped more bags onto the living room floor of Harrow's End, 6 Nash Lane, Bromley. She peered around in dismay at the mass of packing boxes, heaped clothes on hangers, and bedding.

Don't worry about it, she told herself. *You can sort it*

out later. All in good time. Some mess is inevitable on days like today.

All the same, she hated the disruption and disorder of moving house. It wasn't that she didn't enjoy Melissa and Lucy's company, but life had become too complicated in the three bedroom Dulwich apartment. She had lost Albert, the ghost who watched over her like a guardian angel, and nothing could be worse. Klaus, the rugged, blond, German agent with whom she was smitten, had been called away on a covert operation in Iraq. Even with the girls around she had felt too vulnerable. With three living together there was always somebody coming or going. Never a moment's peace. Never a minute when she knew her surroundings were unchanging. Tyler needed control, needed her own space, now more than ever, and this was her way of making that happen.

She thanked the removals men and waved them off as their lorry lumbered from the drive. Everything was in. It was now only a matter of making sense of it. The kitchen bore an unpleasant, stale odour. She cleaned and polished every surface, scrubbed tobacco smoke stains from the walls and sprayed copious plumes of air freshener. An hour later she brewed tea and sat at the kitchen table, sipping from her favourite mug and surveying her work with the back door wide open, the smell much improved.

Finishing her tea she checked her watch and sought new places for her cutlery, china, pots and pans. She frequently plundered the boxes in the living room for missing items and more than once wondered if refusing help from her closest friends, Melissa and Lucy, had been the right thing to do.

No. I can't get everything straightened out with them

17

*running around and tripping me up, having to ask where
everything goes. Better to do it all myself and know where
everything is.*

The sudden noise of thin parcels dropping through
her front door startled her out of the pantry.

What a way to spend your birthday.

Still, she wasn't exactly in the party mood. *Nineteen,
a spy and a ghost haunter with her own ghost machine.* It
wasn't as glamorous as it sounded. Most of the time, it
was boring. The rest of her life was just plain terrifying.
Ghosts and foreign agents were out for her blood, not to
mention the insidious gloves: those infamous Nazi ghouls
joined with stolen, innocent children. Three remained.
Three were out there, somewhere. Three never left her
waking mind.

She collected the brown paper packages from the
doormat and ditched them on the pile on the sofa. They,
too, could wait until later. She noticed one of the
packages was out of line with the others and shoved it
back into place, frowning. *Not like me to leave it like that.
I must be losing it.*

As the sun edged towards the horizon, she peered
out approvingly from an upstairs window across the fields
and roads that backed onto her Victorian house. It was a
nice enough view, but that wasn't why she liked it. It
afforded her an uncompromised view of her surroundings. The nearest woodland was a quarter mile away.
The closest house lay across the adjacent farmland. On
all sides she could see exactly what approached the
property, day or night. *That* is what she liked, although it
would be a day or two before the surveillance cameras
were installed and then she would be able to see all
approaches from one bank of monitors. The deep, cool

wine cellar, another appealing feature, would make an acceptable panic room once her planned alterations were installed.

She allowed herself one disruption to the otherwise pristine white of the kitchen, a single photograph of the ghost, Albert Goodwin, which she stuck to the fridge door. Three months had passed since she had last seen him.

"Wish you were here." She ran a finger the length of the picture feeling like everything was changing, everything was missing.

She picked up a stray teaspoon from the work surface and put it away.

As evening closed in she fantasised about Klaus joining her there in her house and wondered if that would make things better. Through the kitchen windows the badly kept vegetable patch lurked in February's late shadow. The days were growing longer but not quickly enough for Tyler. She flicked on the kitchen light and wound through each of the unfamiliar, box-cluttered rooms and hallways, illuminating as she went. Tonight she planned to work late, organising her home. She liked the light. Memories of dark passages and night-time, covert operations flashed frantically in her mind. Reveries groping towards her. Explosions and gunshots in the gloom. Gloved ghosts with glowing, pale-blue hands and heads, darting in shadows.

Yes, she liked the light.

The light was good.

She glanced at the kitchen clock.

It's later than I thought. Better start work on the bedroom so I have somewhere to sleep. The rest can wait 'til tomorrow.

At eleven thirty-five she took a break, heading to the kitchen for a mug of hot chocolate and sat cross-legged at the table, peering out of the window. She noticed another stray teaspoon on the countertop and with growing concern dropped it into the drawer, sure she had not left it out. Sensing a ghost nearby, she shivered.

Not Albert, so who?

She hurried to the lounge and stared at the present, once again out of line. She shoved it back in its place and looked around at the blank walls before returning to the kitchen.

Nobody there, at least, nobody I can see!

The world beyond the glass of the kitchen windows was fully dark now and she wished she had hung blinds. The room felt stark, but at least it was warm. The window panes, chilled by the night air outside, fogged with the kettle's steam.

She crossed to the sink and reached up to open the narrow top window as a sudden buzzing jolted her heart. She collected her mobile from the table and hit receive.

"Hi, Melissa."

"Happy birthday, you."

"Thanks."

"I thought you'd still be up. How's the new pad?"

"Right now it's pretty creepy, but that'll change when I've sorted things out." She wiped condensation from a window and squinted out into the garden, thinking she had seen movement. Slug-eaten cabbages decayed in sad rows.

Probably just the wind. A neighbour's cat, perhaps.

"Did you open my present?"

"Not yet. I haven't opened any. It's on my list for tomorrow." Tyler turned from the window to put the kettle on again. One cup was not enough tonight.

"We nearly dropped round but you said you wanted to do it all by yourself."

"Yeah. Thanks for understanding. Sorry. I wish you were here, now. Why don't you drop by tomorrow afternoon, around three? I should be more organised by then."

Melissa consulted Lucy at the other end of the line. "Sure. We'll do that."

"Great. Still no word on Albert?"

"Nothing this end I'm afraid." A tense silence. Again Tyler sensed the closeness of an uninvited spirit. Melissa continued. "Our place feels weird without you and I can barely sleep. I'm too busy thinking about what the NVF ghosts might be planning next."

The kettle, still hot from its last use, boiled quickly. Steam hazed the air to cast waltzing shadows across the work surface, and a foreign shadow joined them. Tyler watched it with concern, her pupils dilating.

"Tyler? Tyler, are you there?"

"Hang on, Mel." Slipping a narrow blade from her jeans, Tyler spun around to meet a phantom face on, surprising him with a quick, upwards stab. The ragged ghost of a German World War Two soldier groped at her, pinned by the blade. His eyes widened in shock and he dispelled with a shriek as his blade of gallows iron fell harmlessly to the tiled floor.

"Tyler? You okay? What was that?"

"Nothing. I'm fine. Mel, this is going to be a *very* different war from anything the world has seen before." She returned to the sink, closed the window and latched it.

"You can say that again. In 1939 Hitler started World

21

War Two by invading Poland. This time round he's letting his ghosts do all the work."

"I think he may have put a price on my head."

"If it's any consolation, I don't think you're the only one."

"Any luck with the ring?" A little over three months ago, Lucy had snatched a ring of gallows iron from a packing crate on the Mariana before the crate was lost overboard. Melissa now wore that ring.

"No. I've tried a hundred different things. Read the list of names forwards, backwards, every which way. Tried numerous pronunciations. Worn the ring on every finger I have, *and* thumbs. Nothing. Not a single reverie."

"You think it's a fake, or maybe not real gallows iron?"

"Who knows? I'm wearing it all the time anyway, just in case I think of something."

"Good idea. Listen, Mel, I gotta go. Sorry. I have to lock down the house before I can sleep. Good luck with the ring. We could really use it. Keep safe."

"Thanks. You too. See you tomorrow."

"See you then. Bye."

She dumped the phone and checked that every window in the house was closed and locked. Tomorrow she planned to install wire mesh guards to prevent ghosts from slipping narrow gallows blades into the house when windows were open. She took a power drill and, slipping outside, screwed the letterbox shut with tamper-proof screws before hammering used coffin nails into each of the old, pitched timbers of the house. She didn't know if the nails would truly ward off unwanted ghosts but Izabella was not around to ask. It didn't matter that her letter box would cease to function. As of tomorrow, all her post would redirect to her MI6 office where it would be x-rayed and checked by sniffer dogs before landing on her desk.

Back in the lounge she found the present out of line again and left it there.

Returning gratefully to the warmth of the kitchen, she made hot chocolate and headed upstairs to bed. Tonight she would sleep with her P99 and a gallows blade under her pillow, and the contrap safely around her neck. She muttered to herself as she climbed.

"Stupid, Nazi ghosts messing with my life..."

*

Wednesday

Tyler rose early and set to work on the house again. She took a tea break mid-morning and opened some presents, this time ignoring the usual out-of–place teaspoon, a moved ornament on the fireplace and a book that had fallen from a shelf for no natural reason.

Lucy's gift was a double-sided knife bandolier handcrafted in black, Italian leather. She filled the six sheaths with gallows blades and tried it on. It was on the bulky side but she imagined it might go unnoticed beneath a jacket or coat. Next she opened Melissa's present, a book titled Peace of Mind. Tyler smiled at the thought.

Some chance.

By the time Melissa and Lucy knocked on the door later that day, Tyler had organised the living room and cleared the hallway of boxes, and the house was beginning to feel like home. She made drinks, found biscuits and played host as they sat in the lounge, her friends taking in the unfamiliar surroundings.

"Nice place." Lucy looked awkwardly at the antiquated mouldings around the ceiling and hanging lights.

"Yeah, thanks. Thanks for the presents, too. Very thoughtful."

"You're welcome."

"That's okay."

They sipped. Lucy unpacked a C7 assault rifle from a case and started breaking it down into its various oily components on Tyler's coffee table. "I brought a little homework. I hope you don't mind."

"Is the fireplace original?" asked Melissa.

"I think so."

"I was thinking, we should split up the remaining artefacts so that at least we all carry one part for each of the remaining gloves," suggested Melissa.

The others nodded and they pooled the remaining artefacts onto the coffee table: two finger bones from Reinhard Heydrich's skeletal remains, two from Josef Mengele's, and a pocket knife and comb once belonging to Adolf Eichmann. They decided Tyler should keep the pocket knife and a bone each from Heydrich and Mengele. Lucy cut a section of the comb small enough to fit into one of the silver money capsules she wore around her neck. Melissa kept the larger remaining part. Lucy cut the other bones in half with a knife she pulled from her boot, and handed Melissa her share for safe keeping before dropping her halves into their respective capsules. Tyler and Melissa put their shares of the artefacts into their respective zip-lock forensics bags.

"At least we'll be ready if any of them show up." Lucy resumed polishing the C7 barrel interior with a cleaning rod.

"Except for Angel. Mengele's bones didn't work on him, so we still need a Hitler artefact if we're to catch Hitler, Mengele, Angel, the oppressor—whatever you call him—with the contrap's draw."

Tyler had learnt enough about the enemy they dubbed Angel to know he was originally the *gloved* ghost of Joseph Mengele. When Tyler had temporarily lost the contrap, Mengele's *glove* had taken on board the ghost of Adolf Hitler, rescuing him from the *Ghost Portal*. The ghost of Hitler also had history. He was the same ancient spirit who had dwelt amongst the Egyptians when they enslaved Israel, and the Babylonians when they took Jerusalem in ancient times. He coerced the Syrian king, Antiochus Epiphanes, into the sacking of Jerusalem and the murder of her people. He led the Romans in their campaigns to enslave the nations. He inhabited the murderous emperor, Nero and he brought about the crusades.

Conversation reverted to mundane comments about Tyler's new house until Melissa changed the subject.

"Listen, Tyler, we didn't just come to see the house. We need to talk. Something odd's going on."

"What?"

"Have you heard from Chapman recently?" asked Lucy. She oiled the trigger mechanism and rubbed it dry with a grimy, yellow cloth.

Tyler shook her head. "No."

"Neither have we. Check your phone."

Tyler fetched her mobile and checked for messages.

"I have a text from MI6, but it's not from Chapman. It's from Yash. That's unusual."

"Yeah. He's calling us in, first thing tomorrow morning."

"You think there's a problem with Chapman?"

"Maybe. I guess we could be leaping to conclusions but he usually lets us know if he's away for any reason."

"When was the last time he contacted you?" asked Lucy, snapping her gun back together with practised speed.

"About two weeks ago. I figured he was just busy or leaving me to get on with this." Tyler gestured at the house around them.

"Thing is, when he's busy, we're usually busy."

"Yes. What about Freddy? Weaver? Have they heard anything?"

"They're out of the country on operations. Even *we* aren't allowed to know where, or what they're up to."

Lucy finished reassembling her C7 with a loud click that made Melissa jump. Tyler stared into her cup.

"Great."

*

When Melissa and Lucy had left, Tyler shopped and returned to work manically on the house. The girls had been called in and that could only mean one thing: they were going to be sent on another mission. She wanted, needed, her house to be in order before she left.

She unpacked more boxes and stowed away linen and clothes, reserving the second bedroom for her operations gear. At first glance the room appeared as any other, but sliding back the full-width closet doors revealed armoured cases, black bags, several guns and an array of gallows blades all in a locked unit along with her Taser. To one side, hangers held a range of Kevlar jackets and other special ops clothing with boots below. She finished organising and cleaned the room before closing the door and moving on. By late evening she had finished unpacking and was again cleaning compulsively, the TV on in the background as company.

A war correspondent told of harrowing attacks in Palestine during ropey footage of bombing raids and buildings reduced to rubble. A series of updates from twelve other war-torn locations followed. Egypt's borders changed daily. Syria was under constant bombardment. Russia was invading Kazakhstan. Britain and the USA were targeted daily by terror attacks. The broadcasts had ceased to name those killed in the spreading conflicts long ago, opting instead to quote death-toll figures for individual zones. Thousands of new UK conscripts were packing up and shipping out to the many and various front lines. Tyler knew some of them personally; men and women with meaningful lives to live, fathers, brothers, daughters and wives; people who did not deserve this.

The casualties of this war already extended to several family members: Tyler's Uncle John, her nephew, Joshua, and her two cousins, Regina and Marshall. Everyone else she knew had a similarly depressing list.

She swallowed guilt as the images rolled. The world had gone mad and she wasn't doing enough to prevent it. When the report switched to Iraq her interest heightened.

Klaus! He was out there, somewhere.

Video footage cut from levelled buildings to American and British ground troops, mass graves and mourning Iraqi citizens, and Tyler had to look away. The program concluded with a story covering the growing number of disappearing heads of state and politicians across the globe. She knew what, or rather *who*, had caused it all to blow up like this, and she intended to find them and stop it. The most frustrating thing was the waiting, but perhaps tomorrow's meeting would tell her if she was to get another chance to take out Angel and the other gloves. Her stomach flipped at the thought.

Trying to shake the images from her mind, she ordered pizza, ate and began work on the kitchen blinds, kneeling up on the worktops to drill holes in the walls and screw in the fittings. She glanced outside, this time sure she had seen a figure at the edge of the garden. Dropping her tools, she slipped her P99 from her shoulder holster. She bolted out into the night in time to see a shadow leaving the stone wall at far end of the garden. She sprinted down the path and mounted the wall to stand peering across the dark fields on the other side.

"Who are you?" she called. "What do you want?"

Feeling suddenly vulnerable, she drew the contrap from her shirt and set it to the *ghost portal*, ready to collect any sinister presence, but the night around her was quiet and she sensed she was alone with only the grass stirring in the slight breeze.

Ernst Packmann

Thursday: MI6 Headquarters, London

Tyler, Melissa and Lucy exited the lift and turned the corner towards the department briefing room. They stopped suddenly when Weaver entered the corridor from another room a few doors further down. Weaver was a few years older than Lucy but they had fallen for each other on sight. She looked him over, meeting his fiercely intelligent eyes through the fringe of dark hair that swept from his brow. Her gaze settled on his strong wiry shoulders and ran the lengths of his arms and gracile hands.

"Weaver!" She bolted to him as his mouth broadened into a grin.

"Lucy, I didn't know I'd see you here." They embraced.

"Me neither. I thought you were out of the country."

"I am. I mean, I got back last night, but I'm off again later today. I thought it might be less frustrating to not tell you I was back at all. We can't meet up anyway. Too busy I'm afraid."

Tyler and Melissa exchanged glances.

"We'll see you in there, Mojo. Good to see you, Weaver."

"You too, girls." Weaver flashed a charming smile their way.

Tyler and Melissa entered the briefing room and Yash surveyed the gathering, his eyes betraying an unusual nervousness.

"Thanks for attending promptly. Take a seat." He closed the door, swept a speck of dust from his pristine charcoal suit and straightened his cobalt tie. His tightly-bound, black turban needed no adjustment. In all her time with MI6, Tyler had never seen it an inch out of place.

She glanced behind and noted the usual resentment smouldering in the eyes of the older agents. For a few, Tyler, Melissa and Lucy were far too young and inexperienced to carry the authority and responsibility of MI6 officers.

Along with the girls, several officials installed themselves in the incident room, busy with iPads. The more familiar agents gathered nearer the front: a large man named Perkins, an expert in computer forensics and IT tracking; Jenner, an attractive, sharply-dressed thirty-something, the department communications specialist; and three experienced field officers, the first a short, balding man named Harrow, next to him a spindly woman in her forties named Jade, sporting a secretarial appearance, and Blithe, a well-built man in his late twenties. All would remain in-house as part of the operations support team.

Yash continued with a stroke of his well-groomed beard.

"Don't mind our guests. I've asked them to sit in on your briefing." He nodded to the department heads and managers at the back of the room.

"What's this about?" asked Tyler.

"I'll tell you when everyone's here. Where's Lucy?"

"On her way. She's, er, been detained."

Jenner handed Yash a file.

"Here's the report from the last twelve hours, Sir."

Jenner waited for several minutes in a stilted silence while Yash perused the report. Lucy entered and Yash nodded. Jenner walked back to his seat.

"You're a disgrace to the service, Denby," he whispered as he passed.

Lucy yawned in his face and approached Yash. She opened her mouth to speak but Yash looked up from the pages to cut in.

"You're late, Denby."

"Where's Chapman?" she asked, glaring at the unfamiliar officials. "I only take orders from Chapman." She took a compact mirror from her bag and poked at her smudged lipstick.

"Mr Chapman is otherwise detained," explained Yash. "I'm standing in for him until his return."

"His return from where?"

"I'm not authorised to release that information at this point. Please take a seat."

"Okay. Let's hear what you have to say."

Lucy dropped onto a chair next to Tyler and plonked

her heavy Goth boots up on a desk, watching Yash with distrust and exchanging unsettled glances with the girls.

"All right," said Yash with forbearance. "Lucas Streicher, believed to be the main man behind the mechanics of the GAUNT machine." He swept a grainy image of Streicher onto the large touchscreen at the head of the room. "Modus operandi unknown. Location unknown. That is, until rumours of his recent movements reached us. If they're true, he's currently operating under the name Ernst Packmann. Commit his face and the name to memory. You'll need to recognise him and we think he's using disguises to move more freely."

Tyler's heart sank. *So no news on Angel, Adolf Eichmann or Reinhard Heydrich. What a waste of time.*

"Apparently, we're not the only ones after him. The NVF are trying to chase him down, though we're not entirely sure why. They might be hoping to re-recruit him, or kill him. We just don't know. It's conjecture, but we think he may have acquired something of great interest to them. We want to know what. If possible, you are to recover it and bring it home.

"What we *do* know is he's dangerous. We must get to him first. We can't risk him falling into enemy hands and, well, you've seen what one GAUNT machine is capable of. I don't need to tell you what a second could do for our enemy."

The girls nodded.

"There's something else: a single document has been retrieved, a letter he discarded." On the screen an image of a previously crumpled page appeared, the writing a crazed mass of jutting lines. "There's not much we can glean from this but one thing is of interest to us. The writer refers to someone in the letter called Sceloporus. Sceloporus is clearly someone important within the NVF network, but it's obviously not his real name. We need to know who he is."

Melissa sat up in her chair and looked from face to face of those around her. She finally settled her gaze upon Yash.

"You do know what sceloporus is?" She typed the word into Google on her tablet and hit search.

"No. Care to enlighten me?"

She turned her iPad to show Yash the resulting search images.

"Sceloporus is a class of spiny lizards. They live in America. You'll notice some of the images here show it with a blue head. That's one of the species. Do you know how many animals have naturally occurring blue heads?"

"I don't suppose there are many."

"It has to be a moniker for one of the gloves," continued Melissa. "The coincidence is too great. I know you haven't seen them in person, but in the dark they're really quite striking, their heads and hands glowing blue because the rest of their skin is hidden beneath their clothes."

"It could be Adolf Eichmann's glove," suggested Lucy. "Perhaps he's in America, hence the name. We don't know where he is or what he's been up to all this time."

"Nothing good," muttered Tyler.

"Fine," said Yash. "Look into it. In the absence of Mr Chapman, it falls to me to make some critical decisions. Our latest intelligence can't be ignored. Tell me, Melissa, how are you with Slavonic languages?"

"So so. My Croatian's not great. Why?"

33

"Because we believe Lucas Streicher will be smuggled into the Czech Republic. If we're wrong then someone has seriously gone out of their way to deceive us. At this point we don't think that's the case. I want you three girls to go after him. Confirm when you have a visual. With the recent increase in hacking capabilities we've noticed the NVF are leaning heavily upon old-school methods of espionage, so keep your eyes open."

"You want us to capture and extract him?" asked Tyler.

"Just report back when he's in your sights and observe. As far as the rest of the world goes, you're three university students of architecture on a field trip. Do your homework on your cover stories and use them well. Make it look good."

"You gonna give us any more clues?" asked Lucy. "The Czech Republic's a big place. We're not likely to bump into him by chance."

"Quite. A room has been booked in the name of Ernst Packmann at the Four Seasons Hotel, Central Prague." Yash passed manila files to each of the girls. "These photo-fits will give you an idea of his possible disguises, but Tyler's seen him before. There's a good chance she'll recognise him anyway. He's a portly fellow and he can't do much to hide that. He travels the day after tomorrow." He passed air tickets and a passport to each of the girls and handed Tyler a slim case full of banded wads of Czech Koruna. "I want you there ahead of him, waiting. You're going to need transport over there. Any preferences?"

"A car?"

"Yes. Your choice. We'll have it waiting for you at the hotel."

Tyler looked to Melissa and Lucy.

"I don't care as long as it's fast and reliable."

"We require a Ford Mustang Shelby GT500," gabbled Lucy. She shrugged and met Tyler's questioning gaze. "It's fast and reliable."

"But would three students be driving one in Prague?"

"Yes," said Lucy, unequivocally. "If one of them had a rich daddy."

*

The house was cold when Tyler arrived home. She turned up the wall-mounted thermostat at the bottom of the stairs, shoved a frozen lasagne in the oven and packed her luggage with obsessive precision. When she had eaten and had only to add her wash bag to her case, she wrapped herself in a blanket, opened the door beneath the stairs and descended the steps into the cool of the cellar. A team of technicians had worked all day installing the new system and she found it up and running. She sat on a black leather swivel chair and surveyed the exterior of the property through multiple wall-mounted screens, flagstones cold beneath her feet. Newly fitted motion sensing lights illuminated anything that moved and night vision cameras showed her all unlit areas.

She smiled. *This is more like it.*

A *cloaked* ghost carrying a single blade alone would trigger the alarm, send lights flashing on all relevant monitors, and instigate a tone that could be heard throughout the property. Her TV in the lounge was also rigged to automatically override any channel with the security system source when triggered, displaying the monitor feed in a small square in the corner of the screen. With a flick of the remote she could maximise the monitor image to full screen, if she wished. Single monitors rigged to the same feed serviced every other room in the house. If anyone or anything ever approached the property she would know about it. At least, that was the idea.

No, she would never feel *safe*, exactly, but she felt safer and more prepared to defend herself than she had for a long time. She locked up and checked the windows with their newly fitted, steel mesh guards. She armed the state-of-the-art alarm system and, reassured she had done everything possible to protect herself, went to bed, falling asleep in the greenish glow of the monitor mounted high in the corner of her bedroom.

*

Friday: Prague, 13:45 hours

The girls walked around the silver Ford Mustang Shelby on the hotel forecourt, admiring its form.

"Gangster glass. Nice touch." Tyler popped the boot and checked the gear Yash had sent with the car. They collected their guns and Tasers, quickly tucking them away into shoulder holsters beneath their coats.

"Can I try it out?" asked Lucy, with a wolfish smile.

"Be my guest." Tyler closed the boot and tossed her the keys. "Be back in ten minutes."

Lucy climbed in and roared away, returning precisely eleven minutes later to park the Mustang in a side road opposite the hotel. Tyler and Melissa crossed the road to the car. From here they would have an excellent view of the main entrance.

"Nice." Lucy tossed the keys back to Tyler before heading around to the back of the hotel.

*

Tyler scanned the faces of visitors outside the hotel through her field glasses, referring to the open file on her lap.

"He's the right side of tubby but it's not him. Why is it that when you're looking for a fat man, suddenly every man seems fat?"

More people entered the Four Seasons, passing brass luggage carts beneath the national flags flying from the wall. A suited footman in a peaked cap stood on duty by a set of revolving glass doors, hands behind back.

"He has to come through here, right?" Melissa squinted at pedestrians through a crack in the car window. "I know he's expected around three but are you sure we have the right hotel?"

"That's what the sign says." Tyler passed Melissa the binoculars, swapping to the *Present Eye* of the contrap and focusing through the solid walls and rooms of the hotel to the rear. "Mojo's parked up out back. She's watching the back door, pretending to tinker with her bike."

Lucy's matching helmet rested on the rear of her matt-black, modified Aprilia motorbike. She crouched at its side with an open tool roll laid out on the saddle. She reached into her leather jacket to take out her phone and study the screen.

"Someone texting you, Pointer?" asked Tyler over the Bluetooth comms set against her ear. Lucy and Melissa wore identical pieces.

"Just Weaver."

"Send him our regards."

"Will do."

"What do you have TAAN doing at the moment?"

Lucy had amassed a considerable membership of

TAAN, *The Activists Against Nazism*, contactable en masse via a single text from her mobile phone. She spent time each day spreading the word and growing the list.

"They're still on graveyard watch, though I've specified any disturbance is to be reported directly to the local police for them to handle. The NVF are still plundering for gallows iron."

"Can you get word out that we need a Hitler artefact? Maybe someone from TAAN can help us. We could post a reward."

"I'll get on it."

For the next few minutes Tyler and Melissa watched the front doors, Tyler continuing to peer through the *Present Eye*.

"Anything yet, Pointer?" Tyler asked.

Lucy's voice crackled over the system. "Nothing definite. Several, shall we say, *large*, old men but I don't think I've seen Streicher. Will keep you posted."

"Wait, that's him!" Tyler telescoped in with the *Present Eye* to get a better look at the portly man in a duffle coat and pork pie hat as he hauled baggage and dragged a wheeled suitcase towards the hotel. She peered at the open manila file on Melissa's lap to study a grainy, enlarged photograph of Streicher before squinting into the contrap's crystal again. "He's grown a nasty little beard, but that's him all right." She swapped for a long-lensed camera and rattled off several pictures, closing in on Streicher with each shot.

"Okay," said Lucy. "Standing by."

"So what now? I guess we wait," said Melissa, watching Streicher wrestle his bag through the rotating doors before disappearing into the hotel.

"Yeah." Tyler followed him with the *Present Eye* as

he signed in at the reception desk, took the elevator to the third floor and entered his room. He dumped his bag on the bed, deposited some money and a thick envelope in the room's safe, and ran the shower. Tyler stopped observing when he began to undress, and called Yash.

"Do you have news for me, Ghost?"

"Yes, Sir. We have visual on the mark. What are your orders?"

"Just observe for now. I want to know what he's doing there."

"Yes, Sir." She ended the call and gave Streicher a good half hour before she focused into his room again with the contrap. She found him tucking clothes into drawers and hanging shirts in the wardrobe.

"He's making himself comfortable. Looks like he intends staying a while."

An hour later, Streicher left the Four Seasons carrying a russet leather briefcase, and crossed the road.

"Pointer, the mark is carrying a briefcase, heading west. Leave the bike. He's walking."

"On my way."

Tyler and Melissa glimpsed Lucy joining the chase as they left the car and crossed the road to the corner where Streicher turned out of view past a restaurant.

"Keep right, Pointer. We'll stay left. Do you have visual of the case?"

"Yes. You think it's a drop?"

"Could be. Go buy a replica. Cog and I will stay on the mark."

"Seriously? Why can't one of you two go?"

"You have a motorbike. You'll be quicker."

Lucy huffed. "Okay, I'm going." She turned back.

Tyler and Melissa followed Streicher along the

pavement, threading between pedestrians and skirting a long frontage of tall, cream buildings. The noise of Lucy's Aprilia kicking into gear reached them through their ear pieces. Passing bars, banks and shops they shadowed Streicher deeper into the centre, arriving at the old town square with a cobbled open space and a dominating memorial statue.

"That's Jan Hus," explained Melissa, pointing out the tall statue of a bearded man cast in sweeping robes. "He was burned at the stake in 1415 for heresy against doctrines of the Catholic Church."

"Nice," said Lucy.

"Not that I don't appreciate the sightseeing tour, but do you think we can stay on track?" asked Tyler.

"Sorry."

"How's the shopping, Pointer?"

"I found a place that sells bags. I'm going in now."

"Wait. Where's he gone?" Tyler searched for Streicher in the crowd of tourists he had joined. "Cog, do you have visual?"

"No. He's vanished."

"We better split up. Cog, go that way." Tyler pointed towards the back of the memorial. "How did he do that?"

"He's sneaky," said Melissa. "He's made a living from being a sneaky dirt bag and he's good at it."

"He *must* be here somewhere." Tyler circled the memorial as Melissa entered another road. "This is useless. First chance we get, we put a tracer on this guy."

"They have an identical bag. I'm buying it now." They heard Lucy's brief exchange with the shopkeeper."

Twenty minutes of searching the square and surrounding streets of tall, ornate buildings turned up nothing until Lucy called over the comms.

"I have him. The clock tower, opposite Jan Hus. There's this amazing clock, lower down on the wall. Our mark has a weird fascination for it."

"That's the astronomical clock. On my way," said Melissa. Tyler crossed the square to the base of the brown stone clock tower. At the top of each side of the tower, large clock faces showed the time, but a more interesting clock near the base displayed the cycling months. She spotted Lucy carrying the new case among the milling crowds and soon after located Streicher.

"I see what you mean, Pointer." Tyler took out a sketch pad and pencils from her bag and began sketching the clock. Melissa joined her and played along to blend in with the other tourists and art students, riffling through her bag for her sketchbook. They worked away, sketching its two circular faces and the little curving roof that jutted from the sandstone tower to protect its intricacies from the worst of Prague's weather. The clock faces themselves were complex, the upper one showing a smaller dial denoting the positions of the Sun and Moon in the sky, surrounded by a larger time of day dial. On the calendar dial of the lower clock face, illustrated medallions picked out in gold represented each month.

While they sketched, Streicher stood back from a small cluster of tourists photographing themselves in front of the famous clock. He gazed, transfixed by the upper of the clock's two embellished faces and placed his case on the ground to take several photographs with his mobile. A few minutes later, satisfied with his study, he walked back into the square, bought a newspaper and headed towards the memorial where he sat at one end of a bench beneath the statue, depositing his case on the cobbles at the side. He opened his paper and read as the girls observed from a distance.

Tyler had a feeling something was about to happen.

"It's the drop point. Pointer, stay with the bag. Swap it the instant he's gone if you get the chance. I'll stick with Streicher. Cog, stay and back up Pointer."

Streicher folded his paper and left the bench.

"Okay, this is it. He's left the bag. You're up, Pointer," said Tyler, following Streicher out of the square. "Wait! Get a tracer on the case before you make the swap."

Lucy strode towards the bench, case in hand, as more tourists flocked into the area.

"Don't worry, Ghost. I'm way ahead of you."

The Astronomical Clock

Lucy threaded through the crowd and sat on the vacant bench where Streicher had sat. She checked around to see if anyone was observing her. As far as she could tell, they weren't. Around her tourists chattered in a cacophony of varying languages and snapped photographs. Behind this living screen she grabbed Streicher's case and slipped the replica in its place. She milled among the sightseers as their tour guide led them away to the next spectacle and, moments later, she headed off alone.

"Ghost, I'm getting this case out of here."

"Good work, Pointer. Cog, watch the decoy. Document the collection and follow. I want images and an address."

"I'll do my best," said Melissa.

Tyler shadowed Streicher back to the Four Seasons

and sat in the car while he drank beer and watched television in the hotel bar. She observed him through the *Present Eye* until Lucy startled her by rapping on her window six inches from her face. Tyler let her in and they stared at the brown case on Lucy's lap.

"What do you think it contains?" asked Tyler.

"Only one way to find out." Lucy tried to slip the catches but the case was locked.

"We have tools back at the hotel."

*

Tyler passed a screwdriver beneath the locks and prised them open one after the other.

"Here goes." She opened the case and took a long look at the contents. "That's disappointing."

"Old newspapers." Lucy lifted out a paper to study it. "It's local, only a few days old." She took another. "The same. It's ballast, to make someone believe there was something in the case. You think he knew he was under surveillance?"

"I don't know. Maybe it was just a test." Tyler tipped the case upside-down, emptying the contents onto her bed. "Nothing but newspapers." She checked for a false bottom and, finding only the solid case edging and polished leather trim, dumped the case back onto the bed. "What a waste of time."

"Like Mel said, that man's a sneaky dirt bag."

Melissa knocked and Tyler let her in. She pushed past into the room and shuddered as Tyler closed the door.

"I really don't like fieldwork. When I get home I'm asking Chapman for a desk job."

"If he's there."

"How did it go?" asked Tyler.

"I waited for an age and thought nobody was coming for the bag, but then this tall blonde in a fur coat bustled up and sat on the bench. She smoked a cigarette with one of those long holders and when she'd finished she left with the bag."

"Photographs."

"Of course, and here's your address. She's in a hotel across town, a nice place." Melissa offered her notebook with the hotel details and showed the others her best photograph of the woman on her iPhone.

"Vivid lipstick."

"She's quite the vamp, I'm telling you."

Tyler studied the image of the blonde sitting at the bench, smoking, her hair elegantly fixed up high with a clip, black boots ending above her knees.

"Well done, Mel."

Melissa sent the images from her phone to HQ for identification.

"Yeah, but it gives me the creeps." She shuddered again and perched on the edge of Tyler's bed. "I could have been followed. I might have given us up and I nearly wrecked the entire operation. You know I suck at this surveillance stuff."

Lucy nodded but stopped at Tyler's glare.

"Do you think you *were* followed here?" asked Tyler.

"I can't be sure but I don't think so. What's in the case? Papers?"

"Yes."

"Just old papers. Nothing of any help," said Lucy, heading for the door. "I need coffee. Are you girls coming?"

*

Streicher ordered a second beer and perused the bar

menu. The game show on the TV was almost over and soon the bar would be open for food orders.

"So he just came straight back here after dropping the case?" asked Melissa, glancing around nervously. "He didn't meet up with anyone on the way? Didn't bump into someone at the hotel?"

"No. He didn't even go to his room. Just came right here to the bar and ordered a drink." Tyler was sure she had missed nothing. She had watched him for so long with the contrap that she feared it would soon run out of power, the ghosts within exhausted. She was glad to be able to observe him from their table on the opposite side of the room without need of the *Present Eye*. At least the contrap was now set to the *Safeguarding Skull*, resting, the ghosts within recuperating.

"There must be something," continued Melissa. "Why would he walk all that way just to drop a dummy case? And it was collected, too! It doesn't make sense."

"Okay, it doesn't make sense," said Lucy between sips of coffee. "So what? Maybe he's an idiot."

"I want to see the case again," said Melissa.

"What, right now? We just got here."

"Yes, right now. There has to be something about it. Something we missed."

"All right." Tyler set her coffee cup on the table. "I'll come with you. Lucy–"

"Yeah, yeah. I'll keep an eye on old sweaty face over there. It has to be said, I get all the best jobs."

Tyler accompanied Melissa back to the room where Melissa spent ten minutes examining the case in great detail. She took fingerprints from the handle and every inch of the outer surface with the scanner on her phone before entering them into her laptop for analysis. She double checked each of the filing compartments in the lid to be sure they were empty and took swabs for chemical analysis. In frustration at finding nothing of interest, she took a lock knife and prised its blade between the case's hard edge and its soft fabric lining. Tyler watched, wondering if Melissa had finally unhinged. But once Melissa had worked all the way around the lining to the opposite side of the case, she plucked out a miniscule flash drive and showed it to Tyler.

"I knew there had to be something. Let's see what's on it." Melissa slotted it into a USB port on the side of her laptop. A moment later a new window popped up on the screen.

"There's data on the drive but it's encrypted."

"Of course it is."

"I'll set a program running to sort this out. We can leave it working while we go eat."

Melissa's phone bleeped announcing a received message.

"That'll be HQ with the ID on the blonde." She checked her phone. "Name's Katalin Mészáros. A Hungarian national. She's been around a bit: Germany, Australia, New Zealand, Bulgaria and Russia."

"What's she doing here, dealing with Streicher?"

"That's what Yash wants us to find out."

They joined Lucy in the bar to order food and update her.

"Glad it wasn't an entire waste of an afternoon. Well done, Mel."

Melissa gazed at Lucy, slack-jawed.

"I'm sorry, did I hear you right? Its sounded like you said *Well done*."

"I did."

"Are you feeling okay? I have a thermometer in the forensics kit. I could take your temperature if you like. There must be a doctor in town somewhere."

Lucy checked her phone. "I'm perfectly well, but point taken. Thank you. I was merely congratulating you on thinking of something that no one else thought of. But then again, that's why we let you tag along in this little outfit, isn't it?"

"Aaaand she's back."

Tyler intervened. "Lucy did a good job this afternoon. Mel did a good job finding the drive. We're actually a pretty good team when you two aren't at each other's throats. One day perhaps you'll see that. Lucy, what's Streicher done in our absence?"

"Not much. He finished his beer, ordered another and some food, and then took out a piece of paper. Ever since then he's been staring at it like it's a crossword puzzle." Lucy glanced at her phone again.

"Maybe it *is* a crossword," said Melissa.

"If it is, he's not doing very well."

"I wonder what's on that paper," said Tyler. She had an idea. "I'm going to the loo. I'll be right back." She left the bar and found the closest toilets. Locking herself into a cubicle she drew the contrap from her shirt, set it to the *Present Eye* and focused through several walls until she found Streicher. He stared at the paper in his hands and she edged the contrap's lever slowly around to close in, but he was holding the paper at such an acute angle that she failed to read a word. She tried the cubicle at the far end and managed to glimpse the start of each of four lines, all handwritten in an unfamiliar language.

Tyler abandoned her spying and returned to the girls as a waiter served their food. When he had gone she turned to the girls.

"One way or another I have to know what's written on that page."

*

Six hours later, Streicher left the hotel, heading back towards the old town square. Softly glowing pearlescent streetlamps lit the night. Tyler left the girls with instructions, grabbed her coat and scarf, and followed at a distance. Streicher led her along the same route he had taken earlier in the day, the streets now quiet and all but empty. A sprinkling of snowflakes meandered from the inky sky to glint in the lamplight, and soon it thickened, falling faster and settling on every cobble and ledge.

Streicher's squat form was easy to track. He strolled at an easy pace, pausing only to fasten his duffle coat and adjust his hat. He turned right at the end of a road and skirted the block, bearing left until he arrived once more at the astronomical clock.

What is it with you and that clock?

*

Melissa forced herself into the ill-fitting uniform and glared at her reflection in the full length mirror. Her waist bulged at the top of the navy trousers and the buttons of the light blue blouse were nearly bursting open.

"Cosy," said Lucy, already comfortably dressed in her stolen housecleaning gear.

"I can't go like this. *This* is a joke!"

"All for queen and country. Stop faffing. We don't know how much time we have."

"Okay, okay!"

"How's it going?" asked Tyler via comms.

"We're just preparing," said Lucy. "You?"

"He's back at the astronomical clock. I'm observing from a distance."

Lucy and Melissa left the room and descended in the lift to collect a cleaning trolley from the basement services department.

"You need to chill," Lucy said. "You look like you're going to hyperventilate."

"If you mean *breathe abnormally fast and deep*, it's wishful thinking. In this thing I can barely breathe at all!"

They rode the lift to Streicher's room keeping their heads down as they passed hotel guests. At the door Lucy inserted the key card Melissa had rigged having firstly hacked the Four Seasons' computer system. Streicher's door opened first time and they slipped inside with the trolley, hanging a housecleaning sign on the outer doorknob.

Melissa reported to Tyler

"Okay, we're in."

*

Tyler crept closer, hugging the wall and slipping beneath the picturesque arch of a shop front. Between her and Streicher a couple walked the cobbles hand in hand. Streicher made another cursory study of the clock and loitered as the square slowly emptied of visitors. When he thought the last of the tourists had departed he checked around to be certain before approaching the clock. Tyler retreated to the depths of the arch and watched through the *Present Eye*, hardly believing what she was seeing as he began to climb one side of the clock tower. Surprisingly agile, he heaved himself up the sandstone architrave, gripping the fluted columns with apparent ease. Using every crevice and ledge he continued to nimbly scale, carefully avoiding the delicately carved figures at the clock's edge.

*

Their hands clad in latex gloves, Lucy and Melissa searched Streicher's belongings. Melissa booted his laptop and set to work breaking his password and copying files. Lucy cracked the room's safe and photographed its contents: money, traveller's cheques and several passports in various names, none of which were Lucas Streicher or Ernst Packmann. Three minutes into their invasion she stopped to hiss at Melissa.

"This is it. I have the note!" She clicked off several photographs using her phone. "Ghost, how are we for time?"

"You guys won't believe this. He's climbing the clock!"

*

As Streicher drew level with the clock's huge calendar dial, the soft crunch of footfalls in the snow echoed from the square. He waited, silent and still. When the sounds waned he climbed on, reaching the two figures to the right of the complex time dial. He examined the carved skeletal figure of Death, studying the back of its skull. Apparently content with his work, and ignoring the neighbouring carving of the Turk, he began his descent as more footfalls sounded from across the square.

Tyler swung her view onto the approaching newcomer and was surprised to see a police officer. He peered curiously at the clock and muttered into his radio before shouting at Streicher and sprinting towards the tower. Streicher rushed the last few metres, almost slipping from the wall, and fled as the officer pursued. Two more officers arrived at the clock and followed.

Soon Tyler was alone. She ventured out from the

arch and into the empty square.

"Cog, Pointer, get out now! He's heading home."

"We're leaving."

She walked to the clock front to peer up at the pale figure of Death with his little bell and poignant hourglass. Pulling the contrap from her shirt she set the switch to *Flight* and drew the lever, taking off into the flurry filled air. She guided herself up to the carved skeleton and studied it. On the back of Death's skull someone had drawn in black pen a symbol resembling a ring with a lump, or perhaps a gem stone.

So the figure of Death has been marked, but why? And what does that mean to Streicher? Is that what you were seeking, Lucas?

Conscious that she could easily be spotted flying in the centre of town, she descended quickly and headed back to the hotel.

Prague is His Origin

Tyler paced her hotel room as Melissa, working at the glass-topped dressing table to one side, translated the four lines of text from Lucy's photograph. With Streicher sleeping off his escape from the police, the trio had time to work.

"It's Czech, as you might expect, but look, I checked it for hidden messages by heating the page under the bulb of the desk lamp. There's this other word written across the smaller writing. Angličtina. That's *English*, to you and me. I swabbed it and tested it. The hidden word is written in human blood serum."

"Someone used their own blood as invisible ink?"

"Yes, directing the recipient of the note to translate it into English for reasons unknown."

"What do the four lines say?"

"One minute. Almost done." Melissa scrawled more words on a page of hotel notepaper. "Here. This is the most accurate translation I can get. It still doesn't make much sense though." Tyler took the page. Melissa and Lucy gathered round to study the words over her shoulder as she read aloud.

Follow death's row
Three houses of the skull
Prague is his origin
Next in line to sacrifice

"Are you sure this is the same text you glimpsed from the toilets?" asked Melissa.

"I'm sure."

"What the heck does that mean?" asked Lucy.

"Haven't a clue. Mel, any ideas?"

"Yes, *Mel*! Any ideas?"

"Be quiet, I'm thinking. It could mean *death row* as in a prison." They waited in silence. "No. *Follow death's row* means we need to find a row and follow it. But a row or a line of what? *Death's row*. You said there was a ring symbol on the back of Death's head. Maybe that's one in the row. I mean one of the *three houses of the skull*."

"Of course, a row of three houses. Streicher's been working on this riddle for ages and he's found the first house of the skull. That's why he was so interested in the clock. That's why he's in Prague! But the clock tower isn't a house."

"It's close enough, surely," said Lucy, checking her phone for messages.

"Technically it *is* a house," Melissa explained. "It houses the astronomical clock."

"What about the next line?" asked Lucy.

"*Prague is his origin*. Taken literally it means Death

comes from Prague because the only persona mentioned so far is Death, but it's written in an obscure way which means it's probably cryptic. Death originates in Prague? Death starts in Prague?"

"Do you think the NVF is planning a terrorist attack on Prague?" asked Lucy. "A plot that Streicher is helping with? Maybe he's created some kind of secret weapon that's going to level the entire city. He could be trying to locate the weapon."

"Perhaps," said Melissa. "I'm not sure."

"Surely if he had created the weapon he wouldn't be trying to locate it from a bizarre riddle on a scrap of paper," countered Tyler.

"But it could have been stolen before he had a chance to use it. Maybe he's trying to get it back."

Melissa continued. "I'm not sure. The last line is the most interesting. If it's a clue to the whereabouts of something valuable then it's not much help. *Next in line...* Does that mean the next house of the skull in the line of houses? Is the object hidden in a fourth house?"

"Here." Tyler handed Melissa the page. "Can you write it out again but give us your best interpretation of its meanings, knowing what we know? I mean rather than a direct translation."

"Okay." Melissa scribbled for several minutes before passing her notes to Tyler.

Follow the line of three houses
Each has a marked skull
Death begins in Prague
The location is a church within the line, or possibly next to the third house?

"Don't take too much notice of the last line," added Melissa. "This is conjecture, but the end of the riddle mentions sacrifice. Sacrifices take place on altars and a house with an altar surely has to be a church."

Lucy stared at the page. "The location of what?"

"Yes. That's the big question. The riddle doesn't even give a clue. Find that out and maybe we can all go home, I can have a word with Chapman, get a nice desk job, and we all live happily ever after."

"Wake up and smell the coffins, Mel. It's World War Three, Chapman's gone and at this rate we'll be lucky if there's a London to go home to. There is no happy ever after." Lucy slunk away to glower out of the window.

Tyler met Melissa's unsettled gaze and shrugged. "Anything interesting in Streicher's laptop?"

"I copied his emails but everything else on there is protected. I'm guessing he has at least one other email account that's secure and hiding away somewhere but I can't locate it. He's a clever chap and has a serious firewall. If I had more time I might be able to break into more of his files. I took a cursory look through his mail but didn't see anything of any real interest. It almost appeared as though he was expecting that to be hacked. You know, too clean.

"He's ordered some pretty hard-core computing manuals and visits some dodgy websites, but that's about it. I've copied everything to HQ for further analysis. My system has decrypted the protection on the flash drive, though, the one from the case. Take a seat. You'll want to see this."

*

It swarmed around him, growing, pulsing and gushing. The black, stifling fog swamped Albert's essence as he pressed deeper into Sheol. He felt its weight dragging at his essence and heard its rasping, faceless voice.

"I know you, Albert Goodwin. This is not the first time I have tasted your soul. You will not escape me a second time!" It swirled like black water, excited by his presence. Gathering up before him, it formed a heaving mass that morphed into the shape of a gigantic, ragged skull, dripping with decay. The skull watched him hungrily from empty sockets.

"You can't 'old me in 'ere. I'm appointed to pass," called Albert. "I order you to retreat!"

The skull shrieked and cackled with laughter and a terrible rushing sound filled his ears as the blackness tore about him with renewed frenzy. It roared, its fluid substance quickening through its form.

"Who are you to command the Keeper of Abaddon, you who would contend with Death?"

"I'm tasked to watch over the Hope Bringer. Let me pass. This ain't my appointed time."

The skull hissed its reply.

"But this *is* your appointed time or you would not find yourself in your present predicament. You are in Sheol. You are dead! I will take you and bind your eyes, your voice and your ears. No more shall your tongue dance within your head. No more shall your spirit roam the earth." The serpentine voice grew in volume, swelling with outrage as the skull bore down on him. "No longer will you speak in the tongues of men and walk as the living. I am Death! Behold my realm!"

Fronds of liquid darkness tore around his arms and legs to bind him, but a soft glow grew from his centre and Albert closed his eyes feeling a hidden power surge from his being. A dazzling light erupted from his core in response to the fog and another's voice flowed from his mouth, a voice that took even him by surprise at its potent depth and power.

"I am an agent of the hallowed light! The power of your master dwells within me. Return to your farthest haunts and hinder me no more!"

With a hiss the skull recoiled and retreated, driven into obscurity, and soon the light waned and vanished, and Albert was left alone, shaking, full of fear and awe.

*

Tyler took a seat at the desk and Melissa clicked open a file on her laptop. The screen filled with horizontal sections, each containing a faded black and white mugshot of an agent and, beneath, several lines containing his or her personal information.

"The photographs are old."

"Yes. I've checked. Not one person here is still living. Clicking on each section opens up a full personnel file on that individual. They're all dead Nazi agents who were very active during World War Two."

"I don't like where this is going," said Tyler.

"It's Streicher. The man behind the GAUNT machine. Where did you think it was going?" asked Lucy, returning to peer over Tyler's shoulder at the screen.

"So, what?" asked Tyler. "He's planning to bring all these agents back from the dead?"

"He can't. Can he?" asked Lucy.

"If he built another GAUNT machine he could," said Melissa. "He'd just need an artefact from each of the deceased agents and enough kidnapped kids to glove with the ghost agents."

"Maybe that's what Streicher's after with the riddle. Artefacts."

"But he didn't build it all by himself surely. There was a whole bunch of scientists working on it." Lucy folded a stick of gum into her mouth.

"He'd only have needed access to a photocopier to copy the GAUNT file, the one we took five years ago. Everything he'd need would be in that file. I took a copy before we handed it in to the police. I still have it somewhere."

Tyler watched her with concern.

"Don't worry. It's in a secure location."

Tyler scrolled down the list of dead agents and stopped at an image of a particularly gruesome thug. She read his name. "Jürgen Schwinghammer, AKA die Vieh."

"Wow, that guy's built like a tank!" said Lucy.

"The Beast," translated Melissa. "Seven feet, two inches. Speciality strangulation and torture beatings." She speed-read the first paragraph of his personal data. "Seems they used to send him in to clear houses of Jews who were deemed a threat, the ones the Gestapo thought might be problematic to arrest. He had a reputation for leaving no one alive. Let's hope they don't bring *him* back from the dead."

"Er, Mel, I don't mean to alarm you," said Tyler, pointing to a status box beneath Beast's name and photograph that read REANIMIERT. "But I think they already did."

*

Albert viewed his surroundings in a daze. The visitation and his struggle with the death fog had left him exhausted. A long, dank tunnel stretched ahead of him, its low ceiling of solid rock arching claustrophobically over his head and dropping to the ground in solid walls at his side, almost brushing his shoulders.

He took a few slow paces forward, unsure if the deathly miasma would return. When nothing happened he walked more boldly, hoping to see signs of the tunnel's end but it appeared to flow on into a deep pitch, its fetid air unmoving. It had the feel of an ancient tomb, untrodden by the living, buried in the crust of the earth, a cave carved for one purpose alone; to contain the spirits of the dead. He reached out to test the wall and found it solid. Here, ghosts were trapped and confined amid the stale and fetid stench of rot.

Remembering Tyler and the lost ghosts, Albert trudged on into the suffocating darkness as sweat beaded to chill the nape of his neck.

Houses of the Skull

Melissa surfed multiple browser windows to research buildings in Prague containing skeletons or skulls while Tyler FaceTimed Yash.

"Ghost, it's late. This had better be worth it." She watched a dim image of Yash peering back, bleary-eyed.

"Yes, Sir. We intercepted a briefcase dropped by the mark. Cog found a flash drive full of personnel files about dead Nazi agents. It's bad news, Sir."

"I'm listening."

"Twelve agents on the list are already marked as being reanimated."

"So they've created a second GAUNT machine as we feared. That *is* bad."

"Looks like it. And our mark is definitely searching for something. I'll send a full report in the morning but I thought you should know."

"Thank you. Is that all?"

"Yes, Sir."

"Then goodnight, Ghost. I'll be in touch."

"Goodnight, Sir." Tyler was about to end the call when Yash spoke again.

"Ghost?"

"Sir?"

"New orders. Seek and destroy the machine at any cost."

"Yes, Sir." Tyler ended the call.

"We're in the right place if we want to see skulls," said Melissa. "Prague's full of them. My problem is there're too many. She gestured to a map of the town on the laptop's screen with multiple location markers. "Any of these could be the designated sites."

Lucy stared at her phone and pocketed it, frowning.

Tyler checked her watch. "It's two a.m.. We'll have to call it a night soon or we'll be useless tomorrow."

"Maybe Streicher knows something we don't. We can follow him in the morning and see where he goes. He's had more time to do his research, and without a second house of the skull we have no idea in which direction the row goes. We don't even know if the astronomical clock is the first one in the row."

"Yeah, I guess it could be any one of the three. Okay, we'll follow him in the morning, but we need to get ahead somehow. If we can get to the second marker before him maybe we can erase it and leave him guessing."

"Sounds like a plan."

Lucy took her phone out again and stared at it, as though that might make it ring.

"What's with your phone?" asked Tyler. "You've

been checking it every three seconds all day."

"It's Weaver. He's not returning my calls."

"Isn't he on operations?" asked Melissa. "He won't call or text if the operation's classified and he's in a war zone."

"That doesn't *usually* stop him."

"I'm sure he'll be in touch when he can," said Tyler, feeling a pang of jealousy. Klaus barely ever called or texted, and never when he was on a mission.

When at last they stopped working, Tyler lay staring at the curtains in her room. *Albert would normally be standing there. Albert should be there, my guardian angel, watching over me while I sleep.* She wondered what he was doing and if he'd ever return from Sheol. How could he? No, Albert was gone for good, and she would have to get used to the idea. Feeling a deep loneliness, she took out the contrap and set its switch to the *Ghost Portal*, desiring company, wanting another Albert but knowing he was irreplaceable. The grey memory mist greeted her as always but the portal revealed no one. She waited for a moment but with a click the crystal blackened and the mist vanished. She turned the contrap over. The switch was set to the *Brimstone Chasm*.

That's odd. I didn't move the switch and I don't sense any ghosts around.

Feeling vulnerable, she placed the contrap back into its lead box and closed the lid. The hotel walls would keep no enemy ghosts out and there was nobody but herself to even warn of their presence. Without Albert, sleeping was a scary proposition.

"Come back to me, Albert," she murmured. "Come back to me before I'm murdered in my bed."

*

Albert fought the desire to rest. Navigating the dark passages and tombs of the underworld by little more than touch alone was exhausting. He thought back to the time he and Tyler had dived into the Shivering Pool and remembered a similar feeling. Sheol emanated a deep and binding need for sleep and the endless darkness only accentuated it. With every step into the palpable gloom he urged himself not to succumb. He had a notion *that* would be the end. He would lie down and never rise again. The deathly miasma would return to find him in slumber, an easy target. He would be wrapped and bound in fronds of Death's liquid-mist like a spider's dinner waiting to be eviscerated.

He found a new chamber and stole in. In a carved recess a single spirit lay blackened with fog, bound and unmoving in shadow. Albert approached slowly and peered down into the lifeless face, touched the black binding substance and felt its dust-like texture sapping his energy. Somewhere down here Zebedee, Izabella and the rest of the Ghost Squad rested, all of them sleepers in the dust.

He left the chamber. This sleeper was no one he knew and beyond help. Turning from the doorway he crossed to another passage and stood gazing at the open expanse beyond. There, in an array of platforms and niches that reached into the far distance, slept thousands of souls.

"Hold on, Missy. This could take a while."

*

"We have to get a three-bed suite. I can't take another night like last night. We'll be safer all sleeping in the same room."

"Agreed," said Melissa.

"Wuss." Lucy put the finishing touches to her Goth makeup and blew herself a kiss in the dressing table mirror. "Do you two have gallows blades?"

"Uh-huh."

"Yeah. Six of them."

"Good."

"I have my Taser," said Melissa.

Lucy smirked. "Good luck with that."

Tyler shifted focus with the contrap's lever and watched Streicher put on his coat.

"Streicher's preparing to leave. Are you ready?"

"Yes."

"Ready as I'll ever be."

"Good. Let's go."

They headed out of the hotel to loiter in the street across the road from the main entrance. Streicher emerged from the revolving doors and turned left into the street. The girls followed, Melissa tracking their progress on her phone's satnav with interest, wondering which of the possible targets he might visit first. Several streets later, Streicher boarded a red tram and they rushed to catch it before it left the stop. Two minutes later they crossed a bridge over the Vltava River and Melissa voiced her prediction.

"He's heading for Prague Castle. That has to be a hot contender for one of the houses of the skull. There's a sculpture called Parable with a Skull by Jaroslaw Rona in the east end of something called the Golden Lane. It's a huge skull sitting on top of a crouching man."

"It's like living with an encyclopaedia," muttered Lucy.

Streicher alighted the tram in a busy cobbled street and walked up the hill towards the castle entrance.

"Don't lose him. The castle's massive. It's supposedly the biggest castle complex in the world," said Melissa.

"Who's going to follow him?" asked Lucy. "We can't all do it. It would be too obvious in there."

"Agreed. I'll do it. The contrap might come in handy. You two look for the marked skull. Check the sculpture first and if there's a mark photograph and erase it before Streicher finds it."

The girls checked their Bluetooth comms units and Tyler followed Streicher up the street. He paused to purchase a castle guidebook and studied the intimidating entrance. On either side of an arch decorated with gilded swirls, gargantuan sculptures fought on broad sandstone plinths, joined beneath by wrought iron railings. Armed sentinels stood guarding, statue-like, sheltered within narrow, chevron-emblazoned huts. Streicher entered the sprawling castle grounds mingling with hordes of tourists. Fearing she would soon lose him, Tyler fought through the crowds to close on him. Using the *Present Eye* was out of the question. Too many people.

Melissa's voice came through Tyler's ear piece.

"We found the skull sculpture. We checked it. No symbol."

"Maybe it's not the castle."

"Maybe. We'll keep looking anyway."

"Okay."

For the next hour Tyler tailed him through the castle's courtyards, annexes and buildings until he reached the sculpture at the end the Golden Lane and examined every inch of it, taking photographs as he circled. Finding no mark he left the Golden Lane and threaded through the crowds out of the castle grounds.

*

Albert descended steps cut into the cold bedrock and reached the first cluster of spirit shelves. Not knowing what else to try, he began searching one sleeper at a time for the faces of his friends among the many levels. For an age he paced from shelf to shelf, sometimes climbing more steps, sometimes descending. Thousands of death-veiled faces, but not one of them familiar. He crept along a solitary, narrow passage that led into another chamber, vast and filled with countless more of the sleepers. This chamber led to another. And another. Back aching, feet throbbing, Albert shook his head at the futility of his endless task.

*

Melissa gawped at Tyler.

"He's not checking St. Vitus Cathedral?"

"No, he just left the castle grounds. So you didn't find any symbols?"

Melissa shook her head.

"It doesn't make any sense. I'd have checked the cathedral first."

"Why?" asked Lucy, as they passed the gate with its sentries.

"Duh. Think about it. We're looking for houses of the skull. A cathedral is a house of God, packed with tombs and burials under the floor. No shortage of skulls."

"So why *didn't* he search the cathedral?"

"My point exactly."

"Maybe he's discounted it for some reason."

"Or he had his hopes on the sculpture being the marker. He could have better targets in mind. You said yourself Prague has many possible houses of the skull."

"I need to do more research. We're missing

something."

"Okay. Mel, you go back to the hotel and research. Lucy and I will stay with Streicher. We'll see you later."

Streicher descended the hill to the tram stop and waited as Tyler and Lucy watched secretly, ducking in and out of the shops along the street. A tram arrived but quickly filled up with passengers, Streicher among them. Tyler and Lucy waved down a taxi.

"Follow that tram and I'll double your normal rate," Tyler told the driver as the tram rattled back towards Prague's old town. They crossed the bridge and Streicher left the tram at the next stop, a few blocks from the Four Seasons and walked.

"Where's he going now? The hotel's that way." Lucy pointed in the opposite direction.

"I don't know, but we're going to find out."

*

Albert drifted off to sleep as shadows shifted in the cavern's murky depths. The Death-mist wormed closer, a black fog oozing along the stone floor; a hungry, fluid snake, twisting through lightless passages and hollows. It found him and began its work, entwining its dark miasma around his essence.

Albert stirred and blinked, saw the mist and stood, scraping at the fog as it swirled around his arms. He felt its strange, heavy texture, grainy and more solid than real fog, like a mixture of gas, water and sand.

He stepped away, shaking off the mist. Retreating up a set of steps, he avoided its grasp and watched it flow by. He continued, chamber after chamber, face after face, passing thousands of lifeless forms. Hours of hunting. Days. Who knew how long he had been here in 'real' time? And still no sign of his friends. He continued searching, checking every face, never missing a single one. Endlessly exploring. Fruitlessly seeking.

Sleepers

Tyler and Lucy huddled against the frozen wall of the café beneath the tram cables and arching streetlamps. Inside the café Streicher, in shirt sleeves, savoured a cappuccino.

"We could risk going in, I guess. I wouldn't mind thawing out."

"No way," said Lucy, shivering. "We'd be way too obvious. We've been following him all day and he's not an idiot, or blind."

Streicher had killed half the morning at the castle. Now the mid-afternoon light ebbed weakly. Beyond the broad road the tree-lined Vltava flowed, a fat, sluggish snake. Snow tumbled from the greying sky, twisting in the growing wind as Tyler located a street sign and phoned Melissa.

"Are you at the hotel? He's taking a break but he's been heading north along the river." Tyler made a brave attempt at Czech pronunciation. "We're on a street called

71

Sme-tan-ova Ná-bř."

Hang on," said Melissa, fingers clicking away on her laptop keypad. "Here we go. I have a map. He could be heading for Charles Bridge. It's the oldest bridge in Prague. Dates back to 1357."

"Any houses of the skull there?"

"I'm searching."

Lucy risked a walk-by of the café entrance to keep tabs on Streicher and returned to warn Tyler.

"He's paying the bill. Will be out any minute."

Tyler nodded.

"The bridge is protected by three towers: two on the other side, one on the old town side. The old town bridge tower is a bit special. It's rated as one of the best civil gothic-style buildings in the world. I'm guessing that's where he's heading."

"Thanks, Mel. Gotta go. He's on the move."

They followed Streicher's to the old town bridge tower. Tyler and Lucy watched as he photographed it, walked through its enormous arches spanning the width of the bridge, and jotted notes in a pocket book. The tower displayed a plethora of decorations above its arcade: crenellations, complex arches and mouldings. Above a line of heraldic shields, vaulted recesses housed statues and detailed sandstone embellishments, but the girls could see no sign of a skull among them. Tyler noticed tourists entering the tower's side door beneath the main arch.

"You go in and take a look around ahead of him."

Lucy nodded and left her to join other visitors in the tower, passing a black, iron-studded door and following the stone stairs up and around to a high chamber.

Tyler's phone buzzed. *Melissa calling.*

"It's certainly a possible house of the skull. I've been digging. On the twenty-first of June 1621, twenty-seven leaders of the anti-Habsburg revolt were executed. Their severed heads were hung on the tower's walls to deter others from rebelling against the royals."

"Yes, but are there any skulls?"

"No actual skulls as far as I can see. But there could be a mark somewhere on the structure."

"Thanks, Mel." Tyler slid her phone into her pocket as Streicher entered the tower. She jogged beneath the arches to the other side and examined the walls there. No skull. No symbol. Nothing but weather-beaten, city-blackened stone.

*

Another passageway led Albert to the deepest cavern yet. He stood at the edge of a ledge and gazed down from a colossal height, predicting what he would find down there. He followed a pathway spiralling down around the chamber's edges, sinking lower with each step, until reaching more of the sleepers laid out on their rock shelves. He searched, all the while watching and listening for the Death-mist. With the last of the sleepers checked, he had to accept the brutal truth: His friends were not in this chamber either. No doubt there were more he had yet to reach.

He sat down cross-legged on the cold ground and rested, the cavern around him deathly quiet and gloomy. A voice whispered softly, words too distant to distinguish, but slowly the words grew louder and clearer until he recognised the voice in his head: Izabella. She had spoken before entering the *Brimstone Chasm*.

"Your greatest weapon will, therefore, be hope. You must find hope in all circumstances. You are going to need

it–mark my words!"

Perhaps, *if that were true of the Chasm it might be true of Sheol.* Attempting to cheer himself, he tentatively sang a few words of a ballad he had known when he had been alive. It was a melancholy song but he liked it and, at first, its sweeping melody brought fond memories to mind.

> *"Oh London town I see thee sleep*
> *and sorrowfully mourn,*
> *For winter's cruel and bitter chill*
> *doth reach beyond the dawn..."*

As the tune mounted he sang louder, knowing it might bring the Death-mist but not caring. He had to try something. Memories of cheer filled his thoughts, images of him with his sister, Molly, materially poor but rich in love, care-free, dancing under the streetlamps of old London, opening Christmas gifts lovingly carved by their father, and storytelling around an open fire in their claustrophobic, rented room in Nine Abbey Place. *Yeah, my ol' man really knew how to tell a story...*

> *"Do you recall the day when once we met*
> *and danced a merry step,*
> *Upon the twelve days, feasting high,*
> *when Solstice bells were born?*
>
> *Come lamp-lighter with hasty tread*
> *upon the cobbled street,*
> *And in my doorway huddled so*
> *I dance with icy feet,*

For in my head and in my heart
I'm safely sheltering,
And merry in good company
before a fire's heat."

Finishing the song he covered his face with his hands and muttered.

"I'm sorry, Missy. There just ain't nothin' I can do." The last verse always brought it back to him, the way his sister had died. He hugged his knees tightly to his chest and relived the horror of his sister's death.

Porlock, their landlord had kicked them out onto the street when their father failed to pay the rent. A bitterly cold winter raged outside, the ground hard as iron, the water like stone.

"You ain't stayin' 'ere, no matter what ya' say! Ain't no good beggin'. I got my own debts to pay! I've to get someone in 'ere with coin or I shall end up in the debtors' prison. Be gone now and ne'er return!" Porlock had bellowed from the steps of the house.

They had been homeless more than once before and it hadn't killed them. The last time it happened his father begged a room from Aunt Rosa. Rosa wasn't their real aunt but an old friend of their deceased mother. In pity, Rosa had taken them in but this time there *was* no Aunt Rosa. She had passed last summer from a hideous disease that had rotted her mouth and nose.

Albert and Molly huddled in doorways begging for food from toffs passing by, while their father hunted for work. They walked windswept streets to the poorhouse as snow fell, just as their father had said to do. With holes in their shoes and freezing feet they rapped at the tall poorhouse gate with its grand, brass ring knocker.

The burly gatekeeper opened the gate briefly to stick his head through the gap.

"No room for the likes of you! Be gone!

"But please, Master Dobner, we ain't got nowhere else to go," Albert pressed. "It's only for a night or two until Da finds work. We'll soon be on our way. At least let us speak to Old Brander!" Albert had not known if Brander was the Beadle's proper name or a sinister nickname others called him behind his back, but Brander *was* the man in charge of the poorhouse. If anyone could get them in, it was him.

"I can't help you. I got my orders. I'm to let none pass. There's no more beds."

"We can sleep on the floor! We're not asking for much, not even bread," said Molly, but the gatekeeper closed the gates and with finality turned the key in the lock.

Albert recalled staring at the gates.

"Let's go," said Molly, taking his hand. "He ain't comin' back."

"But we 'ave to find shelter. It's gonna get even colder soon."

He remembered the sad acceptance in Molly's face as she had squeezed his hand. "It'll be all right, Albert."

They spent hours knocking on doors, hoping to appeal to the kinder side of someone better off than they. Most would do nothing for them and simply turned them away, but by four o'clock as the light began to fade, an old maid brought them out two slices of stale meat pie, glancing nervously over her shoulder and drawing a finger to her lips.

"I can't let you in," she whispered. "But take these and God keep you."

They thanked her and moved on to the next doorway, quickly devouring the crusty slices of pie. Stale or not, it was the best pie they had ever tasted.

Albert left Molly huddled in a doorway. He trudged through the snow to the Dog and Duck seeking his old boss, Tommy the sweep, hoping to beg back his old job.

Tommy, soot-blackened from the day's work, yet as cheerful as ever, greeted him with a broad smile displaying a patchwork of missing teeth.

"Young Master Godwin! How are you, my dear lad?" He stooped from his considerable height to crush Albert's hand in a vice-like grip.

"I'm well, Master Sweep. I'm well. My folks is on the streets, though. Da lost his job last Thursday and Porlock gave us the heave-ho. I need my old job back. Just for a couple o'days. You know, just until Da brings in a few bob."

"Oh, Albert, you know's I can't do that. When you's too big for a chimney, you's too big. I can't shrink ya' now, can I?"

"I can still get up the broader ones in the grand 'ouses across the river. Couldn't you send me up them stacks and use the younger kids for the rest? I'm an 'ard worker. You know's I am."

"Yes, yes. You always worked 'ard. I won't deny it. One of the best."

"So wha'd'ya' say? Will ya give me a few days more? Maybe a week?"

"Look, Albert, it ain't that simple. That ain't my patch no more. I sold it on to Archie Rogers." Tommy rubbed at his stubbly chin, weighing Albert with a look. "I suppose I could 'ave a word with 'im."

"Go on, Sir! I'll work twice as hard as the rest."

Tommy stared at his feet for a moment before lifting his head and nodding.

"All right, Master Goodwin. I'll call in a favour. But if he runs out of the fat stacks he'll let you go and I won't be able to stop 'im."

"Thank you, Sir. Thank you a hundred times!" Albert dipped his cap and left, grinning. Maybe one night in the cold wasn't so bad. Tomorrow he would climb the insides of chimneys again in the employ of Rogers, able to pay for a room for his family.

Smiling, he hurried back to the doorway with his news. He called out as he approached but Molly, curled in a tight ball clutching her blanket, remained motionless. He reached out. Her arms and face were icy and frozen solid, and he understood. He sat there for hours, arms wrapped around her frigid, lifeless body, not understanding why he did so, trying to warm her even though he knew she was gone.

"I'm sorry, Molly."

Less than a week after they buried Molly in a pauper's grave, Albert's Da was committed to an asylum. Molly's death sent him plummeting over sanity's already-fraying edge. He blamed himself for everything. Albert worked up in the big chimneys across the Thames and was able to rent a room. He visited, but his Da barely said a word, failing to recognise his own son.

Three days later, Albert found himself sweeping a *fat* chimney and became trapped halfway up in a dogs-leg. He hollered down to Archie Rogers, a scrawny, unkempt sweep in his fifties with cold eyes, a crooked nose and no front teeth, who croaked persistently with a death-rattle of a cough.

"I'm stuck fast, Master Rogers! I can't go up nor

down!"

"What you do that for, you idiot?" Archie's words choked into a minor coughing fit.

"I'm sorry, Master Rogers. I didn't mean to."

"All right, all right. Don't you worry. We'll get ya' down." But Archie was more hopeful than accurate and his attempts to free Albert became ever more frantic. Finally, oozing with goose fat and aching painfully, Albert peered down through a small gap near his left elbow to glimpse the red glow of Archie's smouldering clay pipe in the darkness of the fire box below.

"It's no good, Albert. You'll just 'ave to stay up there until you get thin from hunger. Then you'll slip out like a greased pig."

"No! Master Rogers! Don't leave me 'ere!"

"There's nought I can do, lad. The owners are away. We're supposed to sweep while they're gone. I can't knock their house down to get you out. I just can't. It would cost a fortune to break open the stack and have it rebuilt, and the bankers are already bearing down heavy on me. You'll come out. Just you wait and see. A day or two with no grub and you'll thin right down."

"No, Master Rogers! Please! Don't leave me!"

"I'll drop by tomorrow. They're not back for another week. We got time to starve you out."

"Archie, no!" Albert was little more than skin and bone as it was. He greatly doubted he would become any freer by fasting.

"Sit tight, lad. I'll return."

Albert continued to plead as Archie left and closed the front door. Unoccupied and unheated, the house and stack were already chilled. Albert had stripped down to his shirt to climb up to the high smoke shelf. Caught

79

between the shelf and the stack lining, he couldn't move and had no means to keep warm. A new level of cold settled over the place as night rolled in.

Archie was good for his word. He returned the following afternoon to see if Albert had managed to wriggle free but, unwilling or unable to help further, turned his back on Albert's increasingly desperate pleas and left again, promising to look in the next day. Albert shouted late into the evening, trying to raise a neighbour, but either they could not hear him or chose to ignore his calls. The cold of the second night in the stack was worse. He did not know the hour of his death but he recalled the tremendous chill of his bones. They felt like old sticks from the snowy grounds of the park: numb, brittle and dead. His incessant shivering passed as he neared exhaustion and soon the icy flesh of his fingers and toes lost all sensation. The very breath in his lungs felt like the ice-blown waters of the Thames and, at last, he felt his heart slow and beat its last. A brief moment of startling anxiety flooded his mind, but he was already tipping into a spiralling blackness: a sleep that drew him relentlessly, insidiously, on.

Albert stirred from his memories to look around at the cavern of sleepers. He waited, trying to shake the image of his frozen sister from his mind. *Is Molly here somewhere, swathed in the fog and sleeping?*

There were too many sleepers for him to search, endless numbers of the dead, collecting here since Adam.

How am I supposed to find the Squad in 'ere? An' even if I could, how would I get us all out?

A small, distant sound broke the silence, a thin, female voice, gentle, little more than a whisper. Albert looked up, wondering if he had imagined it, but the voice had gone.

"Now I'm 'earin' fings, Missy."

Again the voice peeled distantly, echoing from a labyrinth of walls and caves, now clearer.

"Hello? Is that you?"

He turned, trying to track the sound. A few moments later it repeated.

"Is that you? Hello? Where are you? Hel-lo-oh?" The voice distanced further and vanished. Albert stood and followed, dashing down passages and through sleeper caverns. If someone else was awake down here, he wanted to meet them. He called out as he sped on through more caverns.

"'Ello? Can you 'ear me? I'm 'ere. I'm right 'ere!" For several frustrating minutes he thought he had lost the voice altogether when it stopped but, as he relinquished hope, it resumed more loudly than before.

"Hello? Hello? Albert, is that you?" A girl's voice. Not Izabella with her overbearing Russian accent, but a soft, young sound.

He pressed on, searching, following each delicate note when it came, calling out when it faltered and died. Whoever she was, he was sure she was as desperate to find *him*.

"Yeah, I'm Albert. Who are you? Do you know me?"

"Claudia. I'm Claudia! I know you, Albert Goodwin!"

Claudia! The Roman slave! She sounded even closer, perhaps one or two chambers away. He rushed. The last time he had seen her, Claudia had been torn away from him by the violent, black water of the *Brimstone Chasm*.

"Keep comin' this way. Not far now!"

Following each other's voices they met in an

entrance to a low cave of sleepers, and embraced.

"I thought I'd never see another waking face," said Claudia.

"Me neither." Albert gazed in disbelief at her. Slim and dressed in a loose, drab tunic, Claudia was attractive and stuck as a teenager, already two thousand years old. Around her brow a twine headband kept her hair from her pretty, yet slightly pinched, features. Her perpetual scowl was strangely absent, though her eyes remained as dark and sunken as ever.

"Have you been down here long?"

"Yeah, too long. What 'appened to you? I thought the black water took you in the *Chasm*."

"It did, Albert! It took me and carried me away. The river flows all the way from there into this place. It must do. It took me underground and washed me into a cavern. It left me shrouded in black mist and I slept. The black river and the mist, it's the same thing."

"Where's Tyler? She must hate me! I was rotten to her. How long has it been since the *Chasm*?"

"A couple o'years. Missy don't hate you none but how did you escape the mist?"

"You woke me from the sleep, of course."

"*I* woke you?"

"Yes, your singing woke me. I knew your song, knew your voice. I awoke, fought free of the mist and came looking for you."

"My singin' woke you?"

"Yes."

"Do you think it could wake the others?"

"What others?"

"The rest of the Ghost Squad. They're down here somewhere." Albert explained all that he understood about the Ghost Squad's disappearance.

"Then they could be anywhere down here."

"Wait a minute. My song woke you but none of the other sleepers around. Strange! Why?"

"Tell me something that isn't strange about this place? Perhaps it was because I recognised your voice. No one else did because they don't know you, so it didn't affect them."

"Which would mean my singin' might wake the rest o' the Squad!"

"If that's true all you need do is roam the rest of the caverns singing. Eventually, all those who know your voice will rise. We can gather everyone together and try to find a way out of here."

"Claudia, you's changed. What happened?"

"Have I?"

"Yeah. You's changed a whole lot. You was kind o'selfish before. Now you're... You're nicer."

"It must have been the *Chasm* that changed me, seeing all those poor, wretched souls trapped, suffering in there. What did they all do to end up in there?" Claudia drew closer, her eyes widening as she lowered her voice. "Albert, I don't want to end up back in the *Chasm*. I can't. I couldn't endure it!"

"Wake up, Claudia! You're in the full knowledge. You knows why they're in there. It's what they done and what they ain't done. They chose their own path when they rejected redemption.

"Come on. I got a plan, and whatever you do, don't fall asleep."

The Tavern

Lucy found Tyler outside the tower in time to see Streicher leave the arch and head back the way he had come.

"Anything?"

"No," said Lucy. "You?"

"Nothing, and I don't think Streicher's found a symbol here either. He doesn't seem particularly happy."

They followed him back to the Four Seasons where Tyler watched him through the *Present Eye* from Melissa's room. Streicher ordered a meal from room service and seemed set to stay in his room for the night.

"We can get ahead while he's resting up. Mel, where should we try first?"

Melissa maximised a browser window on her laptop.

"We can't visit the cathedral today as the castle grounds are now closed."

"We could break in," said Lucy.

"We could, but the security will be pretty tight. Probably best to visit tomorrow when it's open. Other than that, my money's on this place." Melissa pointed to an image of a grime-worn tavern on the screen. "It's supposedly the oldest medieval tavern in Prague. It opened in 1375. I've checked through a bunch of images on-line. I can't find a reason why they're there, but at least one part of the building has a load of skulls coating the walls and ceiling. It's like Mojo's bedroom or something. Pretty creepy, right?"

"We'd better check it out," said Lucy, smirking. "Maybe we can eat while we're there."

Half an hour later they turned into a narrow street lined with black iron bollards and mosaic pavements. They climbed as the cobbles rose steeply towards an old lane where the dusty tavern lurked. One left turn at the top brought their goal into view and a few strides later the girls arrived. A palpable reek of bygone ages issued from its smoke-stained walls: soot, beer, candle wax, roasting meat and a thousand other less obvious scents. Three iron hands grasped unlit fire brands to punctuate the frontage and, cluttering the ancient window arch below, a scatter of modern signs announced the current available services.

Tyler stared at the tattered Germanic script emblazoned in red and black over the door and windows, and tried to read the name. Melissa corrected her pronunciation.

"U Krále Brabantského."

"Okay. Whatever it's called, we're going in."

"Be careful. There could be others seeking the mark."

Tyler and Lucy looked at Melissa.

"Do *I* have to go in? I could wait out here, right?"

Lucy rolled her eyes and with a final glance at the yellowed wall and carved stone entrance arch, grabbed Melissa's arm and opened the door.

*

"Death will be seeking us by now! We got to move fast. Follow me, and sing." Albert walked deeper into the subterranean labyrinth and resumed his song.

Claudia sang a song she had known before her Roman master had ended her mortal life, the old Latin swirling to an ancient rhythm, once played with drum and pipes. The melodies mingled among the sleepers as the singers roamed but the searching of cavern after cavern yielded no waking ghosts. They stopped to rest, Albert perching on a step and Claudia on the edge of a sleeper's niche. Grimly she peered down at the blackened, motionless sleeper.

"It's not working, Albert."

"Maybe there just ain't no ghosts 'ere who knew us. We got to keep tryin', Claudia. We got to, for Missy's sake."

"You're right. We'll rest a while and try again."

"For sure. Not much else to do 'ere anyway. I wonder how long I've been down 'ere. It's 'ard to know without a glimmer of daylight."

"Do you think we'll ever see daylight again?"

"I 'ope so. Tell ya what, you rest. I'll keep watch."

Gazing into the gloomy reaches of the cavern, alone and exhausted, Albert eventually let his weary eyes close.

Just for a few moments, he told himself. *Just a little rest. That's all I need.*

*

A turn from the entrance hall led onto a scene that might have been four hundred years old if not for the scattering of modern-dressed customers in seats, eating and drinking at the tables. Tyler took a cursory look around and shrugged.

"No skulls."

"There're stairs back that way." Lucy nodded. Waitresses in medieval dress served robust platters of flame-grilled food and tankards of sloshing beer. "There must be another room."

The girls backtracked to descend curving wooden stairs into a vaulted, crypt-like chamber lit with candles and lamps. Tarnished skulls rose from the stone walls in tightly packed formations, a macabre blanket decorating the room's arching ceiling. They found a table beneath a cartwheel candelabra and sat down, leaning in close to whisper across the table top.

"This place is awesome." Lucy glanced around at the candles and skulls.

"Do people actually come here to eat?" hissed Melissa. "Surrounded by bits of dead people? That's gross."

"I'd come here all the time." Lucy checked her phone yet again and grimaced.

"Still no word from Weaver?" asked Melissa.

"No."

Melissa's phone chimed. "It's Freddy. Hi Freddy... Yes." She giggled. "Always... I'm missing you, too... No, *I* miss *you* more... Yes, I like green... Of course. I'd like the brown one or green, or maybe the–"

Glowering, Lucy snatched the phone.

"Green. Get her the green one! Goodbye, Freddy." She pressed the red bar and handed back the phone.

"Hey. Not nice."

"We better order food and wait until the other customers have gone," said Tyler, leaning in. "We need to check every skull for the mark."

"How are we going to do that with the staff coming and going and the other customers hanging round? We need to do it without unwanted attention."

"We'll just have to wait until all the other customers have gone. We'll stay late and one of us can distract the staff while the others search."

A buxom waitress in a tavern-girl costume arrived to welcome them with practised, smiling charm while handing out menus. She returned a few minutes later with drinks and took orders. Lucy's phone buzzed. She whipped it from her leather jacket to glance at the screen.

"Sorry, I have to go. Katalin Mészáros is on the move with the case."

"The Vamp? Huh. You would have thought she'd have smelled a rat and ditched it long ago."

"Yeah. Weird. I've been keeping an eye on the tracer I planted. She never ditched the case. It's been in her hotel room until a few seconds ago."

"Do you think she wants to meet up?" asked Melissa.

"With us? Maybe. I don't know what to think." Lucy rose to leave. "I'll go find out."

"What about your food?"

"Have them bag it up, Mel. I'll see you later."

*

Albert opened his eyes to see Claudia's panic-stricken face staring down at him as she shook him.

"Albert, wake up! The mist is here. We have to move!"

He sat up to glance around. Death-mist seeped

across the ground towards them, a serpentine, rolling force, and Albert wondered what would happen if he allowed it to overpower him.

Would the blinding light revisit to drive it back?

Not waiting to find out, he scrambled to help Claudia up the steps beyond the mist's reach. They fled through a narrow passage and into the next sleeper chamber, a long low tomb with niches on all sides, floor and ceiling. They wove a path, carefully avoiding the unmoving, fog-bound ghosts beneath.

Again they sang as they walked until Albert glimpsed movement in the shadowy distance of the cavern.

"What was that?" asked Claudia, pausing.

"You saw it, too!" whispered Albert.

They waited, studying the darkness before them for any sign of a waking presence.

"Has it gone? I thought the mist was behind us," said Claudia. "Is it ahead of us too?"

"I surely hope not. Wait 'ere." Albert toed his way forward, nimbly picking a route between the many hollows and balancing on the narrow edges of rock.

A grey figure emerged from the pitch of the chamber. Albert stopped, debating whether to approach or flee but, as it drew nearer, he saw the paled features of a ghost. Not Death in any of his forms but the ghost of a mortal man. Albert shook his head and wiped his eyes.

"Naw. Can't be."

"'Ang on a minute! Is that...?"

Albert closed the gap as the other ghost neared.

"Tommy the sweep! Is that *really* you?"

"Young Master Goodwin! My, my. What you doin'ere, m'lad?"

They clasped hands before embracing briefly,

Tommy grinning and lifting Albert clear of the ground.

"Wait a minute. Who's that with ya?" asked Tommy.

"This is Claudia. Claudia, meet my old boss, Tommy the sweep."

Tommy offered his hand as Claudia bowed her head in greeting.

Albert explained what had happened to him and Tommy nodded and tutted his way through the story, but appeared to understand perfectly well.

"So you're stuck down 'ere with the rest of us?"

"Aye, but I 'ave t' find a way out somehow. I 'ave to get back to Missy. She needs me."

"Right you are, old son. Of course, and I'm coming with ya. I'm sorry, by the way. Sorry for what 'appened, with the chimney an' all."

"That's all right, boss. It don't matter. We'd best get movin'. Sing somethin'. It wakes the ones who know you."

"So that's what 'appened. It was *you* who was singin'?"

"Yeah. You see, free people *free* people. We got to wake more ghosts, as many as we can. This way. These caverns go on and on. There's a ton of ground to cover and a billion sleepin' souls."

*

Lucy phoned Tyler from outside the tavern.

"Heads up. I just passed Streicher as I left the tavern. He's heading your way."

Tyler swore. "Okay. Thanks." She told Melissa what Lucy had said.

"So, what? Is he following *us* now?"

"Maybe."

Streicher walked into the skull chamber, still puffing

from his hike up the hill. Sweat beaded on his face. He took a seat at the end of the room and gazed at the skulls before snapping several photographs. A waitress interrupted his work to take his order and returned fifteen minutes later with a tankard of beer and a plate of pie and chips. When she had left, Streicher watched the girls with a smile, inclining his head and lifting his pork pie hat in an unspoken greeting. Tyler flashed a half-smile and grabbed a menu to hide behind.

"He's on to us!" she hissed. "He's definitely on to us!"

"Should we go? If he knows about us we could be in danger."

"When aren't we in danger? No. We sit tight and wait until he goes. I'm not running from that horrid little man."

"There's nothing he can do to us here, right?" asked Melissa. "Not with witnesses." They exchanged anxious glances as other customers paid their bills and departed, leaving only Streicher and across the room a honeymooning Swedish couple. She thought about Klaus and then felt guilty because she wished he was with her instead of Melissa. Pushing Klaus from her mind, she tried to discern Streicher's thoughts.

"Okay, we'll wait him out. Maybe he'll get bored and give up before *we* do. What do you really think he's looking for? I mean, what's behind the three houses of the skull?"

"I thought it was probably an artefact the NVF were trying to track down, but now I'm not so sure. What if the GAUNT machine's been stolen and he's trying to get it back?"

"What? A two-ton machine the size of a bus,

stolen?"

"Well, you wouldn't need to steal the entire thing to stop it working. One crucial part would do. Maybe a part that's really hard to replace."

"So you think someone's playing around? It seems a bit of a tease to lay clues to... To whatever it is we're all after."

"I don't know what else to think. How else has he been set on this crazy treasure hunt?"

An hour later the Swedish couple put on their coats and left, arm in arm.

"You *do* have your gun, don't you?" asked Melissa. Tyler nodded and slipped a hand into the breast of her jacket to feel her P99 nestling snuggly in its shoulder holster.

Streicher left his table to stroll slowly around the room, peering at the skulls playing the inquisitive tourist. He clicked off several more photographs and returned to his seat to drain his tankard dry. He settled his bill, donned his coat and scarf, and followed the waitress up the stairs. The girls waited, listening to his footsteps as he ascended.

"Great! Now's our chance," said Melissa, standing. Tyler rose and began checking the skulls for the strange mark. A canister bounced down the stairs, quickly followed by a second as a smoky, greenish gas rushed from them to spread across the room. They heard Streicher securing the door at the top of the steps. Tyler pulled her gun, half expecting him to reappear in the doorway through the thickening haze.

"He's trapped us. Gas!" gabbled Melissa. "Get down low to the ground." They smelt an unpleasant taint, like that of burning garlic.

"We should try to get up the stairs. Hold our breath."

"No. He's locked us in. We'll die before we can break out." They backed away as the deadly smoke billowed closer, enveloping all in its path. Tyler wrapped her scarf over her mouth and nose, and helped Melissa do the same.

"We have to do something! The shutters! Over there!" Squeezing past tables and chairs they fled to the end of the room where several steps, with chains for handrails, led up to an alcove and a high, shuttered window. A nauseating sense of doom overtook Tyler as she felt the ghosts closing in with speed from all around. She stopped to take the contrap's lead box from her pocket and hang the contrap around Melissa's neck.

"It's set to the *Safeguarding Skull*. It'll keep you alive."

"What about you? No! You have it!"

"We don't have time to argue. They're coming!"

"Who?"

The two girls turned to watch as figures gathered in the room before them, a ramshackle gathering of enemy ghosts brandishing gallows blades. More coalesced to join the small army, some of them ancient warriors in chainmail, tunics and iron helmets, others in the helms and battledress of roundheads. A scatter of unkempt brutes, murderers and lawbreakers leered among them and the rising smoke.

The girls backed towards the shuttered window as the ghost mob closed on them. Melissa tore her phone from her pocket to call Lucy as Tyler pulled a blade from her bandolier and fronted up to the ghosts. The closest of the knights stabbed at her. Tyler parried his blade and thrust hers into his neck. He staggered and dispersed like falling dust.

"What're you doing? Arm yourself!" she shouted to Melissa.

Melissa took a gallows blade from her coat, fumbled and dropped it.

"Mel!"

Lucy answered Melissa's phone call.

"Mel? You okay?"

"Mojo, help us! We're trapped in the tarvern! He's gassing us!" Melissa pocketed her phone, stooped to retrieve her blade and joined Tyler.

"Go! Get to the window and break it open!" said Tyler, lunging at a ghoulish, chain-mailed thug with a long gallows blade. She dodged his thrust and sliced his arm, stepping back as he crumpled into a vapour that vanished into the fog. Watching the others she pulled a second blade from her bandolier. "Leave now or go the same way!"

Melissa scrambled up the steps to heave at the shutter doors. Tyler remained to ward off the ghouls as the gas reached her.

"They're locked shut! I can't budge them."

Tyler took a long last breath of clean air, held it and launched a blade at an oncoming roundhead. It penetrated him and the outlaw behind him, and both ghosts dispelled into vaporous dust. The others were less confident now. They lingered, several backing off, but a few came in to fill the new gaps in the rank. Desperate to breathe, she fought on. Two more ghouls received her thrusts and vanished before the breath burst from her and she gasped a lungful of the poison. It hit her lungs like a burning injection of acid and she slumped to the floor. Vision waning, she glimpsed the high shutters explode and heard a shotgun's sudden blast as fragmented glass rained around her. Gallows blades flew over her head and phantoms shrieked. A moment later, Lucy's face was hovering over hers and strong hands grabbed her under her arms to drag her away.

The Chapel

A sleeper rose from his shelf, brushing at the encumbering mist. He placed his feet on the cavern floor and stood, gazing around at the surrounding gloom. Claudia's and Tommy's songs echoed from the far-reaching sleeper halls.

"Well, I never. Where am I? What *is* this place?"

Albert stared up into his father's baffled face. He appeared to have lost the crushing stupor of his last mortal days.

"It's Albert. It's your Albert, Da."

"Albert? Is that really you, my son?" Mr Goodwin stepped closer, squinting, but Albert ran to embrace him.

"It's really me, Da."

"Bless my soul! Where are we?"

They drew apart.

"We're in Sheol, Da. You gotta 'elp us." He briefed his father urgently. "So you gotta 'elp us, see? You gotta sing!"

"And Molly's down 'ere somewhere?"

"I reckon she must be, and a whole bunch of others we know. We just gotta find 'em."

Mr Goodwin joined the searchers, singing a jovial rendition of *Come into the Garden Maud* as he walked while Albert rekindled his own song. In the next cavern they found Claudia with three other risen sleepers, all Roman slaves. Mr Goodwin found friends there, also, and their numbers swelled. A short while later Albert's small team of singers had grown to a lively throng of Londoners, Romans and ghosts from many nations, their voices entwining in a raucous cacophony of mismatched rhythms and melodies as they purged chamber after chamber of sleepers they had known in life.

*

Tyler opened her eyes and tried to focus on the figure looking down at her. Her lungs felt seared and stung each time she inhaled. Gradually her vision cleared and the doctor in the white coat spoke.

"Ah, she wakes! How do you feel, my dear?"

She recoiled, pressing up against the headboard of the hospital bed.

"Don't touch me or I'll kill you!" She didn't know where she was or why Dr Josef Mengele was leaning over her. She squinted at the two blurry figures beyond him.

"Mojo? Mel?" She focused and scrutinized the doctor. *Not Mengele.* "Sorry. I... I thought you were someone else. Your accent, you sound German."

"That's quite all right. You have had a bit of a shock. I am Dr Stransky. Now, I need you to take a few deep breaths from this, if you please." Stransky placed a hosed ventilator mask over her mouth and nose. She inhaled, watching him study the monitor at the side of her bed. "Good, good. You are recovering quite well. Your blood tests show your body took on very little of the poison you inhaled. I will keep you here for a few more hours just to be sure there are no residual concerns. Your friends tell me you do not wish to file a police report."

"No police," said Tyler.

"Very well." Stransky nodded curtly and smiled before leaving the ward.

Tyler put a hand to her chest and felt the contrap nestling there.

"You got me out. Thank you."

"That's all right," said Lucy. "Mel put it on you as soon as she was clear of the gas. You passed out. I think the contrap saved you."

"You two saved me. I remember that much. Where am I?"

"A private hospital in Prague."

"What was the gas?"

"The doctor found traces of arsenic in your blood, but the contrap kept you alive. Either that or you didn't breathe enough of the gas for it to cause any lasting damage."

"What happened with Katalin Mészáros? Any new leads?" asked Tyler.

Lucy shook her head. "She ditched the case with the tracer and returned to her hotel. I think she's a dead end." Lucy studied Tyler's medical notes briefly. "Let's blow this joint. You're perfectly fine and *I'm* starving."

*

At the Four Seasons Tyler sipped hot chocolate in their three-bed suite. The burning in her lungs had eased in the short time since waking in the hospital bed and she checked the contrap to make sure the switch was set to the *Safeguarding Skull*.

"You'll be all right, you know," said Melissa. "You were only in the gas for a few moments. It could've been a lot worse."

"We could have died," said Tyler. "What's Streicher up to? Has anyone been keeping tabs on him?"

The others shook their heads.

"We've been busy with you," said Lucy. "But my guess is he returned to his room to get some sleep. He probably thinks we are dead."

"That would be good. I'd better check on him." Tyler reached for the contrap hanging around her neck.

"Oh no you don't," said Melissa. "Leave that on and keep it set to the skull, at least until morning. We can catch up with Streicher another time. You're more important. It's late. Get some sleep."

Reluctantly, Tyler nodded.

"Yes, boss."

*

Albert's gang grew by the second and he wondered if it would ever stop. Every raised sleeper woke ten, twenty, a hundred others. After only a few hours singing they had gathered and multiplied to more than he could count, their crowds expanding into Sheol's dim reaches.

Claudia had woken almost fifty Romans, both slaves and free citizens. Those few had each in turn raised the same again and so they grew, spreading from cavern to cavern and breaking the deathly silence with their songs as word spread.

Tommy and Albert's father had raised similar numbers who now sang bawdy cockney songs while searching. Others Mr Goodwin had known in life mostly comprised miners and quarry workers, but he found and woke Mary, his wife, and searched on, feeling invigorated. Each time a new sleeper awoke the entire process delayed while old friends and family clasped each other and cried, laughed or hooted with joy. All past demeanours were forgiven and a newfound delight in company arose. Little by little the deathly ambience of the underworld altered as it grew into a glad reunion of yesteryear's masses.

Albert forged ahead rousing new sleepers of his own until at the far end of a gargantuan cavern he caught sight of a towering wall of blackness. There, no sleepers rested and no features lurked. It seemed as though Sheol itself had ominously reached a close. As he stared, the blackness shimmered and he understood. The black mist had gathered itself up and was advancing on him and the others in a vast wall of death, enveloping everything in its path. Somehow, this time Albert knew it would not retreat, not from the thousands of spirits he'd stirred. It had come to take them back. Death had seen and comprehended what was happening, and his fury burned.

Albert turned to warn those around him.

"Run!"

Ghosts fled from the light-engulfing mass as Albert realised a new problem. He knew they had to get away but *where?*

"You said the black water washed you into Sheol from the *Chasm*," he shouted across to Claudia as they ran. "We got to find the way through."

"To the *Brimstone Chasm*? Are you mad?"

"No, I ain't mad. Trust me!" They ran on until Albert glimpsed a small perplexed figure with a grubby, pale face standing motionless amongst the stampeding spirits. He fought his way through to her and stared, slack-jawed.

"Molly!"

*

Tyler woke early to spy on Streicher through the *Present Eye*. He showered, dressed and visited the hotel restaurant where he ate breakfast before returning to his room.

"Get ready. He's preparing to leave," she told the girls, watching him brush his teeth. "Lucy, you'll have to tail him today. He'll be looking out for Mel and me. He probably knows no one died last night." Tyler felt a tremor from the contrap and its crystal lens darkened to a smoky scene of swirling memory mist. She turned it to examine the back and stared at the switch. "That's weird. I'm sure I didn't touch it but it's now set to the *Ghost Portal*."

"Maybe you knocked the switch without knowing." Lucy pulled on chunky, black Goth boots, fluffed her hair in the bedroom mirror and tested her Bluetooth comms with the other girls. She left the hotel lobby to start her bike and sat in wait. When Streicher exited through the front doors to hail a taxi, she pulled out onto the road several cars behind.

"In pursuit."

Tyler and Melissa listened via their comms.

"Keep us informed of his movements. We'll follow at a distance."

"Wilco."

Streicher's cab crossed the bridge and a few streets later dropped him off near the castle. Lucy relayed the news.

"What did I tell you?" said Melissa. "He's going back to check out the cathedral."

"You were right. I'm parking up. I'll catch up with him inside." Lucy locked her bike up and ran up the cobbled hill into the castle grounds. She located Streicher's chocolate coloured duffle coat and pork pie hat easily and followed him through crowds of the complex to St. Vitus' Cathedral, where he spent a good hour circling and studying its walls, playing the tourist with a fascination for architecture. Lucy took out her sketch book and pencil and sketched ornate masonry while keeping an eye on Streicher.

Six pages of drawings later, Lucy reported again to Tyler.

"He's been pacing around this one chapel for an age, taking a serious interest in it. The public aren't allowed in but you can look from the doorway."

"Which chapel?" asked Melissa.

"The St. Wenceslaus Chapel."

"Wenceslaus as in *Good King Wenceslas*?" asked Tyler.

"Yes," said Melissa. "Although he was only proclaimed a king posthumously. He was really a duke, murdered by his brother. His bones are in that chapel. His skull's a venerated object, housed in a secret chamber below along with the Bohemian Crown Jewels."

"A house of the skull," said Tyler.

"Precisely. That said, it's going to have some pretty good security so I don't know how he intends to get anywhere near it. Of course, we've the same problem."

"That explains all the waiting around. He's lost, doesn't know how to gain access without getting caught. Cog, research the security. Pointer, as you were."

"Wilco."

"On it," said Melissa.

A long interval passed and nothing much changed except the migrating crowds of sightseers. Melissa called in via the comms.

"Pointer?"

"He's still hanging around the chapel." Lucy watched Streicher munch unceremoniously on a BLT sandwich. She folded a new stick of gum into her mouth and continued sketching.

"I have intel. on security measures."

"Listening."

"They're a closely guarded secret. There's not much on-line about it except the door in has seven locks and the seven keys are held by seven different officials, likewise the iron safe within the vault. Yash dragged a few details from another source. There're cameras secreted around the chapel. Don't bother looking for them. You won't find them. They're well hidden, and there's a state-of-the-art security alarm on the door to the vault beneath. There's only one way into the vault below and its exact location is a secret. If anyone breaks the cathedral rules and crosses the barrier into the chapel an alarm will trigger, bringing armed guards."

"Feels like stalemate."

"Yeah, I know."

Tyler chipped in. "Hang in there, Pointer. Stay with the mark and report any movements. There's not long until closing time. He may feel pressured to act."

Lucy checked her watch. "Wilco." Tyler was right, in less than forty minutes they would be locking up for the night.

The tourists gradually thinned and soon Lucy and Streicher were the only ones lingering. He threw a suspicious glance in her direction before taking a last look through the chapel entrance and wandering away across the expansive cathedral nave.

"He's on the move." Packing up her pencils and sketchbook Lucy ran to the St. Wenceslaus Chapel to peer through the archway. The room was incredible, its lower walls adorned with semi-precious stones and gilded and coloured mouldings. Every inch was decorated with gold, marble or frescoes portraying biblical and medieval scenes. From the ceiling vaults hung a dominating golden chandelier and to one side, beneath, stood a solid, candle-laden tomb bearing a lavish reliquary; the resting place of the Wenceslaus bones. Resisting the desire to dash in and search the entire chamber for the symbol, she turned to creep after Streicher in time to glimpse him slipping into another of the many side chapels. Devoid of sightseers, the cathedral echoed with every small sound she made, her soft footsteps reverberating from the lofty walls and arches. She crossed the nave and peered into the chapel after Streicher but he was nowhere to be seen. A swift glance around told her this arch was the chapel's only entrance. Here he had gone in and had not come out.

Where are you, Streicher?

A whisper of noise behind her broke her thought. Lucy turned to see a tall, dark, spectral shape drifting in from the shadowed arches of the transept. She drew a gallows blade from the bandolier beneath her jacket and hissed into the comms microphone.

"Ghost, Cog, get in here, now!"

The Good King

The phantom halted at the edge of the nave across from Lucy, nothing but a dim, menacing form. She watched it warily, awaiting Tyler and Melissa, and glanced from her wristwatch to the chapel door and back to the looming shade.

Why have you stopped? Who are you and what do you want?

To ask aloud would have alerted Streicher to her presence, so her thoughts remained unspoken. Echoing footsteps stole her attention. Tyler and Melissa approached from out of the cathedral's thickening gloom. Lucy met them a few strides from Streicher's chapel to whisper.

"He's in the there. There's no way out but he's disappeared so I guess he's found somewhere to hide. There's a tomb and an altar. He could be behind either. I think he's waiting until the place is locked up so he can take a proper look at the Wenceslaus room without the crowds."

"But he'll never get in without being seen on the cameras," said Melissa.

"Maybe he doesn't know about the cameras."

"Maybe he has a plan," said Tyler, focusing the *Present Eye* through the wall and into Streicher's chosen chapel. She found him crouching on the other side of a blocky tomb. "He's there all right. Wait, something's not right. I can feel a presence. We're being watched!"

Lucy gestured towards the shadowy figure opposite the chapel entrance.

"Over there."

"Who is it?" asked Tyler.

"I don't know."

"Is it one of ours or an enemy?" Melissa took a step away from the entity.

"I don't know," whispered Lucy. "I haven't asked. Why don't *you* do the honours?"

More footsteps sounded further down the cathedral.

"Hide!" hissed Tyler. "The guards are locking up. We mustn't be found!"

*

All around the cavern ghosts hastened from the encroaching black wall. Molly locked onto Albert's widening eyes and spoke.

"Of course it's me. Who else would I be?"

Albert took in his little sister's simple face; soft, round and still bearing the grime of a street urchin. She appeared unchanged, down to the gaps where she had lost milk teeth and the snags in her thin, mousy hair. Seemingly unaffected by her icy death, she peered back at him with a mixture of gladness and compassion.

"Molly, I'm sorry, about... You know..."

"I know, Albert. It weren't your fault, but it don't matter now, anyway. What's done is done."

"Did it hurt, when you died?"

"Not for long and then I fell asleep." Around them ghosts rushed on.

"Hold on. Da's here somewhere. Have you seen him?"

"Our Da? Here?"

"Sure as the pitch. 'E's here." Albert turned on his heel, calling. "Da! Da! It's our Molly!" Mr Goodwin stepped from the rushing crowd to stand rigid before Molly. For a moment he only stared but, slowly, his care-worn features spurred to life and a wide smile bloomed across his face, igniting his eyes. Embracing her, he lifted her from the ground to spin her around.

"Molly, my girl! My princess!"

Albert interrupted. "Da, we gotta go! The mist..."

Mr Goodwin looked back at the void edging closer and nodded.

"Right you are, son. Let's get out of here. Quickly, Molly, my dear!"

He put her on his back and joined the fleeing multitude of spirits exiting the cavern, funnelling through a bottleneck gap in the passage.

Albert fought his way up through the ranks of other ghosts. He led them through a long, narrow passage, worrying the wall of mist might catch them as they slowed. The next cavern was deep and broad and they made short work of it using every inch of space to run. At the end of this cavern he was less worried about the wall although it remained, a distant threat.

The Brimstone Chasm is connected to the caverns of Sheol, but how and where? It would, doubtlessly, be a small gap in the rock, a single insignificant little doorway or even a puddle of the black water into which they would need to plunge one at a time. But somewhere, somehow, there *was* a passage. He was convinced.

And if there was a way through to the *Chasm*, there was a way through to the *Tower of Doom*.

If the way *was* small, the entire gathering might be forced to wait while a few squeezed through to the *Chasm* beyond and if they survived that the real trouble would begin.

"Claudia?" He searched for the Roman slave girl in the fleeing crowd and she came to him, exhausted and breathless.

"Albert, we need to rest soon. We can't keep running like this forever."

"We'll stop soon. If that cloud reaches anyone they'll be wrapped and returned to their graves and we'll not be able to reach them again."

"I'm so tired."

"Soon. We'll rest soon. Where does the black river enter Sheol?"

Claudia shook her head.

"Sorry, Albert. I haven't a clue. I suppose it must be somewhere near my resting place but we've come such a way, I don't know where that is anymore."

"Don't worry. Look for anything that could be the river channel, or a chink of light, anything that could show us the way through to the *Chasm*. Spread the word."

*

The girls each took a chapel, Lucy dashing into the one

beyond Streicher's and Tyler sprinting for another as Melissa entered one in between. They hid behind tombs until the guards' footsteps and sweeping torch beams passed by. Tyler radioed the other girls.

"Cog, Pointer, keep the mark in hiding. If you come out and pace around a bit he'll think the guards are checking around. Shine your torches around, that kind of thing. Keep him hiding while I search this chapel."

"Wilco."

"Okay."

With the contrap primed, Tyler left her chapel and crept closer to the lurking, unknown presence. Two words would send it shrieking into the *Brimstone Chasm*, but for now she ventured out into the darkening nave, wanting to know its purpose.

"Who are you, spirit, and what do you want?" she asked.

The ghost remained still, regarding her calmly. It spoke with a soft depth, words coloured by an ancient tongue.

"Come closer, child, and I shall tell you. In life I was the Duke of Bohemia. You will know my name." With his face hidden by shadows, it was in his voice that she detected a hint of smile.

"You are King Wenceslaus? *Good King* Wenceslaus."

The spectre gave a subtle nod and beckoned her closer with a wave of his hand.

"There is something different about you, child. I feel it."

"Tyler. My name is Tyler. Yes, at least, I *have* something special." Tyler studied the contrap in her hands, the orange heat of the *Chasm* glowing from its crystal. With another step closer the otherworldly light bathed the ghost's features eerily and she knew she had nothing to fear. His expression was serene, his eyes welcoming. He was handsome, bearded and wearing royal, crimson robes but no crown. She switched the contrap to the *Safeguarding Skull* and let it hang from her neck.

"I thank you for your trust, but no, Tyler, it is not the intriguing object you carry, to which I refer. No matter. Follow me. There is something you need to see." The Duke drifted away from the arch of the nave to close on the St. Wenceslaus Chapel, pausing at the entrance only to wait for her.

"Wait," she said, stepping near to him. "I can't go in there. There are hidden cameras."

"There are, indeed." With regal grace, Wenceslaus waved a hand and a scatter of other medieval ghosts coalesced around the chapel's interior, servants, maids and house guards, some hovering near the ceiling vaults, others floating lower. They each dashed away at his signal. "My retinue, goodly fellows, one and all. Be assured, every security guard in the building is this very minute being thoroughly distracted. You will not be noticed, but be quick!"

"Why are you helping me?" Tyler scrutinised his face.

"You mean to thwart the evil that preys upon this land, do you not?"

"I do. Yes."

"That is enough for me. I have heard tell of the oppressor and his tyranny. You will find what you seek on the reliquary holding my bones. Remove it, if you will. It is a blight and an ignominy."

Tyler took a sketchbook from her bag and began

scribbling on a new page. "Is there a mark that looks like this?" She showed him the ring symbol she'd sketched.

Wenceslaus nodded. "That is the mark. A man came here a while ago to despoil my shrine with it."

Tyler gave Wenceslaus a nod and he waved her through into the chapel, adding "I shall remain to keep watch."

Tyler would have liked to wander the enclave at ease, marvelling at the many fascinating images and embellishments. One swift glance told her it was an amazing room, but against time and with Melissa and Lucy in mind she pressed on, running straight to the tomb. The reliquary on top was roofed and curtained in red velvet. She searched, lifting the cloth to look beneath at the glass sided, sealed box of bones. She found the mark hidden at the back and, taking an eraser from her pack, scrubbed at the ring symbol. She feared it would not move but as she rubbed, the image smudged and receded until it could barely be seen on the glossy surface. She removed the last lingering patch of pen or paint, she was not entirely sure which it was, with a little spit and her shirt sleeve. With all trace of the symbol gone, she returned to Wenceslaus to thank him.

"Thank *you*," he replied. "Know this, Tyler, you are not alone." He waved a hand and his retinue of ghosts returned to the chapel.

Tyler bowed her head briefly before jogging back to the other side of the nave where Melissa and Lucy paced, shining their torches into Streicher's chapel from time to time. She beckoned them away with a finger to her lips. Switching off their torches, they followed, throwing backward glances at Streicher's hiding place.

At the far end of the cathedral they gathered behind

the high altar, listening as distant guards locked final doors. The entire cathedral fell into silence.

"What do we do now?" whispered Melissa. "How are we going to get out of here?"

"We could hand ourselves in," suggested Lucy. "We could try explaining what we're doing here. Maybe they'd just let us go."

"No, they wouldn't!" countered Melissa. "They would try us as foreign spies, at the very least for attempting to steal the crown jewels."

"Wait," said Tyler, with a knowing smile. "Any minute now Streicher's going to get caught on the hidden cameras. By the way, I found the mark. The St. Wenceslaus Chapel is the second house of the skull."

"But Streicher is about to find it, too!" breathed Melissa.

"No, he isn't," said Tyler. "I erased it."

"Excellent!"

"I have to get back to our room," said Melissa with a new urgency. "I need to see the riddle again, and a map."

They waited in the dark until a distant alarm blared and security guards rushed to unlock and enter through an outer door. The guards tore by and as their clamour distanced towards the St. Wenceslaus Chapel Tyler, Melissa and Lucy slipped away through the open door.

*

Gathered in their room at the Four Seasons the girls ordered room service. Melissa studied the page of notes on the translated riddle.

Follow death's row,
Three houses of the skull,
Prague is his origin,

Next in line to sacrifice

Beneath this Melissa had added her own interpretation.

Follow the line of three houses
Each has a marked skull
Death begins in Prague
The location is a church within the line, or possibly next to the third house?

"Wait, wait, wait." She tapped the page. "I may have got this wrong. We have two of the three locations, correct?"

"Yes," said Tyler, crossing the room to look at the riddle. "The clock and the chapel." Lucy joined them with growing interest.

"So it stands to reason, if the three locations are in a line, I mean a straight line, the first two will point to the third. We need a map. We need a big map of Prague and the entire Czech Republic."

Lucy rummaged in her suitcase and produced an area map which she unfolded and spread on her bed.

"But you said you had something wrong," she said. "What did you mean?"

Melissa took a marker pen and drew red dots on the map, marking the astronomical clock and the St. Wenceslaus Chapel.

"It's one of the riddle lines. I thought that *Prague is his origin* may have meant Death begins in Prague when taken in context with the other lines, but now I'm not so sure. I think it's a reference to help locate the last location, the most important one. It could mean the line begins in Prague. Do you see?"

"That would change everything," said Tyler.

"Exactly." Melissa cleared a space on the floor and dragged the map off the bed.

"What are you doing?" asked Lucy.

"The bed's too spongy. I need a metre rule or something else long and straight so I can draw a line through the two locations. By extending the line we can see likely options for the third location."

"You could use your personal collection of uninteresting facts and figures. That's pretty long and straight," said Lucy.

Tyler punched Lucy on the arm.

"Do something useful and get the laser sight from your M4." Tyler glared.

"Okay, okay." Lucy fetched the laser sight and returned to hand it over. Tyler held the laser against the map to shine the fine, red beam along the line of the two marked locations.

Melissa met her gaze.

"We need to cross-reference with my list of potential houses of the skull. Any that don't fall in line are irrelevant. Somewhere along this red line sits what this whole thing is about, the last house of the skull. Find *that* and we find the reason Streicher is in Prague."

Kutna Hora

Melissa worked through several locations remaining on her list, places that lined up perfectly with the first two houses of the skull. She stopped and peered up from the map where she knelt.

"This has to be it, the Bone Church, Kutna Hora. It lines up perfectly. It's around seventy kilometres from Prague, but look at this." She stood and woke up her laptop to Google Kutna Hora. Search results swiftly filled the screen. She clicked on a link and played a YouTube video titled 'The Sedlec Ossuary' showing the interior of an old church decorated with thousands of bones, including numerous skulls. The camera view passed a variety of sculptures, each made from the artistic piling of bones, and paused to show details of a vast bone chandelier. Lucy gazed at the images with fascination.

"It's certainly a house of the skull. This place is crazy."

"It's my best bet. All the bones used inside as decoration used to be buried in the graveyard. Back in twelve seventy-eight the abbot of Sedlec Monastery returned from a visit to the Holy Land with a handful of Golgotha's soil. He sprinkled it around the cemetery grounds kick-starting its reputation as holy ground and causing it to grow in popularity as a place for burials among aristocrats. During the Black Death thirty thousand were buried there. It became so overcrowded the monks began exhuming old burials to make space for new ones. Over the years they collected the bones of between forty and seventy-thousand people and, later on, a woodcarver used the bones to make all these sculptures."

"That's creepy," said Tyler. "Get some sleep. First thing in the morning we're going there." She smiled to herself. "Finally we're one step ahead of Streicher. Let's keep it that way."

*

Albert followed Claudia beneath a low ceiling, scrambling over the recessed beds of sleepers.

"This way!" she called back to him over her shoulder. "I'm sure I saw a bead of light. It was the smallest glimmer, but I saw it."

"Keep going," Albert implored. Behind him massed the gathering of woken sleepers. Some were singing again, well ahead of the black wall. Albert had given up his song, now focusing on their escape, and he ran, not stopping to check the motionless faces of the sleepers he passed. Part way down this low chamber, he tripped and stumbled into a pit, coming face to face with sleeper. He scrambled out but looked again and stared in disbelief. The face in the grave was one he knew.

"Zebedee? Zebedee Lieberman? Wake up!" He stooped to shake the sleeping figure. Zebedee Lieberman was a bony figure of a man who, in his distinguished beard, black top hat and tailcoat, was a picture of the perfect funeral director. From a buttonhole in his waistcoat glimmered a gold chain that secured his pocket watch.

Ahead of him, Claudia paused. "Sing, Albert! You have to sing!"

Albert hurriedly sang a verse of his song and Zebedee stirred. With Albert's help he sat up and painstakingly climbed out of the recess, brushing at the cloying death-mist and sweeping it from the brim of his top hat.

"My dear boy, it's good to see you." Zebedee checked his pocket watch and brushed down his tailcoat. "Have I been out long? My pipe! I must find my pipe!" He riffled in his pockets and drew out a pipe with a long, curving stem. "Ah!"

"Too long. We can't 'ang around, Zebedee. There's a black wall of death-mist a'comin' this way and it's moving fast."

"Then there's no time to lose. We have to find Izabella. She must be here somewhere."

"Right, then sing!"

"Sing? Why the devil would I do that?"

"It's what wakes the sleepers. Izabella will know your voice. Mine too. Sing." Albert sang another verse as he searched about. He hesitated again. In a double sleeper cell at his feet rested Kinga and Danuta. A moment later his song woke them and they freed themselves of mist. Before Albert could explain what was happening, more figures rose from the beds. Marcus, the mute fiddler wearing shorts, a plain shirt and cloth cap, climbed to his feet. A moment later, Izabella, a rotund, elderly Russian in a flowery dress, clambered out to join the others and Albert helped more of them up from the pits: the Saxon warrior, the slave with his iron neck-ring, the British infantry man, the Jews and every other member of the Ghost Squad.

"Follow us!" he cried, as still more ghosts awoke and the entire Ghost Squad gambled along behind him. "'Ang on, Missy. I'm bringin' you an entire army!"

*

"Do you think we should've split up?" asked Tyler from the passenger seat of the Mustang.

"Yes," said Lucy, without pause.

"No," said Melissa. "Definitely not. We should stick together and, anyway, Katalin Mészáros seems to be pretty inactive right now. It's no loss that we don't have anyone on her."

The girls had been travelling through open farmland for over an hour since leaving central Prague, passing through the occasional village. The countryside around them bristled with lines of stark, leafless trees.

"Still, she could be up to something. I'd feel better if we could cover all bases."

"Well, we can't. We just don't have the resources and Chapman would've had us focus on this Streicher thing. Anyway, I expect she and Streicher have fallen out over the missing flash drive, the one we intercepted. Maybe that could be why she's so inactive. She's been cut off. How much longer?"

Lucy checked the satnav.

"Ten minutes. This is Miskovice coming up, the last village before Kutna Hora."

They passed broad log piles the size of small houses at the roadside and entered the village. On the other side of the modest settlement the road rose gently to cross a brow before curving towards Kutna Hora.

Tyler tried to swallow, dry-mouthed. It all led to this one place, this ancient and peculiar Bone Church, and she wondered what they might find there. She glanced behind at the road they had travelled, checking cars for any sign of Streicher and knew she would not feel so nervous if Albert was with her. She sipped coffee carefully from a cardboard cup as Lucy drove them through Kutna Hora, crossing roundabouts and passing town houses, restaurants and office blocks.

"Doesn't seem much different from any other town," said Tyler, watching the benign streets go by.

"Don't worry," said Lucy, glancing from the road. "There's nothing normal about the place we're heading."

Several turnings later they pulled up outside a café and, across the road, a pale rendered wall topped with terracotta tiles. They glimpsed the Sedlec Ossuary Bone Church rising beyond the bust-crowned wall pillars, the ornate baroque entrance arch and the tall trees within its grounds. The girls climbed out of their car and pulled white coats over their clothes. Ignoring inquisitive glances from the coffee-drinking living they prepared to enter a house of the dead. Melissa collected an aluminium hard case from the boot.

"All set?" asked Tyler, trying to suppress the malaise that was creeping over her. There were ghosts here.

Many of them.

She could sense them clustering, a dormant hive of the departed. Melissa paled and shot glances up and down the quiet street. The skull and crossbones marked in white cobbles on the path outside the gates did little to steady her nerves.

Lucy nodded. "Let's do it."

They ventured in through the gates and Lucy closed them, hanging a sign from their curling wrought iron that read CLOSED FOR CLEANING in both Czech and English. She worked her way around the church's side and through the well-kept and brightly flowered graveyard to leave another similar sign on the other entrance.

Few tourists visited this early in the day. The girls entered and passed a gift shop to one side offering a choice of postcards, fridge magnets, guidebooks, wine, and plastic skulls arrayed on shelves and beneath a glass-topped desk with a till drawer. At one end a CCTV monitor with a four-way split-screen displayed various aspects of the interior. Between them, the girls ushered several unimpressed sightseers out through the second gate and shut themselves in the bone-encrusted sanctuary where a cashier with curly, brown hair and wearing a blue suit hastily clipped across the hexagonal floor tiles to accost them. She babbled something in Czech that only Melissa understood. Melissa responded promptly in Czech and pulled out a laminated ID card with a photograph. While the woman stepped closer to squint at the details, Lucy stole silently behind her to jab her in the back of the neck with a hypodermic needle. The cashier gave an involuntary roll of her eyes before slumping in Lucy's arms. Tyler helped drag her limp body around to the gift shop where they laid her out of sight, behind the counter.

Tyler disengaged the CCTV hard drive from the camera feed and watched the monitor screen fill satisfyingly with static.

"Do you have the degausser?" she asked Melissa.

Melissa nodded and, unclasping the aluminium case, raised its lid and took out a degausser, passing it to Tyler. Tyler switched it on and erased the contents of the CCTV unit's hard drive, sweeping the device along the black casing several times.

With the degausser back in its case they descended broad steps into the heart of the ossuary.

Tyler stood for a moment on the cool flagstones of the dim interior, breathing the lingering scents of centuries of use: stale incense, wood polish, dust and damp.

"Okay, let's get to work," said Tyler, peering around at the bone sculptures and feeling the heavy, stifling aura from the mass of surrounding ghosts. She strained to sense their natures, only able to receive vague impressions. Some were benign, others less so, but ultimately she distinguished none she thought were too dangerous.

In the centre of the church four tall spikes jutted from the floor, each of their sides stacked with skulls and crossed bones. She began by checking every one of these skulls, climbing onto the spike plinths to reach those at the top. The entire place had a dusty, aged patina.

Lucy worked her way around one side of the central chamber to examine the bones of a giant coat of arms. In the bottom right-hand corner, small bones depicted a raven plucking the eye from a ginning skull.

"This place is awesome!"

"This place makes me feel odd," countered Melissa, standing in the open floor at the centre, slack-jawed.

"Come on, Agent Cog," said Lucy. "Make yourself

useful."

Melissa gingerly walked to a transept where metal grillwork closed off a section of the church from the public. Beyond the grill a stocky pyramid of neatly piled long bones and rows of skulls faced her. At its centre an open arch ran the pile's full depth. She inadvertently placed a hand on the grill and, thinking better of it, withdrew it to wipe it on her coat. She shivered.

"Do you think the symbol could be in there somewhere? There must be thousands of bones just in that one pile."

"We can't reach it easily so check the ones we *can* reach," said Lucy. "Get moving! We don't know how long we'll have before we're interrupted."

Melissa began searching the bones of wall decorations but couldn't resist taking her notes from her pocket to re-read the riddle, hoping for a clue to speed them.

"There's a ridiculous number of skulls in here. Whoever wrote this riddle surely couldn't expect someone to search every skull for a symbol. Surely that would be madness."

"And what part of this wild goose chase would you call sane?" quipped Lucy, clambering up steps to check more skulls.

"I don't know. I just don't think it makes sense. The answer must be here on this paper."

"Fine," said Tyler from the top of a spike. "You work on that while Lucy and I check the bones."

"It has to be something to do with the last line," said Melissa, thinking aloud. "*Next in line to sacrifice.* What *does* that mean?"

"Sounds like somebody's gonna die, to me," said

Lucy. She finished checking a turret of skulls and stood peering up at a bone chandelier clinging to the ceiling like a monstrous upturned spider. "Don't suppose anyone brought a ladder."

"Forget the chandelier and skulls draped from the ceiling. Work your way around that side," said Tyler, crossing to a corner where a niche housed a chalice sculpted from bones and mounted on a plinth, and edged by more columns of skulls and crossed bones. "I can fly up there later if I need to."

Sensing a presence nearby, she stopped.

"*Next in line to sacrifice*," continued Melissa. "It doesn't make sense, not taken literally anyway. Sounds like we should be looking for a list of sacrificial victims."

"I don't think you'll find one of those down here."

"So it's cryptic," said Lucy. "Like a crossword puzzle."

"That's exactly what it is. It's cryptic," concluded Melissa.

Tyler's senses worked frantically. A hidden ghost was close by. She felt it as surely as she felt the bones before her. A movement in the shadows of the niche opposite captured her attention. There a dark, hooded figure glided slowly back into obscurity leaving her to shiver and wonder.

"Let's hope Heydrich doesn't show up. I get the feeling there're enough reveries around here to drown us."

They worked in silence briefly, Tyler and Lucy checking skulls while Melissa wrestled over the last line of the riddle. "Next in line. If you rearrange the letters 'next' could read 'ten' with an X."

"X marks the spot," said Lucy. "X *always* marks the

spot."

Melissa began to gabble manically. "So it could mean ten in line next to sacrifice. Or an X in a line of ten. No. Not that. Ten skulls in a line. There's no shortage of them here. Wait, X is ten in Roman numerals. Why didn't I see that before? I don't think it's a line of ten. It's the *tenth* in a line. You make sacrifices on an altar." She turned to Tyler and Lucy. "Stop what you're doing. We're looking for the tenth skull in a line of skulls next to an altar!"

*

Again Claudia located the speck of light in the murk ahead and shouted across to Albert as they picked their way quickly between sleeper beds.

"This way. I see it!"

He changed tack and the other ghosts followed, ducking low beneath an overhang of rock and diving into a new chamber to be greeted by more sleepers, more pits and more darkness. The light was visible to all now, a pinprick at the very end of the cavern like a single, dull star in sky of pitch.

"Do you really think it's the way through to the *Chasm*?"

Albert squinted at the meagre glow.

"I 'ope so, for all our sakes." He turned to the fleeing mass of spirits. "Faster. Make for the light!" Albert and Claudia were the first to reach the end of the cavern where the ground fell away into what seemed a bottomless crevasse. They stopped, teetering on the edge as a barrage of followers rushed on to thump into them like a tsunami tide. They fell from the lip, tumbling uncontrollably in a waterfall of screaming ghosts as more dashed blindly over.

*

Melissa found the altar easily, its single candle keeping a lone vigil at the centre before it. Beyond the guttering flame, steps rose to a platform, overshadowed by a prominent crucifix, and on the time-battered walls either side climbed columns of toothless skulls.

"This is it!" hissed Melissa, awed by the sight. "Check the tenth skull on either side."

"Tenth from the top or tenth from the bottom?" asked Lucy, stepping over the barrier that sectioned off the altar from the rest of the interior. Tyler swung her leg over, heading for the column on the right.

"Check both." She counted up nine skulls from the lowest and examined the next one on her side, standing on her toes on the top step and stretching up as high as she could to see. "Nothing." She counted down but found nothing on the lower skull either.

"Got it!" said Lucy, tilting her head at the tenth skull down the column on her side of the altar. "This skull has the mark, something like a ring. Wait, there's something inside it!" She hooked a finger in through an eye socket and coaxed a small scroll of paper out through the gap. She unrolled the scroll to glance at it before handing it to Melissa across the barrier. "Here, I think it's in Czech."

A scuttling sound echoed from somewhere near the main entrance. The girls turned.

"What was that?" asked Melissa.

"I don't know. Check it out."

"I'll go," said Lucy, slipping her P99 from her shoulder holster. "You girls finish up here." She climbed free of the altar and left them to investigate.

Melissa glanced nervously at Tyler before staring at the scroll.

"It *is* Czech."

"Translate it!"

"Fourth from the centre of the X. Red."

"Another riddle. Great."

"Don't worry. This one's simpler. Even Lucy could get this one..." Melissa pointed to the floor at the feet where worn tiles spread out across the expanse in drab shades of red and black. "...eventually. Whatever's hidden here is beneath the fourth red floor tile from the middle of the cross, the cross being the crucifix."

Tyler found the centre of the altar and counted four red tiles out towards the middle of the church, ignoring the black tiles. She slid a gallows blade from her bandolier and scraped away at the grout around the edge of the tile, only to find it was not like the hardened stuff around the other tiles, but was softer, like putty or modelling clay. With a little effort she cleared the entire circumference and felt the tile come loose. Forcing the tip of the blade into the narrow gap she prised the tile up a few millimetres before the blade broke with a sharp snap.

"Here, let me help," said Melissa kneeling at her side and taking a gallows blade from her coat while Tyler slid another from her bandolier. It was easier with two blades. The tile lifted an inch but slipped back into its hole, slipping from the tips of the iron blades. They tried again, this time succeeding in raising the tile high enough for Tyler to slide the broken blade underneath. She levered the tile up and lifted it out. Placing it down on the floor at her side she peered into the hole where a small shaft ran down into the foundations of the church. At the bottom nestled a flat object wrapped in oil skin. She reached in as a man's voice close behind her froze her blood.

"You know, you're not the only capable spies in the vicinity."

Almost

Tyler and Melissa turned. Standing in the entrance arch at the base of the stairs Streicher greeted them with a broad, piggish smile. He gestured with the gun, telling them to rise and set the silver case on the floor. Tyler and Melissa stood and backed away.

Behind Streicher a huge man towered clamping Lucy in an unbreakable grip. One enormous hand covered her mouth as her eyes bulged with fury.

Tyler recognised him as the agent from Streicher's file, the one nicknamed Beast. He was even more brutal in real life; a burn scarred the left side of his hard-boned face and a short knife scar divided his jutting chin. The master stroke on this human work of art was the long, pink smile running half way round his neck, a failed garrotting hastily repaired with amateurish stitches. A heavy layer of powdery foundation barely concealed the faint blue glow of his skin.

"Drop the blades and step away from the hole,"
Streicher ordered. The girls obeyed. Tyler felt the weight
of the contrap around her neck as she retreated. *You're
not taking it, whatever happens.* She scanned frantically
for somewhere she might hide it.

"You two, up against the grill." Streicher turned to
his monstrous companion. "Put her over there with the
others. Watch them."

Beast shoved Lucy towards the grill. Standing with
their backs to the giant bone pyramid, the agents watched
their captors. Streicher passed his gun to Beast and
walked to the hole. He knelt to retrieve the object within
while Beast trained the gun on the girls.

"Don't move," he said, his booming voice
unmistakably German. Straightening, Streicher unfolded
the oil cloth to examine its contents: an old, leathery
book. He grinned. Intrigued by the book, Beast
momentarily took his eyes from the girls. While he
glanced away, Melissa pulled the gallows ring from her
finger and swallowed it with a sharp glance at Lucy. Tyler
snatched the contrap from her neck and tossed it through
the grill behind her into the void of the piled bones. Lucy
understood, coughing loudly to mask the sound of the
contrap's impact.

Beast spun his attention back on the girls.

"What was that?" His eyes darkened.

"I have a cough," said Lucy. "It's all this dust." She
coughed violently as evidence.

"Shut it!" Beast barked. He turned to Streicher who
pawed obsessively through the book with an insane grin.
"They're up to something. Should I search them?"

"All in good time. It's quite all right, my friend," said
Streicher. He wrapped the book in its oil cloth, placed it

into his case and cuffed the handle to his wrist. He crossed to the girls, smiling unpleasantly. "I have what I came for. Thank you, girls, for your kind help in locating what was lost. It's been challenging, tracking this little thing down." He waved the case in their faces. "But, utterly worthwhile." He turned to Beast.

"Keep the gun on them while I search them."

Tyler considered making a grab for her gun but quickly abandoned the idea. Convinced he had been deceived by their actions once, Beast watched the trio closely while Streicher pulled Tyler's gun free of her shoulder holster, shaking his head and tutting in her face.

"Anything else hidden away in there?" he asked, widening the neckline of her shirt with the tip of the gun to peer inside.

Tyler pinned the shirt to her chest with one hand.

"Nothing that'll ever be yours." She spat in his face. His reprisal was swift and emphatic. The butt of her gun impacted the back of her head with jarring force. She crashed to the floor, vaguely aware of Melissa's distant scream.

*

"Tyler? Tyler can you hear me?" The gentle feminine voice sounded a million miles away. "Tyler, open your eyes."

She tried, closing them when it was too much effort, too painful, the world beyond her lids too bright and too cold. She was too cold. Shivering. She became aware of a nauseating motion. Someone was rocking her.

"Stop it," she muttered. "Leave me alone." Icy, rusting iron pressed hard against the side of her face.

"Tyler, no one's touching you." She recognised Melissa's voice. "Tyler, you have to wake up. We were

133

drugged. The water's rising."

"The what?" Tyler opened her eyes again, this time forcing them to work despite the pain. Frigid liquid lapped at her feet, seeping into her boots and socks. She smelled salt and rust. A piercing crack of light blazed from above Melissa's bleary silhouette. Lucy moved into view, obscuring part of the glare.

"I'm so cold," muttered Lucy, through chattering teeth.

"Where are we?" Tyler knew the sensation, now. Nobody was rocking her. It was the motion of the sea. "Are we in a boat?" She battled to rise, hampered by the rolling of the waves, the odd angle of the iron floor and the residue of the drug in her system. Lucy helped her up.

"Of sorts. A shipping container, to be precise. We're being murdered by Streicher and Frankenstein's monster, so any time you feel like getting with it..."

"I think I'm with it now. We're going to drown." She put a hand to the void beneath her throat where the contrap usually hung.

"Very good."

"Can you see where we are?" Tyler scrambled up the sloping floor to squint through a crack in the door. Mile upon mile of billowing waves stretched out beyond. "I can't see land. Nothing. Not even a ship."

"The ship's long gone," said Melissa. "They scarpered as soon as our container hit the water."

Tyler sat down as a thunderous pain rolled around the back of her head. She glared at Melissa and Lucy, both sodden from the waist down. Water inched closer.

"We'll have to find something to prise the doors open with. What's under the water down there?

Anything we can use?" At the sunken end of the chamber, water continued to rise up the wall as the container sank lower with the spill from another wave. After an unbearable moment Melissa broke the news.

"There's nothing! Lucy and I already searched."

"Right." Tyler returned to the high end and rattled the doors, shouldered them and stamped at them. They held fast. She sat again, dismayed. "So there's nothing we can do."

"Not really," said Melissa. "We could try to stuff the gaps around the doors with our clothes to keep the container afloat for a little longer but that would only delay the inevitable. We're already dead. I'm sorry."

"It's not your fault." The water reached Tyler's feet.

"Oh, stop it!" shot Lucy. "Stop pretending. We all know whose fault this is: mine. Okay? I know! It's my fault. We all know. I stuffed up and now we're all going to die."

"I didn't say that," said Tyler.

"Admit it! I screwed up. I let Streicher and Beast get the better of me and I've as good as killed us all, and you, the *big heroine*, there's nothing even *you* can do about it."

"Is that what you believe? That I think I'm some kind of hero? Well I don't. I'm not. I didn't ask for any of this!"

They sulked in silence, huddled on the high end as water rose to their ankles.

"I'm not giving up." Tyler removed her coat and began forcing a sleeve between the submerged doors. She glared at the others. "Are you going to help, or what?"

They stood and joined her working to tightly pack the gaps with their clothing. The water reached the doors, streaming in despite the wadded clothes. Within moments it rose to their chests and the container lurched, tipping in the wake of a wave. They hurried to the sealed end to gather in the last remaining air-pocket, now a dwindling two feet deep.

"Well, it's been fun," muttered Lucy.

Tyler pounded on the roof and shouted.

"Help! Help us! We're trapped in here!" She continued to shout as Melissa and Lucy joined her in a desperate last hope.

The low throttling rumble of a motor silenced them.

"A boat!" It grew louder and, when it sounded like it was right outside the container, died. Waves lapped. The girls turned to each other and resumed their pounding and calling. Lucy hushed them to shout.

"Hello! Who are you? Can you get us out?"

A sudden, heavy thump boomed on the creaking metal above their heads. Footsteps thundered with a dull echo as someone on the roof stomped across towards the doors. A grating groan of iron replaced the thumps and something beyond their view snapped at the doors. One of the doors opened, flooding their space with wave-displaced aquamarine light. In the moment before the container filled, Tyler glimpsed a pair of bolt croppers and Klaus' face through the water. The girls gulped air into their lungs and swam.

"Klaus!"

"Grab my hand," said Klaus. He dragged her free as the container tipped again, belching the last of its air and sinking below the surface. Tyler clambered up onto its roof and helped Klaus pull Melissa and Lucy from the sea. He hauled on a rope at his waist to bring in the Zodiac Hurricane, as the container continued to sink, the sea past their knees. The girls hauled themselves aboard, dripping. Klaus pulled himself up into the boat and pulled blankets and a flask from a storage hatch. He passed the blankets and the girls wrapped themselves while he poured hot coffee from a flask, passing around the flask's single cup.

The red container descended silently into oblivion beneath the waves.

"Good riddance," said Lucy, with a curl of her lip.

"What the hell are you doing here?" asked Tyler. "I mean, don't get me wrong, I'm very grateful, but I was under the impression you were on operations in Iraq."

"I *was*, believe me. But Yash called me back home and reassigned me."

"To do what? Follow us?"

"Pretty much. I was ordered to follow at a distance, observe and report your movements."

"To spy on us? Great. He doesn't trust us but he trusts *you*, a foreign agent?"

"Yash knows me. We've worked together before."

"So have we!"

"I know, but not directly. Chapman's always been your section chief. Listen, there's a lot you don't know. A lot I need to tell you. Right now Yash doesn't trust anyone, *you* included. I'd like to say he asked me to watch over you, you know, to make sure nothing happened to you, but I'm afraid that couldn't be further from the truth. He gave me strict instructions not to intervene even if you *were* in trouble."

"Well, thanks for breaking protocol," said Lucy. "It's nice to know our superiors have our backs."

"My pleasure." Klaus threw a concerned glance at Lucy, cranked the outboard into life and steered them away, salt spray dashing their faces. He drove and for a while no one spoke. Tyler joined him at the wheel as land came into view through a low sea-haze. Lucy and Melissa remained huddled beyond earshot at the stern.

"Where are we?" The salt-laced wind stung Tyler's face.

"The Baltic Sea. That's Poland." Klaus pointed to a distant, grey line on the horizon. "And Germany's over there."

"There's something you're not telling us isn't there?" she asked, squinting through the far mists at the sliver of land.

"Like I said, I need to fill you in, but not here. I have some bad news, but first I'm taking you somewhere safe, warm and dry." Klaus throttled-up the motor and sped the Zodiac across the open water.

*

Albert landed in a heap as other ghosts rained down around him shouting complaints and groaning. Zebedee bounded to his feet with surprising agility, all elbows and knees, and straightened out his crumpled top hat.

"By Jove! What a shambles!"

"You shouldn't complain," muttered Izabella, rolling over onto her back. "You landed on something soft. And mind your cane in future!"

"Oh, dear." Zebedee helped her up. "My sincerest apologies."

The light was marginally brighter here. It illuminated the chamber with a dull sheen, highlighting the figure of a wiry ghost climbing out of a deeply-carved sleeper bed. As Albert struggled to his feet and dusted himself off, the rising sleeper turned slowly, revealing a thoughtful, handsome face and military-style hair.

More ghosts landed around Albert and he stepped

closer, clear of the fallout at his back.

"Naw, it can't be." He edged nearer doubting his eyes as the other ghost straightened. "But *you* can't be 'ere!" said Albert, blinking. "Not yet. Surely not!"

The wiry ghost peered down at his feet, through his transparent hands, and blinked back.

"Albert, am I dead?"

*

Klaus studied the readout of his handheld GPS and killed the outboard. Expectantly, he peered at the water beyond the Zodiac's bow. Tyler turned to him.

"What are we waiting for?"

"Shuush. I'm listening." Twenty metres ahead of them bubbles broke the surface. Moments later, the water churned and boiled as the bridge of a military submarine emerged.

"*That* is what we're waiting for," he said, yanking the outboard's starter chord and steering them closer to the stabilising submarine as it rose. Water cascaded from its exterior decks. The hatch wheel spun and a German officer opened the hatch to peer out. Klaus quickly moored the Zodiac to a railing and boarded the submarine with the girls, rushing to get through a hatch and down a ladder, out of the freezing air.

In the belly of the vessel they warmed, waiting as Klaus reported briefly to the captain. When he returned he was unable to meet Lucy's eyes.

"Lucy, sit down. It's about Weaver. Bad news." He gazed at one of the many airlock hatches and allowed his eyes to trace the line of pipes and pressure dials on the wall to one side.

Refusing to sit, Lucy glared at Klaus.

"What is it?" She stepped closer, her face draining of

colour. "What happened?"

"Weaver's dead, killed in action two days ago. I'm so sorry, Lucy."

Bad News

"Yes, Weaver, you's dead all right. When did you get 'ere?"

"I don't know. Last thing I knew I was running from a bomb blast outside a safe house in Jerusalem. Next minute I hear this distant singing and I'm waking up with this grainy gloop all over me. Where am I, Albert?" They stood motionless, an island amid a flowing sea of ghosts.

"You's in Sheol. You's in the grave. But now you's awake you gotta move. Come with us. Follow the light."

"Why? Where are we going?"

"No time. Follow the light!"

Albert and Weaver joined the tide heading for the narrowing tip of the cavern where a hot light dawned from a low entrance in the dank wall of stone.

*

A bearded German submariner brought in a pile of clean, dry jumpsuits and towels to deposit them on a bench near the hatch of their chamber.

"You should find some that fit," he said. Klaus thanked him and the submariner left. Melissa took one of the orange suits and Klaus turned his back while the girls changed out of their wet clothes.

"How? How did Weaver die?"

"He was undercover in Jerusalem, on a crucial mission. Successful but... He died a hero's death."

She glared at him, eyes burning.

"And what is that, Klaus? What exactly is *a hero's death*?"

Klaus sat on the bench and exhaled a long sigh, staring at his folded hands.

"I don't know, Lucy. I guess it's just something people say when they don't know *what* to say. I'm sorry. I'm sorry I don't know what to say."

"Were you with him?"

"No. I was on another op. I don't know much about it but it comes from a reliable source."

"Yash?"

Klaus nodded guardedly, his eyes alighting on Lucy and the other girls.

"He won't tell you while you're in the field. You aren't his next of kin and his mission was not pertinent to yours. There'll be a formal letter awaiting you when you arrive home."

"*Not pertinent*? And when will that be?" It was Lucy's turn to glare at the wall.

"I don't know that, either, but we need to get one thing straight. We're not here and you never saw me. I'm going to help you out, give you what information I have and set you on your way, but you're still on the Streicher Op. He clearly has something of great value to the NVF. I don't know what, but you should find out. Get back on his tracks and take it out of his hands before he leaves Prague, if he hasn't already gone."

Lucy shuffled closer to Klaus and let her head slump against his shoulder.

"I'm sorry," she murmured. "I know it isn't your fault."

Klaus instinctively wrapped a comforting arm around her.

"You don't know where Streicher is now?" asked Tyler, looking away when he met her gaze.

"No. When I followed the container from Kutna Hora I had to leave him and his henchman behind or risk losing you. Use the contrap. Track him down again." He released Lucy, glancing at Tyler's neckline as she paled. "They took the contrap?"

"No. At least, I don't think so. I tossed it into a pile of bones in the Sedlec Ossuary. I don't think they noticed. Beast was supposed to be watching me but he's pretty dumb. Streicher was obsessing over the book he took from beneath the ossuary floor.

"Do you know anything about the GAUNT machine?" she asked him.

"Of course. You mean the machine Streicher created; the one he and Bagshot used to bring back some of the Nazis? Yes."

"No, not that one." Tyler shook her head. "There's a new machine. He's made a second one. That huge guy hanging with Streicher is a gloved ghost. His name's Jürgen Schwinghammer, also known as *the Beast*. So

Yash isn't telling *you* everything either."

"Why would he? As you pointed out, I'm a foreign agent."

"I don't know. It's just... You seem to know more than we do about everything else. Is that everything, or is there more?"

"There's more but it can wait. I think Lucy could use a strong drink. Let's face it, we could all use a drink. I'll see what's on offer. The captain always carries brandy for such occasions."

The captain obligingly surrendered brandy, glasses and the use of his office quarters for Klaus and the girls and he left them to talk. Tyler sat at the small round table, sensing the only ghosts in the near vicinity were the drowned souls of the ancient dead who lingered beyond the life bubble of the submarine's rounded, steel hull. Klaus closed the hatch.

"What else?" asked Tyler, weary from recent events but steadily warming. "Are you going to tell us Yash thinks we've been turned? That we're working for the NVF or something?"

"No, it's not that simple. There is a mole in MI6. Someone's been leaking information, and Yash wants to be sure it isn't you. Don't worry too much. He's giving everyone the same treatment. He's brought me in and other trusted agents from outside sources to help."

Tyler sat back and sipped brandy feeling its liquid warmth burn her throat. Lucy was already on her second.

"So your mission was...?"

"To observe you three and report all movement, eyes only. Strict orders not to reveal myself or interfere in any way, even in the event of threat to life."

"Well you've blown that one," said Melissa.

144

"What can I say? I'm human."

"More human than Yash," muttered Lucy.

"Thank you," said Tyler.

"You're welcome." Klaus rolled the brandy in his glass and took a sip. "Do you have any idea who it might be?"

"The mole? No," said Tyler. The others shook their heads.

"I'm pretty sure it's no one from our office," offered Melissa.

"Maybe not but it has to be someone from your section."

"Why?"

"The information leaked can only have come from a source in your section, Chapman's section."

"Perkins, Jade, Harrow, Blithe. It could be any of them."

"Wait a minute," said Lucy, with sudden interest. "Weaver's death. Information leaked?"

Klaus gulped brandy to steel himself and held her gaze.

"Weaver's operation may have been compromised by leaked intelligence. I can't confirm it, but you can't approach Yash on this. Not yet. You can't say anything. You didn't see me and this meeting never took place. I presume you haven't told Yash about the shipping container and being drugged as I'm guessing Streicher took all your phones."

"Correct," said Melissa.

"Good. You can doctor your story."

"What about Chapman?" asked Tyler.

"What about him?"

"Do you know where he is? What he's up to?"

145

"He's missing."

"But what does that mean? No one will even talk about it."

"It means he's missing. He left London via clandestine means and hasn't returned. If Yash knows any more, he certainly isn't saying, but there's a good chance he doesn't know. Chapman could easily have been on an operation so secret that no one else knew of it. It wouldn't be the first time."

"Right."

"Did you hear about Tabriz?"

"What?"

"The Russians are pressing down ever closer to Saudi Arabia. They've taken Georgia and two days ago passed through Azerbaijan. Now they're pushing into Iran. It's assumed their motive is oil, but NATO is trying to halt their flow and re-establish order. We were overpowered at Tabriz when thousands of ghosts appeared, flooding into the suburbs. They massacred our soldiers."

"With gallows blades?"

"There have been other reports of sporadic, smaller groups armed with gallows blades but not at Tabriz. We sent drones to scour the battlefield when it was all over. Not a single blade was recovered, and it appears the dead had been killed with their own weapons."

"Reveries?"

Klaus nodded.

"It's the only logical conclusion."

"There's no defence against reveries," said Melissa. "The soldiers turned their weapons upon themselves."

"So Heydrich was there at Tabriz."

"There's something else," said Klaus.

"What now?"

"Streicher and I aren't the only ones who've been watching you lately." Klaus pulled a photograph from his inside pocket and handed it to Tyler. She studied the image of a swarthy man with wavy, raven hair combed tight to his head. He wore a long leather coat that Tyler thought might have been a war time relic judging by its state. "I first saw him at the tower on the bridge. He's been tailing you ever since. He may have also been among the crowds by the astronomical clock. I don't know who he is or why he's tracking you, but he is. He could be a malign presence, though I can't see a connection between him and Streicher so far."

"Great. Any more good news? I'm getting an inferiority complex." Tyler swigged the last of her brandy.

"No. I think that's about it. This man, I'm not convinced he's a threat. Either he's a rookie or he's trying to get caught. I'm surprised you haven't noticed him."

"Right. Pass the brandy."

*

The captain knocked and poked his head into the room, muttering in German. Klaus translated.

"There's a hot meal awaiting us in the mess."

Tyler and Melissa ate a bolstering meal of beef stew and grainy bread while Lucy poked at her food. After coffee they changed back into their civvies, now dried and warmed through. Klaus climbed with them to the submarine's upper deck to board the Zodiac and they motored towards the low slab of landmass as the sky glowered with velvety shades of burnt-amber. Behind them, the submarine submerged with a boil of foaming water and quickly vanished from sight.

The voyage to the port of Rostock took less than an hour and from there Klaus drove them to Rostock Airport where he produced a black bag from the boot of his car and accompanied the girls inside. In the departure zone he handed the bag to Tyler.

"New passports, phones and a little cash to see you safely back to your hotel. I presume you still have most of your gear back there."

Tyler nodded. "Unless our room's been compromised."

"If you do need anything else you'll have to call in to Yash for it. This is as far as I go. I'll be following you, but I can't be seen with you on the other side of this flight. I've risked enough as it is."

"What should we tell Yash? We better get our stories straight."

"Tell him the truth as far as possible. Just leave me out of it. You were drugged and dropped at sea in an old shipping container. You escaped and were rescued by a passing ship. You made your way back to Prague. I'll leave the details to you. I'll tell him I lost you in Kutna Hora."

"I can do that," said Tyler.

"Chapman would have sent someone to rescue us. He would have tracked our journey via satellite. Why didn't Yash?" asked Lucy.

"Good question," said Klaus.

"Maybe he lost the satellite feed," suggested Melissa. Klaus turned to Tyler and drew her close.

"Get back to Prague. Revisit the Bone Church. Find the contrap and trace Streicher."

"Yes, Sir." Tyler lent in to peck him on the cheek, wanting to take it further but resisting because Melissa and Lucy lingered close by. She settled for a whisper in his ear. "I'll miss you."

"I'll miss you, too," he breathed. He aimed a wink at her and headed for the exit.

"Good luck."

*

Weaver and Albert fought their way through to the front of the crowd along what appeared to be an ancient river bed. Amid this, a narrow ravine split the cave floor, its depths glistening with black water. The other ghosts stopped and stared at a small, neat doorway carved in the wall at the far end of the cave. From the doorway an orange glow wavered and everyone sensed it; this was the very end of Sheol, the close of a gargantuan realm. Beyond this point other powers ruled. Other dynamics applied. All around, ghosts peered at one another with a quickening mix of fear and excitement. A short way before the door, the ravine ended and the black river streamed into the ground beyond their view.

"The river running beneath here comes from the *Chasm*," said Albert.

"This is it," said Izabella, turning primly to him. "This is either a chance to escape, or the doom of us all. Who's to go first?"

Albert gazed above the doorway where shapes chiselled into the rock's surface caught in the frail light. Leaning closer, he saw two hands sculpted in relief and meeting at the tips of their thumbs and forefingers. The fingers of each hand were curiously spread into pairs. He looked back into the gloom of the cavern behind him where the black wall entered, like oil oozing in to fill a bottle.

"We don't have much time. I'll go ahead to check it's safe," he said and, with a lingering glance at the growing assembly of ghosts, he stepped towards the door. Weaver caught his arm.

"Wait! I'm coming with you."

The Death Ships of Hakan

The new tomb glimmered with an otherworldly light and Albert recognised it at once.

"The Cave of Sorrows." He paused to pinch the flesh of his forearm and found it more solid than his previous substance, as before when he'd entered the *Chasm* with Tyler to seek out the Mordecai chains. Here, he understood, he could be injured like the living, could feel pain, hunger, the cold, and even die a second death. As with Sheol, the Chasm did not allow ghosts to *cloak*. With an unnerving cocktail of terror and hope, he looked around as Weaver entered.

Across the rough stone floor lengths of chain lay scattered, glimmering softly and a flash of white light caught his attention deeper in the tomb. Albert dashed after it, hoping for a glimpse of its origin. He chased it through the passage to the outside but whatever had made the light had already flown.

A resonant peal of thunder greeted him and he halted in cold rain, panting and leaning on the great stone disc that had once sealed the tomb's entrance. A deep gully dipped away from the secluded tomb and the shadow of the thunderclouds overhead, and beyond, the fruitless cracked lands of the *Chasm* writhed and rolled like a living creature, broiling and shimmering with its strange fire. It rumbled and groaned beneath the lively patter of the rain.

"I know you're there!" he shouted, glaring along the ravine and up at the angry, blood-red and fiery-orange sky. "Why do you run?"

Weaver poked his head out of the tomb into the drizzle.

"What *was* that?" he asked, sniffing at the air. Albert smelt it too, the sulphurous reek of brimstone.

"A seraph. They guard the way but they let us through for some reason. You *is* in the full knowledge, right?"

Weaver nodded. "Of course."

"Good. Then you'll know you can't talk to anyone living about the seraphim. Go back an' tell the others we found the way. Quick!"

Weaver ducked back into the tomb and soon hundreds of ghosts streamed out from the entrance to blink in the hot light of the *Brimstone Chasm*. Izabella and Zebedee found Albert contemplating the gathering army.

"This is a lot of spirits to drag through the *Chasm*," said Izabella, fixing Albert with her clouded stare. "I trust your plan is to reach the *Tower of Doom* and pray Tyler chances upon you there."

"Yeah," said Albert, fearing a barrage of ridicule for the notion. "Somethin' like that."

Izabella nodded slowly while appraising him with candour. She stilled, a subtle smile blossoming on her wrinkled lips.

"It is an idea at least. I suppose it could work."

Zebedee stooped close to Albert.

"What she means is you really *are* a *brilliant* boy!"

"It ain't gonna be easy." Albert scanned the boiling horizon beyond the ravine's sheer edges.

"Indeed! The *Chasm* is fraught with perils, but we've survived it once before. We shall endeavour to do so again." As Izabella spoke, a deepening mass of cloud rolled nearer to obscure the pale, low sky. They peered at it uncertainly.

"What *is* that?" asked Albert.

Zebedee removed his hat and wiped his forehead with his sleeve.

"I'm not sure we should wait to find out."

"I'll gather the others." Albert turned. His ghost army spewed from the tomb door in single file and had already filled the little plateau outside. They talked, cried, babbled and jabbered in a chaotic din.

"Listen up!" he bellowed. "I know you's all wearied and wantin' rest but we ain't there yet. We 'ave t' keep moving, ya' see? Somewhere in the *Chasm* there's a tall tower with battlements. It's surrounded by a wood of twisted trees. It's the only patch of land that don't writhe. We 'ave to find it if we're ever to escape. See that?" He pointed up at the gathering mass in the sky. "That ain't nothin' good, and it's comin' our way! Grab as many of those glimmering chains as you can from the tomb and follow me. Run!"

They fled. Through panic or obedience, Albert was unsure, but he cared not. The mass in the sky closed fast, its details emerging into stark reality. Numerous, wide, crimson sails extended outwards from plunging galleys of iron-studded clinkers. Thick smoke swelled from beneath broad hulls where circular iron outlets vented fire and ash and along the sides of each ship's bow, lines of oars swayed in time to the boom of an unseen drum. Each oar ended with a wing that ballooned as it caught the air on the backward sweep and thinned on the forward stroke as grime from the fires drifted in an ugly haze in their wake, clouding an area of sky the size of a small city. More than that, Albert and the others dashing through the valley below failed to see, nor did they stop to make closer examination, but remote words reached them on the heated wind from above as they paused to catch breath.

"Heave, you vermin!" The crack of a whip followed the familiar gravelly voice. It was the voice of a contra-passo and, with it, memories came flooding: Albert fighting for his life in a horrific prison camp, freezing near to death in the dead of night, eating rotting bread crusts cast over the smouldering dirt ground and knowing a torturous thirst in the stifling midday heat beneath the *Chasm's* high, red sun.

"I didn't know the contrapassi had sky ships," puffed Zebedee at Albert's side.

"Who'd have thought?" panted Claudia, flashing the whites of her eyes.

"What's the contrapassi?" asked Weaver.

"*What's the contrapassi*, he says!" Zebedee muttered. "Suffice to say they're twice as high as a man, hairy and have the heads of temperamental jackals. They are always armoured with impenetrable plates of bronze and invariably armed with machine guns or whips, or staves, blades or other instruments of pain. Their very raison d'être is to torture. They're loathsome creatures devoid of anything worthy. Take it from me, boy, they're trouble!"

Purple-faced and gasping, Izabella glared at her friends.

"Unless you wish to meet one I suggest you save your energy and RUN!" She set off again with renewed vigour, the skirts of her flowery dress flagging from her wobbling thighs.

The ghosts left the confining slopes of the ravine and spilled out on to the banks of a black river. Past the snaking water the first ship landed with an almighty deluge of steam and smog from its vents.

Claudia screamed at the sight of the unnatural water and skidded to a halt. She scrambled away and back-tracked until Albert shouted.

"No! Not that way. Follow the bank!" He waved the others on as he turned to flank the water's edge. Weaver pulled his gun from his shoulder holster and aimed at the closest contrapasso.

"Young man, that's not going to work down here," warned Izabella. Weaver took a shot and found the gun clicked harmlessly like a child's toy. Across the water the beast roared and gnashed its teeth, hackles quivering with rage.

"Of course. What was I thinking?" Weaver returned his gun to its holster.

Other contrapassi leapt from the bow of the grounded ship and a second vessel came in to alight with a belch of noxious fumes.

"Interesting," mused Zebedee, mastering a bandy-legged, high-kneed jog. "I don't recall seeing any with bows and arrows before."

"Yes, *fascinating*," quipped Claudia, her eyes bulging at the sight of more jackal-headed monsters streaming from the ships. Hapless ghosts, prisoners of the jackal crew, peered out helplessly from the gunnel balustrades, their feet shackled to the decks. Behind the first of the landing vessels, others dropped their ropes and contrapassi zipped to the ground ahead of the descending hulls. The hulking creatures swaggered out from the fleet to edge the river, the twin lightning bolt insignias gleaming from their breastplates. Some loosed arrows from their roughly-hewn bows while others waded, thigh-high, into the viscous black flow.

Albert wondered at the death-water, knowing that if he, or any other of the ghosts there, were to venture in they would be swallowed and dragged away by an overwhelming undercurrent, only to wash up amid the binding death-mists of Sheol. Not so the Contrapassi, it seemed. To them the water appeared benign.

Albert's ghosts fled, avoiding the black waters.

"Don't go near the water! Keep away from the river!" he shouted as he ran.

The river snaked beyond its bed, hungry for spirits to consume. The banks at its edges rose and fell in a slow, unpredictable undulation as they ran. Rounding the slope of the valley end, a forest heaved into view, trees swaying with the pitching ground.

"The forest! Head for the trees!" called Albert, tacking around to his right. The mass of ghosts behind turned to flock towards the trees. Behind them the contrapassi quickened like a startled herd of lumbering wildebeest, their manes and forelocks tussling, their enormous clawed feet pounding the barren ground. A sudden volley of ropes and nets shot from their lines, coming down to trap ghosts. Other ghosts fell to the arrows unleashed in wave upon wave and the giant creatures slowed to secure their captives.

Scowling with fury, Albert pressed on at the head of the survivors to plunge into the woodland leaving the monsters behind. A quarter mile in, he collapsed, planting his back against a tall pine where he remained panting as the others gathered round. A long process of checking followed to ascertain who was missing from the army. Albert counted names as they were called by the various ghosts who could not find certain individuals among their number and, after personally searching at length, he returned to his tree and cradled his head in his hands. By his calculations at least fifty of them were now *guests* of the contrapassi and the true number was probably much higher. A paltry handful of Mordecai chains had made it with them. The ghosts who had managed to bring them were exhausted from their weight.

"We'll have to take turns carrying the chains," he told the survivors. "They're too heavy for one ghost to carry for long. Now listen up! You all need to know 'ow to use them chains. We don't know who'll end up with 'em if the contrapassi attack again. You throw the chain as you say the command: Mordecai obligo. The chain will bind whoever it meets. To release the chain you just say Mordecai resolvo. Got it?" Ghosts nodded.

Zebedee came over, lit his long-stemmed pipe and puffed away on its tip.

"Izabella's gone," he said. "Couldn't keep up. The contrapassi have her."

"It ain't just Izabella," said Albert. He released a low,

mournful groan. "Marcus is missin', too. So's my Da and, worst of all, my Molly."

*

No one spoke for a long time while everyone absorbed the knowledge of their losses. When rested and feeling stronger, Albert roused the remaining army and set off again, this time at an easier pace. They tramped through the forest. It seemed to have a mind of its own, growing larger and diving into vales and obscure slopes at random intervals. Even the leaf-strewn floor shimmered with the strange flames Tyler had called fire-fog.

"They'll be in a prison camp by now." Zebedee strode nimbly at his side. "We'll have to find them and break them out somehow."

Albert removed his cap and used it to wipe sweat from his face. The *Chasm* heat reached every nook during the daylight.

"Agreed, but first we find the tower. It's our only hope. From there we can gather ourselves, rest, eat, even mount an attack when we're ready. When we've found the tower we'll send out search parties for the others. Make a plan."

"Jolly good!" chortled Zebedee. "I knew you wouldn't let us down." He tousled Albert's hair before leaving to converse with the remnants of the Ghost Squad as they trudged. Albert replaced his cap and explained to Claudia all that had happened since her entrapment by the black lagoon.

"So you see," he said in conclusion, "the under realms are growing stronger and the magic of the mortal realm builds. The contrap ain't the only magical artefact any more. There's others comin' out of the woodwork left, right and centre and there's more ghosts roaming the mortal world than ever before. The livin' stopped trying to deny their presence long ago. The world's been plunged into chaos and war by the spirit of the oppressor. They're callin' it World War Three. And just look at this place. Do you see it? It's changed since we were last here, grown stronger, more powerful. I sees it. I feels it in my essence. The whole place smoulders with it."

"Do you think *that* was his purpose all along?"

"No, 'is purpose runs deeper than that. The war's merely 'is means to another, darker end. I fear 'e wishes to tear a rift from the mortal world into the under realms."

"But that would–"

"Yeah," said Albert, meeting her eyes with a steeled gaze. "Exactly."

*

Izabella glared through the net at the distant heat haze and twisting black river, her humiliation complete.

"Retched hairball," she muttered, amid the clink and rattle of bronze armour. The net dug into her skin painfully.

Her captor, a thick-set contrapasso with broad hackles, dragged her and Marcus along the smouldering dirt towards the grounded fleet. It hauled them up a rough gangway into a ship where it spilled them out onto an iron-clad deck.

"Man the bellows!" it roared to the sneering crewmembers lingering beyond the companionway. "Full sails and cast off. Commander, let's have this old cog off the dust before Hakan has us flogged."

Two other contrapassi stomped closer. They stooped and locked manacles around Izabella's ankle and wrists. Seizing the opportunity, free of the net and with the other beasts busy, Marcus dashed for the gunnel in a desperate, last-ditch attempt at escape. He slipped and slid on the iron deck and grappled his way closer to the gangway, losing his violin in the process. At the boom of deep, throaty laughter, he turned. Three hulking contrapassi clomped over to block his way, hemming him in. One bent to shackle him as another snatched his violin from the deck.

"Can you play this thing?" the contrapasso thundered.

Marcus gave a dour nod.

"The Master will hear of this." The contrapasso marched away, the fiddle and its bow dwarfed in his hands.

The remaining beasts bundled Marcus and Izabella to the edge of the companionway and kicked them down the stairs.

Below deck, Izabella and Marcus rolled to a stop, squinting around in the half-light and nursing their wounds as best they could. Izabella examined the tears in her dress and her bleeding elbows. Blood streamed from Marcus' temple where he had landed against one of the deck supports and he flexed an agonising, twisted ankle.

As their eyes adjusted to the gloom, they made out the sorry shapes of other imprisoned ghosts and, in the glare of a furnace deeper in the heart of the ship, witnessed contrapassi feeding the flames through a circular fire door twice as broad as a man. Hideous screams split the choking air. The fire-feeders manned positions either side of the furnace to heave on immense bellows, fanning the inner fire with roaring blasts and, with each gust, a new plume of blackened smoke and ash rolled from the fire door. One of them snarled to workers somewhere above on the upper deck.

"More oil!"

Izabella leant in close.

"There are many others down here, Marcus. Other prisoners like us."

The manacled ghost of a French aristocrat sat within the chained ranks nearby. His once-prim and bleached wig of curling ringlets perched, soiled and askew, over his leaden brow and his fine coat and frilled shirt bore the stains and grime of an age in the *Chasm*. He peered up to correct Izabella.

"No, Mademoiselle, we are not prisoners." He turned to look down the hold at the monstrous fire-feeders, dread glowing from the whites of his eyes. "We are fuel. We are fuel for the death ships of Hakan."

Beneath the Skin

Collapsing on her bed in the hotel, Tyler felt her world crumbling. *I've lost the contrap, lost Streicher, lost all leads on the remaining gloves. Weaver's dead. I will never see Albert or the Ghost Squad again. I'm tired beyond bearing, beaten, aching and I need to see my shrink. Is life really supposed to be this hard?*

Underlying this, she harboured a stupefying fear that the contrap may have already fallen into the hands of the enemy. The dread brought beads of sweat to her brow. She wished she could turn to Albert for a few shrewd words of encouragement, but she couldn't even call Klaus, not when Lucy grieved silently across the room.

She watched them, Melissa with a comforting arm around the stone-like figure of Lucy, the pair perched on the edge of a hotel bed. Weaver's death had brought Melissa and Lucy unexpectedly close, forcing Tyler to constantly bite her tongue each time Klaus came to mind.

She took a compact mirror from her bag and dabbed at the wound on her head with cotton wool and iodine. When satisfied the wound was clean she rummaged through black armoured cases until she found her spare gun. She slotted a full clip into the handle before slipping the gun beneath her pillow, along with a couple of gallows blades.

Lucy hadn't cried, not yet, but it would come and they all knew it. In the meantime an unspoken law prevailed; romantic relationships were to be closeted. Lucy's gaze was cold at the best of times but right now she seemed to reserve the bitterest looks for Tyler, who hated treading this fragile ground of fracturing shells. She wanted to get on with things, get back out there to reclaim the contrap with all haste, if that was possible, but practical issues clouded her path. The late night flight back to Prague had thwarted her and sleep was necessary whether time allowed or not. She stripped and slid beneath the soft covers of the bed grateful, at least, for Klaus' rescue and a comfortable room.

*

Lucy needed time out, time away from the other girls.

Time away from everything.

She rose at dawn and took the Aprilia out on the open road, leather-clad, desolate and incensed. Speeding every mile of the way, she arrived in Kutna Hora long before Melissa and Tyler pulled up outside the Sedlec Ossuary in their taxi. They found the Mustang parked where they had left it the previous day.

Lucy sat dourly on a bench in the graveyard beyond the iron gates. The ossuary itself was closed, yellow police tape strapped across the double doors. She looked up at Tyler's approach, and curled her lip.

"I haven't touched anything, but the place is clean. I staked it out for forty-five minutes before you got here. Thought I'd wait until the lock-picking expert arrived."

"At least we won't need to sedate anyone this time," said Melissa.

"The local police are obviously investigating what went on yesterday. You two keep watch while I get us in." Tyler ransacked her replacement bag for the slender, steel tools she would need. The lock mechanism was nothing unusual or challenging. She picked it in seconds and opened the church door.

"Mel, with me. Lucy, replace the tape once we're in and wait out here. Warn me if the police or anyone else turns up. This shouldn't take long."

"Okay."

Feeling her nerves unravel, Tyler slipped into the ossuary, followed by Melissa. Tyler checked the CCTV system as she passed the gift shop. The hard drive unit was gone, in the hands of the police, she supposed. She and Melissa descended the stone steps, their footfalls echoing in the deathly quiet.

"This is it, Mel. In a few moments we'll know if they found the contrap or not. We'll know if the oppressor has what he's been after all along."

Melissa stopped before the grill demarking the mammoth collection of bones into which Tyler had tossed the contrap.

"First we have to get in there."

"Give me a second." Tyler, viewed the top of the wire caging. The grill stopped short of the ceiling, ending three metres from the tiled floor. Three wooden arches extended to meet the larger stone arch of the niche. A short climb and she would be up and over, among the bones. She felt the unsettling sensation of ghost eyes watching as she scaled the grill and clambered over the top.

"Come on, Mel. It's easy." She waited near the top on the far side while Melissa ascended, and helped her over through one of the wooden arches. They climbed down and began their search.

Skulls clattered and rolled as Tyler pushed her way into the arched tunnel beneath the bone pyramid while Melissa searched from the other end. Here skulls had been packed cheek to dusty cheek, covering the entire floor. It felt wrong to clamber over the remains, but Tyler didn't have time for superstition or reverence. She squeezed into the tunnel and rummaged for the contrap at the exact spot she thought it had landed.

Nothing.

A shock of panic rocked her.

"I think it's gone. It fell right here. I'm sure, but I can't see it, Mel." The sensation pulsed more strongly. Her gut told her she should go. The little voice in her head screamed 'Get out now!' Ghosts were closing in. She sensed their creeping shadows edging around the church grounds

Not now! I can't stop now. I have to find the contrap or...

"Keep looking." Melissa grimaced at the other side of the bone archway, blocking the light. With Tyler's body shadowing the front, the passage between was dark. Tyler wrestled a small Maglite from her pocket, switched it on and passed its beam over the skull floor. Domed shadows lengthened and shrank as she worked.

"It's not here. I knew it wouldn't be. We've lost

Streicher and without the contrap we've lost our only way of finding him. I don't know why I–" Tyler trembled.

"Okay. Let's do this systematically," said Melissa with a calming voice. "Check every gap between every skull. You start at that end and work your way in. We'll meet in the middle. Urgh. This is gross. I should have swapped places with Lucy." Melissa took out her torch and searched as Tyler backtracked to the first line of skulls. "Do you think it could have slipped right underneath one of these skulls?"

"Who knows? I guess it's possible. Mel, I'm getting ghost-blind, like in Chacarita. There are ghosts moving all around."

"Of course there are. Look where we are. Right. Back to the beginning. Lift every single skull one at a time to be sure we haven't missed it somewhere."

"Mel, you're not listening! You *do* remember Chacarita, right? Reveries swarming out of the trees, feeding on your life-force, Heydrich carrying you off through the tombs–"

"I get the point but we *have* to find the contrap. It *has* to be here or we're screwed."

"Agreed. All right, work faster and let's get out of here. I'm sensing some bad ghosts, some *very* bad ghosts." They quickened their efforts, urgently searching every inch of floor within the arch only to meet midway empty handed.

"See? I told you. It isn't here."

"Then Streicher has it," Melissa concluded, "and this mess just got a whole lot worse."

A burst of noise from the main doors startled them out of the bone stack. A black-haired, middle-aged man in a worn leather coat blundered into the ossuary, hands raised and groaning. Tyler recognised him as the man Klaus had described as their mysterious shadow.

"Okay, okay. You do not need to hurt me!" he gabbled in a heavy Czech accent. Lucy appeared, silhouetted in the doorway behind him, shoving him forwards, her P99 trained on the back of his neck.

"Get in there and quit complaining. I hate whingers. Keep your hands up." She prodded him with the gun's muzzle. "Higher!"

Tyler and Melissa scrambled over the grill and out of the niche as the man approached.

"I am not a whinger. You nearly broke my skull."

"Yeah, yeah. You've mistaken me for someone who cares. Get over there, face down on the floor, hands on your head. Spread your legs. No funny business. I'm already in a bad mood so I won't muck about."

Her captive obliged, nodding and puffing a wordless protest of wind as he clambered to the ground and laid his face against the cold, grimy tiles.

"Why are you following us?"

"I told you I mean you no harm."

"Answer the question!" Lucy took a short run up and booted him in the ribs with one of her substantial, glossy Goth boots. "Who are you?"

Tyler and Melissa joined her, standing over the wincing prisoner. Lucy prepared to strike another blow as he waved his palms submissively.

"Woa, woa, woa! I can help you. Give me a minute to explain," he pleaded, showing her his open hands before rubbing at a lump on the back of his head.

Lucy delayed her next kick. "Explain what? Search him."

"Don't you think we should hear what he has to say?"

asked Melissa.

"Search him! He may have a gun!"

Melissa searched him begrudgingly.

"It's gone, by the way," Tyler told Lucy while Melissa worked. "The others must have found it."

"I don't have a gun or any weapon. I need to stand up," said the man.

"He's clean," said Melissa, opening the wallet she'd taken from his inside coat pocket. She studied credit cards and a driving licence.

"My name is Lumir Barak. I'm a citizen of the Czech Republic, a nationalist and a humble cartographer. My friends just call me Barak."

"*You* have *friends*?"

"He's telling the truth about his name, at least. Either that or he stole Lumir Barak's wallet."

He spoke with an easy going manner, unperturbed by Lucy's threats. "I need to show you something. I admit I've been following you but I can explain, honestly. Just hear me out."

"You seem pretty calm for someone with a gun to their head."

"I'm a laid-back guy. Everyone tells me so. I am no threat to you."

"All right," said Tyler. "Get up. No sudden moves or my friend here will shoot you." Barak slowly climbed to his feet and held his hands aloft. He glanced at his captors in turn and shrugged. He gave a brief, uncomfortable smile, the leathery edges of his mouth creasing, and moved a hand towards his coat pocket.

Lucy pressed the muzzle of her gun into the back of his neck. "Just give me a reason."

Barak froze.

"What I have to show you is in the inside pocket of my coat, but I don't want to show you here, anyway. It's not safe."

Melissa stuffed Barak's wallet back into his coat pocket.

Tyler nodded and looked at the other girls. The weight of the lingering phantoms close by was oppressive and worrying.

"He's right. Too many ghosts."

*

Barak climbed awkwardly from the back seat of the Mustang, hands cuffed at his back. The girls left the car and took him through a dilapidated farm gate and further on into an expansive, bleak field. A bank of hedgerow hid them from the road and the distant farm house.

"This'll do," said Tyler, training her gun on Barak's chest. She nodded to Lucy. "Take a look. See what he's got."

Lucy slapped Barak hard across the face and jabbed a finger towards his face. "Don't try anything." She opened his battered coat to delve into an inside pocket and drew out a small, red notebook.

"Is this it?"

Barak nodded. "Read it."

Lucy took the book to Melissa while Tyler watched Barak. Lucy and Melissa flipped through several pages.

"It's a journal of Streicher's movements," said Melissa, after a moment's study. "I have a similar one in my pocket. He even has Streicher's fake name written in here."

"You see," said Barak. "I've been tracking him, too. You and I are on the same side."

"And what side is that, exactly? Why are you

following Streicher?" asked Tyler.

"He already admitted he was following us," said Lucy.

"I was only following you because you were following him."

"The journal proves nothing," said Lucy.

"Like I said, whose side are you on and why were you following Streicher?"

"It's complicated. I'm looking for something, something that belongs to my brother. Streicher knows something about its location. Listen, I suggest we get some coffee, sit down somewhere comfortable, somewhere safe, and I can tell you all about it."

Tyler gave Barak a long measuring look, deciding he seemed honest.

"Coffee does sound good," said Lucy, watching him.

Tyler took a chance and went with her gut.

"Okay, but you look the wrong way and we'll drag you back here to finish you off."

*

Tyler sat down opposite Barak and set her coffee on the circular table in the quiet end of the cafe. Barak visibly relaxed amongst other civilians. Melissa and Lucy settled either side around the table so they could talk quietly enough not to be overheard.

"Well?" demanded Tyler, watching him impatiently. *If Streicher has the contrap, I need to track him down and get it back asap. I'm useless without it.* "You'd better not be wasting our time."

Barak glowered back at Tyler as he considered where to begin. He spoke with a brisk, accurate inflection.

"It concerns my brother, an antiques dealer. He holds internet auctions, some of them attracting

171

worldwide custom. Sometimes the lots are precious antiques or ancient, valuable and rare items." Barak paused to stir cream into his coffee. He peered out of the café window across the busy Prague streets where the midday sun glistened from snow-trodden cobbles and played against masonry in golden tones. "This whole thing began when my brother, Řezník, acquired an ancient and highly valuable book."

"What book?" asked Lucy, the gun in her jacket pocket pointed firmly at Barak beneath the table.

"A one of a kind. A book so rare that general consensus purported it to have never been written. At first we thought it a forgery, but Řezník had it scientifically studied in secret and the results proved it genuine. It's certainly old enough and writing comparisons with an existing book by the same author convinced the specialists. It's happened before, an important artefact previously unknown to the world rises from obscurity, a lost van Gogh or an undocumented Ming of supreme antiquarian value."

Tyler caught Melissa's brightening gaze and gave a subtle shake of the head.

Don't mention that we saw Streicher take a book from the floor of the church. Not yet.

Melissa remained quiet.

"Go on," prompted Tyler.

"This book was written by an alchemist who lived sometime before the Fourteenth Century. His name was Abraham Eleazar."

Astral Theorem

Barak sipped hot coffee and replaced his cup on the saucer with calm precision.

"To those initiated in these matters, this name is synonymous with that of the famed alchemist Nicholas Flamel, for another of his books, a volume titled The Book of Abraham the Jew, was the inspiration for much of Flamel's work. But this book, the one in my brother's possession, was an unknown work by the very same Abraham and its sudden emergence caused a stir among collectors."

"What has this to do with Streicher? Is this about money?" Tyler grimaced. *We're wasting time here chasing a dusty, old book while Streicher is winging the contrap into the hands of the new Führer.* She swore below her breath, privately damning Yash for ever sending them on this barren mission. Barak shook his head and smiled knowingly.

"No. This is about more than money, potentially a great deal more."

"What do you mean?" Lucy scowled.

"What's the book about?" asked Melissa.

"The book is titled Astral Theorem. It's an ancient work on astral bodies and concerns the creation and manipulation of certain theoretical artefacts. The text itself is full of obscurities, is highly complex and difficult to comprehend. It also contains a plethora of bizarre diagrams and illustrations. There was a bidding war when my brother announced its availability online. That was the start of the trouble."

"Trouble?"

"People started following my brother, strange foreigners, fanatics.

"And spies.

"He was harassed in the street, dragged into dark alleyways and offered underhand deals for the book, threatened during anonymous phone calls and through nameless text messages and emails. He confided in me. He was afraid the book would be stolen before it ever came to auction, but I thought him paranoid. I told him it was just a worthless, old book and that he was losing his mind. What happened next proved I've never been more wrong."

Barak raised his cup and took a deep swig before dabbing his mouth in his constrained, exacting manner with a white paper serviette.

"My brother had every right to be concerned. It was then he hid the book. He told no one, not even me, where he had concealed it. Shortly after he did this, he disappeared. I've been looking for him ever since. Over the following few months I learned a few things that led

174

me to that man calling himself Ernst Packmann. I'm not surprised to hear this is a fake name. He is a spy, is he not?"

Tyler turned to the other girls.

"We need to talk."

"Wait a minute," Barak interrupted, rubbing at his five o'clock shadow. His dark eyes locked onto Tyler's with purpose. "I've told you why *I* was following that man. Now it's your turn. What do you know about him and my brother's disappearance? Do you know where he is?"

"Wait there and don't even think about running," said Tyler, drawing Melissa and Lucy away from the table to conspire. Barak sat back, shrugged with resignation and drank coffee.

"What do you think?" asked Tyler, almost bumping heads with the other girls.

"He seems genuine," said Melissa.

"That's what I thought."

"I don't trust him." Lucy glanced sideways at Barak. "He could be hiding something. His whole story could be invented to help him break in to our team, to win our confidence. He could be a spy after the contrap."

"You don't trust anyone," said Melissa.

"I trusted Weaver."

Tyler glanced at her friends in turn during a brief silence.

"We have to decide somehow."

"Can I make a suggestion?" asked Melissa.

"Fire away."

"Bring him in but *need to know* only. Let him believe we want to help him find his brother. We've lost the contrap anyway so he can't take it from us."

Tyler nodded. "See what he tells us and take it from there."

Lucy shrugged. "I guess."

*

They resumed their positions at the table.

"We'll help you, you help us," said Tyler.

"I don't know who you are or who you're working for. You're obviously not Czech and I never asked for your help. You attacked me and marched me out into a field at gunpoint. Even now this girl here," Barak nodded at Lucy, "has a gun trained on me beneath the table. Why should I trust you?"

"He has a point," nodded Lucy. "We could just take him back to the field, dispose of him quietly."

Tyler took a further gamble.

"What do you know about the NVF?"

"Nothing. Should I know about them?"

"We're British intelligence. The real name of the man you've been following is Lucas Streicher. He's a spy. As far we are aware, he's working for the NVF, the Nazi organisation behind the war. We were sent here to observe his movements." Tyler turned to Melissa.

"Show him the note."

"Tyler?" Melissa's jaw dropped.

"It'll be okay. I trust him."

"Even so, I can't show him." Melissa's frown betrayed her annoyance. "Streicher took it."

"But you remember it, right?" Tyler tore a page from her pocketbook and passed it to Melissa along with a pen. Melissa quickly scribbled out the riddle and shoved the page across the table for Barak to read.

Follow death's row
Three houses of the skull
Prague is his origin
Next in line to sacrifice

"These words were written by my brother. This is him. This is exactly what he would write if he wanted to get a message to someone. Wait a minute. It's as though this note were for me, as though he was trying to get word to me, to tell me where to find the book. This is bad news. It means he's trapped somewhere or else he would just come home and collect the book himself.

"Three houses of the skull. Let me guess, the astronomical clock, the St. Wenceslaus Chapel and finally the Bone Church. Yes, I would have recognised these as the three houses of the skull and my brother knew it. So that's what Streicher and the giant took from beneath the church floor. I couldn't quite see from my hiding place but now it all makes perfect sense. They already have the book."

"You mentioned the book concerns the creation and manipulation of certain theoretical artefacts. What exactly did you mean by that?"

Barak poured more coffee and added cream.

"I'm not sure I can help you there. I spent only a few moments perusing the manuscript and I'm no scholar."

"You mentioned pictures, illustrations."

"Yes."

There was a pause while Tyler took the paper from the table and sketched the contrap on the blank side. She slid it over to Barak.

"Did anything in there look like this?"

Barak's eyes sparked when they fell upon the image,

but he shook his head.

"There was nothing like this in the book of Astral Theorem."

"Are you sure?"

"Yes."

"Have you seen this somewhere else?"

He looked again at the contrap sketch and then back at Tyler.

"Perhaps. I'm not sure."

"What *were* the pictures in the book?" growled Lucy.

"Strange drawings: odd symbols, dragons, hills, caves, trees and rivers. Some were of flasks, like vases or bottles. There were various winged creatures and many oddities. I can't remember them all."

"What about a ring?" asked Melissa, quickening. "Was there a ring?"

Barak paused, frowning momentarily.

"Yes, several rings. There were some forged from creatures, a snake with its tail in its mouth, forming a loop."

"It's called an ouroboros," said Melissa. "It's an ancient Greek symbol, the one we've been searching for. Tyler, this book could be incredibly important to the NVF. We need to speak privately."

They broke away once more as Barak rolled his eyes.

"You think the book may have something to do with the rings of gallows iron?" asked Tyler. Melissa nodded vehemently.

"You know I swallowed the ring when Streicher caught us? Well, I got it back."

Lucy sniggered.

"Stop it. It's not funny." Melissa eased the ring from her finger and held it in the flat of her hand for the others to see. "Do you see it, next to the seal?"

Tyler took the ring between her finger and thumb to study it more closely.

"I wouldn't touch that if I were you," jibed Lucy. Melissa cuffed her shoulder.

"Yes, I see it," said Tyler. "The faint markings of a snake's head. I would never have noticed unless I was looking for it. They almost look like random scratches. Where the seal rejoins the ring, the snake's tail enters its mouth. The ring is an ouroboros, so it's possible Heydrich's gallows ring is also an ouroboros."

"Not possible, highly likely. And Streicher just claimed a mysterious ancient book of magic about a ring of gallows iron. You see my point?"

"You're right."

Melissa shoved the ring back onto her finger and they rejoined Barak at the table.

"We need that book from Streicher but that's going to be so much harder without the contrap."

"Pardon me, but what is this *contrap*?" asked Barak. Tyler tapped the drawing.

"This is the contrap. It's about so big and made from silver. It hangs on a chain."

"Why would this help you take the book from Streicher?"

"It has certain properties that would help me to track him."

Barak nodded pensively and picked up the sketch.

"We must return to Kutna Hora," he sighed.

"Why?" asked Tyler. "We only just got here. Without the contrap there's no point in going back."

"You said before that you trusted me."

"Yes."

179

"Did you mean it?"

She studied his face momentarily. *I don't think your eyes are lying.* Tyler nodded.

"Then take me back to the Bone Church."

"You said it wasn't safe there."

"It isn't."

*

A mean-eyed contrapasso surfaced from the shadows to tower over Marcus. He grabbed Marcus by the shoulder and half-dragged him to the end of a row of grim prisoners. The beast stooped to link Marcus' shackles to the line. It spoke with a rumbling growl, its rank, hot breath in Marcus' face.

"Sit, scum. Await your doom."

Marcus complied while trying to see what was happening with Izabella. Another contrapasso had led her away into the cheerless reaches of the hold. He glimpsed her as her accompanying contrapasso pushed her down and chained her in place.

For a long time Marcus sat there watching the eclectic mix of ghosts from many ages chained in row upon row all around. Every so often the fire feeders would select their hapless fuel and toss several writhing ghosts into the flames, and the screaming would begin again.

The Fiddler

The doors of the Bone Church were closed, its insides cold and lifeless. For the second time Tyler peeled away the police tape and eased open the door, giving Barak a nod. He slipped through. Melissa quickly followed. On the threshold Tyler turned to Lucy.

"I know." Lucy cut in. "Same as before, right?"

"Thanks." Tyler closed the door leaving Lucy to replace the tape and stand guard, while she descended the steps to join Melissa beneath the vaulted ceiling inside. She checked her P99 was loaded and flicked off the safety catch, pointing the barrel at the floor, ready in case she was wrong about Barak. He walked to the centre and peered around. At mid-afternoon on this winter's day the ossuary was in near-complete shadow, unlit by lamps or candles and dim in all its corners except where the late, pale sunlight streamed in static pools from the high windows.

"I will need a torch," said Barak.

Tyler took her Maglite from her bag and tossed it to him. He switched it on and began combing the far end of the chamber, walking among the marble pyramids adorned with skulls and crossed bones. He swept the light across each pinnacle in turn before finally settling on one topped by a golden winged cherub cradling a skull.

Tyler stepped closer.

"This one, I think," said Barak, handing the torch to Tyler. "Here, give me some light."

Barak climbed the pyramid, careful to avoid dislodging any of the bones and using their plinths as foot and hand holds. Stretching to the top he plucked something from the between the crowning skull and the cherub's lap. He descended.

"Take it."

Tyler shone the Maglite over his outstretched hand where the silver contrap gleamed, its crystal casting bright dabs around the vaults. She met his unwavering gaze.

"You were right to trust me. Now I think it is time you at least told me your names."

*

A contrapasso unlocked the shackles as the massive clawed hand of a second beast descended to grasp Marcus painfully by the scruff of his neck, hoisting him from the line.

"The Master wants to see you, little grub," the hand's wolfish owner guffawed. "He must be bored, or hungry."

Marcus swung in time with the lurching gait of the contrapasso as they left the hold. The monster climbed the stairs out into the glowering, red twilight of the

Chasm. Marcus watched the deck go by while, beyond the ornate railings of the gunnel, the burning sun sank ever lower. He glimpsed the distant, broad spans of Hell birds coasting on the last of the day's thermals and heard their screeching calls resound. The ship's bat-like wings stretched from the bow into a field of sulphurous clouds above an oily stream of smoke from the vessel's gigantic vents. The contrapasso bore him to the timber forecastle where it stood, hammering its great, clawed fist against a set of iron-studded doors. More of the creatures swung open the giant doors from inside.

"What is it?" snarled the largest.

"I have the whelp Hakan requested." Marcus' carrier hefted him up to show the door guards. Marcus glimpsed the inside of the forecastle. A long feasting table spilled over with bread, fruit, cheese, roasted flesh of all kinds, and carafes of wine. Contrapassi seated at its edge ripped into joints of meat with their claws and teeth, and quaffed wine from deep goblets. Seated at the far end, a monstrous contrapassi outweighing all others sat enthroned on a chair carved with the many flowing forms of tortured beings.

"Bring him," he bellowed, beckoning them closer with a formidable shaggy arm. At his sides, other contrapassi stood guard, watching the feasters with narrowed eyes, machine guns cradled at the ready.

Marcus' creature stomped the length of the chamber in a few quick strides and dropped him at the feet of the master. To Marcus' surprise, the master leaned forward in his throne and produced his bow and fiddle. He dangled them before Marcus.

"You can draw music from these things?"

Marcus dared to peer up and nod.

"Good," growled the master so slowly and deeply that Marcus felt reverberations through the insides of his semi-ghost body. "Take. Play."

Marcus turned at the screech of iron hinges. Beyond the long table the studded doors boomed shut.

*

"You were watching when I ditched the contrap," said Tyler.

Barak nodded. "And when I retrieved it I wondered what it was, wondered why you were so concerned to keep it from Streicher. Its markings are peculiar.

"Streicher and the large man were making me nervous. I feared I might be caught following them, but I didn't have much time to think. I hid it up there and left to track Streicher. I picked up their trail and knew you three were in danger. I followed for miles but lost them when I had a flat tyre. I was relieved to see you back at the ossuary the next day. If you had been killed I would have blamed myself. I guess you were searching for that." He gestured toward the contrap clasped in Tyler's hand.

"Now I have it back I can track Streicher." She hung the contrap's chain around her neck and took out a notebook where she scribbled with a pen.

Melissa crossed to her. "Tyler, we don't have much time. The police could turn up any minute and that's a complication we don't need."

"Nearly done." Tyler completed her list and read it back.

Locate and destroy the new GAUNT machine
Locate and acquire Abraham Eleazar's book on Astral Theorem
Free all gloved children

It was a short but weighty list. A new list of the gloves at large would have to wait until later.

She switched to the *Past Eye*, the uneasy feeling about the spirits around the church lingering. For the meantime they were keeping at bay but she suspected ghost spies watched her every move. She focused the contrap on the area with the loose floor tile and wound the lever a quarter turn to watch time reverse through the crystal lens. For several moments she searched the past, watching shadows grow and shrink and soon she arrived at the point when Streicher first appeared in the ossuary.

Shifting the lever back a little allowed the seconds to tick forward in real time. She watched him pass his gun to Beast, commanding him to put Lucy with Tyler's other self and Melissa. She saw Streicher kneel to take the oilcloth-wrapped book from the recess and, swinging her view back towards the bone pyramid, caught the moment when her other self lifted the contrap from her neck to toss it through the caging into the bones. She focused back onto Streicher, slowing and halting time on an image of the book, free of its cloth, in his hands. She stepped closer with the contrap to see more detail.

Its cover was age-worn leather, cracked and splitting at the edges and at the centre a large ouroboros was embossed and stained with a darker substance. Within this ring a leafless, craggy tree stretched angular branches outwards. Around this flowed embossed, complex, scalloped patterns forming an intricate frame. The entire cover was fastened by two clasps tipped in a dull and discoloured metal.

"I can see the book. Streicher just took it from the hole." She described the cover to Melissa and adjusting the lever, studied the spine as Streicher turned the book in his hands. "If there's writing on the spine it's too faded to see. But I'm pretty sure this is Řezník's book because of the ouroboros on the front."

"Bit of a giveaway," said Melissa.

"Yeah."

"It probably never had writing on the front or the spine. Really old books don't."

"So Streicher has my brother's book."

"It looks that way. I'm going to track him now. This could take a while but in the end the contrap should lead us to Streicher, wherever he is."

*

Albert and the remnant of his ghost army stalked unseen through the forest. In the clearing thirty metres ahead, a band of weary contrapassi yawned and scratched as they lounged on logs around a camp fire. To their side, ten ghost prisoners sat shivering, bound in chains, too far from the fire to draw its warmth.

"They must have tracked them as they fled into the woods," whispered Zebedee, leaning on his brass-handled cane at Albert's shoulder. "These few took a different path. By the time the contrapassi caught up with them they were miles from the ships. No doubt they're planning to hike the prisoners back to a death camp first thing in the morning."

"Good," breathed Albert, his face glowing softly in the night shadows beneath the lofty pines.

The sky beyond the highest branches lurked a deep shade of smoky blue. The temperature had plummeted once the *Chasm's* vengeful sun retreated below the horizon and ice crystals soon formed on the extremities of each ghost and every pine needle.

Albert brushed frost from his eyebrows and rubbed

at his chilled nose. Zebedee seemed unaware of the small icicles forming on the tip of his beard. He tried peering at the camp ahead through his monocle but ice clouded the glass and he slid it back into the top pocket of his tailcoat. Albert counted the contrapassi.

"We outnumber 'em. We'll creep round an' attack from all sides, surprise 'em. By the time they knows what's 'appenin' we'll be away with them there prisoners. Zebedee, you take a group around left. I'll take a chain and go right." He collected a Mordecai chain and slung it around his neck.

"Then what?"

"I don't know. We try to free the prisoners. Fight off the contrapassi as best we can. There are a few branches lyin' around. Get your ghosts to arm 'emselves."

He watched the hulking creatures snapping branches from the surrounding trees to throw on the fire while several huddled against the cold, wrapping themselves in their cloaks. Others reclined around the fire, shrouded and already sleeping, their snores and the growled complaints of those awake mingling with the snap and crackle of the flames. A dank animal smell drifted from the camp.

"Perhaps we should wait until they're all asleep."

"Nah. The longer we waits, the greater the chance they'll spot us. An', anyway, they'll leave a few to keep guard for sure."

"Right you are, Master Goodwin." Zebedee tucked his pipe into his breast pocket and, with much hushing and many low whispers, gathered his team of ghosts ready for the assault. He led them in a broad, sweeping arc around the left flank of the camp, stealing between trees and freezing to the spot each time a contrapasso glanced their way.

On the opposite side, across the forest, Albert headed closer. He caught Zebedee's eye, signaled for him to wait and, creeping to the edge of the clearing at the mountainous backs of the nearest contrapassi, stole in to search for the manacle keys. He found them hanging from the leathery belt of a snoring contrapasso who rested against a tree, and nimbly unhooked them without disturbing the creature. From there he skirted the ring of log-benches towards the gathering of chained ghosts.

One of the giants glimpsed movement in the corner of his eye and turned to scan the shadows, peering directly at Albert. Albert paused, flattening himself against the end of a gigantic log. In the waltzing light from the fire and the curling smoke and shadows, Albert's semi-ghost transparency hid him well, but the chain glimmered. He dropped it behind the log and waited until the contrapassi turned away before sneaking over to the captives, drawing a finger to his lips. Pressing a key into the manacles of the nearest prisoner, a wave of disappointment swept over him. Neither Molly nor his father were there.

He freed the nearest, a Saxon maid with long, braided hair, and sent her scurrying into the woods. A Roman slave boy soon followed with a curt nod of thanks. The third, a coal blackened miner, was seen and, with a sudden lurch, a guard clambered to his feet, bellowing with steamy clouds of breath.

"Wake up, you dogs! The vermin escape!" He lumbered through the edge of the fire stack, scattering flaming logs around his path. "Awake, you laggards!"

Albert flashed Zebedee a double nod. Zebedee ran from the forest cover trailing a stream of ghosts as fire from a burning branch caught the hairy ankle of an unwitting contrapassi. Others pointed, laughing as several of his fellows attempted to damp the flames, but the helpers took flame and staggered away trying to snuff the fire. The stink of burning hair bloomed. Waking contrapassi staggered up, bleary-eyed, to see their flaming companions and ghosts dashing here and there. Albert snatched a flaming branch to ward off the approaching guard. The guard baulked at the brand and stepped backwards onto a stray, smoldering log. He danced to keep balance and, righting himself, retreated to join the others, growling. Albert retrieved his chain and launched it.

"Mordecai obligo!"

The chain flew to encompass the contrapasso with coils, felling him like a sawn tree.

Zebedee neared the camp, dashing unnoticed from shadow to shadow. He approached a gangling contrapasso from behind and swung the knobbed end of his cane upwards between the creature's legs. The contrapasso howled and keeled over, writhing on the ground.

"Ups-a-daisy."

Zebedee joined his team of ghosts as they entered the ring. They formed a line, each brandishing a flaming branch stolen from the scattered fire.

The rest of Albert's team reached the camp and more chains flew. Contrapassi fell, enveloped and bound. The newcomers helped Albert to release more of the prisoners while Zebedee's ghosts held most of the contrapassi at bay, jeering and waving their brands.

Three contrapassi ran, burning, into the woods trying desperately to smother their flames, their shrieks echoing among the pines. They rolled on the forest floor and tore down great branches to bash at their burning legs, only fanning the flames and setting fire to the nearby trees.

Seeing the fate of their comrades, the remaining contrapassi hesitated at the growing line of fire-wielding ghosts and, as the last of the prisoners' shackles fell loose, the ghosts hurled their flaming brands and fled from the growing forest fire. Behind them the beasts howled.

The Tower

They gathered, exhausted at the fringes of the forest an hour later. Albert scanned the quiet woodland behind him. No sign of the contrapassi. The *Chasm* appeared to be resting. Zebedee drew alongside wheezing and collapsed in a heap on the forest floor to recover. When his breathing eased, he refilled his pipe with tobacco and lit it with a Lucifer, puffing plumes of smoke.

"Are you thinking it may be time to cut our losses? No one would blame you. If we were to find the *Tower of Doom* before too long we might still be of some assistance to Miss May and her cause. That is, of course, if she happened to see us at the battlements, if by chance there *are* any battlements. Delay long and she may be killed and we could be trapped in here until the end of days. No wonder you have the morbs."

Albert fixed a stony gaze upon Zebedee.

"I lost Molly once before. I ain't losing her again an', anyway, there's still a load o' souls with them jackals. We ain't leavin' anyone behind. You got me? Not one!"

A subtle smile emerged on Zebedee's face.

"Jolly good. I knew you wouldn't abandon the others."

For several hours the remnants of the ghost army sat huddled in groups to stay warm among the tall frosted pines. Now and then part of the forest lurched into life, heaving, groaning and shifting around them ominously in the murk beyond. Albert set up a guard shift, placing watchers every few metres around the outskirts of their camp and managed to sleep for a while.

He woke at the sound of a soot-stained chimney sweep running to them through the crowd of other ghosts. The sweep stopped before Albert and Zebedee, doubling over to catch his breath.

"Boss, come quick! One of our number just found us. Was wounded at the river but survived. Her name's Ba and she wants to talk to you. Says she's seen things."

*

Tyler tracked Streicher painstakingly. The *Past Eye* first showed his movements from the ossuary in Kutna Hora driving in a white transit van to a dilapidated farm at the outskirts of Prague. She watched her other self bundled with Melissa and Lucy into the battered, red shipping container bound for a freighter at Rostock. Streicher passed a padded brown envelope to the haulage driver, no doubt a payment for his underhand services, and headed into central Prague with Beast. Once, along the way, the contrap's crystal blackened and Tyler lost her quarry. She turned the contrap to find its switch inexplicably set to the *Ghost Portal*. In frustration she set it back to the *Past*

Eye and spent a further irritating hour searching for Streicher's vehicle before she could continue tracking.

Returning to the Four Seasons, he hurriedly packed and took a taxi to the airport. Through the *Past Eye* Tyler checked the departure time and destination on the flight schedule board. She glanced at her watch, made a quick calculation and turned to Melissa.

"He left for Qaanaaq about twelve hours ago."

"Why would he go to Greenland?"

"Who knows? But we have to follow him." Tyler returned her gaze to the contrap only to find the crystal dark and smoky. She checked the switch and found it still set to the *Past Eye*. She tested other settings and swore. "The contrap's out of power. I couldn't track him anymore even if I wanted to."

"It doesn't matter. We'll have to pick up his trail later anyway. Right now we have to go home." Melissa, nodded towards Lucy. "Look at her."

Standing apart, Lucy was a vacant mess of smudged eyeliner. She turned away, shoulders quivering, and tried to straighten her makeup with a tissue.

Tyler whispered to Melissa. "Meltdown. Guess it was bound to happen sooner or later. It's the first time she's cried since Klaus broke the news."

"She just took a call while you were tracking Streicher. Weaver's funeral is this Friday. They're flying what little remains of his body back to London today."

Barak joined them, bringing a cardboard tray of coffee in disposable cups.

"Before you go home there is something I'd like to show you."

*

"You wants t' see me?" asked Albert, stooping over the

bedraggled African slave woman named Ba, amid the ghosts tending her wounds. A contrapassi arrow protruded from her side and her left arm lay at an unnatural angle. To one side of her a group of miners and sweeps debated how best to remove the roughly-hewn shaft from her bleeding ghost-flesh. "What did ya' see out there?"

"Terrible things. I fled from the jackal sky ships. I passed camps of prisoners, thousands of prisoners, all skin and bone, everywhere the jackal-heads tormenting. I ran for many miles until I found a cave where I rested. When I left the cave later I saw the ships again, but many more, an entire fleet numbering hundreds, if not thousands. They seemed to fill the sky."

"Jackal-heads?"

Ba nodded and winced in pain.

"There is something else, something screeching in the skies. I saw them, great shadows sweeping in with giant wings. I did not like the look of them."

"Hell birds," said Albert, his interest fired. "Was they circlin' a tall tower set amongst blackened, twisted trees?"

"Not birds, Master Goodwin. The creatures I saw were not birds, though their wings were like those of a bird's, but I did pass the tower."

"She's seen the *Tower of Doom*," said Zebedee. "It can't be far."

"Can you lead us there?" asked Albert. "When you've rested."

"I will do my best, though this land turns upon itself, writhing like a bed of serpents. By the time I lead you to where I last saw the tower, it may have gone."

"Don't worry, Ba. The tower is the only place that doesn't move."

Albert had ghosts rig a makeshift stretcher ready for Ba while others carefully removed the arrow from her side, and they carried her while she murmured directions. Retracing her steps through the forest and across the barren plains, they reached the cave she had mentioned and rested briefly as the *Chasm's* cruel sun rose to wash the land in long shadows and fiery hues. For a few blessed moments the ghosts warmed but all too soon craved shelter from the heat of the red fireball as it climbed higher in the blazing sky.

*

The house sat in darkness, lurking at the end of the steep path like a hungry creature of the night. Barak went ahead through the late evening shadows playing beneath the untrimmed bushes and trees of the long garden. At the end he paused, fumbling with keys from his pocket.

His brother's house was much as Tyler imagined. A love of antiques and all things curious purveyed: the gothic moulding of the architraves, the arched windows and carved stone relief and pinnacles, the select and various well-placed artefacts behind the unlit windows, and its unusual location for such a stately home on the outskirts of the city.

"Řezník gave me a key some time ago." Barak slid the key into the lock but before he could turn it the door yawned open, creaking softly. "Someone got here first."

Taking a Maglite from her pocket, Tyler squeezed past him to illuminate the dim hallway within. She slipped her P99 from her shoulder holster and crept in. At the base of the stairs a side table lay overturned, a marble statue of a Greek goddess shattered on the polished hardwood floor. She rounded a doorway into a front room once resplendent with choice antique furniture, marbles and paintings, all of which now lay in disarray and ruin. Drawers strewn across the floor spilled their papers, files and office bric-a-brac.

"Streicher and his Beast," suggested Lucy from the doorway.

"I guess so. If not them, who?" Barak crossed to a crooked oil landscape hanging on the wall and lifted it from its hanger to find a wall safe, its steel door wrenched away. "They've taken everything. Wait, maybe not everything." He left the front room and climbed the stairs with the girls close behind, dodging fallen and broken antiques along the way. He led them into a spacious bedroom with a medieval four poster bed, and dragged a Persian rug from the floor. Beneath, three floorboards were shorter than the rest. He prised them up with the blade of a pocket knife and delved between joists to draw out a box file.

"He had a habit of keeping things here, things he considered too valuable to put into an obvious safe. I know he made copies of some of the plates in the book. They're what I brought you to see. He may have kept them in here." He unclasped the box file and opened the lid. "Look."

Tyler took the box and lifted a photocopied page filled with odd symbols.

"That's the ouroboros again," said Melissa, peering over her shoulder at the torch lit images.

"Barak, may I borrow these?"

"As long as I get them back and on condition they are in no way published."

"Thanks. Mel, get these copied to Yash for analysis and give the originals back to Barak right away."

*

196

Weaver's funeral was a smart affair attended by a select few. Lucy remained stony-faced throughout, saying little even when it was all over. Tyler dropped her and Melissa back at their apartment and drove home alone in the Beetle.

Parking on the gravel driveway she sat for a long time with mixed feelings, looking at the house. Its tall bay windows, still unfamiliar, daunted. She had never meant to end up living here entirely alone. She had thought Albert, at least, would always be with her. Feeling isolated and uncertain if she was glad to be home, she locked the car, walked to the back door and slid the key into the Yale lock. She paused. Stepping around to the back she opened the gate and peered at the rows of last season's cabbages and the unloved garden ending at the old stone wall. Nothing had changed.

Inside, she turned off the intruder alarm and cranked up the heating. All appeared as she had left it, everything except for that single misaligned teaspoon on the kitchen counter.

"Hello?" She wasn't sure why she called aloud, but if there was a ghost haunting the house she wanted to know who it was. No one answered.

She switched the kettle on, unpacked, and shoved a load of dirty washing into the machine.

In light of the funeral and in consideration for the girls, Yash had ordered two days recuperation before allowing them back in the field. Even then he was non-committing when it came to Lucy. She was to attend a psychological evaluation which she would have to pass satisfactorily before commencing with duties, so Tyler had a little time to sort her gear and prepare for Greenland. With her washing machine thumping away in the background she perused her wardrobes, picking out arctic clothing and several pairs of boots including spiked ice-trekkers. She made a start on assembling a kit bag for the trip, throwing in two ice picks, climbing gear, gallows blades, grenades, smoke grenades and a range of tracers. A set of NanoSects, the artificial insect surveillance drones, also went in. Memories flooded her mind: the mosquito-like drones buzzing around her while she fled clinical hallways of the NVF's jungle lair, explosions, the taste of blood, metallic in her mouth, wanting to die, wanting it all to be over.

She shook off the notion. Right now she felt a deep need to stay alive. The washing machine stopped its distant throbbing and the house fell deathly quiet.

Perhaps I've made a mistake. I should have asked to stay with Mel and Lucy.

Tyler searched for her phone and found it near the kettle. She phoned Melissa's number while the kettle boiled again.

No signal.

That's odd.

She put the errant teaspoon away in the cutlery drawer and padded down the cellar steps to study the greenish aspects of her house exterior in night vision mode on the CCTV monitors. *Nothing out of place there.* She toggled through the interior rooms camera views and saw the teaspoon already back on the kitchen surface.

Dashing up to the kitchen she drew a gallows blade from a pocket and turned around the room seeking the ghost, knowing it was lurking close by. She sensed a malicious presence strongly. She had left her gear unlocked in the spare room. Panic welled from her gut. Upstairs a small arsenal of weapons lay arranged on open shelves and in her bag.

"Who are you? Show yourself. What do you want?" She brandished the blade.

She tried her mobile again. Still no signal. She stole up the stairs and into her room, every moment expecting an attack, a sudden apparition flying at her with a cold iron blade, a murderous glint in its eyes. In the room her kit remained undisturbed. She hastily counted her gallows blades, bundled her bag into the lock-up and secured the doors. No blades were missing. No ghost appeared or answered. She tried to calm and returned to the kitchen for her drink, carried it to her bedroom and curled up in her bed with an extra blanket, her P99 and a gallows blade beneath her pillow.

With the contrap set to the *Ghost Portal* she waited, watching for someone who might help, hoping for a new Albert. It had helped her before. Mist swirled irritatingly empty of souls.

Who am I fooling? There'll never be another Albert.

Thinking of her new list and wondering how badly she was progressing, she switched to the *Tower of Doom*. The little tower in the crystal viewfinder confirmed her fears, less than half built and slaking like quicklime. Hell birds glided in lazy circles over its ruins, silhouetted in the glow of the moon. Recalling a time when she and Albert had sheltered there, nestled together for warmth against the *Chasm's* freezing night, she huddled down under her covers and tried to sleep, aware of every creak and groan of the old house.

*

Zebedee saw the creatures first. He dropped his monocle and stood to get a better view, pointing with his cane.

"Look there, flying over the forest. Ba was right.

They're not Hell birds."

Albert joined him.

"They're bigger than Hell birds. Maybe two or three times bigger."

"Contrapassi with wings?" ventured Zebedee, as distant screeches reached them from the sky.

They exchanged concerned glances.

"Let's hope not. I'm going for a better look. Stay 'ere and keep an eye on the others."

"Mind yourself, Albert. Don't let them see you."

"I'll do my best." Albert left the cave entrance and ducked around the hillside, threading a path down a boulder-strewn slope. When the land levelled out he bent towards the forest to risk the open, broiling plain between him and the winged creatures, and dodged patches of shifting ground. Before him a single, jagged mound rose from the fire-fog plain. He made for this with a last mad dash and came to its side, glad to be hidden from the skies beyond. Climbing a short way he spied from his vantage point.

The creatures were not winged contrapassi. They were different, though every bit as fearsome. Their feathered spans stretched, black and broad like eagles' wings, and their powerful talons hung, curled and clawed, ready to strike. The rest of their bodies by comparison were curved, tanned and exquisite, the seductive forms of beautiful women with long, black tresses of hair, and barely clothed in the sheerest of fabrics, but from each of their temples sprouted horns like those of a goat.

Albert was instantly mesmerised. He glimpsed several contrapassi between the trees and realised the winged creatures were stalking them. One of them dived into the forest releasing a piercing screech and attacked the contrapassi, raking with her outstretched talons. Others followed in its wake plummeting through the trees to swoop on their prey. The woods echoed with the growls and snarls of the contrapassi as they battled. They drew bows and fired their rough arrows at the winged attackers as they in turn took bows from their shoulders to return fire.

Another of the creatures perched in a large tree, wrapping her claws around a branch and clinging to the trunk with one arm. Jutting her face at the contrapassi below, she breathed a storm of fire upon them.

Albert turned away as the beast's howls shook the forest, and he fled back to the other ghosts, hoping he would not be caught by the sky terrors and roasted alive.

Caged

Lucy woke late and in a sullen mood, reliving the funeral. She sat around in her pyjamas, staring at the wall, yesterday's makeup blotching her face.

Melissa slid a mug of obscenely strong coffee across the breakfast table, followed by a plate of bacon and eggs, hoping to bring Lucy round. *Life goes on*, she wanted to say.

"You should eat something. It's nearly lunchtime."

Lucy poked at the eggs and chewed unenthusiastically on a sliver of bacon.

Melissa needed to distract Lucy. The alternative was living with a morose zombie-Goth.

This could go on for ever!

"I've been thinking about Yash and Chapman's disappearance. I still find it odd. Don't you?"

"I guess." Lucy ditched her fork in favour of the

coffee. "The only other time Chapman went missing was when his family was abducted."

"I'm going in to HQ to do some poking around. Coming?"

Lucy stared at the steaming coffee in her hands and Melissa realised she would not answer.

"I want to get into Yash's office. It would be much easier with your help."

Lucy looked up.

"Okay."

*

Albert reported all he had seen to Zebedee, the twins and the rest of the remaining Ghost Squad.

"They can only be one thing: liliths," Zebedee informed them.

"What?"

"Liliths, winged she-demons with talons for feet. Their legend dates back to ancient Babylonian texts. Imagine a flying grizzly bear with a headache, only ten times worse. Breathing fire, you say? Hmmm, fascinating."

With the ghosts rested, Albert roused them to follow Ba's directions. Carried by her bearers, she guided them away from the forest, the cave and the plateau, and down on to a rambling course of jagged hills. Their winding path undulated treacherously beneath their feet, rolling and tilting, but the rugged peak of the highest mound remained solid enough for them to gather and peer out across the land ahead. Ba pointed to a distant area beyond a river that was dark with blackened trees. From the centre of this scattered forest a tower pierced the crimson skyline and around the tower's unfinished walls, Hell birds soared.

"That's it, Zebedee. The *Tower of Doom*."

Albert turned to the gathered troops.

"We got to get to that tower."

*

Busying herself around the house, Tyler's day passed quickly. She drank copious amounts of hot tea to fuel her as she unpacked the remaining boxes from the move, keen to reclaim the space they consumed at the end of her lounge. By late afternoon she had flat-packed the last of the boxes and carried them out into the twilight to stack them around the back in the woodshed.

For the first time the house felt like hers. Every room was as she wanted it and everything had its place, except for the teaspoon that continued to appear in the kitchen as frequently as she tidied it away.

At six she watched the BBC World News for a war update. Jerky footage of a war zone on the boarders of Iraq and Syria showed UN soldiers running for cover as shells landed nearby. Dust filled the air and the foreign correspondent informed of the latest hundreds of deaths in the area, of those made homeless and the thousands of starving refugees fleeing, unwelcomed, into Syrian jurisdiction. The footage cut to a view of a roadside lined by shrouded corpses awaiting burial.

"The scene behind me is one repeated throughout the region. Many of the dead will never be buried because it is simply too dangerous to linger here."

The next zone of terror and destruction was Gaza where the old war raged on.

More footage swiftly followed. Libyan troops pressed into Egypt, a path of devastation, injured civilians, refugees, and the unburied dead in their wake.

In Columbia and Venezuela, civil war pockmarked

the lands, the cities' streets empty except for the burning wrecks of petrol-bombed cars and looted shop fronts. Disorganised guerrilla mobs led by cartel rulers invaded Nicaragua while US troops set up barricades alongside the woefully under-prepared local police.

Terrorist attacks across the USA and Europe peppered each famous city. London, among the worst hit, lit the night with an orange glow as emergency services fought to control fires, tend the injured and apprehend terror groups. Extremists marched the streets chanting demands for a change of rule, their clashes with police shield-walls turning violent.

Tyler switched the TV off and cradled her head in her hands. She left the lounge and descended the steps into the cellar to see what improvements she could make to security down there.

*

Through the office window Lucy watched Yash leave the building. She hurried down a corridor to a security room in time to see him getting into his car. James, the young officer at the desk, greeted her.

"All right? You need help?" He allowed his eyes to roam Lucy's figure.

"I'm okay, thanks." She humoured him. "Just checking on my bike."

"Yeah, that's a sweet ride."

"Oh, there was something. My parking card has been playing up. Can I swap it for another?" She handed him her card.

James nodded. "I'll have to fetch one from the store. Give me a minute."

While he was gone Lucy crossed to the locked wall box behind the desk and used a bump key to open it. She took the spare key card to Yash's office from a hook, replacing it with a dummy key from her pocket, closed the box and skirted the desk.

James returned and handed her a new parking card.

"Here."

"Thanks."

"My pleasure."

She left the room, closed the door, and called Melissa on her mobile.

"The bird has flown."

"Okay. Green light."

Lucy took the lift down a level and paced the corridor while she waited for Melissa. She slipped the key card into Melissa's hand and stood guard at the far end of the corridor. With the patch Melissa had rigged into the CCTV cameras covering this corridor and the Section Chief's office, all James would see was a replay of thirty seconds of unattended, unlit zones.

Melissa paused at the door and read the words etched into the frosted glass panel.

Section Chief
JIC

In Chapman's absence Yash ran the department from here. She used the key and entered the office, locking the door behind her.

After ten minutes of nervously watching, Lucy phoned Melissa again.

"Anything?"

"Yes. I'm nearly done. Two minutes."

Across from Lucy the door of the lift opened and two agents from a neighbouring department stepped out.

Lucy walked. It would not do to be seen lingering.

"Two red lights." She hissed into her phone before pocketing it. She headed for the lift, nodding a greeting to the agents as she passed.

In Yash's office, Melissa finished photographing one file of interest for later examination but three drawers remained unsearched and she wanted to be thorough. Lucy's abrupt end to the call concerned her. She killed her torch beam, shoved the file back into the drawer and slid it shut. She ducked beneath Yash's desk to hide, and waited.

A moment later her phone buzzed again.

"All clear," said Lucy.

"Thank God!" Melissa glanced through the contents of the remaining drawers, wiped down every surface she'd touched and left as quickly as possible. Lucy met her at the door.

"Let's get out of here."

*

Albert and his army trudged between a sprawling forest and the river's floodplain, the tower's broken walls visible above a smouldering ridge of fire-fog beyond the river.

"Of course," said Zebedee, stepping nimbly beside him, "reaching the tower might only be the start of our problems."

"Meaning?"

"Even if we reach the tower we won't get in. Do you recall? We left its doors closed and barred from the inside, and there's no other entrance."

"Then we'll 'aft to use the Hell birds."

"Begging your pardon, Master Goodwin, but how are we to do that? They are ferocious."

"They helped us before."

"Ahh, but that was because they knew we had food. This time we don't have anything."

Albert peered into the shadows of the forest to his side. The trees here were different, a mix of deciduous species with a tall jungle canopy and hanging creepers.

"I know. And everyone's hungry." He stopped before changing tack and headed for the forest as an unnatural cloud drifted into view over the horizon behind him. Ghosts nearby shouted, pointing to the mass.

"It's the sky ships."

"The jackal-heads!"

"They're coming!"

"Quickly," called Albert. "Into the woods before they see us."

The troop bolted for the cover of the trees and gathered a short way in, hidden by the canopy. From the shadows they watched as the ships approached, blotting the air with their filth. The stench of burning oil and flesh descended and a silence settled over the ghosts as the ships passed overhead. Albert waited until the sky fleet became a distant cloud once more.

"Gather vines for rope and branches for caging. We 'aft to build a trap."

"A trap for what?" asked Claudia.

"A trap large enough and strong enough to catch a Hell bird."

"Have you lost your marbles?" said Zebedee. "You can't *catch* a Hell bird and even if you could, it would not do what you wanted."

"We'll make a saddle for it, and reins so's I can steer it. We 'aft to get inside that tower somehow. In there we can eat, rest and get stronger. From there we can launch our mission to rescue the others. An' only from there can we be summoned out of the *Chasm*."

"Very well, we can try, but I'm warning you: Hell Birds cannot be tamed," said Zebedee.

Ghosts gathered creepers, tugging the looser ones down and climbing trees to wrestle others free. They brought fallen branches and dumped them in a growing heap before Albert and soon he had a team of volunteers binding branches together with lengths of creeper to build a rough cage the size of a hansom cab.

"With what will you bait the trap?" asked Zebedee, watching the ghosts work.

"I don't know. I haven't thought about that yet."

Claudia stepped out from the gathered ghosts.

"I'll do it," she said. "I'll be the bait. I'm small enough to slip through the bars once the bird is inside and I'm quick when I want to be. I'm a good runner."

"I don't know." Albert looked her up and down. "You could get hurt, even killed. Then we'd be waiting around for you to come back from the second death and we could be waiting ages."

"I won't get killed. I promise. I can be fast. *Really* fast."

He watched her uncertainly.

"Faster than a Hell bird?" He put a hand to his shoulder where a scar remained from his first encounter with one of the birds.

"I can try. Let me do something to help. I've a lot to make up for."

"She's right there," muttered Zebedee, through a cloud of tobacco smoke.

"All right, Claudia, but don't blame me if the bird claws your face off. We'll bind a length of vine around one of your ankles. Anythin' goes wrong we can drag you to safety."

*

Claudia trod the broiling, cracked dirt of the open plain in full sight of the soaring birds. A rope of creepers trailed wherever she walked, leading out across the plain and into the forest. Albert and the other ghosts had not needed to modify her looks for the part. Her simple slave girl's dress was already torn, filthy and ragged from her journey through the *Chasm*. She had been a thin, undernourished girl in life and now, half-starved, she appeared appropriately on the verge of starvation and dying from thirst; a vulture's delight. She staggered and fell, dragged herself up to her feet and repeated the act, circling the trap. Three Hell birds descended to fly closer, orbiting above.

I've caught your eye. It's working.

The heavy cage sat propped with its back edge on the ground, the weight of its front supported on the opposing side by a long branch that could be easily kicked away to bring the cage down.

The nearest bird dropped closer and moments later plunged after her with a sudden turn. Claudia dashed for the shelter of the cage. The bird tore down on her from the sky, a streak of black lightning, clawing at her leg as she dived into the trap. She shrieked, abandoning her performance. Fighting for her life she backed up into the far end of the cage, scrambling away as the bird's sizeable beak stabbed at her from the entrance. She tried to kick the support away, if only to drop the cage and keep the bird on the outside but, fearlessly, the great bird raked its way inside and, trembling, Claudia found herself staring into a pair of black, soulless eyes.

Blackout

The Hell bird shrieked and lurched closer, one wing dragging on the edge of the cage. The cage shook and the support toppled. Claudia bolted through the bars as it crashed down, trapping the bird. Her safety tether pulled tight, caught around the branches of the trap. The bird stabbed at her through the cage as she fought desperately to rid herself of the rope. Dragging her foot painfully from the noose, she fled back towards the forest, leaving the trapped bird behind.

"It worked! Albert, it worked!"

Albert and the others ran out from the treeline as an explosion of splintering and cracking sounds caused Claudia to turn.

The bird stood amid the flattened and broken remains of the cage. It cocked its head to one side, watching her purposefully, and screeched before making a waddling pursuit.

"Run!" bellowed Albert, speeding towards her. The other ghosts closed, too, forming an arc around her as the bird closed. It slowed, seeing the troop gather. Claudia faced the bird, backed by the other ghosts. The bird took a hesitant step forward, mauled the ground and let fly a bone-juddering shriek of fury.

"What did I say, Master Goodwin? A Hell bird will not be tamed."

"Wait there, Zebedee," said Albert, observing the bird closely. It appeared nervous of the crowd as it continued to watch Claudia, neither daring to venture an attack nor provoked to fly. "All of you wait exactly where you are. Claudia, come to me slowly."

Claudia backed away from the bird as Albert walked out to take her place. The bird switched its focus onto him, twitching its head to the side and clacking loudly. Albert slowly raised an arm to point to the tower still some way off across the river.

"I can get you food. You remembers the tower food, don't ya, that fresh bread an' all that juicy, ripe fruit? Take me to the tower and, I swear, I'll give you all the food you can eat."

*

Tyler gazed at the teaspoons, increasingly unsettled. She considered getting in her car and heading over to Melissa and Lucy's place. Where one spoon had repeatedly appeared, now lay two. She snatched them from the worktop, irritation mounting, and shoved them back into the cutlery drawer. Returning to the room five minutes later she found three spoons on the side.

"This is ridiculous. Who are you? What do you want with me?"

Instantly the entire cutlery drawer wrenched out from the unit to spill on the floor with a crash. Stainless steel implements scattered. She knew only a powerful ghost would be able to move the whole drawer like that. Unnerved, she shouted.

"Leave me alone! Get out of my house, whoever you are!"

A woman's disembodied voice startled her.

"I don't think so."

With a heart-jolting stab of fear she recognised the voice.

Silvia Bates!

Cold sweat beaded on her brow as she fought a panic attack.

"Get out, Bates. You've no business in my house."

"On the contrary, Tyler. You *are* my business. You took the contrap, my contrap, and killed me in the process."

"I didn't kill you."

"You're splitting hairs, my dear. You know exactly what I'm talking about."

Tyler backed up towards the door, trying to plot Bates' invisible position.

"Show yourself, you coward." She slipped a gallows blade from the sheath beneath her jacket.

"All in good time. You can't deny the cat a chance to play with the mouse."

Why now? What have you planned for me?

"I've brought a friend to see you, Tyler, an old acquaintance. You remember Violet."

The name quickened a new fear. *Yes, I remember Violet Corpe, the knife-wielding, Tudor murderer I set loose from the Ghost Portal.* She remembered Violet coalescing briefly in the air before rushing in to occupy Bates' terrified body. Violet was a mad hag with missing teeth, crazed hair and sunken eyes. A white bonnet topped her straggled thatch of greyed hair. She wore a tightly laced bodice over a grubby, stained shirt, and the mere sight of her was enough to instil fear.

Of course, when Bates died Violet's ghost was set loose again.

Another voice entered the room.

"Hello, Deary!"

Violet appeared before her with a sudden rush, as ghastly as ever and with her hand raised, ready to stab down with a ghostly carving knife.

Tyler ran for the door as Bates' *cloaked* ghost slammed it shut. She heaved it open and dashed through into the hall as Violet cackled insanely. Tyler grabbed the hall phone and held it to her ear.

No dial tone. Someone's cut the line.

Turning to the front door she stared in horror at the steel mesh guard she had fixed over the letter box. One end was now buckled and twisted where someone had forced a gallows blade through. Ignoring Bates' haunting laughter from the hall, Tyler bolted for the passage beneath the stairs. She secured the door behind her with its original old lock and its two new deadbolts, hit the light switch on the wall, and fled down into the strongroom to frantically check the surveillance monitors as strip lights blinked to life.

At first glance everything outside the house appeared normal. She skimmed over the interior room screens and found nothing moving, no ghosts or anything else out of place. In the kitchen the spilled cutlery remained on the floor.

The green night-vision displays showed the sides of the house where nothing moved. At the front, plants along the garden edges swayed in the wind, and the driveway and lawn were still and empty. The rear was much the same. No living soul anywhere to be seen.

I guess that's something to be grateful for, at least.

As though reading her mind, figures emerged through the darkness. The first came from the green gloom at the end of the drive, a ghostly man, too indistinct in the camera's limited resolution for much detail. The ominous figure and the flickers of slim blades gliding towards her front door quickened her pulse. Squinting at the screen, she wondered if this was a gloved ghost, a man or a regular enemy phantom.

Her mobile displayed three bars of signal. She speed-dialled Melissa. No one answered. Neither did Lucy, Klaus nor Yash when she tried them. In desperation she phoned Freddy, unsure if he was even in the country. To her surprise he picked up.

"Tyler, is everything okay?"

"No, it's not. I'm under attack, locked in my house. There are ghosts everywhere and possibly men too." She glanced at the front-of-house screen where more figures lurched up the drive. To the rear, several men were climbing over the stone wall at the end of the garden. "Yes, definitely men. Bates' is here. I'm scared, Freddy."

"I'll get a team there asap. I'm on my way. You have a blade?"

"Several. I've shut myself in the cellar."

"Great. Stay there and do what you can to protect yourself. I'm hanging up so I can call it in."

"No! Freddy, talk to me. I'm all alone here. I tried everyone, even Yash. No one answered."

"That's odd. Even if his line's busy every call to that number is answered."

"I know, right? I'm worried I might have a panic attack and pass out. I'll be easy pickings if that happens."

"Listen, it will be all right. Just sit tight and focus on the things you can get on with. Keep your mind busy on doing stuff." The rumble of Freddy's car engine came over the phone. "I'm coming to you now but I can't call for backup while I'm talking to you. Hold the line." A static tone replaced his voice.

Tyler turned on the spot checking for the tell-tale flashes of a gallows blade in the hands of a *cloaked* ghost. Scratching sounds from above warned her someone had reached the house. On the front-of-house screen, a figure lurked in the doorway, trying to break in. Other less solid figures passed through into the hall unhampered.

"They're coming for you," whispered Bates, close by.

Tyler dropped her phone. Bates appeared across the room with a sudden flourish, producing a gallows blade and holding it ready to bear down. Running at Tyler she shrieked with bared teeth, her crazed eyes narrowing. Tyler dodged the blow and struck out with her blade, missing Bates by millimetres. Bates snarled, turning for a second attack. Their blades clashed, gallows iron hissing. Bates *was* a strong ghost. Tyler felt her weight behind the blade as they wrestled. She broke away, twisting to the side. When Bates flew at her again, Tyler aimed for the blade and knocked it from Bates' hand. It hit the floor and skittered into a far corner. Bates vanished with a growl.

In her place Violet appeared, a lopsided smile splitting her haggard face. A long, gleaming gallows blade replaced her previous weapon of choice.

Tyler grimaced.

"Hello, Violet, how *nice* to see you."

*

The Hell bird peered sideways as Albert acted out the breaking open of a melon. Albert pretended to take great bites of the fruit and dangled imaginary grapes, taking them into his mouth one at a time. Finally, he tore apart an invisible loaf of bread to chew on its crust.

The bird clacked and clawed at the ground again, a hunger glinting in its eye.

"I do believe it's working," muttered Zebedee, watching with the others. "Keep going, Albert. The beast seems to understand."

Again Albert pointed to the tower and renewed his acting. The bird took a tentative step forwards before releasing its loudest screech yet. It spread its wings, wafting dusty fire-fog into the air and took off, leaving Albert and the ghosts on the plain below. Zebedee watched it go.

"Oh, what a shame. I thought for a minute there–"

"Wait, it's coming back," said Claudia. Up in the sky the Hell bird circled round before descending towards the gathering. The ghosts backed away, panicked by the bird's sudden plunge. Many ran for the cover of the trees. Albert braced himself.

This is it. It's all or nothing. Either the bird will carry me, or it will tear me to shreds.

The great bird folded its wings to dive. Extending its talons, it cawed, rushed in to grab Albert by the shoulders, and carried him up into the sky. Pounding the air with its massive wings, it climbed, crossed the river and banked to head straight for the broken tower.

Below, Zebedee whooped with delight and tossed his

hat into the air.

"It worked, my boy. It worked!"

*

Violet rushed forward, screaming as Tyler wished she had grabbed the contrap instead of the blade. She risked a shot with the blade but Violet veered to the side and dodged its path, speeding closer. Tyler slipped a new blade from her bandolier and met the attack face on. For a few hideous moments, Violet's demented stare burned only inches away. Tyler smelt the fetid, clammy taint of the crone's foul breath. She forced Violet's blade away from her face and muscled her own blade closer to Violet's heart. Violet *cloaked* into invisibility and suddenly pulled away, her blade dropping to the floor. Tyler snatched up the blade.

She turned to her bank of monitors and watched her front door give as men at the back of the house smashed in the windows. At the side of the house, figures kicked at the back door. Their banging echoed down through the rafters of the old cellar, displacing dust. Movement triggered the sensors on every monitor. The alarm blared and the surveillance system lights blinked rapidly, casting the walls in red flashes.

Violet was still somewhere in the cellar, perhaps Bates, too. Tyler sensed it as she collected her phone from the floor. Backing into the wall, she scanned the room before trying Yash's number again. Still no reply.

A floating blade levelled and shot through the air at her. Tyler dropped her phone and spun to the side, lashing out at the space where she thought Bates must be. The blade came at her again, stabbing down. Tyler parried and her opponent's blade snapped. Bates cursed and Tyler felt her withdraw.

"And don't come back, you old hag." Tyler glanced around the cellar as she felt Bates and Violet retreat further. She was alone, but knew her reprieve would not last long. She took out the contrap and set it to the *Tower of Doom*. The tower remained a ruin.

Great.

Hell birds soared over the rubble and beneath the large moon one carried something in its talons that resembled a branch. She switched to the *Ghost Portal* and whispered into the swirling fog beyond the crystal. *What was it Albert had said before entering Edwina's grave? When you need me, seek me out.*

"Albert, if you can hear me, I could really use your help right now."

*

Her phone screen, smashed by the fall, lit up. Its casing vibrated against the stone floor, a struggling firefly in a spider's web. Letting the contrap hang around her neck, Tyler snatched up her mobile.

"Freddy."

"How are you doing, Tyler?"

"I'm still here. I think Bates has gone for the time being but men are in the house. The ghosts will have told them I'm down here by now." She crossed to a wall safe, tapped in the code and opened the steel door. "They'll soon break down the door." She took a P99 and a spare magazine from the safe and closed the door. Drawing the contrap from her shirt she set it to the *Brimstone Chasm* and forced the lever full circle.

"Vorago expositus."

"Tyler?"

"Just preparing a little reception for Bates. If she tries anything again I'll put her and her friend into the

Chasm."

"Right." A deep hammering sounded from the stairway. "What's that?"

"Sounds like they're sledgehammering the last door. They'll be in any second now." She aimed the contrap's crystal at the cellar's stone steps. The strip lights flickered and died, followed by the red flashing indicators and the monitors' green hues. She swept the *Chasm's* fiery glow around the room. "They've cut the power. It's just me and the contrap now."

"Hang in there. Help's on the way."

"Thanks, Freddy." She pocketed the phone and listened to the footsteps and clamour overhead. A metallic wrenching sound told her the intruders were bending the reinforced steel plating of the under-stair walls and door. A stream of flickering blades danced into view down the cellar steps.

"Phasmatis licentia!" cried Tyler.

Unseen spirits screamed into the *Chasm*, ripped from the air in icy streaks of blue light, their blades left to clatter on the flagstones. Tyler dashed forward and collected the blades, shoving them quickly into a back pocket. She resumed her position, guarding the entrance. The noise above intensified with shouts, yelps and gunshots. Visible ghosts dashed into the chamber and again Tyler shouted the command. The phantoms morphed, spinning into the *Chasm*, a cluster of shrieking whirlwinds. Gunshots blasted.

And then the stillness came, a quiet pause of thirty seconds or so in which Tyler felt as though time itself had frozen. Footsteps on the cellar's stone steps broke the silence. Human footsteps. Tyler lowered the contrap and levelled her gun instead. Torch beams bounded around the walls of the stairway like searchlights as she backed into the wall and screamed.

"GET OUT OR I'LL KILL YOU!"

Freddy and Lucy breached the stairs, with Melissa close behind. A blinding torchlight settled on Tyler's face.

"That's a fine way to greet your saviours!"

Denby, Watts & May

Freddy Carter, bearing the unfortunate code name of Pratt, smiled sheepishly. A year younger than Tyler and the girls, he stood a hand taller than any of them, his gangling body topped with a mop of red hair. Once gloved with the ghost of Heinrich Himmler, he still bore a pale scar across his nose from Tyler's bite. She thanked him for driving over and examined what was left of her front door.

Hanging from a single twisted hinge, it was missing the lock and surrounding area. The steel mesh around the letterbox was a gnarled mess and the remaining wood was scarred, beaten and riddled with bullet holes. A gallows blade remained lodged near one edge. She pulled the blade free and turned to Melissa and Lucy accusingly.

"You didn't answer my calls. Nobody did, except Freddy. Where were you?"

"I'm sorry, okay?" said Melissa, standing in the shadows of the hallway while Lucy texted beside her. Freddy watched from behind. "We've been busy. We broke into Yash's office. Then we were coming over to see you about what I found and we didn't notice the calls."

Tyler's cracked phone buzzed, signalling a text message from Lucy.

SORRY

"I could have been killed. I very nearly was!"

"You can't stay here tonight. You'd best come back with us."

"I'm not going anywhere. This is my home. I'm going to repair it, only I'll make it stronger this time."

"What happened?"

"It was the ghost of Silvia Bates and she brought friends. She arranged it all, must have joined forces with the oppressor. She's taken her accidental death pretty personally but don't worry, Lucy. She's blaming me entirely so you're off the hook."

Lucy cringed and resent her text apology.

Tyler checked her phone again.

"Will you stop doing that?"

"We did kind of rescue you," Lucy pointed out. "I got through to Yash. I guess the lines were all busy." Beyond the threshold the bodies of Tyler's human attackers lay strewn around the drive. From where she stood she could see at least six more inside.

"SOCO are going to kill us," said Melissa, surveying the dumped corpses.

"There won't be any police if I have anything to do

with it. This house is so remote that we can shut this whole thing down before anyone sees or hears a thing about it. Yash can deal with it."

"Does your kettle still work?" asked Lucy. She headed for the kitchen.

"I guess." Tyler glared after her.

"Let's sit down," said Melissa, taking Tyler by the arm. "We need to update you."

Two unmarked vans sped up the drive and screeched to a halt. A tactical assault team rushed out, slowing at the bodies.

Tyler glowered at them, hands on hips.

"Oh good. Here's the cavalry, just in time for tea and biscuits."

*

When the clean-up team were gone and the bodies bagged and taken away, the girls and Freddy gathered around the plaster strewn kitchen table. A cold breeze blew unhindered through the damaged house.

"I've had this feeling about Yash for a while now," began Melissa. "I guess it started when Chapman vanished but it's intensified over the last couple of weeks."

Tyler cut in. "By the way, he called me to check everything was okay a few minutes ago. Sounded surprised when I answered my phone. I'm really feeling the love."

"Yeah, I think we all know what you mean," said Lucy.

Melissa continued.

"Since we came home I've been waiting for the analysis of the pages I copied from Barak. Get this: Yash hasn't even passed them on to anyone. He's just sat on

227

them. It's like he doesn't want our investigation to go anywhere."

"So that's why you wanted to check his office."

"That and his silence on Chapman's disappearance, his inability or reluctance to help us, the way he had Klaus spy on us... I mean, Klaus is one of us. Yash knows that. It's like he's trying to fracture the team."

Tyler nodded. "I've felt the same ever since he sent us to Prague. It never seemed like anything worth chasing. No sign of the gloves or anything but, as it turned out, we just happened to dig up something of interest."

"Evidence of a second GAUNT machine and Abraham Eleazar's book of Astral Theorem," added Lucy.

"Wait a minute," said Freddy. "What are you talking about? Who's Abraham what's-his-name? A book of Astral what?"

"Astral Theorem, or *cosmic metaphysics* if you prefer." Melissa brought Freddy up to speed with their jaunt to Prague while he dipped biscuits in his coffee, stuffing them into his mouth one after the other.

"Wow, this changes everything." Freddy shoved the biscuit tin away. "If we could harness the power of the gallows ring we could combat Heydrich's reveries and probably double our strength against the insurgents. It should have been his top priority."

Melissa nodded.

"You would think so. But let me show you what I found in his office." From her bag she drew a file bearing a *Top Secret* stamp and opened it on the table. "It's a compilation of documents and notes I copied. I don't have proof, but I think most of this was from a project Chapman was working on before he disappeared. Look at this. I found it shoved down the side of a filing cabinet drawer." She unfolded an official document and smoothed it out on the table for the others to read. They examined it during a brief silence.

"It's governmental acceptance and confirmation of a proposal to set up a new MI6 sub-department," said Freddy. "One headed up by you three girls. Check the date. That was three weeks ago."

"I know," said Melissa. "And Yash has hidden it all this time. The Department of Investigation in Response to Paranormal Threat, internally known as *Denby, Watts and May*. It details the advancement in authorised powers for the three of us. If Chapman was still around we would now be in charge of our very own handpicked team of intelligence officers. We'd be working from our own department office."

"Hang on. Why's her name first on the list?" Tyler nodded towards Lucy.

"I like it," said Lucy. "*Denby, Watts and May*. It has a certain charm."

Tyler rolled her eyes. "What else is he hiding?"

"I'm getting to that. When we got home I made a quick study of everything I copied from the office. Most of Chapman's notes are in his unique style of shorthand. Basically I can't read a word and it would probably take the world's leading codebreakers four months to crack, but there *is* this." She drew a page free of the pile and slid it across the table. The others studied the document.

"I see what you mean about the shorthand," said Freddy. Chapman's scribbly writing filled the page with indecipherable words. Half way down, a break in the scrawl was bridged by a line of numbers he had overwritten in red pen.

78043829

"What's with the red numbers? A phone number?"

"It had me foxed for a while but I figured it out on the way over here. It's an eight-figure grid reference. For some reason Chapman made a note of it. You'll never believe where it is."

"Where?"

"It's North Ice, an abandoned research station in Greenland. It was in use from nineteen fifty-two to fifty-four."

"It's surely too much of a coincidence for us to ignore," added Lucy.

"It's in a barren zone of ice sheet, roughly eight hundred kilometres east of Qaanaaq, the airport Streicher just visited. There's nothing near it except miles and miles of ice."

"Mel, you'd better tell them about Barak," prompted Lucy.

*

The Hell bird set Albert down on the dusty rubble wall of the old tower. As soon as his feet touched down, rock and mortar began assembling of its own accord, the tower building around him as he watched.

That's a good sign.

He peered out across the gnarled trees, the plain and the river towards the tiny figures of the ghosts he had left behind. He waved them on, unsure if they could see him from this distance. It was hard to check their progress but the more he squinted, the more certain he became.

Yes, them ghosts are coming this way. Good. Now to get that old door open.

He skipped from wall to wall as they rose, and leapt

across onto the unfinished spiralling stone staircase leading down to the lower levels. Jumping from its highest steps he descended.

This part of the tower was empty, still and quiet. It felt safe and he made short work of the steps, leaping the last dozen three at a time to stop a few feet from the curved wall on the ground floor. There the tower's great arched door stood solid and thick, its many and varied bolts still in good order.

Another good sign. No one had tampered with the door or tried to break in.

He backtracked up several stairs to the lowest of the tower's arrow-slit windows and sat, watching for the arrival of his ghost army.

Outside, the afternoon's heated glow subsided into scorched tones. Fire-fog rose from the charred fringe of misshapen trees and an unearthly screech split the sky. Albert pressed his face into the slit to shout.

"Hurry! The liliths!"

Beyond the trees the ghosts quickened their pace, bolting for the protection of the clawed branches. A shadow swept over them, followed by another.

Albert watched helplessly as the first of the liliths plunged towards his troop. Ghosts lurched aside, scattering like startled field mice as more shadows swooped overhead. A second lilith dived, its outstretched talons raking at a hapless ghost. The she-demon clutched but missed and the fallen ghost scrambled, attempting to escape as the lilith gathered itself for a second lunge.

A sudden, smaller shadow darted from the sky, the quicker, darker form of a Hell bird. It hit the lilith at full pelt, knocking her from the sky. In an instant the sky clouded with more birds, all massing against the liliths as battle erupted.

That's interesting. The Hell birds and the liliths are enemies.

The ghosts fled through the trees, ducking limbs and branches. As the first of the ghosts neared the door, Albert descended to draw the bolts and heave it open. Alone he struggled to dislodge it but as ghosts ploughed in from the other side the great door groaned and opened in a crack wide enough for them to enter. A moment later they pushed it further still and they streamed in. Behind them the liliths spewed fire at the warring birds as blazing trees threw flames into the air.

*

"What about Barak?" asked Tyler.

"Surprise, surprise, he's not who he says he is," explained Melissa. "When we came home I did some research. The real Lumir Barak, the real brother of Řezník Barak, was murdered in Bulgaria a month ago."

"So who's the imposter?"

"I don't know but he clearly lied to get close to us and he wasn't after the contrap, so the question is what did he want with us?"

Tyler phoned Klaus repeatedly until he answered. She told him the news, explaining all about her encounter in the house, Barak, Yash and Chapman's Greenland grid reference.

"I agree. We need to get there and look into it. Keep it to yourselves. We can't tackle Yash while he's the section chief. He's just too powerful. This will need to be a closely guarded secret."

"So you're in?"

"I wouldn't miss it for the world. Would you like me to arrange transport? I can have my guys air-drop our kit somewhere on the ice sheet. That'll free us up to travel by more conventional means, but we better move quickly. Streicher's been there a day or two already, and who knows what he's doing?"

"Do you think Chapman went after something?"

"Perhaps. Short of confronting Yash with Melissa's file there's only one way to find out."

"Yes. In Qaanaaq I can pick up Streicher's trail with the *Past Eye*."

"But let's see what's at this grid reference first. Tracking Streicher could take years. If we don't find him at the reference point in Greenland, we've always got the *Past Eye*."

"Okay."

"I'll be in touch when I have some things in place and, Tyler, I'm glad you're okay. I'm sorry I wasn't there to help."

"It's okay."

"Still, if anything happened to you, I don't know what I'd do."

She ended the call and with help from the others worked boarding up her front and back doors for the night. At one o'clock in the morning she took a return call from Klaus and stuck her head into the living room where Melissa, Lucy and Freddy dozed in spare bedding and sleeping bags.

"It's on. Klaus has organised everything. We leave from Heathrow at thirteen hundred hours. He's going to meet us in Qaanaaq Airport."

Qaanaaq

Ghosts massed against the door forcing it shut and Albert swiftly drew the heavy bolts home to secure it. He led his troop upstairs and found to his delight that the tower had grown while he had been below. The penultimate floor, however, had yet to be built and with it the room of abundance that had fed him and Tyler on their previous visit. All the same, the tower's edges were building still, creeping almost unperceivably towards the next level and his stomach grumbled at the thought of the fresh food and cool jugs of clear water that would manifest when the level was complete. He gathered the troops in the shelter of the level below.

"Soon we'll be able to eat but for now rest 'ere and recover what strength you can. We still 'ave a lot t' do before we can get out of 'ere."

When most were either asleep or resting, he climbed

to the top of the tower and pushed open a wooden hatch. Above him the *Chasm's* dusk descended, its cold air chilling his semi-ghost bones. He perched on the wall and watched. The liliths were gone, along with the Hell birds and, in the far distance of the horizon, pinpricks of flame flashed against thunderclouds as blue lightning split the night.

Where are you Tyler?

*

Qaanaaq, North Greenland

Tyler released Klaus from her embrace and grabbed her baggage. Leaving the airport they took a taxi to a local hire centre and collected the white snowmobiles Klaus had booked; one each for him, Freddy and the girls.

"Wouldn't it be quicker to hire a small plane?" asked Lucy.

"Too obvious. If time allowed it would've been nice to do a fly by, see what's down there, but even then there's only one way to be sure and in a plane everyone for miles around would see us."

"But we'll be driving for days."

"Believe me, it's the best way. I spoke with my contacts here. There's been a spate of missing aircraft over the ice sheet. Small planes and helicopters, all non-commercial flights. They go out and are never seen again. There's not a ban but they're strongly advising not to fly while they investigate. We'd better hurry." Klaus glanced at the heavy sky and passed around snow goggles. A brisk wind blew in from the sea, snatching snow and ice from the ground to swirl it out of the compound onto the open expanse of the ice sheet. It drove on relentlessly, a persistent, beckoning voice compelling Tyler to join its flow. Somewhere out in the featureless, frigid void an unnameable NVF horror lurked, awaiting her arrival. It loomed in her mind like a mountainous shadow.

"We need to reach the ice sheet before we set camp. It's best if we find somewhere away from any prying eyes." He checked his watch as Tyler and the others fastened their white, fur-lined Arctic parkas. "It'll be dark soon. Just over two hours until the drop and it would be best if we could get there before touchdown."

"It's funny. Somehow I figured Greenland would be greener," muttered Lucy.

Melissa smirked.

"Try picturing an entire island smothered by over one and a half million kilometres of ice sheet and you'll get a rough idea of what to expect."

"Right," said Lucy.

They hauled rucksacks, tents, gear and fuel onto the back of the snowmobiles. Tyler finished first. She drew up the hood of her parka and watched through the loop of its wolfish trim as the others prepared to leave. Klaus strapped a bear gun over his shoulder and the team followed him out of the gates.

They drove into the twilight, learning the peculiarities of the unfamiliar vehicles and stopping only to don more layers and add furry trapper hats beneath their hoods. With practice, the vehicles grew easier to master through their thick Arctic-mitts. Lucy took to her snowmobile effortlessly, leaning back and looking like she had been riding all her life while Melissa crashed into the first snow bank. They paused to drag her free, right her snowmobile and dust her down.

An hour into the seemingly empty void of the ice sheet, Klaus called a halt and tugged a GPS from his pack to chart their progress.

"This is close enough. The drop zone is two hundred metres east."

They dismounted and set camp by the light of several lamps, their smaller head-mounted lamps chasing beams in the darkening air. All around, the ice sheet dwindled into grey obscurity.

With the tents erected and their baggage stowed inside, Klaus called them out.

"It's time. We need to leave a guard at the camp, so who's coming with me?"

"I'll go," offered Tyler.

"I'm up for a jaunt, too." Lucy stepped forward to receive a glare from Tyler.

"Great," said Klaus, rubbing his mitted hands to warm them. "That's good. We might need three snowmobiles to bring back the kit anyway."

"I'm sure two would manage," said Tyler.

"Fine," fired Lucy, with a curl of her lip. "You stay here if you like." She stomped past Tyler and mounted up. "Let's go. I'll feel a lot safer when we get our guns from the drop and when we've set up the perimeter alarm. I've a feeling it's not just the bears we need to worry about out here."

Tyler mounted and started her snowmobile, scowling. Klaus passed Freddy the bear gun and mounted up.

"Ready?"

"Good to go."

"Affirmative."

They set off at an easy pace, guided by Klaus and his GPS. Soon the greyness of the night swallowed the camp behind them and Tyler had a strange feeling that they might have been the last three people on the face of a frozen planet. The soft grey of the night surrounded a tight zone of light from the headlamps of their churning vehicles. She was glad the noise of the engines made it hard to talk.

At least I'll have some respite from Lucy's tongue while we ride.

Klaus paused, checked the GPS and switched off his snowmobile.

"We're close enough. The gear should drop over there." He pointed to a patch of ice ahead at the limits of the snowmobiles' lamp beams. "I guess we sit and wait. I have a little coffee in a flask if anyone's interested." Lucy left her snowmobile to join him.

Tyler killed her headlamps and dismounted to wander a short way. With her back to them and her head-mounted torch off, she stood amidst a fine dusting of driving snow, wind the only sound. Unarmed except for the contrap around her neck and with nothing but the clothes she wore, she felt incredibly small and insignificant in this alien landscape. She remained there for several minutes absorbing the feeling and finding it strangely liberating.

I'm insignificant. I do not matter. I'm superfluous and the world will keep spinning with or without me.

She scanned her bleak surroundings for other entities, wondering if she was being watched. She reasoned that, if the NVF were operating somewhere out here, they might well have placed sentry ghosts on guard. Qaanaaq was the only civilian airport in the northern sector of the island. If enemies of the NVF were to approach undercover, it would most likely be from there.

Turning back she felt lonelier still. Over by the

snowmobiles Lucy was nestled in Klaus' arms.

I'm losing him. No. Wake up, you stupid girl. You never had him in the first place!

She turned away to search the sky for signs of the incoming stealth plane. Here and there stars carved pricks of diamond light and to the north traces of a green aurora glowed in a single, sweeping wave.

Before long it came; the soft drone of the aircraft, though one of the quietest she had ever heard. Little more than a fleeting shadow overhead, it was gone in an instant and suddenly parachutes weighted by aluminium canisters fell from the pitch of the sky, catching in the lamplight of Klaus' snowmobile.

*

Albert slept fitfully below the upper trapdoor, waking cold and hungry to a room of dozing ghosts. Beside him Zebedee snored loudly, whiskers swaying with each exhale.

Albert climbed the stairs to the door and heaved it open. The *Chasm's* early morning light flashed into the room. He squinted out onto the tower's top where Hell birds feasted from a table laden with fresh fruit, crusty bread and rich cheeses. They careered and crashed around in a feeding frenzy, knocking flasks of water to the floor and casting food across the unfinished room. A large, black wing passed in front of Albert's nose and he recoiled, quickly drawing the trap shut again.

After a moment, he tentatively reopened the door a few inches. When no attack seemed imminent he prised it up further and grinned as a glossy, red apple rolled within reach. He snatched the fruit, took a large bite and descended to shake Zebedee by the shoulder. The old ghost stirred.

"'Ere." Albert shoved the remaining apple into Zebedee's hand. "I'm going back for more."

Other ravenous ghosts awoke at the excitement in his voice, and gathered inquisitively. Before long a team formed, taking turns to dash out and risk assault by the feasting birds. Some returned empty handed. Others scampered back to the stairs with arms fully laden, their faces beaming with success. They passed around the scavenged food, sharing it as best they could and everyone ate at least something to ease their aching bellies.

"Just you wait 'til the roof's on. Then we'll *feast*."

Come on Tyler. Just a little closer to your goal.

*

Back at the camp, Tyler and the team unloaded the new gear from the snowmobiles. Klaus was right: they had needed three to carry all the canisters back. They unpacked five C7 assault rifles, their P99s, spare magazines, boxes of rounds, grenades, surveillance kit, gallows blades and rations. Klaus stopped to rest and swigged water from a bottle.

"We going to be heavily loaded from here on in, but it'll be worth it. We don't know what we'll find."

Tyler opened a new canister and with Klaus' help dragged out the lead box of Mordecai chains, wondering if it had been a mistake to bring them. The box alone would weigh down a snowmobile enough to slow its progress.

Lucy approached an unopened canister at Klaus' side and he stayed her with a hand.

"Not that one. Here." He slid a newly opened canister over to her and strapped the unopened one onto the back of his snowmobile while she watched him suspiciously.

"Freddy, give us a hand setting the perimeter sensors."

For the next few minutes Klaus, Freddy and Lucy worked around the edge of the camp, jamming metre-long sensor spikes into the packed snow and ice. When finished, a circle of twelve spikes ringed the tents. Klaus took the alarm console from the canister and powered it up.

"Okay, Mojo." He gave Lucy a nod.

Lucy slid a gallows blade from her thigh bandolier and tossed it twenty metres out into the ice sheet. A ring of LEDs on the top of the spike closest to Lucy flashed red, accompanied by a high-pitched bleep. Klaus flicked the reset switch on the alarm console and peace resumed.

"All set." He glanced at Lucy near the perimeter. "You'd better retrieve the blade." Lucy trudged away.

Klaus turned to Tyler.

"Where's Mel? It would be best if we all knew how this works."

"I'll fetch her." Tyler left to find Melissa. She unzipped the girls' tent and stuck her head in. Melissa sat cross-legged on the floor, engrossed with the screen of her laptop.

"What you doing?" asked Tyler. "Klaus wants to take us though the perimeter system."

Melissa leaned across to see if anyone was with Tyler at the opening. When she saw Tyler was alone she beckoned her over.

"Can you keep a secret?"

Tyler gave her a withering look. *Of course.*

"Okay. I bugged Yash's office."

Tyler raised her eyebrows. "You did *what?*"

242

"You heard."

"You do know you could get court-martialled for that? Does Lucy know?"

"Nobody knows, but us. *Someone* had to watch him. I don't trust him."

Tyler joined Melissa behind the laptop to view the screen. She watched Yash sitting at his desk sorting through files. A moment later he picked up the phone and put it to his ear.

"No sound?"

"I only had time to install a single camera. I wasn't expecting much of a signal out here, but tonight I got lucky. I've been watching him whenever I can. All the data's recording to my hard drive. I have spare batteries for the laptop and a solar charger so I can check the footage each night. In theory."

"Nice work. Anything suspicious?"

"Not yet but it's early days."

"Okay. Klaus is waiting. We'd better go."

The rest of the team gathered around Klaus to look at the alarm console while Lucy searched for the thrown blade. Above rows of switches, buttons and LEDs, a small screen divided into twelve blocks showed thermal images of the ice sheet radiating from the camp perimeter. In one of these camera feeds, Lucy's figure shone with pinks and yellows against the midnight-blues of the ice.

"How reliable is this thing?" asked Tyler.

"As far as technology goes, it's as good as it gets. Of course, it can be damaged, batteries can run down and the weather can interfere."

"Like a snowstorm or something."

Klaus nodded. "In good weather it'll work perfectly. In a whiteout it's next to useless. The spike sensors detect motion. They're good for thirty metres or so and they're set to react to anything larger than a snowflake. The alarm is also triggered by hits on the thermal cameras. You can select an individual camera with this button and this one here toggles between thermal imaging and night vision." He took her through each of the controls. "It's important Lucy brings back the blade. We need to keep things tidy where weapons are concerned. The system won't warn us of any ghosts if they come unarmed so we need to be careful where we leave any blades, or they could use them against us." He turned to Tyler. "Right now, you're our only warning system for unarmed ghosts."

"Yeah, but I could be affected by the weather, too. I could freeze to death."

Klaus grinned and wrapped his arms around her while Lucy traipsed by, silently clutching her retrieved blade. She busied herself, neurotically, taking inventory of every weapon and round in their arsenal.

*

Marcus played before Hakan. Over time, he noticed the usually growling and dour contrapassi were partial to his merrier tunes and, whenever they gathered to feast, he played these until his fingers were sore. During the night, when Hakan and most of the other monsters retreated into the gloomy compartments of the lower decks, Marcus was allowed to sleep on the floor of the forecastle, chained and guarded by the two sentries at the doors. They never fed him wilfully, but every so often a nub of chewed bone or a crust of bread would tumble from the bestial feast and, behind turned backs, he snatched and fed on those that fell within reach.

This night as the contrapassi feasted, Hakan's mood

turned particularly grim. He downed several jars of wine and searched the table for more.

"Wine," he growled to his guards. "More wine, now."

A guard left his post to fetch more from the ship's store and the feasters roared their approval as he tossed them the keg. The closest contrapasso slammed a blade into the top and prised off the lid to dip his tankard.

Hakan rose from his throne to tower over the unwitting offender as the room quietened with a sudden tension.

"You dare to drink before your master, Gaw?" breathed Hakan, drawing the long, curving sword from the scabbard at his belt. With one powerful stroke he sliced through Gaw's substantial shoulder, cleaving armour and flesh to the belly. Gaw fell dead across the table, dashing food and several jars of wine to the floor.

Marcus grabbed a rolling jar and after wiping dog drool from its lip, drank its dregs. While the contrapassi argued and raged he pilfered a hunk of unspoilt bread and shoved it into his shirt.

A challenger shoved his chair from the table and rose to his feet. Hakan snarled and stamped forwards to wrestle and hoist him from the floor. He threw the challenger against the wall with a sickening thud. The broken contrapasso slumped to the floor, blood dripping from his hackles as Hakan turned back to the others.

"Does anyone else care to challenge their king?"

Marcus spotted another find. Not far from his chains, at the edge of the throne, a joint end of meat and bone rolled to a stop. He checked his captors and found them still busy glowering at each other distrustfully. Marcus grabbed his violin bow by one end and used it to nudge the morsel closer. Hakan lurched to the table and dipped his tankard into the wine keg. Marcus slid the morsel closer still and covered it with his foot as Hakan turned back to the throne.

"Play!" growled Hakan, scowling down at Marcus. "Play us a merry tune."

The Leap

When all but the guards had left for their beds, Marcus devoured his meagre scavenged meal. He chewed and gulped quickly in fear of the contrapassi's return. He knew that if they discovered his food, it could mean death. Nibbling the meat away he sucked the splintered bone clean of roasted flesh, admiring the pointed tool it left in his hands. Glancing at the doors to be sure no one was watching, he jammed the bone point into the key hole of his manacles and began picking the lock.

*

0700 Hours

Tyler peered out from her tent at the surrounding, endless white of the ice sheet as dawn flooded the camp with light. Klaus was already up and heating breakfast on two camping stoves between the tents. She checked the thermometer hanging on the tent exterior and sniffed the air.

-24°C

"What's that?" She stepped out of the tent and zipped it up behind her.

Klaus stirred sludge in the bottom of a ration pack. "The army's idea of a good breakfast. Personally I'd prefer bacon and eggs. There's more water on the boil for tea or whatever."

Tyler rummaged in the supply bag next to Klaus and pulled out a foil pack. "What do I do?"

"Just add hot water and stir. Are the others awake?" Tyler poured and stirred as a strange, eggy smell rose.

"Mel is. Lucy's still asleep."

"Better wake her. We need to make the most of the daylight."

"Okay." Tyler returned to her tent, unzipped the entrance and nudged Lucy with her boot. "Wake up. We need to eat and go."

She returned to the stoves where Freddy now sat across from Klaus chewing on a bacon sandwich.

"Where did you get that?"

Freddy gulped down his mouthful. "It's bacon jerky. I smuggled a pack through customs."

"Happiness for you. You could have got caught and every inch of our baggage would have been searched. You jeopardised our mission for a bacon roll?"

"Somethings are worth the risk. You want some?" He offered the roll.

Tyler shook her head and glared.

"What do you think we're going to find?" he asked.

"I don't know," admitted Tyler. "Maybe the second GAUNT machine, maybe something else. One thing's for sure, it's the NVF. Do you think Chapman's out here, locked away in an NVF prison camp or a lair beneath the ice?"

Freddy shrugged. "Why would they bring him here? I mean, why would they bring anything out here into the middle of nowhere? Surely it's the GAUNT machine. They're trying to keep it a secret so you don't destroy it like last time."

"I'm going to destroy it this time, too, and they can thank Streicher for that."

Freddy chuckled and raised a steaming mug of tea in salute.

"I don't doubt it, and we're going to give you all the help we can but, Tyler, I'm afraid they may have already killed Chapman. If he was on to them and was caught, why would they keep him alive?"

"Don't, Freddy." Tyler paled. "Don't even *think* it. Chapman would find a way. He'd give them a reason not to kill him. He's alive and we're going to find him." She forced down a spoonful of the eggy mixture.

"If you say so, but I think you should prepare yourself for the worst. If he *is* dead, he wouldn't have wanted you to get upset and jack in the fight. Whatever's out there, you'll need to carry on. We need to be prepared for anything, all of us. Okay?"

She stared him down.

"Chapman's not dead."

"I hope not. Did it occur to you that if they have all the information they need to build a second GAUNT machine they could build as many as they like."

Tyler nodded grimly.

Lucy and Melissa joined them, bleary-eyed, and Klaus tuned in a radio. They ate while listening to reports from the war zones: more countries siding with the Russian threat, the impending shadow of nuclear escalation. The UK, now with more enemies than friends had allied with Europe and the USA to declare an official state of war.

They packed down the camp in silence and, with Klaus guiding their caravan of snowmobiles, set off, pushing deeper into the ice sheet.

*

Izabella watched her row of shackled ghosts slowly deplete. When the contrapasso had chained her, ten ghosts sat in the line ahead of her and, in front of them, another entire row. Now a trifling four ghosts remained between her and the flames of the engine's burner.

The hulking fire-feeders turned from the furnace.

"More fuel," growled the one she had learned was named Ruk. The other, a broader beast named Grar, stomped to her line and collected the next ghost to fuel the fire. The ghost, a pretty maid in a once-glamourous medieval gown, screamed, kicked and fought. Grar hoisted her with ease, her flailing ineffectual against his giant, muscular limbs.

Trembling and unable to watch, Izabella peered at the doom-shadowed ghosts behind her.

What have they done with Marcus?

*

The iron loop clicked open and Marcus withdrew the bone spike from the keyhole, gawping in surprise. His ankle was free. He glanced at the door, wondering if the contrapassi outside had heard the manacle open. He waited, listening to the quiet rumble of the ship. When no one came, he tied his fiddle and bow together with string and strung them over his back.

Alone in a feeble shaft of moonlight falling through a narrow window, he considered what he might do with his new-found freedom. He couldn't escape through the doors. The guards outside would catch him. He scanned for a potential hiding place thinking he might wait for a better opportunity. Perhaps if they thought he had already gone they would cease to guard the room.

Roughly hewn cupboards offered only a delay in his inevitable recapture. The sparse, basic furniture around the chamber would not hide him well. He considered the long table. Beneath that he might evade the returning contrapassi for a few minutes but eventually he would be caught because it would give him no means of escape from the room. The gap between its far end and the doors was too great.

Left with nothing to try but the windows, he dragged one of the beasts' massive chairs over to the closest one and clambered up to inspect its fastening. The window was held shut by a simple latch. He hopped down to visit the table and, pocketing handfuls of bread, fruit and meat, he drank his fill of water from a huge jug before returning to climb the chair.

The latch gave easily and with a gentle push the window inched open letting in a stream of bitterly cold air. Shivering, he spied out through the gap at the dormant upper deck. Beyond the gunnels the night sky boiled with cloud and the ship's filthy vapours. He opened the window wide and eased himself through to climb down the other side, hanging from the windowsill and listening for the contrapassi. He let go and dropped to the boards below, where he flattened himself against the forecastle wall.

The ship groaned, its massive lateral masts creaking against the wind.

Voices from above startled him. The captain and one of the crew muttered in low growls beyond his view, somewhere at the bow of the forecastle. Their murmurs grew louder and Marcus knew the contrapassi were approaching. He dashed to the gunnels and peered over the side. Between curving sails he glimpsed other ships below. The closest rode the wind to one side, its sails almost touching Hakan's ship but lingering a short distance beneath.

Marcus climbed nimbly over the gunnels and inched down to the lateral mast below. Hugging the beam with all his limbs he inched towards the neighbouring ship. The growling voices drew closer. Marcus scuttled around the mast and hung from rigging to hide below its breadth.

"Give the lads another half hour and then wake 'em. I want this old cutter shipshape before the master rises. He's in his cups so there'll be no mercy today."

"Same as usual, then."

"Aye, same as usual."

Marcus waited, clinging on with ever-more aching arms, until the two contrapassi walked away. When the only sound was the thump of the ship's engines and the drone of the others in the sky nearby, he heaved himself back on top of the beam to continue his treacherous journey.

Every few feet he reached a thick sail rope lashed to the mast and had to clamber over. Half way he stopped to rest and spy on the neighbouring vessel. The first of the deck crew emerged, stomping up from the lower decks to work the rigging and man their posts. At the stern, a captain bellowed orders as the sun roasted the horizon. For a few minutes of respite from the cold he felt its warmth as he hurried to reach the other ship before any more crew appeared. He neared the end of the beam and surveyed the scene beneath. The neighbouring sail wavered closer before drifting away.

Climbing to the very tip of the mast, he waited until the sail swung back again to fill the space beneath him and with a deep breath and a surge of terror he leapt to freefall to the lower ship, his fiddle trailing after on its string. The fall seemed to last forever and he felt himself drift on the wind. Hitting the sail a short way from his target, he grabbed and grasped for a hand hold, slipping and tumbling. He rolled perilously close to the edge, where he clung, panting.

The captain's loud horn blast summoned the remaining crew from below and soon the deck of the new ship crawled with contrapassi. Other horns sounded across the fleet, reverberating throughout the sky.

Marcus lay flat on the sail, clenching its edge with white knuckles and wondering what to do next. Perhaps if he remained undiscovered and if the ship landed he might slip away without being noticed, but he felt sure he would be found before that happened. Splayed on an outstretched sail he knew he would be easily spotted from the higher ships. It was a wonder they had not already seen him. He edged closer to the hull, hoping to find a better hiding place.

A roar from the deck startled him.

"There! Shoot the vermin!" A battle-scarred contrapasso pointed to him.

More shouts followed as the crew fetched bows and gathered at the gunwale. They unleashed arrows, peppering the sail and mast, and Marcus rolled away, trying to evade the lethal rain. The end of the fabric lolled unexpectedly into view and he tumbled over the side to hang, clinging one-handed to the edge. An arrow thwacked into his arm and with a silent scream he let go and fell.

From the deck, the archers watched him drop.

"He's a gonner," muttered the jackal-headed captain. "Back to work, boys."

Marcus passed several ships unnoticed by their crews. Plummeting through the fleet he wondered if his imminent death would result in his reappearance sometime later, like the second death as he had witnessed previously in the *Chasm*. He hurtled towards another of the ships, dreading a crushing death on the hard deck. With a sudden jarring impact he landed on sail cloth and bounced to a stop. A moment later he came to his senses and peered up at the hull. The sail he had hit was a lower sail and from here the deck was hidden except for the gunwale's curving edge. He crawled in closer to the hull and lodged himself between the mast and the clinkers. Peering down, he realised if he had missed this ship he would have fallen all the way to the fire-fog below but now, here on the lowest ship of the fleet, he sat with his back to the hull, concealed from all contrapassi eyes.

Steeling himself, Marcus yanked the thick arrow shaft from his arm, tore a strip from his shirt to bind the wound, and waited.

*

Albert watched the walls grow slowly, stone by stone. By the time the sun neared its zenith the beams and boards of the tower roof started to assemble. The Hell birds clacked and gawked, reluctant to enter beneath the first slivers of ceiling.

"See?" he said, turning to the other ghosts and pointing to the birds. "Soon they'll leave the food alone altogether 'cause they's scared o' getting trapped when the roof's done."

As the afternoon drew on, the birds became scarcer. He and the others took turns, each bolder than the last, to scavenge from the table of plenty and each time food was taken, more appeared. By mid-afternoon the ghosts had gathered a surplus of food and had eaten their fill. To keep the birds away they scattered hunks of bread and pieces of fruit over the spreading tower roof, nursing an uneasy bond between ghost and bird.

While the ghosts mostly remained below, resting, eating and recuperating, Albert set his mind to a plan of action, whispering with Zebedee and the remnants of the Ghost Squad.

"We can stay 'ere a day or so, but no longer. Just until we're stronger, all right? We can gather supplies for when we leave."

"All well and good, Master Goodwin, but how are we going to rescue the others when we don't even know where they are?" asked Zebedee.

"I don't 'ave all the answers."

"We could send out scouts, have them spy out the death camps and the ships," suggested Kylie. "Maybe the birds could help."

Albert nodded. "Aye, they 'elped before. Now we control the food they'll do what we want. Say that works, an' we learn where the captives are. What then? There's the contrapassi to deal with, the prison wires and gun towers, the archers an' swords of the ships, and let's not forget the liliths. If we run into a bunch of them without

255

cover we'll burn."

"Let's take one thing at a time," said Zebedee. "Send out our spies. We can discuss what to do next when we know what we're up against."

"All right," agreed Albert. "Organise some volunteers. The smaller the better. Make sure they're well fed an' watered. I'll take some ghosts t' make a store downstairs. The tower could crumble at any time so we best be prepared. The bread should keep for a few days at least, an' we can store water in jugs from the table."

An hour of preparation and briefing followed and Albert led the volunteer spies, twenty-four in all, up onto the roof. Flecks of mortar and heavy flagstones gathered into place on the far portion of the unfinished floor. Without a single battlement in place, Albert felt precarious on the rooftop. One strong gust of wind, an irritated Hell bird or a chance stumble might send a ghost slipping over the side and deplete their number further.

"Keep away from the edge," he warned them. He scattered grapes and chunks of bread to draw in the birds and they swooped in, their keen eyes targeting the food. They pecked and jabbed, squabbling for morsels as the spy ghosts threw more food. Soon, the gorged birds lingered on the roof edge, sensing their services were expected in payment.

"They know. Don't ask me how, but they know we need them." Albert tempted the boldest of the birds closer with a bunch of grapes. The bird considered the fruit and cocked its head to watch Albert before hopping forward.

"We need you to take us out into the *Chasm*. We need you to carry these ghosts. They are our spies. Take them to wherever the jackal-heads are and wait for 'em.

When they are ready, bring them back 'ere. Do you understand?"

The bird clacked and blinked its glossy eyes. It strutted closer.

"Spread out," Albert told the ghosts. "Find a bird each. They'll do what we want because they know's we control the food."

He turned to the ghosts.

"Show 'em you 'ave food with you."

The other ghosts took bread from their pockets, their shirts and bags and presented it.

"You will be given food while you wait for us and all the food you can eat when you return. Now go."

With a sudden burst of energy, a bird at the far edge of the roof stretched its powerful wings and took flight. Grasping a ghost in its talons, it rose from the tower and carried the ghost away, a shrinking silhouette against the fiery sky. Others followed and for a few chaotic moments the roof flashed with black wings and rising ghosts.

Albert watched them go, calling after them.

"Godspeed!"

The Follower

Snow fell in large heavy flakes to blanket the ground ice. Its white patter blurred the mid-distance in an obscuring mist. A surging squall blustered at the expedition as Klaus stopped his snowmobile. The others pulled up alongside.

"What's wrong?" asked Tyler, as Klaus took a GPS reading.

"We're near the Petermann Glacier. The ice sheet here can be highly unstable and with this poor visibility. We need to rope-up or we might lose someone down a hidden crevasse." Klaus scanned the ice ahead through field glasses. "It looks rough. If the ice gets too treacherous for the snowmobiles we'll have to go the rest of the way on foot. Refuel. I'll get the ropes."

"Klaus–"

"I know. We have a company. Is it man or ghost?"

"A ghost, I think. I've glimpsed it several times now. At first I thought my eyes were playing tricks but then this grey shape always lurking some way behind us, mostly hidden by the snowfall."

"If it's an enemy ghost why doesn't it *cloak*?"

"It probably has, but it takes a lot of energy for the more powerful ghosts to remain *cloaked* for extended periods of time. Albert told me. If it's been following since we left Qaanaaq and has been invisible for most of that time it would try to use the snow. Earlier it ventured too near and I sensed it. That's when I started looking for it."

"What do you want to do?"

"Nothing, for now. One solitary ghost can't do much to us, especially if it's tiring. Carry on. I'll keep an eye on it, so don't make it obvious we've noticed. Okay?"

The others nodded.

"Does everyone have a gallows blade to hand?" asked Freddy.

Again they nodded.

"Right." Klaus fetched the main safety lanyard from his gear and linked the chassis of the snowmobiles together. When they were ready to move out, Klaus called them together.

"Buckle-up. If you hit a fissure you don't want to come off your snowmobile or we won't be able to haul you out."

For the rest of the day they drove in a slow, single column, hampered by the linking ropes of ten metre lengths. An hour before sunset, Klaus stopped and switched his snowmobile off to dismount. He circled a small area of ice testing it every so often with an ice pick.

"It seems solid enough. We'll camp here for the

night."

They erected the tents and drew up the snowmobiles to form a windbreak as a storm mustered.

Klaus, Freddy and Lucy set the perimeter sensors while Melissa and Tyler cooked rations and heated snow in a pan. Lucy finished with the perimeter and joined the girls at the stoves to make a strong coffee. Freddy and Melissa left to sort out their gear in the tents. Klaus, Tyler and Lucy sat around the stoves in an awkward silence. Lucy poured a cup of coffee and took it to a tent, unzipping the door and sticking her head through.

"I made..." She stopped.

Inside, Melissa and Freddy kissed. They noticed her and drew apart.

"Oh." Melissa coloured.

"I made you coffee but you're obviously busy. I'll come back later," snapped Lucy, walking away and muttering. "We should check the ammo again. I don't think we have enough grenades."

Melissa swore.

"Hey, it's not our fault," said Freddy. "He was our friend, too, but life goes on whether she likes it or not. I'm not going to keep away from you forever because Weaver died. Now, pucker up, Blondie."

"Don't call me Blondie. You know it winds me up."

"Yeah," said Freddy, leaning in. "It's just too easy."

"Freddy–"

He cut her off with a kiss.

*

Albert sat cross-legged on the rooftop watching the sky darken, disappointment etching his face. Thunderclouds billowed in the far distance as the rest of the empty heavens broiled with fire-fog clouds and vapours.

Zebedee arrived at the top of the stairs, his face cast in stark relief from the sunset's golden glow. He joined Albert, knees creaking as he sat to lean his back against a newly forming battlement.

"Don't worry, lad. Did you truly expect them to return within the day?" He dug tobacco from a side pocket of his tailcoat to refill his pipe.

"I don't know what I expected. I want to get out of 'ere, get back to Tyler, quick like."

Zebedee lit his pipe and smoked.

"Of course you do. The whole squad feels the same. Still there *is* some good news."

"Yeah, what's that?"

"The tower continues to grow. Little by little, Tyler must be approaching her goal."

"Whatever that is. We've been apart for so long I don't even know any more."

"Oh, cheer up, old boy." Zebedee took a handful of fruit from another pocket. "Here, have a grape."

*

Marcus watched the ground loom closer as the fleet descended through thick cloud. His day, spent balancing on a mast with his back pressed against the ship's hull, was uncomfortable and long. His ship remained the lowest of the fleet, riding the fire-fog only fifty feet or so from the ground and he had seen the prison camp below from some distance away. But he had glimpsed the tower beyond the forest and the sight had sparked a new hope.

Has Albert survived the contrapassi's attack to seek refuge in the tower? Is he there now, watching?

Marcus slipped from the mast the moment the ship's great keel touched down. He landed lithely as other ships lowered to earth, belching their smog. Each ship was equipped with four gigantic wooden lobes the size of trees that stabilised them as they landed and he dashed to hide behind the nearest of these as the hull settled with a groan overhead. He sprinted for the trees and hid in the fringes of the forest long before the first of the contrapassi disembarked. Crouching in the shadows, he observed as the captain growled orders beyond earshot.

Contrapassi lowered the gangway and a gaggle of the crew marched down, heading for the prison camp.

*

Tyler huddled at Klaus' shoulder before the stoves as the others finished eating.

"I've been thinking about our little friend out in the blizzard."

"Yes?"

"I'd like to know who it is." Tyler unzipped the neck of her parka and took out the contrap. "I'm going to use the *Present Eye*. Maybe I can locate the ghost."

"Won't the ghost sense it?" asked Klaus.

"Maybe but they already know we're here. There's a good chance they already know who we are. There's not much to lose."

Tyler searched the dim ice sheet through the *Present Eye* as the others talked.

"It creeps me out knowing there's one following us," said Melissa. "I mean, it's out there right now, waiting. But waiting for what?"

"We could take shifts through the night, guarding the camp," said Freddy. "The storm might whiteout the perimeter sensors while we sleep. We could be murdered in our tents."

Klaus nodded. "We'll work in pairs. That'll be safer."

"There're five of us," Lucy pointed out.

"I'll take two shifts," said Klaus, heading for his tent.

"Greenland sucks," muttered Lucy, looking out beyond the perimeter.

Tyler swept the contrap in a slow arc across an area in the direction they had travelled, finding it impossible to distinguish any landmark in the storm other than the camp and the perimeter spikes. Beyond those the landscape dissolved into eddies of snowfall. She levered the contrap's viewpoint back until she felt she must have covered half a mile of ice and returned the focus to the camp perimeter to start again a few degrees further clockwise. A fruitless half hour of searching with the *Present Eye* passed.

She switched to the *Tower of Doom* and found it surprisingly tall. Straining her eyes she thought she discerned the small beginnings of the tower's battlements. That was encouraging but an oddity also struck her. Where were the birds? The sky around the little tower was strangely empty.

A sudden, repeating bleep shook her from her thoughts. Lucy ran past to check the alarm console.

"Something's triggered the perimeter alarm."

Tyler joined her as they others arrived. Klaus checked the monitor of the perimeter system, toggling from one thermal camera feed to the next. The growing snowfall blurred every image into indistinct shades of deep blue, though Tyler remained convinced that no people were near the camp, none living, anyway.

"What triggered it?" asked Melissa.

"I don't know," said Klaus. "Arm yourselves and check the perimeter."

They separated to walk out from the centre of the camp, peering into the snow. Five minutes later they reconvened by the tents.

"Anyone see anything?" asked Tyler.

"No," said Klaus and Lucy together. Freddy shook his head.

"Nothing," said Melissa, shivering.

Klaus nodded, a flicker of concern in his eyes.

"Okay. False alarm. Maybe the whiteout caused an issue."

Tyler studied him and approached when Melissa and the others returned to the tents.

"Can a whiteout do that? Trigger the alarm like that?"

He turned to her soberly.

"No, but I had to say something. I didn't want to worry Melissa. Keep your eyes open."

"I'm going to stay out here and search again with the contrap."

"Good idea." Klaus left her.

Fruitlessly, she studied the surrounding stormy snowscape for a further ten minutes, while around her the wind battered the camp. She found Klaus sheltering in his tent, studying a geological map of the ice sheet.

"It's not working with the *Present Eye*. I'm going out to see if I can find anyone."

"No, you're not. Not in this. That would be madness. Come in and close the flap."

She stepped inside, zipping up the tent behind her.

"What's all this about?" asked Klaus, cradling a thermal mug of coffee.

"I can't locate our tail. I need to go in person to have a good look."

"No way. The storm's building. If our shadow's still there it would be too dangerous. You could get caught out with this poor visibility. You'll barely see your hand in front of your face."

"What hides him can also hide me."

Klaus stared at her, dumbfounded.

"I'll be careful," she said. "I have to know. I won't sleep thinking there's a spy hanging around. If I can just deal with him I'll be all right."

The conversation paused while Klaus considered her plan.

"I guess I can't stop you so I'll have to go, too. But if we're going to do it, we should do it soon. It's getting dark."

Tyler flashed a half-smile.

"You know it makes sense."

"Just a quick look. Get a rope. We don't want to get separated in the storm." They put on snow goggles and drew up their parka hoods before Tyler unzipped the tent.

Outside they tethered themselves together allowing twenty metres of leash between them before walking out past the perimeter to battle the tempest at every step. Klaus shouted over the wind.

"Split up. We'll cover more ground. I want to be back in my tent before it's fully dark. Give the rope a tug if you see anything."

Tyler quickly lost sight of Klaus as the maelstrom enveloped them both. Her last glimpse was of him shielding his eyes and staggering against the wind with a gallows blade outstretched before him.

What on Earth am I doing?

She nearly called it off then and there, but a hardened determination from deep within drove her on. She stumbled forwards, squinting into the driving snow, unsure which weapon she might need. Beneath her coat, her bandolier held six gallows blades. Her Taser nestled in its shoulder holster and, on the opposite side, a second holster carried her P99. She took out the contrap, fumbling with her heavily-gloved hands, and switched it to the *Ghost Portal*, deciding that would deal with most threats. She had not seen a blue glow emanating from the follower and so doubted it was a glove. Another fear plagued her: If she glimpsed Klaus in this morass of snow she might mistake him for the enemy and put him into the *Ghost Portal* before blinking.

She pressed on, periodically glancing at the trailing rope. It slackened and stretched as she and Klaus travelled and, every so often, tightened to the point that she was forced to stop and alter her course. She soon realised their lack of planning had doomed the exercise. They had not set a course or even discussed a general direction in which to work. She called to Klaus but her voice was lost in the wind. She called again pulling herself towards him with the rope.

"Klaus?"

The rope suddenly tightened, dashing from her hands and pulling her to the ground. She screamed as it dragged her along the snow for several feet before falling slack. She sat up and tugged it without resistance.

She scrambled to her feet to trace the rope through the snow, calling for Klaus. Ten metres later she found the end and stooped to examine it. The outer sheath ended cleanly leaving a little of the inner filaments to protrude. They, too, ended in a neat, hard line. The rope had been cut.

She studied the storm ahead, watching for any sign of movement. She thought she heard a voice and pulled back her hood to listen. The squall pelted her head with its icy ammunition. It tore around her in the growing murk and all she wanted was to get back to camp and fetch help.

She turned about, hoping to locate a tent or a perimeter spike, but found only the driving snow. She swore. The storm had swallowed Klaus, the camp, the whole world, and she was lost. Calling was futile. The volleying wind would drown out every sound.

A dashing grey movement quickened her. Not Klaus. What she had seen was the fluttering, temporal transparency of a phantom.

Whiteout

Tyler ran several metres and stopped. Standing in the whiteout she waited, feeling scooped and duped in an alternative, blindingly-cruel netherworld.

A second glimpse of the grey figure in her peripheral vision made her turn. A face flashed between gusts of the storm. She recoiled, shaking her head.

It can't be. Bates!

Tyler chased the phantom only to lose sight of her again, doubting her own vision. Was it *really* Bates, or was the storm playing tricks on her?

Cautiously she paced on, the contrap outstretched and the command ready on her tongue. With her free hand she drew a gallows blade.

Come on, then, Bates! What are you waiting for?

The phantom came, rushing out from the swirling snow to drive at Tyler. Not Bates, but Violet Corpe. Tyler spun to face her.

"Phasmatis licentia!"

Violet slid to the side, sweeping in close with her blade. Avoiding the draw of the *Ghost Portal*, she stabbed downwards at Tyler's flank, grunting at the effort. Tyler stepped back and brought her blade in to parry the strike. There was a shrill scrape of metal and Violet was gone.

Tyler turned.

Where's the camp? Where are Bates and Violet? Where's Klaus?

A fleeting void in the blizzard ahead revealed a new figure, grey and hulking. It watched her with a solid gaze through a veil of wind-born ice particles.

Okay, not two but three attackers!

Tyler stared back, straining to make out details. This ghost was tall and broad-shouldered, swathed in a long dark coat with wide, tattered tails fluttering in the wind. Atop the ghost's unmoving shoulders sat a head that was almost square, with hair closely cropped. Or perhaps he was bald. Tyler could not tell. She thought she saw the suggestion of a heavy jaw but the thick neck behind eclipsed it.

She glanced to her sides, expecting another attack from Violet or Bates, and all the while the Tall Man watched, statue-like. For a moment they faced off and Tyler judged he might be close enough for the contrap's draw.

"Phasmatis licentia."

The Tall Man darted to his right, vanishing into the storm. Tyler set off, knowing she had to keep moving. He knew where she was but she had already lost him. She searched fruitlessly, hands shaking, adrenaline coursing.

Show yourself!

A terrifying minute passed. She halted when a bulky shape appeared dead ahead. She tensed, aiming the contrap.

"Phasmatis..."

The figure turned towards her.

"Klaus! Thank God!"

"Someone cut the rope."

She was shaking and her face was so cold she could barely talk.

"Yeah. I noticed."

Klaus checked the GPS. "It's this way."

Together they staggered back to the camp and found Lucy, Freddy and Melissa conversing in the girls' tent.

"There're three of them," she said, as Klaus zipped the door closed. "Bates, violet and a new freak."

"You've been out in this?" asked Melissa. She fetched a blanket as Tyler sat on a sleeping bag, shivering. "Are you insane? In the first place, that was really stupid. Secondly, you could have at least told someone."

"I told Klaus."

*

Albert scanned the sky, squinting as a distant dot appeared over the horizon.

"I fear it's nothing but a Hell bird," said Zebedee, standing with him and Weaver at the tower's edge.

The shape grew, two wings beating the cold night air.

"It's carrying somefing. A spy returns!"

"Oh, jolly good."

In silence they watched the bird fly in and circle round to deposit one of Albert's old acquaintances before them.

"What did you see, Briggs?" asked Albert.

"A prison camp. Some of our own are there. It'll be a hellish job to get 'em out," explained the boy, a skinny lad of seven years, who Albert remembered polishing the boots of gentlemen on the streets of London. Briggs had a cheeky face and stood, by habit, with his thumbs tucked into his braces.

"I think I can find it again as long as the ground don't shift too bad."

"How many? How far?"

"About two miles that way." Briggs pointed towards the spot where Albert had first spotted him in the sky. "Not so far. There're hundreds of ghosts, too many to count, all trapped inside."

"Are there many guards?" asked Weaver.

"I counted twenty-five, all armed, but we can take 'em, easy, especially if them Hell birds help. Of course, we'll 'ave to get in and steal some weapons first. I found a spot in the corner of the camp where they can't see the fence. There're jackal buildings in the way." Before Briggs finished speaking, a second spy returned in the clutches of a bird. It dropped a girl onto the roof and settled with the others, folding its wings and awaiting rewards. Zebedee scattered fruit for them as the newly arrived ghost, a wide-eyed, spritely slave girl named Lucretia, ran to Albert.

"I found the sky-ships. I watched them set down over there, beyond the forest where the clouds are thick. I reckon they've stopped for the night, but we'll have to be quick if we're to try something. I don't suppose they'll stay long."

"How far is it?" asked Weaver.

"Less than a mile."

"How many ships?" Albert asked.

"Forty-three. They set down near a prison camp."

"This is it, Zebedee," said Albert, a fire kindling in his eyes. "We 'ave to make our move while they're grounded. It's now or never."

He descended the steps into the feasting room and called those eating to gather in the level below. Here other ghosts huddled, wrapped in tapestries and anything else they could find to help themselves keep warm. He studied them, wondering at the eclectic mix. Among them stood Victorian ladies and gentlemen, chimney sweeps, miners, English infantrymen, Roman slaves and free men, Vikings, Saxons, Jews, Africans and Russians. When every ghost was present, waiting with anticipation to hear his plan, Albert began.

"This won't be easy and there's too many of us for the birds to carry. If we're going to move on the ships we need to go now. It will be dangerous so I'll not make anyone go. Volunteers only. Those who want to go raise your hands."

"We'll stand a better chance against the contrapassi if we all go," said Briggs.

Every ghost put up a hand.

"Great, though we need one or two to stay in the tower t' guard it an' watch for the other spies."

The gathered ghosts muttered amongst themselves but no one put themselves forward. Albert turned to Zebedee.

"Someone needs to look after the place. Zebedee?"

"If it helps."

"That's settled, then," continued Albert. "Weaver an' I will go first. Lucretia, you'll come wiv us to show us the way. After the ships there's the prison camps holding the rest of our ghosts, but we 'ave to take the ships first."

"Lucretia knows a blind spot on the fence," added Weaver. "She'll lead us there and we'll find a way in. Once inside we'll need to arm ourselves or we won't stand a chance against the contrapassi."

A murmur of fear and excitement rippled throughout the gathering. Weaver turned to Albert.

"Albert, I've some experience with this kind of thing. I'd like to help lead."

"Of course," said Albert. "You can lead us all if ya' likes. I don't know why they've been following me. I never asked to be in charge."

"They follow you because you're driven. You know the way."

Albert offered his hand.

"Glad to 'ave you on board, Weaver." They shook hands. "Stick wiv me." Albert addressed the crowd.

"Follow me."

He led them down the spiralling stairs to the ground level and enlisted help to unbolt and heave open the door. He stood, gazing out into the bluish haze of the night and the charred trees. For a moment he doubted, wondering what terrors awaited beyond the threshold.

What chance do we truly have?

A cold breeze rocked branches and carried fire-fog in milky swathes to veil the horizon while unearthly sounds caused his eyes to dart.

Gritting his teeth, he stepped out into the murk.

"Stick close."

The ghosts spilled out into the night. Albert stooped to pick up a branch that had fallen from one of the blackened trees.

"Arm yourselves with anything you can find."

*

While Lucy and Freddy took their turn on watch and Klaus and Tyler slept, Melissa booted up her laptop. She clicked to open an icon named Forager 6; surveillance software of her own creation, and the product of several years of training in MI6 and GCHQ. A video link window opened up and filled with static and an overlaying message.

No signal

She waited for several minutes and triggered a signal search. She was giving up and closing the laptop when the video screen blinked to a live feed. She watched Yash pace his office floor and sit at his desk.

Troubled, are we?

With Greenland three hours behind, it was close to two a.m. in London.

You're working late tonight. Something worrying you?

She scrolled through the past twenty-four hours of footage to catch up and check his movements. Learning nothing of interest from the day's video, she switched back to the real-time camera view and briefly thought Yash had gone home. Inspecting the shot more closely she found a tell-tale shadow near the bottom left corner of the screen. Yash was standing at the door.

What are you doing?

He remained at the door for several moments before walking to his desk, accompanied by an agent Melissa had seen around the MI6 building. She did not know the agent's name but she captured a decent screen shot and saved it. Cursing the lack of audio, she watched the two converse in silence. She marked the time frame and noted that a good five minutes passed before their meeting ended and the agent departed.

So what was all that about, Chief?

*

Lucretia guided Albert and the other ghosts out from the tower, through the trees and onto a plain of fire-fog. The ground pitched and rolled as they stalked towards the forest, ears straining for the faintest signs of an approaching threat through the dense miasma around them. Remembering the deadly liliths, Albert watched the sky for fear of attack. He wondered if the sky-ships were close and shuddered, dreading what new monster might be lurking beyond sight, waiting to devour them. The open ground made him nervous.

"Hurry!"

They sped up, rambling closer to the forest ahead, but Albert raised a hand to halt them some twenty feet from the treeline. The mist thinned near the trees and in the shadows beyond he saw movements. He tensed. Raising a finger to his lips he waited for a full minute, studying the forest. The movements were too low to be those of the towering contrapassi or the liliths. As he stared, he recognised the greyish forms of ghosts. A girl left the deeper shade where others lingered to softly venture out, peering at him.

"Albert?" she called quietly.

"Danuta, is that you?" He stepped closer, fearing a trick of the *Chasm*.

"Yes. Kinga is here, too. One of your spies found us in a camp. There was a fight but most of the ghosts broke out. They're sheltering behind me."

"How many of you are there?"

"I haven't counted. Sixty or so."

"Great. Join us. We're going after the ships."

"We passed the ships on the other side of the forest. We thought they might see us and capture us again."

With excited whispers, the two groups of ghosts continued into the woodland with renewed speed, slowing only when the grounded ships came into view on the plain beyond. There, at the forest edge between them, a small figure stepped out from the cover of a tree to stand framed between two broad trunks. The figure scrutinized the approaching ghosts as they stopped, every one of them staring back at him. A sly smile spread over his face.

Fire

Albert recognised Marcus at once and ran to him. Marcus pointed to the closest of the ships and Albert read his mind. Long ago he had discovered the curious ability to know what Marcus was thinking when close and he had long since ceased to wonder at it.

"Izabella's on that ship," Albert told Zebedee, Weaver, Kylie, Danuta and Kinga. "She's shackled on the lower deck along with a whole room full o' others. The deck's guarded by two contrapassi who feed the engine's fire. Many of the crew 'ave left to bring in supplies. Their leader also left the ship, but they'll return soon. We 'ave to go now!"

Armed with sticks from the forest and pockets full of smouldering stones from the plain, the ghosts poured out from the trees with Albert and Weaver at their head.

"You take another ship," Albert hissed to Weaver.

"I'll go after Izabella. We need her."

Weaver gave a nod and waved a group of ghosts his way, leaving Albert beneath the hull of the ship holding Izabella. Albert gestured for the ghosts to scale the props, and climbed. Other ghosts clambered onto one another's shoulders to grab at the lower sweeps of the lateral sails. They heaved themselves up and scrambled across the sailcloth to the towering side masts.

Albert was the first to reach the deck. At first glance it appeared utterly abandoned. He wondered if the entire crew had left for supplies, but spotted two contrapassi guarding the forecastle next to a coiled rope. He flattened himself against the gunwale before dashing to a stack of barrels. Unwilling to take on the two guards alone, he waited for backup.

Other ghosts slid over the gunwale onto the deck close to the guards.

*

Izabella's time had come. She had come to terms with the fact long before Ruk muttered the words.

"More fuel."

Grar stomped across to her, stooped to unlock her shackles, and threw her onto his shoulder like a sack. Winded, she gasped for breath and helplessly watched the floor go by. Grar slid her from his shoulder and prepared to launch her into the furnace. Izabella fainted, a rag doll in the giant's hands. A disturbance reached them from the upper deck.

Stoking the flames, Ruk paused. "Hold it! What's that?"

"I dunno," muttered Grar, dropping Izabella. "Wait here. I'll go see."

*

On the upper deck the contrapassi bellowed an alarm.

"Filthy ghost scum! Ghosts on the loose!"

Albert felt the booming voice vibrate through the decking. He charged, raising his branch with a yell.

"Attack!"

The contrapassi stepped away from the forecastle, adopting warrior stances and drawing curved swords.

"You're gonna die, scum!"

"Bring it on! I'll cleave you to ribbons."

Shouts went up from the decks of nearby ships as other guards saw the invaders. The ghosts released their first volley, filling the air with a lethal hail of stones that battered the contrapassi. Across the fleet guards stumbled and fell.

A wave of ghosts flooded the deck, washing with increasing speed towards the guards. The contrapassi swept their blades, slicing attackers with every swipe, and still the ghosts came. Ghosts climbed the foresails and crested onto the higher forecastle deck. They leapt down unto the unsuspecting contrapassi below, blinding them with the stub ends of branches and clobbering their heads. A chance strike knocked one unconscious and he fell, slamming to the deck like a felled oak while his attacker rolled off unscathed. The remaining, dazed guard roared in fury as a group of ghosts ensnared him in a rope. He toppled, flailing wildly as ghosts overwhelmed him, beating him with sticks, stones and their bare fists. One of them took up his sword and hacked at him until the monster lay motionless.

Albert left the fray in search of Izabella. He bounded the steps to peer into the lower deck where the engine's fire cast light from the depths. Dozens of weary, manacled prisoners looked up from their rows. The two fire-feeders were already half way up the deck and stomping closer to investigate the commotion coming from the upper deck.

Albert fled back up the steps, calling.

"Two more heading this way!" He collected stones and readied himself for the emergence of the fire-feeders as a ghost gang gathered around him. To his right a large Roman slave wielded one of the contrapassi' swords. On his left a well-muscled Viking tested the other's blade.

A tense silence settled over the ship as they waited for the inevitable counter attack. The fire-feeders charged out, whips cracking. They thrust and sliced at the ghosts with short swords, clashing at the top of the steps in a rain of stones. The first received a rock to his forehead and reeled back into the dimness of the lower deck. With a skilful sweep of his sword, the Viking severed the remaining contrapasso's whip. The monster dropped its useless handle and battled out onto the deck, stabbing and thrusting madly with a short blade. Ghosts roped and pummelled him with more stones and sticks, finishing him with thrusts of salvaged blades.

On the lower deck, Albert and his army hammered at the prisoners' manacles. They smashed the manacles apart with stones, swords and any heavy bludgeon they could find. He found Izabella slumped in the glow of the furnace and shook her until she opened her eyes.

"Get up! You 'ave t' get out. Now!"

She peered at the surrounding chaos as ghosts smashed at chains, ran for stones or freedom amid the din of battle.

"Then help me up, boy!"

He hauled her arm as she clambered up, dazed. Guiding her to the stairs he watched her go, and returned to peer up at the engine furnace.

"Burn it down," he ordered. "Burn the ship."

They fished embers from the fire, spreading them across the decks and folded sails until the ship was ablaze.

Across the fleet the ghosts fought their battles. As burning ships toppled, torched sails kissed dry wood. The blaze danced across the fleet until three galleons were alight. Then four. The fire consumed masts and keels, licking at munitions stores. Explosions rocked the night as galleons blew apart.

The freed prisoners fled the ships, scrambling down lateral masts, landing supports and gangways. They plucked burning arrows from the timbers and hurled them into the sails of the ships not yet alight. One by one the ships blazed. Prisoners leapt to safety as ships ruptured, tipping and splintering open with great roars of flames. An engine exploded, shooting a host of flaming shrapnel across the fleet. Contrapassi fled, their pelts alight. They leapt overboard to die in screaming balls of fire, fortunate if the ground snapped their necks and ended their agony quickly.

Close to the forest an army of ghosts gathered watching the sea of pyres while newly freed ghosts swelled their ranks.

Izabella observed the mayhem and straightened her tattered dress. She turned to a fellow ghost.

"I don't suppose you have anything to eat?" she asked, her Russian accent as pronounced as ever.

He grinned, presenting her with an apple from his pocket.

Albert and Weaver joined the gathering from the burning fleet. They recovered their breath and took stock of the army as a Hell bird appeared through the smoke. It carried a sweep's boy in its talons and swooped in to set him down with the others. The bird flew back towards the tower while the boy pushed his way through the crowd to Albert and stood before him, doffing his cap.

"There are contrapassi with wagons, only a few minutes away, Boss. They've seen the fires. They're coming."

Lucretia appeared next to him.

"I can show you where the prison camp is. We can creep round through the woods."

Fiery arrows rained impotently down around them from the few surviving contrapassi, their aim hampered by the smoke and fog. Beyond the burning fleet a single ship belched fumes and rose from the ground.

"Into the forest!" shouted Albert to the last of the stragglers. He stayed Weaver with a hand to his chest. "Not you. You and I 'ave a job to do."

*

Melissa closed Forager 6 and clicked open the image she had saved to the desktop. She enlarged it, cropped the agent's face and ran it through an image enhancing software program. She logged onto the GCHQ database through the satellite link and searched for a match, making a mental note of the name when it popped up on the screen. She read the agent's resume. Pretty standard for an agent in middle management at MI6: an impressive education, a background in the military and several years' experience in the field overseas.

I'll be looking into you, Staff Sergeant Abigail Dodd.

*

Albert and Weaver backtracked to the closest burning wreck of a ship and dipped branches in the blazing pitch that oozed and dripped between the clinkers. With their brands burning, they turned back to the forest to rejoin the ghost army as the solitary airborne ship loomed nearer. Flaming arrows pelted from the gunwales at its bow. One of the missiles brushed Weaver's shirt, setting him ablaze. He dropped to the ground to roll as Albert ditched his brand to help smother the flames. Weaver sat up to examine his burn and brushed ash from his arm. Albert reached out a hand as fleeting shadows swept across the sky overhead.

"You're all right."

Weaver grabbed his hand and Albert pulled him to his feet.

"Thanks," said Weaver. "What was that?" He glanced skywards.

"I don't know. Too big for Hell birds."

"It must be liliths."

A few fast strides brought them into the shelter of the forest, now peppered with small fires where trees ignited from arrow flame.

"They're going to burn the whole forest," said Weaver. "We have to get everyone out of here."

Collecting their burning brands, they sprinted through the trees to rally the ghost army. Albert found himself running alongside Izabella as behind them the forest burned.

"What is it they say?" she puffed. "Out of the frying pan...?" Albert forced a grin. The old woman had not lost any of her indomitable spirit in the belly of the ship. He took her arm as she battled to catch breath and keep up with the others.

Lucretia led them through the forest and stopped in the deep shadows at its edge. Beyond, a sprawling prison camp broke the line of the open plain. A tall wire fence ringed the camp, sharp barbs bristling from its crest, and six tall, timber watchtowers punctuated its circumfer- ence. Albert thought he saw the bulky shapes of contrapassi guards at each of the towers' viewing points. He had seen another camp like this one up close before, and that one was protected by mounted machine guns in each of its towers. He shuddered. *This ain't goin' t' be easy.*

His eyes darted to the burning brand in his hand.

"Burn the towers. We'll stand a better chance without them tower guns picking us off. We need six ghosts to carry the fire. I'll go."

"Me too," said Weaver at once.

"No," said Albert. "If I get shot the others will need you to lead them. Who else volunteers to fire the towers?"

A plethora of ghosts pushed through to the front and Albert pointed out the first five. He commandeered five other branches and smeared their tips with burning pitch from his and Weaver's brands.

"Now, go. Hurry! Set light to the towers before we're noticed."

They ran out, illuminated by their own burning torches, heading straight for the tower bases. Albert made for the furthest tower as the contrapasso above startled awake with the glimpse of fire at the base of the neighbouring tower. He roared a warning.

Albert smeared burning pitch up the side of a thick supporting leg and watched as it caught, flames quickly licking up the timber. He turned and bolted away into the night, hoping to be lost amongst the broiling mists of the plain.

A search lamp flickered into life as an alarm droned, echoing to the forest. Momentarily outlined by the circle of light, he sprinted for cover. Machine guns rattled the night and he glimpsed other fire-bringers escaping around him. He reached the woods, doubling over breathless, relieved to have survived the hail of bullets.

"The towers are burning," said Weaver, coming to his side. "What now?"

"Let'em blaze. When all the contrapassi are up an' occupied fighting the fires, we attack. Make sure every ghost is armed with somefing. I'll look at the blind spot. Keep the army 'ere." Albert found Lucretia and took her by the arm.

"Show me the place."

She led him closer to the camp and paused at the edge of the trees. She pointed across the compound as embers floated by and the tower fires rose higher to fill the sky with flames and smoke. Contrapassi swarmed out from their dwellings within the camp to gaze helplessly on.

"There, on the other side behind those jackal buildings," said Lucretia. As they watched, liliths passed overhead, drawn by the fire. Smaller, faster shapes darted in the sky; Hell birds dived as liliths spewed fire defensively and a new battle erupted as contrapassi on the ground fought off the plunging Hell birds and liliths.

Albert scanned the hellish scene before him, scrutinizing every detail. He wanted to visit the blind spot to see how they might get in, but the tower fires burned fast. Soon the distraction would pass and the surviving contrapassi would be more vigilant than before, although the liliths and Hell birds were helping for the time being. He returned to Weaver.

"We needs long branches, sturdy-like. We'll 'ave to approach from the other side, which means leading the entire army 'round through the forest and far enough for us to be 'idden by the night when we break cover. Then we runs for it. Those wiv branches lever up the fence while the others slip in underneath. But we gotta move fast!"

Weaver and Albert organised ghosts to break strong branches from the trees. With an eye on the tower fires, Albert led the army through the forest, passing the prison camp. When he judged they were a good distance from the fence, he took them out onto the plain and turned for the blind spot.

Contrapassi hurled barrels of water at the fires and tried to rope off sections of the towers to pull them down away from their dwellings. Further into the complex, they battled the screeching, fire-spewing liliths and ferocious Hell birds. A lilith plummeted to the ground amid a mêlée of black wings and feathers, Hell birds clustering to overpower it. Contrapassi volleyed bullets into the sky at their remaining airborne foes.

Albert and the branch carriers reached the fence and tried to lodge the branches beneath the wire mesh and barbed wire. The branches caught stubbornly at the base of the fence.

"It's no good, Albert," whispered the closest of the branch carriers. "The fence is buried deep."

"Try harder!" hissed Albert. "We 'ave to get in somehow!"

The carriers rammed branches at the fence, hoping to break through, but their efforts only tired them.

"The fence is too strong."

Several branches snapped and the other carriers

turned to him.

"It's not working. What should we do?"

Perplexed, Albert contemplated the camp on the other side of the wire and the ghosts with their branches. The situation felt useless, impossible. There simply was no way to penetrate the perimeter fence.

A mighty crash shook him from his dilemma as a corner tower collapsed in a heap of burning timber. It covered a patch of fence not ten feet from where he stood, flattening the wire to the ground.

"There!" He pointed to the flattened fence and charged over it into the camp, the others close behind.

The ghost army waiting in the shadows saw their chance and rushed out to the opening to pour in. The larger, stronger ghosts attacked the contrapassi with branches and hurled their rocks. Those who had thought to use the fire ran from beast to beast, setting their shaggy legs aflame as the smaller, nimbler ghosts searched out prisoners and rallied them from their huts to join the fight.

Bodies littered the ground. Fallen liliths and Hell birds crashed and died amongst the contrapassi corpses. A remaining few mowed down ghosts with machine guns while those armed with whips or swords were quickly swamped by ghosts, their weapons immediately turned against their own kind. Flaming contrapassi fled shrieking while others collapsed in balls of flame.

Soon the camp swarmed with ghosts, overwhelming and defeating the contrapassi. Albert gathered those present of the Ghost Squad to shout orders as the last of the giants fell beneath a barrage of missiles.

"Take brands an' set every hut an' hovel aflame. Burn this place to the ground!"

NECRO 904

Bright morning light glistened from the ice with a thousand iridescent sparkles. The blizzard had blown out to leave a crystal blue sky. Tyler and her team made good ground for most of the morning. Nearing midday, Freddy took a turn at the front to give Klaus a rest from the onset of snow blindness. The task was simple enough.

"Remember, check your bearings every ten minutes."

After leading for an hour Freddy slowed to a stop and shouted back.

"Sorry. I got to go." He removed his pack and slung it onto the ice. As the bag landed an explosion erupted, shooting ice and smoke into the sky. His vehicle toppled sideways as a great rift of ice collapsed beneath. His snowmobile tumbled into an opened crevasse as he clung to the handlebars and his cry was lost in the thuds of falling ice and compacted snow. On the surface, the tightening ropes dragged the others closer to the hole.

"Reverse!" shouted Klaus. They throttled backwards as, tracks spinning, they continued to slide closer to the edge. One by one the vehicles gained traction until they stopped.

"Freddy!" cried Melissa. "Freddy are you okay?"

Freddy's distant voice answered.

"I'm fine. Just hanging around."

"You'll have to climb up by yourself," Klaus shouted. "If any of us get off the chain, your weight could drag more of us down."

"Okay!" A burst of hysterical laughter issued from the hole. "I'll be right up." Three minutes later Freddy's reddened face poked over the fragile rim of the hole. He threw an arm up over the edge to grip the rope and waved to the others. "Hi there. Just another day in paradise." He dragged himself up and clambered away from the hole as more snow and ice crumbled in.

"What *was* that?" asked Melissa. "A mine?"

Klaus nodded. "It's a good sign really. It means we're close. They must have placed mines all around their base."

"Yeah, it's a *great* sign!" shouted Freddy. "If only we had more signs like that."

"Are you sure you're all right?" asked Melissa. Freddy calmed.

"I'm just bruised and dizzy. I guess the explosion must have been dampened by a good layer of snow or I'd be dead. I think my ride took the brunt. We've lost my share of the supplies."

Klaus drew a sheath knife to cut the line of the dangling snowmobile, and they listened to it rumbling down into the bowels of the fissure. Blood dripped from a wound on Freddy's neck. Melissa ran to him.

"It doesn't matter, as long as you're okay. Hold still." She plucked a piece of shrapnel the size of a fingernail from the wound.

"Ow!"

"Don't be such a baby." She kissed him and fetched a first aid kit from her baggage.

"Let's take a break," said Klaus. "Reorganise."

Lucy trudged by.

"Nice one, Agent Pratt."

"No sign of Bates or the Tall Man," said Tyler.

"We're not far from Chapman's grid reference," said Klaus, letting the binoculars hang from his neck. "I thought I might be able to see something by now."

"It's going to be one hell of a disappointment if there's nothing there."

Klaus smirked and nodded.

"He must have noted it for some reason. I presume Melissa's had no luck cracking his code."

Tyler shook her head.

"She's given up. It's indecipherable, but there *has* to be something there, surely." Tyler drew the contrap from her parka and switched to the *Present Eye*. She drew the lever clockwise to telescope into the distance, ahead. She searched for several minutes before pausing with an intake of breath.

"I see it! There's a complex of some sort. I think it's the old research station." Through the lens she studied a central, domed building on stilts and a scattering of smaller, auxiliary buildings. "No, it's not old." She let the contrap hang and turned to Klaus. "Someone's revamped it."

"Clever," said Klaus. "They've reused the old British

site. No one's going to ask questions. Let's face it, out here no one's even going to notice a change, but if they did, they'd probably presume it was the British resuming research."

"Chapman could be in there somewhere." Tyler focused in onto a doorway of the main dome at the top of a set of checker plate steps. She read the door sign.

"NECRO nine zero four. What's that?"

"Where did you see that?"

"It's written on the dome's door. I'm going to take a look inside." She focused through the thickly insulated walls and stopped suddenly. Inside, Angel, the *glove* containing Mengele's and Hitler's ghosts, discussed something beyond earshot with a man in a white coat.

"Angel's in the dome."

A rumble from the sky stole their attention. From the far distance beyond NECRO 904 a plane approached. She and Klaus watched it fly in to land next to the research facility. Through the *Present Eye* Tyler saw it deploy a parachute and come to a halt on its skis, its twin propellers slowing. Klaus studied it with high-powered binoculars as the drone of the engine died.

"It's an LC-130, a small passenger plane."

"Do you think they've seen us?" she asked.

"No way. From this distance we must appear little more than a smudge on the ice."

"What about the mine?"

"I guess they might have heard that, but I think Freddy's shouts were louder. We'll soon know if they did. Keep your gun ready."

"Always. They don't appear to be sending anyone out for us."

"Good."

They watched soldiers leave the plane and head into the station's hub.

Tyler searched the wider area with the contrap and noticed a crumpled shape protruding from the snow a quarter mile from the station. She focused in on it and made out the details of a crashed plane, half buried in the snow. She found a second wrecked craft, this one a helicopter a short distance from the plane.

"It's a good job we didn't fly." She told Klaus what she had found.

"They're shooting down anything that comes close. And with Bates and the Tall Man working for them, they know we're here already. We proceed with caution from here on, and let's hope we don't find any more mines."

"Aye aye, Captain." Tyler turned to break the news as the Tall Man materialised behind Melissa, a gallows blade poised to strike.

"Look out!" screamed Tyler.

He lunged with his blade as Melissa turned. She screamed and stepped away but his knife caught her sleeve, slicing through. Lucy dashed in, her hand a blur as she snatched a blade from her thigh bandolier to throw across the stove. The Tall Man spun to his side and *cloaked,* discarding his weapon. Lucy's first blade flew on uselessly.

"Where's he gone?" Melissa turned on the spot.

An insane scream caused them to turn as Bates hurtled in from the opposite direction. Lucy plucked another blade in time to meet Bates with a clash of gallows iron. The impact drove Lucy backwards, her boots sliding through snow. They wrestled while Melissa and Freddy groped for their blades and closed in. Freddy fumbled and dropped his blade.

Cautiously, Melissa approached, her blade out-stretched. Violet appeared, sneering. She flew in to keep Melissa at bay. Lucy forced Bates' blade to one side and jabbed at her while Tyler and Klaus ran into the camp.

Outmatched and outnumbered, Bates vanished, leaving her blade to drop to the snow. Violet followed with a cackle of laughter.

"Guess they're still following us." Lucy checked around. She noticed a slice in the arm of Melissa's parka. "You okay?"

Melissa examined the tear.

"Yeah, he missed me."

*

"I don't understand," said Melissa. "If we're that close, why hasn't Bates and the Tall Man gone ahead to tell Angel and the others in NECRO 904?"

"Good question," said Tyler. "Bates knows about the contrap. It's what she wants. She might be working with the NVF but she's gunning for the contrap. She's a law unto herself."

"So they still don't know we're coming," said Lucy.

Tyler nodded. "I don't think they've told them. I think Bates has recruited the Tall Man for her own purposes. He's trying to help her get the contrap."

Freddy turned to each of them in turn, paling.

"What *was* that?"

"The old hag? That's Violet Corpe. She's the one I released from the Ghost Portal. She's been hanging out with Bates ever since."

Freddy sighed. "I'm quitting when we get home. I can't take this anymore. I'm terrified, and we're not even there yet."

"You can't quit," countered Tyler. "So man up and

deal with it. The world's been invaded by an evil that wants to destroy us all and we're all in the fight, whether we like it or not. If you're not fighting for us, you're just helping them."

Freddy stared at the cold ground, a mix of fury and fear distorting his features. He hoiked his pack onto his shoulder and stomped away to the snowmobiles. The team mounted up and drove on without another word.

When a distant dome appeared on the ice sheet dead ahead, Klaus stopped and switched off his snowmobile. He checked his GPS and turned to Tyler.

"That's it. That's Chapman's exact reference."

"We ditch the vehicles and go the rest of the way on foot," said Tyler. "Hopefully that's the last we've seen of Bates and her friends for a while. I wouldn't be surprised if she doesn't come back with reinforcements, but forget about them for now. We have work to do."

"Shouldn't we just phone this in and have the RAF blast the entire site from the surface of the planet?" asked Freddy.

"Phone it in to who?" asked Melissa. "Without Chapman we have no weight with anyone and we can't tell Yash we're here. Anyway, Chapman could be in there."

"I want to take a closer look," said Tyler. "The *Present Eye* can only show so much. I want to hear what's being said and to find out why Angel's here. There's only one way to do that."

"We can't just walk up to the dome in broad daylight," said Lucy. "We'll have to wait until nightfall."

"Agreed," said Tyler. She resumed spying through the *Present Eye*. "Set up a tent. Check your gear and prepare. I'm going to recce the base."

*

Tyler watched as darkness slowly enveloped the ice sheet. She removed her goggles and Arctic mitts. Fingerless gloves would have to serve for the next hour or so.

At precisely one a.m. she nodded to the others huddled behind the tent. She set the contrap to *Flight* and left the ground. She guided herself closer at a height of two hundred metres and descended to set down fifty metres from the nearest block building on the edge of the base, hoping this distance would be enough to prevent Angel from sensing the contrap. She planned to cover the remaining ice on foot and knew this was risky. She might easily be seen if anyone was up and about, but why would they be in the middle of the night?

She switched to the *Safeguarding Skull*, placed the contrap in its lead box and waited until sure she had not been seen before setting off at a light jog. She reached the nearest block.

Is the second GAUNT machine hiding in one of these buildings? With luck Angel is asleep.

She glanced to her right where the plane remained in the shadows a short walk from NECRO 904. No one had left since she and the team had been spying on the base.

Angel is still here. Hopefully asleep.

It was impulsive, she knew, and she heard Melissa's voice in her head telling her it was a mistake, but she ignored it. Pulse quickening, she took the contrap from its lead box and studied the symbols on its back. She switched to the *Present Eye* and swept its gaze through the scattering of auxiliary blocks surrounding the larger hub of the dome. Several, including this one, appeared to be dormitories. People slept in bunks, their chambers unlit.

The purposes of other buildings were less obvious. Several appeared to be laboratories. Some contained scientific equipment and rooms she assumed were isolation chambers. None housed a GAUNT machine. The central hub was one large, unoccupied space with administration desks and computers segmenting its edges like numbers on a clock.

Confident that Angel was asleep, she skirted the dorm block and stole across the open ice to flatten her body against the hub. She edged around to the door and made a quick study of its lock; a standard five-lever mortise deadlock.

Nothing fancy. I guess you think you don't need much security way out here. Big mistake.

She eased a tool roll from her jacket, selected the pick required and slipped it into the keyhole. She took less than thirty seconds to engage the five interior mortise levers and release locking bolt. She opened the door, entered and eased it shut behind her.

Tyler stood stock-still and waited. The heavy silence of the dome unnerved her. She unzipped her parka and pulled her hood down in the warmth of the room.

She radioed the others. "I'm in. The hub is unoccupied."

"Standing by," she heard Klaus reply through her earpiece. Taking a flash drive from her pocket she inserted it into a USB port on one of the computers and booted up.

"The flash drive's in."

"Good," said Melissa. "It will need some time to do its work. It should execute upon password request. Once it's located the password and entered all you need do is double click the Copy Drive icon and let it run. It will tell you when it's complete."

Tyler waited, watching the screen. A window popped up requesting a password and almost immediately figures appeared, whirling across the password field. She left it to work and nosed around the workstations. Data charts and printouts littered the place. They were pinned to the wall between windows, piled on desks and dangled from strings of clips. She picked one up from a desk to examine it.

Cryogenic Density Report: Germanium 5

It meant nothing to her, but she used her iPhone to photograph it anyway. She snapped off several more shots of the other charts and printouts, hoping the flashes would not bring unwanted attention. Returning to check the computer screen she found a new window had opened up with the title 'Lindworm', another of Melissa's software creations. Within the pane several icons formed a row. She double-clicked the one named Copy Drive and let the program run.

She switched the contrap to the *Past Eye* and levered back until she found a point earlier that day. Angel had been in the hub then, joined by the soldiers as they disembarked the plane. What had happened here and where were the soldiers from the plane? Half expecting to see a secret door open up to a complex hidden beneath the ice, she eased the lever back until the *Past Eye* replayed time at a realistic rate.

She watched as Angel welcomed the soldiers, briskly shaking each by the hand. The soldiers appeared to be different nationalities but they were all dressed in the same grey uniforms and trench coats, similar to those of the Nazi Storm Troopers of World War Two. The men gave Nazi salutes as they passed Angel, and formed a line. They waited in an expectant silence while Angel watched them. He inspected them at a leisurely pace, nodding his approval as he saw fit

At last he retreated and addressed them, to Tyler's relief, in English, though his accent was deeply German.

"Troopers, you have been selected to join my most elite force for you are destined to become spies of the highest order. Do you accept this honour and the price with which it is to be paid?"

The soldiers replied in unison, military style, their accents betraying a far-reaching mix of origins.

"I do, my Führer."

"Serve me well." Angel drew a gleaming, steel blade from a sheath beneath his trench coat. "It is my pleasure to baptize you into the Legion of the Black Sun." He stepped up to the first in line who knelt and bowed his head. Angel kissed the soldier's forehead and indicated for the man to rise.

"Die now, and arise, a new creation."

He thrust the blade up sharply beneath the soldier's ribs, plunging it into his heart. The man dropped, bleeding out while Angel moved on to the next. Blood spattered his coat.

Tyler watched the ceremony, grimacing in horror as Angel felled each soldier in turn. Each recruit, though trembling in fearful anticipation, received their immolation with obvious pride. As the final soldier leaked the last of his blood across the chamber floor, Angel stepped back to view his handiwork, a crooked smile spreading across his face. He removed his bloodied trench coat and dropped it into the spreading pool of blood. An aide stepped from the shadows to slip an identical coat over Angel's shoulders. The Führer stepped back into it and raised his right arm in salute

"Now rise, my ghosts. My Legion of the Black Sun."

Ice

She sank to her knees, the enormity of the horror sickeningly clear. Angel's new ghost spies would have all the advantages of the technological age. How many more of these ghosts had Angel created? They would pass through walls of any building anywhere in the world, switch on their host's computers and steal any information they required. Hacking would be a thing of the past. Instead, they would loiter in houses and offices to spy out passwords and key codes. Across the globe no information would be secure. The new ghost army would be unstoppable, stealing unlimited funds from multiple sources and cracking military secrets on a scale previously unknown. She wondered where they were this minute.

A noise startled her and she spun around to see Lucy slipping in through the door.

"Lucy!" she hissed.

Waist heavy with ammo pouches and cradling a C7 assault rifle, Lucy crossed to Tyler. A second C7 hung strapped across her back along with a sawn-off shotgun.

"I figured you shouldn't hog all the fun." She handed Tyler the spare rifle. "Here, I brought you this in case we get into trouble. Found anything?"

Tyler threw the rifle strap over her shoulder and gabbled an account of what she had seen, struggling to keep a panic attack at bay.

Lucy swore. "Do you sense any ghosts here?"

"Not right now, but that doesn't mean they're not somewhere nearby."

"So what happened to the ghosts of the soldiers? Where are they?"

"I don't know. I didn't actually see any ghosts."

Melissa's voice cut in, crackling over the comms.

"Some ancient belief systems say that it can take days for the spirit to leave the body. Time periods differ according to the various accounts, anywhere from the point of death to a number of weeks."

"So, basically, the new spy ghosts could appear any moment."

"As far as we know," said Melissa. "Where are the bodies?"

"I don't know. Any sign of Bates and co?" asked Tyler.

"Nothing yet," said Klaus.

Tyler stared out through one of the hub's windows at the auxiliary blocks.

"Lucy, we have to end this thing right here, right now. The consequences of us failing are unthinkable. Angel's asleep in one of the dorms. He *must* be here, right now."

"What are we waiting for? Let's find him and give him a wakeup call he'll never forget."

Tyler set the contrap to the *Present Eye* and searched through the dorms.

"It's hard to know where he is. Everyone's covered up in their beds."

"Surely the 'great Führer' does not share a room with the lackeys."

"Give me a minute." Tyler searched for a dorm with a single occupant and found one across the complex.

"I have it. It has to be him." She stared at Lucy. "This is it. We can finish this tonight."

*

Albert reached the safety of the tower and collapsed in one of the lower rooms, vaguely aware of the multitude of bedraggled ghosts streaming past to climb the stairs. Many were injured; blistered and burned, beaten, cut, shot and bleeding. Others were half-starved and dying from thirst, but here they could rest and recover with all the food and drink they needed.

We made it.

He watched in a daze and was on the verge of sleep when Kylie appeared bearing bread, cheese, fruit and water. He drank his fill and barely pausing to chew, gulped down a hunk of bread before succumbing to exhaustion.

Ghosts crowded in on all levels. Zebedee had never seen the tower so packed before. He climbed all the way to the top, pausing only to grab refreshments from the table of plenty, and stood at the roof's battlements.

"By Jove, it's nearly complete. Tyler approaches her goal."

A Hell bird flew in to deposit a ghost spy on the

rooftop. The spy, a Victorian street urchin a little younger than Albert, was wounded. His left arm hung broken and twisted. The boy's legs bore him briefly before giving way.

Zebedee ran to his aid.

"My poor boy. What have they done?"

A lightning flash lit the blood-red sky and a peal of thunder roared from swirling clouds nearby, an angry bellow from the *Chasm*.

*

Lucy opened the door and peered out across the ice station. Tyler snatched the Lindworm flash drive from the computer and they paused in the doorway.

"All clear," Lucy whispered, stepping out and crossing to the opposite dorm, a black cat in the night.

Nerves jangling, Tyler followed. She immediately sensed more than one foreign presence. Gallows blades glistened in the shadows either side of Angel's door. Lucy had yet to notice.

"Sentries!" hissed Tyler. She plucked a blade from her coat and hurled it. The sentry's blade flashed up to smash the missile from its path.

Lucy backed up as a siren screeched. Hands shaking, Tyler grabbed the contrap and set it to the *Ghost Portal*. She aimed while Lucy armed herself with the shotgun and retreated from the sentries.

"Get behind me!" Tyler ordered, stepping forward to unleash the contrap's power.

"Phasmatis licentia!"

The sentries materialised, morphing and spinning into smoky threads as the crystal consumed them. Their shrieks died on the breeze. Tyler glanced at the unguarded door, the only obstacle between her and her goal.

"GO!" Precious seconds ticked by. Each felt like an hour. Movement in her peripheral vision warned her others were coming, both ghosts and armed men.

Lucy ran at the dorm to launch herself feet first at the door. It crashed off its hinges. Lucy landed, crouching on its flattened surface. Tyler dashed to the doorway and peered in, the contrap held ready. Inside, the bunk was empty, the sheets thrown open. Angel had fled.

"He was here," said Tyler. "I saw him. He was here just a few moments ago!"

Bullets thumped into the doorway as Lucy and Tyler ducked inside to shelter.

"We're under attack," Tyler screamed into her radio. "Request immediate backup. Repeat, immediate backup!"

"On our way." Enemy shots peppered the outside of the dorm, cutting Klaus off.

Lucy shouldered the shotgun and smashed out a window with the butt of her C7 to give returning fire while Tyler scanned the station through the *Present Eye* for enemy positions.

"We're pinned in," stated Lucy, one eye training down her rifle sights as she ducked at the base of the window.

"There can't be more than forty men. We can take'em."

"Yeah," nodded Lucy, eyebrows rising in mock confidence. "Piece of cake." She sent a heavy volley of bullets towards the gun flashes streaming from across the station.

"Hurry, Klaus. We don't have the ammo to fend them off for long."

A blast of gunfire deafened Lucy and Tyler over the comms.

"We coming! But we have our own issues," shouted Klaus above the din. Louder gunfire drowned out his words. "Repeat, can you reach the plane?"

Lucy switched to a fresh magazine.

Tyler swept the *Present Eye* across the open ice to the isolated plane. Two unmanned blocks stood between, but she glimpsed a wing and the tail.

"I think so."

Sporadic fire continued. Lucy gunned down enemy soldiers. A scatter of ghosts snaked closer, dashing from block to block, visible by their gallows blades. She risked exposure in the open doorway to hurl a blade at the closest and the *cloaked* phantom perished with a howl. Retreating to the window she launched five more blades in quick succession and resumed her stance with the C7.

"In ten seconds run to the plane," said Klaus. "We'll provide covering fire. Ten, nine..."

Tyler counted aloud into the radio while Lucy continued spraying enemy targets with lead and gallows iron.

"...five, four, three..." A hail of fire erupted from the far side of the station, followed by an explosion. "...two, one..." Tyler bolted for the next block, Lucy following, sweeping their rear with fire. They reached the block and sheltered while skirting towards the last block. A second explosion rocked the air.

"What was that?" asked Tyler.

"Don't know. Sounded like a missile strike. Maybe one of the others got lucky with a gas tank."

Enemy fire switched to their new position, blasting fabric from the building. The team's covering fire renewed, a barrage of clamour in the night.

"Ready?"

"Yup."

"Now!"

Tyler and Lucy sprinted to the last block in a mad dash and flattened their bodies against the back wall, glad to feel its solidity at their backs. Bullets whistled past the building, pounding the concrete and smattering it with wounds. From here it was one final dash across open ground to the plane.

"You *can* fly that thing, right, Klaus?" asked Tyler.

"As long as I'm still breathing."

"Okay, we're nearly there. Move. If we beat you the plane will be shot to bits before you can get her started."

Another explosion rocked the ice sheet.

"Copy. Three, two, one."

Lucy and Tyler ventured to the edge of the block, sweeping fire across the station. The rest of the team skirted the hub, attempting to reach the plane. More ghosts approached, materialising amid the bullet flashes. Unaffected, they closed on Tyler and Lucy. Tyler swapped to the contrap and sent the closest phantom into the *Ghost Portal*. The other ghosts paused and retreated, fear in their dead eyes as Lucy emptied two barrels of gallows iron shells into them. Tyler used the balancing spell to stabilise the contrap.

"Compenso pondera."

The remaining team made swift progress, crossing the station and bunching to shelter behind the hub. They waited, watching Tyler and Lucy across the ice.

"Sending grenades," Lucy informed. "In three, two, one." She lobbed a grenade and quickly followed it with a second. As the first exploded in the midst of the enemy,

Klaus waved the others on and they crossed to the plane. Tyler stared at their shadowed forms as they ran.

"What's Klaus carrying?"

"Looks like a bazooka. Ah, the mystery canister."

Klaus and Freddy heaved the lead box of Mordecai chains into the fuselage. Klaus passed the bazooka to Freddy and climbed aboard to start the engine. Freddy launched a missile into a dorm across the station and the rocket's kick sent him flying onto his back. Melissa grabbed him and dragged him in, close to the plane. Together they scrambled up into the fuselage.

Tyler and Lucy backed their way to the plane, spraying enemy clusters with rifle fire. Bullets plinked into the aircraft's flank as Klaus inched it forward. Tyler stumbled on something unseen protruding from the ice. Skidding facedown with her arms braced against the ground ice she swept a path of ice clean of snow and glimpsed a dead face beneath the surface. She had no time to scream. Melissa leant out of the fuselage hatch to bellow.

"Get in!"

She reached out to haul Tyler aboard as Lucy ran out of bullets. Lucy reached the plane in time to leap onto the nearest ski and take hold. Above her, Freddy clacked his C7 at everything that moved on the burning ice station. The plane gained speed, carrying them away from NECRO 904.

Tyler gazed broodingly through the side windows at the ice station's blaze as the plane climbed into the night. Shaking, Freddy clutched his rifle with white knuckles.

"I guess we just lost the deposits on the snowmobiles."

Legion of
the Black Sun

Tyler wondered if she had imagined the face in the ice. What had tripped her? A foot or a knee protruding from the surface?

"You saw it, too. Tell me you saw it," she said to Melissa.

"I saw bodies beneath the ice." Melissa nodded.

"Then I'm not going mad." Tyler detailed Angel's killing ritual. "He's creating ghost spies by killing his own men and hiding the bodies in the ice. It's not a proper burial so the ghosts linger in our realm." She glanced again through a window at the distant ice station fires, glad to be rid of the place.

"I don't understand how Angel got away. He was right there in the dorm." Lucy drained a bottle of spring water she found in the pouch at the back of a seat.

"Me neither," admitted Tyler. "He must have been warned somehow. He must have used a secret door or something."

"No GAUNT machine," said Melissa. "No Chapman and no Streicher?"

"No. Though I guess Streicher could have been there somewhere among the others."

"We wanted to know what they were doing out here. Now we know," said Lucy. Her eyes widened suddenly as she turned to the cockpit. A gallows blade hovered briefly, mid-air, before rushing at her.

"Company!" she shouted, as more blades rose into sight at the head of the plane. She swiped blades from her bandolier and let them fly. Ghosts in grey trench coats manifested, charging down the plane. The first hissed as one of Lucy's blades thumped into his chest. He crumpled and vanished, his blade dropping.

Cries erupted from the cockpit and the plane lurched, throwing Tyler off balance. Melissa tumbled between seats. Lucy followed, landing badly in the aisle and striking her head against an arm rest. Tyler groped for a hold on a seat and dragged herself upright as the next ghost ploughed into her, gallows blade stabbing. He drove it deep into her shoulder before she dispatched him, thrusting her point up into his guts.

The plane plummeted. Tyler rolled in agony, glimpsed Freddy's panicked face and wondered who was screaming.

The plane slammed onto the ice, hurtling across the jagged, frozen plain, scarcely slowing. It tipped, dipping a wing to the ice, and rattled like a baby's toy. The wing ripped away, wind tearing at the gaping hole in the fuselage.

Tyler fought, struggling to her knees as the craft rumbled on. Steadying herself against the seat she groped for a gallows blade and met a new attacker, a stocky, thick-necked grey coat. Iron shrieked against iron. The plane shuddered violently. The ghost hissed in her face, his breath chilling her cheek. The contrap was useless here. Klaus and Freddy were ahead of the ghosts and Lucy was also in front of her. Their spirits would have been unbiasedly swept up into the *Chasm* or the *Ghost Portal* along with the enemy's. The contrap showed no preference for good or bad souls. She opted for blades instead.

From the corner of her eye she saw Lucy lying motionless but for the bouncing of the stricken aeroplane.

Melissa backed into the side wall of the plane, closing her eyes and blindly stabbing at her attacker. Opening them, she gawped at the ghost she had wounded with a chance strike. He disintegrated in a rage, his blade falling an inch from her throat.

The plane slowed and trundled to a halt.

Tyler forced the snarling ghost off her and rolled away. She turned to face him as he prepared to lunge. Gathering the last of her strength, she hurled her blade. It lodged in his chest and in an instant he vanished, leaving a faint miasma on the air.

Cold gusts ravaged the ragged hole in the stationary wreck. Nobody moved. Tyler surveyed the scene of devastation, checking for enemy ghosts.

"Did we get them all?"

Melissa clung to a seat, trembling.

Freddy walked down the aisle towards Lucy, a gallows blade in each hand and a crazed look cooling in his eyes.

"I think so," he said. "Klaus is wounded. What

happened to Lucy?" He stooped to feel for a pulse at her neck. "She's alive."

"I think she was knocked out when she fell," said Tyler. "There could be more coming. We have to go. Collect the blades. Grab anything that could be useful."

Klaus staggered from the cockpit, rubbing his head. His white parka was torn and bloodied from a wound on his neck. Blood trickled from his left temple.

"Tyler's right. We don't have much time," he said.

"What about all our stuff?" asked Melissa, waking from a dazed state of terror.

"Forget it. We can't go back there," said Tyler.

"But all our supplies. Our ammo, our gear."

"Property of the NVF and there's nothing we can do about it."

"But we're stuck in the middle of Greenland without any kind of supplies or protection. We'll die."

"Everybody has to die sometime, Mel," said Tyler.

"Yes, but I'd rather it wasn't tonight. Wait, maybe we should stay here a while. At least the plane will shelter us through the night. We don't even have a tent."

Tyler scavenged a blanket and a first aid kit from a storage bin near the cockpit while Melissa continued to rant.

"In ten minutes this wreck will be crawling with ghosts. We can't afford to be here when that happens." She gathered several more blankets from the seats.

"We'll have to drag her," said Klaus, eyeing Lucy. "Give me a hand, Freddy." They dragged Lucy from the wreck and gathered a short way onto the ice, trying to find their bearings. Klaus fetched his bazooka and his ammunition bag from the wreck. When he returned, Tyler made him hold still while she examined the wound on his neck.

"How bad is it?"

She slapped paper stitches across it and taped a field dressing in place.

"You'll live."

Freddy and Klaus dragged the box of Mordecai chains from the plane.

Tyler traced a line back from the tail of the plane but found no sign of the ice station fires.

"At least we have a head start. The ghosts must've been guarding the plane all along but there's a chance the others didn't see us go down. In which case they might assume we escaped."

"Don't count on it," said Klaus. "They knew the plane was guarded. They'll be looking for us and expecting a report from their ghosts." Klaus scanned the wreck. "Sorry about the plane. It's hard to land when there's a dead Nazi clawing at your throat."

"Can you get us an evac.?"

"If anyone can get a signal. The satellite phone is back with our gear, and so are the solar chargers and the GPS." He checked his mobile. "Nothing. You?"

Tyler looked at her own and replaced it without a word.

"Move out. We're not dead yet."

*

Albert woke to a new sound. The tower rang with the hoots and shouts of celebrating ghosts. He found Zebedee on the rooftop and asked what was happening.

"Down there," said Zebedee, pointing from a battlement to an area below, beyond the forest of blackened trees. "That must be a hundred more, at least."

Below them a mass of ghosts converged on the

tower.

"A bird brought a spy in ahead of them. They escaped from another death camp on the other side of the river not an hour ago."

Albert grinned but sobered as a new concern struck him. The tower could only contain a finite number of ghosts. If many more were saved from the contrapassi, the tower would soon overflow and that could lead to no end of further troubles. He looked around at the cramped rooftop, knowing the other levels were as equally crowded.

"Zebedee, we have to get Tyler's attention somehow. We have to get these ghosts out of here. Fetch Izabella."

Briggs pressed through to Albert.

"Albert! They're here! They made it!"

Albert frowned at the boy.

"Who?"

"Your Da and Molly, they're in the tower!"

Albert nodded, too drained to show emotion. He climbed to the top of the highest parapet and waved his arms in the air.

Seek me out, Tyler.

*

The team trudged for half an hour, cold, tired and taking turns to pair up and drag Lucy on a section of the broken wing.

The first enemy ghosts surfaced from the greyness of the dark ice sheet two hundred metres behind. Freddy alerted the others.

"They're coming."

The spectres drifted in from obscurity to spread in an arc. Behind them, men on snow scooters and snowmobiles rumbled closer, guns slung across their backs. Tyler estimated thirty grey-coated ghosts and ten of the living. Her wounded team was utterly out-numbered.

"That's them, the Legion of the Black Sun," she said. She knelt by Lucy to slap her cheek as the ghosts edged nearer.

"We need you, Lucy! Come on. Wake up!"

"Who has ammo left?" asked Klaus, training the bazooka on an approaching snowmobile.

"I have a dozen rounds or so," said Freddy. "And two grenades."

"I have two P99 mags and one C7," said Melissa. "I think Lucy was out of rounds but she might have grenades."

Tyler checked her ammunition.

"One C7 mag and half a clip. No grenades." She took a grenade from one of Lucy's pockets.

Tyler slapped Lucy hard across the face and grabbed her parka to shake her. Lucy stirred and opened her eyes.

"What the hell?" She blinked up at Tyler.

"Get up and arm yourself."

Lucy squinted at the shapes approaching in the darkness where Tyler pointed, and raced to get to her feet, slipping on the ice. She checked her C7, ditched its empty clip, caught the full clip that Melissa tossed to her, and snapped it into place.

"Give any spare gallows blades to Lucy. She's the best shot. Keep at least one blade each," said Tyler. "Make every shot count. Spread out."

Tyler grabbed at her throat for the contrap's chain. *The* Chasm *will make short work of these idiots.* She gasped as a bolt of panic quickened her blood. Her finger found nothing. She delved into her coat, down into her shirt.

The chain was gone, the contrap lost.

She checked the snow at her feet and glanced along the line of her teams footprints, stopping when she came to the approaching ghosts. Her mind raced with possible scenarios.

Did the chain break? Did I leave it in the ice station? Did a ghost snatch it in the plane? Where is it? No time!

She readied herself with her one remaining gallows blade as Lucy launched her first throw at a stocky, grey coat. The blade missed and purred past the ghost's shoulder. Lucy's second throw found its mark. The grey coat dispelled, squealing. Others closed. Lucy aimed her shotgun at two of the closest ghosts and sent them into oblivion with a blast of fragmented iron.

A war cry rose from the attackers. They surged forward. Gunfire rattled. The men rushed into range of the bazooka. Klaus crouched, adjusting his aim and loosed a missile at an oncoming snowmobile and driver. The explosion blew a crater in the ice, taking out two other snowmobiles with his target. Flat to the ground, commando style, Freddy emptied his clip into four men. Klaus' second missile fell wide. Shards of ice rained across the attackers.

Lucy fired her shotgun again and again, frantically reloading the two barrels.

Tyler pulled the pin on her grenade and lobbed it at the remaining scooter. The blast hurled the vehicle and driver sideways. One living enemy remained gazing at his devastated comrades. He abandoned his gun and turned to run as Freddy opened him up with lead.

"Dead men tell no tales."

Lucy's work with the shotgun had halved the

number of ghosts. She cocked the gun to reload but stared into the bottom of an ammunition pouch.

"I'm out of shells!" She grabbed gallows blades from her thigh and began throwing.

They drove in now, spearheaded by the tallest and strongest of the pack. He singled out Lucy as his target, snarling, eyes heavy with vengeance. *She* was the one. *She* was his prime enemy. A blade in each hand, he tore towards her, smashing her iron missiles aside with swift flicks of his knives.

Lucy threw and threw again, each time only to see her blades harmlessly dashed away as her colleagues watched.

"Regroup!" shouted Tyler. The men and their guns no longer a threat, her team gathered into a defensive arc. Tyler launched her final blade at the charging lead ghost. His eyes locked on Lucy, he failed to notice and it ploughed into his ribs. He toppled, dissolving into thin air.

Tyler watched, defenceless as the remaining ghosts charged.

Lost

Tyler snatched at the oncoming blade as her attacker *cloaked* into invisibility. Others behind him *cloaked*, having saved their energy for the final fight. She battled with the blade as it inched closer to her chest. Her fingerless gloves, damp and icy, slid against the cold iron. She felt the point chill her flesh, piercing her skin and jarring against a rib. Grimacing, she relinquished one grip to snatch at the tip, risking her fingers. She wrenched at the blade and rolled to the side but the ghost's blade remained, pressing in. He *uncloaked* to hiss in her face, his nose millimetres from hers. The blade bit again. The ghost's snarl changed suddenly, his eyes widening and his mouth gaping into a howl. Through the dissolving ghost, Freddy looked down at Tyler. He offered a hand and helped her up. She stooped to arm herself with the vanished ghost's weapon.

"Thanks."

The last two grey coats hesitated in their approach as the team fronted up with blades. The ghosts exchanged a glance and dashed away into the night, back the way they had come.

Melissa gawped after them, wide-eyed with disbelief. "We did it."

"For now." Tyler self-consciously rubbed at her empty neck. "Um, guys? I have to go back."

*

Lying flat on her stomach, Tyler observed the plane wreck barely two hundred metres ahead. A faint snowfall misted the landscape and shrouded the aircraft. She seethed, loathed Angel and the NVF, and hated losing the contrap. She begrudged the loss of time and energy it had meant to backtrack to the crash site. The relative safety of Qaanaaq was miles in the opposite direction.

With dawn casting a silver sheen across the ice sheet, she had argued dogmatically for her lone mission. It was *her* fault. *She* had lost the contrap. *She* should reclaim it.

Alone.

The others had eventually folded. Better one risk her life than five lose theirs. They were exhausted anyway and needed to rest. They reluctantly agreed to wait while she returned to search the aeroplane. The daylight would make it easier for her to mark her route and the present snowfall was light and gave her little concern. The risks were clear, but they were *her* risks.

To see better she pulled her goggles down and let them hang around her neck. The aircraft appeared unguarded. Soft flurries of snow whirled through its broken fuselage. She waited a while longer, watching, wanting to be sure there were no traps or *cloaked* ghosts.

If I lost it during the crash landing it could still be on the plane. Or, if the chain broke during the struggle with the ghosts, the contrap might be somewhere in the snow nearby. There's a chance it travelled down through my clothes and I didn't notice.

Either way, her last recollection of the contrap was on the plane. She was pretty sure she remembered touching it as it hung around her neck when the first of the ghosts had appeared. She had checked her clothes all the way down to her thermal socks and found nothing. The contrap was either lost in the snow, already in the hands of the NVF, or somewhere on that wreck.

Confident that it was safe to proceed, she stole closer. A groan issued from the wreck as a gust of wind played across the gashed fuselage. She ducked low to the ground and waited. Again, the wind rose and the groan sounded. Nerves twitching, she crept on.

She reached the downed aircraft and scanned the surrounding ice sheet. The faint snowfall masked her team's position but she had a good notion of where they were. Back towards the ice station, the landscape dwindled into grey obscurity and she saw no sign of the previous night's fires.

She boarded the wreck, a gallows blade clutched in each hand. Snowdrifts banked against the undamaged interior walls and seating. She stood for a moment, expectantly. When no attack came she sheathed the blades and dropped to her knees to search. She checked beneath the seat she had occupied during the short flight, and around the seats in front and behind. She flattened herself on the floor to peer across the carpet. Recalling her tussle with the ghost further down the plane she rushed there to search and, empty handed, wandered back to the opening.

A line of cold metal in the snow outside caught her attention. She walked to it, half expecting a trap to be sprung. The object was too far in the wrong direction to have been dropped by one of her team. She looked back towards the ice station before stooping to collect the fallen gallows blade.

Who dropped it here?

A sudden notion sent her bounding towards the station. If she was right, time was running out. The NVF had searched the plane, someone had found the contrap and they were taking it back to NECRO 904 right now. She raced towards the research station following faint tracks in the powder-blown surface of the snow. For five more minutes she ran the line pausing only to search the surface when the signs submerged beneath a recent layer of snow. She scanned the area and picked up the trail again, several metres to her left.

They turned here, but why?

She was sure NECRO 904 was somewhere up ahead. And then it struck her: They were armed with the contrap. Someone had decided to abandon the retreat to go after the crash survivors.

My team!

She ran.

The air felt thin and cruel. Each freezing breath burned her lungs but she barely noticed. The hammering of her heart quickened as she pushed herself. She wondered if it would burst before she keeled over with exhaustion. It mattered not. If she failed to reach the contrap and take it back before the enemy used it on her team, all was lost. Head down, she pressed on as cold sweat froze on her brow.

The outlines of men came into view ahead, ghostly in the thin eddies on the air. Tyler threw herself to the ground. The figures ambled on, unaware. One, standing a head taller than all others, drew her eye. The Tall Man.

Great. Bates and the Tall Man have teamed up with an NVF search party and they have the contrap. She couldn't imagine anything worse. This was not the way it was supposed to go and all her nightmares were coming true.

She watched, catching her breath, hoping she still had a chance. If she could skirt the party without being noticed she thought she might be able to reach her team and warn them. But picturing the annihilation the contrap might cause, she quickly ditched the idea. There was no alternative but to locate the contrap herself, right now, and take it back.

Bates. Bates has it! Who else would persuade the party to turn away from the ice station instead of returning to present their prize to Angel? Bates meant to keep the contrap for herself. Once she had eliminated Tyler and the team, Bates would turn the contrap upon her own, sending them into the *Ghost Portal*. She would have possession and be free to roam wherever she pleased.

Tyler's head spun with questions.

Is Bates' ghost strong enough to wield the contrap? How much does she know about it? The contrap would be easily handled if she used the Heart symbol. A ghost brandishing the ghosted contrap. A match made in...

Hell.

Tyler doubted Bates knew about the *Heart* symbol's ability to turn the contrap into its ghostly form. *But perhaps it has not yet gone that far. She may not even be carrying the contrap yet. Perhaps all Bates has achieved so far is to delay the moment the contrap is handed over to Angel, in which case one of the other men in the party carries it.*

She rose slowly to scurry after the ghostly figures, her mind reeling.

*

Izabella waddled up the steps, breathless and in no mood for idle conversation. She forced her way through a line of discontented ghosts clustering around Albert, all of them questioning at once.

"When are we getting out of here?"

"Are all the ghosts free? Are others still in the camps?"

"The table is running dry. What are we to eat and drink?"

"What do you want?" Izabella asked, planting her stocky legs firmly before Albert, and ignoring the others.

"We 'ave to get Tyler's attention. We 'ave to get these ghosts out of 'ere before we runs out of room." As Albert spoke more ghosts streamed in through the mighty, arched door beneath the portcullis at the base of the tower. Izabella understood. She had battled through crowds to reach the roof and squeezed past others cluttering the stairs.

"You think I have some magic spell up my sleeve with which to summon Tyler's attention? You are sadly mistaken, Albert."

"What about your book? 'Ave you checked in there for help?"

Izabella threw him a withering look.

"There is nothing in that evil book that will aid us now, you fool. We are in the hands of God alone. Pray

Tyler finds us, or all our efforts will count for nothing."

Albert coloured and stared at his naked feet. Disregarding a fresh barrage of questions from the clamouring ghosts, he turned to Zebedee.

"Gather volunteers t' man the parapets, one ghost on each. There must be ghosts wavin' for Tyler at all times. 'Ave some ghosts cut flags. Use the tapestries from the walls of the lower levels. We 'ave to do everythin' we can to get her attention."

*

Tyler stole closer, trying to calculate which of the figures held the contrap. She spied Bates and Violet drifting alongside the Tall Man at one edge of the group. Three grey coats accompanied them. Nine men walked in a line, searching the way ahead. Tyler paused when the central man threw up a hand. The others halted obediently.

So you're in charge. And if you're in charge, you probably carry the contrap. I wonder has Bates shown you how to use it? Does she even know you have it?

A shock of nervous energy passed through her. Ahead of the NVF search party lurked more distant figures: Lucy, Freddy, Melissa and Klaus. Tyler watched, her heart in her throat, as the leader took something from his coat. He held up the object and she recognised the contrap at once. He began to speak the command, taking aim with the crystal and Tyler tried to gauge the the contrap's range, unsure at this distance.

"Phasmatis–"

She rushed forward.

"NOOOO!"

The leader stopped to turn. A shot echoed to the far mountains and the man fell to the ice, dead. Klaus and the team turned to see the remaining threat. Moment-arily, Tyler was bewildered.

Where did that *come from?*

A dog sleigh hurtled out of the obscuring mist of fine snowfall to rumble closer with reins lashing. The dogs yelped excitedly. A clutch of men on the sleigh fired volleys at the hesitant patrol. The patrol changed focus and raised their guns to the sleighs as a second dog team careered into view.

A grey coat captain levelled a finger at Tyler and barked an order to his ghosts.

"BRING HER DOWN!"

*

With a cry, Tyler urged Klaus and the team to the fight.

"Spread out. Conserve ammo. Single shots only." Klaus checked his C7 clip and found five remaining rounds. After that he would be down to his last P99 magazine and the bear gun. The bazooka was now useless and abandoned, all shells spent. He knew the others were no better off. Dog sleighs closed in the gap between him and the enemy forty metres ahead, and he wondered who they were as he aimed and fired. His target, an NVF agent busy ordering his men, dropped.

"I'm out," said Freddy, holstering his spent P99.

"Here." Klaus lobbed the bear gun across to him, followed by a box of shells. Freddy caught the gun and continued the fight, popping shells into the twin barrels every two shots.

"With me," shouted Klaus. He ran for the closest sleigh to take cover, Freddy and the two girls on his heels.

*

Tyler reached the fallen leader along with Bates, Violet and the Tall Man to face off with blades over the body.

"Back off or die," snarled Bates. She nodded to the Tall Man. He edged around one side of the body towards Tyler, bullets zipping by, as the men in the sleighs engaged the other agents.

"You just don't believe in a fair fight, do you, Bates?" Tyler scrutinized her three adversaries. The Tall Man's eyes glinted like steel. Bates' crazed look flashed repeatedly from Tyler to the contrap, glistening in the blood-speckled snow almost within reach. Violet cackled joyfully at the conflict and clapped her hands.

"The contrap is mine by right," said Bates. "I'm simply reclaiming what was stolen from me."

"It's not yours. It shouldn't be anyone's. It's dangerous and when my job's done I'm going to destroy it."

"You'll have to go through us first."

Tyler held her gaze.

"So be it."

The Tall Man lunged, his expansive reach taking Tyler by surprise. She sidestepped at the last moment and parried his sweeping blade. Footsteps pounded as someone approached but she refused to look away from her opponent. Another second and Bates would have the contrap. Tyler dropped her own blade to grab at the one bearing down on her. She stumbled backwards. The Tall Man was strong. She caught the cold metal mid-blade, and felt the chill of his phantasm as her flesh passed through his. Gallows iron sliced into her fingers. She slid to her knees. He forced her down, bearing her flat to the ice. Blood trickled the length of the blade and spattered her face as the point closed on her eye.

A shrill scream echoed nearby amid the continuing gunfire.

Tyler felt her blood-greased hands slipping from the metal. The ghost gritted his teeth, lunging his blade closer. Tyler jerked her head to the side, clear of the point, and it sped past her ear to strike hard ice. She snatched up her fallen blade and rammed it sideways into the Tall Man's ribs. A fire flared briefly in his narrowed eyes before he dispelled, evaporating like steam.

Peering up, Tyler gasped. Where Bates had been, Lucy now stood, arms limp at her sides, her face a shock of white. Lucy dropped her blade and wavered before falling face down to the ground, Bates' blade protruding from her back.

"NO!"

As the others ran in, Tyler hurried to Lucy's side, pausing only when she glimpsed the contrap still lying in the snow. She pocketed it, relieved, and dropped to her knees to feel for a pulse. Lucy's blood raced but her wrist and hand were deathly cold. Tyler leant close to listen for Lucy's breathing and heard a succession of ragged, shallow breaths.

Melissa sprinted over.

"Lucy!"

"She's still alive, but she's not good. A punctured lung, I think. What do we do?"

"Don't pull the knife out. Not yet. It could be all that's keeping her alive."

Tyler took the contrap from her parka pocket, her hands slippery with blood. The chain had snapped but it was all there. She switched to the *Safeguarding Skull*, placed the medallion on Lucy's chest and arranged its chain around her neck as best she could. Lucy's breathing eased instantly.

Everything Tyler touched was left bloodied. She tore

strips of bandage from her pack and bound up her fingers.

"Where's Bates?" asked Melissa kneeling alongside.

"I don't know. I think Lucy got her. They must have stabbed each other at the same time. It's the only thing that makes sense. I took out the Tall Man. I don't know what happened to Violet."

A gunman tumbled from one of the sleighs, a bullet hole ripped in his chest. A ripple of shots from those on the other sleigh finished off the remaining NVF agents, and the drivers reined their dogs in to rest. The panting huskies padded around, nosing at the taint of blood on the air.

A man climbed down from a sleigh, dispatched a dying NVF agent with a bullet to the back of the head and removed his snow mask.

"Good morning, ladies."

Secrets

Lumir Barak strode over to the girls, his reindeer-hide jacket flapping in the wind as Freddy and Klaus arrived.

Melissa stood and levelled a gun at him.

"Don't think we're ungrateful for your timely help, but if you don't tell me who you really are I'll shoot you right here, right now."

Clad in reindeer hide gloves and jackets with hide trousers and sturdy boots, *Barak's* seven surviving men gathered around, seemingly unconcerned as *Barak* raised his gloved hands submissively. They smirked at their leader's predicament.

"All right, all right. I'll tell you. You need not fear. I am on your side. I truly am."

Melissa cocked her head to the side.

"Answer the question. Lumir Barak was murdered in Bulgaria over a month ago so, who are you?"

"My real name is Kornel Sova, but in this game one

name is as good as another. I work for the Bezpečnostní Informační Služba, the Czech secret service. I'm investigating the murder of Lumir Barak and the criminal activity surrounding the disappearance of his brother, Řezník. I apologise for my deception. When I told you I was Lumir Barak I was testing you. I needed to know if you were involved in his murder. Clearly you were not.

"Please lower the gun. I'm too young and pretty to die." Looking spent, Kornel Sova lowered his hands.

Melissa chewed her lip, considering his words.

"Why would I come to your rescue, risking my life and the lives of my men if I were not on your side?" he added.

Melissa tucked her P99 back into her shoulder holster.

"You still have some explaining to do. Why follow us to Greenland, and how did you find us? Even *we* don't know where we are."

"When you left me in Prague I was concerned. I had agents track your movements and learned of your flight to Qaanaaq. You seemed to be onto something. All my other leads had fallen flat. I set out to follow you, bringing a few men for backup. We've been tracking your progress via satellite."

"I'm glad you did," said Klaus. "You saved our lives today." He stepped forward to shake Sova's hand firmly. "We're out of supplies, have no tents or transport, we just used the last of our ammunition, and one of our agents has a punctured lung."

Sova gave a succinct nod.

"It will be safe to remove the knife now she has the contrap," said Tyler, taking field dressings and a bandage from her shoulder bag. She tore a larger hole in Lucy's coat around the protruding knife, and lifted it away. She carefully removed the rest of Lucy's clothing from the waist up while the men turned away. With Melissa steadying Lucy's body, Tyler gripped the blade and eased it free, hurrying to staunch the bleeding and pressurise the wound with a substantial dressing. Melissa helped bind the dressing tightly in place with a broad bandage around Lucy's chest. When they finished redressing Lucy as best they could, Sova approached again.

"Bring her. We'll get her to a hospital as soon as possible."

Melissa leaned in. "Tyler, she's stopped breathing!"

Tyler listened unsuccessfully for a breath, felt for a pulse and eventually checked the contrap's switch.

"It's set to the *Ghost Portal*!" She switched it back to the *Safeguarding Skull*. Lucy's breathing resumed with a long ragged breath.

"Who touched this?" demanded Tyler, glaring at the others in turn. "Someone reset the switch." She recalled the contrap switching to the *Ghost Portal* before, all by itself.

Why?

"It was the contrap. We'll have to watch her closely, and the contrap."

Sova and Klaus reorganised the cargo of a sleigh to form a makeshift bed and rested Lucy there.

"The contrap will keep her alive until the doctors can take over, but we're sitting ducks while she needs it. Angel knows it's here and he won't give up. He'll send others after us."

"We have supplies and tents," said Sova, nodding to the sleighs' bulky loads all wrapped in hides and roped down. "We have ammunition, but collect the weapons

335

from the dead anyway. We may need everything we can get."

"Do you have a GPS?" asked Klaus.

"Yes, and a satellite phone. I'm going to call in a chopper. Get us out of here." Sova rummaged in the side of a sleigh for his satellite phone before trudging back to the group. He showed them a bullet hole leaking daylight through the phone's mangled insides.

"Looks like I won't be phoning for help after all." He tossed the phone away. "We need to move. On our way to you we saw them. They're amassing an army of ghosts at the wrecked ice station. We don't have long."

"Bring the chains. Everyone on the sleighs," said Tyler. "Now."

Klaus and Freddy dragged the lead box of Mordecai chains over and secured it onto a sleigh. Sova walked over to peer inquisitively at the box.

"It comes with us," said Klaus, offering no further explanation.

Sova nodded and took his place up front. The dogs yapped in anticipation, straining against the weight of the sleighs. Sova coaxed them on with a flick of the reins.

"We go!"

*

For an hour the team rode the sleighs, weary and in silence. Tyler used the downtime to sleep curled up on top of the skin-clad supplies but a while later was disturbed by the shouts and cries of the sleigh drivers as they fought to bring the dogs back on course. The soporific trundle of the sleigh ceased and wondering why they had stopped she peered out.

Sova passed the reins to another of his men and climbed down. In front, the dogs snuffled excitedly at the snow, padding around and yelping.

"What's the problem?" asked Freddy, squinting at the snow ahead.

"The dogs have found something," said Melissa.

Tyler climbed down and joined the others as they gathered at the head of the team. Sova and two of his men dragged the huskies back to reveal the frozen body of a man lying face down, his arms hugging his chest. Klaus stepped forward and rolled the ridged corpse. Streicher's unmoving eyes gazed blindly at the Greenland sky, his twisted expression betraying the last agony-stricken moments of his life.

Melissa looked away. "I guess we're not the only ones making a bid for freedom."

"Let's hope *we* have more luck," said Freddy.

Klaus stooped to the body.

"He has something in his arms." He worked to loosen Streicher's icy grip and tugged out the object. Unfolding the stiffened oil-cloth wrappings, he stared at its contents.

"It's a book."

Melissa and Tyler hurried to see the age-worn, leather bound manuscript embossed with an ouroboros and a leafless, craggy tree.

Melissa opened the book. "Abraham Eleazar's book of Astral Theorem. It's what started this whole affair."

"I thought Streicher was after the book so he could take it to Angel. Why did he bring it here? There *is* nothing here, so where was he heading?" asked Freddy.

"He must have changed his mind and decided to keep the book for himself. Either that or he presented it to Angel only to steal it back when no reward was forthcoming," Melissa surmised.

"This is bad," said Tyler.

"Why?" asked Freddy. "We have the book. Haven't you and Sova been after it all along?"

"I don't mean about the book." Tyler glanced at Streicher's stiff corpse and tracked a line in the direction he appeared to have been crawling. "Angel seeks the contrap and now he's after the book, too. He'll stop at nothing to find either one. The massing army is the search party and they're coming this way. They know where he was going." She walked ahead of Streicher's line, heading off from the others as Melissa ran to catch up.

"Wait. What are you doing?"

Before them a ridge masked the mid-distance. Beyond, far mountains protruded.

"Streicher wasn't a complete idiot. He wouldn't head out onto the ice sheet without reason." She strode onwards, climbing the rise. Melissa ran after her.

"Hey, wait! Wait for me. What do you think you're going to fi–" As they breached the ridge Tyler dragged Melissa to the ground. A quarter mile ahead a substantial laboratory block perched on squat stilts. At a nine o'clock position an army of grey coats marched across the ice towards it. Tyler estimated at least three hundred ghosts. Behind the block, a chopper and a rank of snowmobiles and scooters dotted the snow.

"There's our ride home."

*

Klaus walked out from one of Sova's newly erected tents.

"Lucy's warmed up and her breathing's eased. I think the contrap's healing her. Here." He passed the book to Melissa. "You'd better keep this safe."

Melissa turned to Sova, who nodded his approval.

"Keep it for now. They tell me you're an expert with languages. Perhaps you can decipher its words, but I'll need it back eventually."

Melissa took the book into the tent to study its ancient, yellowed pages and watch Lucy. Klaus returned to the others gathered around the camp stove as the sun sank below the horizon.

"So, let me get this straight," said Freddy, warming himself and waiting for the water to boil. "We're stuck on the doorstep of some monstrous ghost army who've been sent to kill us, we can't use the contrap for anything other than the *Safeguarding Skull* or Lucy will die, we're outnumbered, and we've barely slept or eaten for days."

"We're safe as long as they don't know we're here," said Klaus. "For now the ridge is hiding us."

"Thought I felt my ears burning," said Lucy, walking in and taking one of the few vacant camping stools across from the men.

"Lucy! How are you feeling?"

"Much better, thanks to this." She waved the contrap briefly and let it hang from her neck. "Sorry to have zoned out for a while. I'm back now."

"Can you shoot?" asked Freddy.

"I guess."

"Good." Klaus and Freddy brought her up to date with their dilemma.

"Where's Tyler?"

"Out on the ridge with Sova, staking out the laboratory."

Klaus poured boiling water into a mess tin and mixed in a ration pack of something claiming to be beef stew.

"Here, you must be starving." He passed it to Lucy.

"We don't have enough tins so pass it to Freddy when you're done."

"Thanks." Lucy stirred the hydrating gunk with a spoon. "So what are we doing?"

"Right now, nobody knows. We can hardly launch an attack with just the twelve of us. Everyone's tired and hungry, and some are injured. We figured we might as well set camp while we plan."

*

Belly to the ground, Tyler focused binoculars on the huge laboratory over the ridge. Ghosts speckled the grounds. Through distant windows she watched the living as they ate and drank inside the buildings. Most occupied a long canteen. At the centre, the large block towered on stilts to overlook the surrounding area, yellow light glowing from its windows.

"Fifty men, maybe more," she said. "Too many ghosts." She searched for the pale bluish glow of the gloves, wondering if Angel, Eichmann or Heydrich were present.

"More coming in." Sova pointed off to the side where hundreds more ghost soldiers marched towards the laboratory.

"What ammunition do you have on those sleighs?"

"Nothing that would deal with this place. A couple of hunting rifles, some machine guns and a few boxes of rounds."

She searched again, seeking any sign of the GAUNT machine she suspected might be hiding there, but without the contrap it was useless.

"I'm hungry and cold." She shuffled back down the slope in the shadow of the ridge.

By the time she reached the camp most of her team

were settling down in Sova's three tents, making themselves as comfortable as possible. The temperature had dropped and, inside her parka and Arctic mitts, she shivered. Two of Sova's men stood guard at the camp perimeter, armed with guns and night vision field glasses. She was surprised to find Lucy sitting by the stoves and sat across from her to warm herself.

"You're awake."

"That's perceptive of you."

"You look like the living dead."

"Thanks. You too."

"I wanted to thank you for ridding me of Bates a second time."

"You're welcome. Let's hope she's gone for good."

"Do you know what happened to Violet Corpe?"

"She fled when I got Bates."

Tyler nodded.

"Have you seen what's out there? I think the other station was just a staging post for this place."

"You think the new GAUNT machine is in there?"

"Yes, and hopefully Chapman, too."

Lucy took off the contrap and handed it to Tyler. "You can have this back now. It's helped me heal. I don't need it anymore."

Tyler reached for a mess tin and ration pack. "You should keep it. You don't know how far the healing's gone."

"No, I've tested it. I'm okay, honestly. And *you* need it now."

Tyler poured water over her dehydrated stew and looked at the contrap as it dangled from Lucy's outstretched hand. Lucy shook it impatiently.

Take it!

Tyler reached out and grasped it.

"If you're sure you're strong enough."

"As I understand it, none of us are likely to survive the night anyway."

"There is that."

They sat quietly as Lucy sipped coffee from a thermal mug and Tyler stirred her unappetising stew.

"I really am sorry about Weaver," said Tyler, unable to stand the silence.

"Thanks."

Tyler watcher her cautiously, seeking reassurance that Lucy was truly healed. Lucy drained her mug and rose to leave.

"Wake me if anything kicks off."

Albert's Army

Tyler sat alone by the fire, unable to rest. Not yet, at least. She turned the contrap in her hands and peered at the ten symbols. *What am I missing? There must be something here to help us.* She knew an attack on the laboratory with so few would end in disaster and the longer they camped there, the greater was the risk of their discovery.

She considered each symbol in turn.

The *Safeguarding Skull* had served its purpose for now.

Using the *Present Eye* might answer two notable questions: Is the GAUNT machine in the laboratory, and is Chapman imprisoned there? She switched to the *Present Eye* but it revealed little. The various rooms of the laboratory block were now unlit. Cloud masked the moonlight and she could barely see anything in the dark interiors. The occupants had retired. Before giving up, she scanned the multitude of grey coats gangling in the night like brain-dead zombies.

With *Flight* she could obtain a bird's eye view of the block. She could descend silently into the centre to take out sentries, or plant explosives.

If we had explosives...

The *Past Eye* could show her what had happened earlier, but that would take time. Something she didn't have.

She contemplated the *Tree of Knowledge*. Zebedee's warnings about that had proved to be true. It simply could not be trusted, even on the odd occasion when it proffered genuine answers to her questions.

The Tower of Doom *might be of use*, she thought although she failed to see how an assessment of her progress to complete her quest might help at this point. She recalled using it in another way. If the owner of the contrap every wanted to know which direction to move in, they had only to walk while watching the tower. If the tower grew taller, the direction was the correct way to succeed. If the tower crumbled, the direction was bad news.

Tyler weighed up her options. Retreat and run from the laboratory, or risk a clandestine visit to spy out the land.

She switched to the *Tower of Doom* and saw with surprise that the tower was high and missing only a few battlements. She stood and took a few paces away from the ridge and the laboratory, all the while scrutinising the tower for signs of decay. She walked for ten minutes before noticing a change. They tower's miniscule battlements were losing stones. She stared at the top of the tower within the crystal, all but pressing it against her eye.

What is that?

Tiny filaments appeared to waver like the hairs of a microorganism. She blinked to clear her vision and looked again. The hairs remained, waving. A sudden, smoky blackness filled the crystal and she recoiled. Turning the contrap she found the switch set to the *Safeguarding Skull*.

What's wrong with this thing?

She reset to the *Tower of Doom* and searched again for the hairs.

With a jolt she realised what they were! The entire rooftop was crammed with ghosts, all of them frantically waving to her.

She sped back to the camp and burst into a tent to find Melissa and Lucy.

"There are ghosts in the tower!"

Melissa blinked and sat up in her borrowed sleeping bag.

"What?"

"There are ghosts in the tower. I think Albert might have found a way through. Do you remember? He said something like *when you need me, seek me out*. It never made sense before, but I think he meant look for me in the contrap. I think he suspected there might be a way through from Sheol into the *Brimstone Chasm*. I think he's made it all the way to the tower."

Lucy climbed from her sleeping bag to look into the contrap's crystal.

"But you said there were ghosts. Who are all the others?"

"I don't know. Perhaps he's found the rest of the Ghost Squad. After all, that's why he went into Sheol in the first place."

Lucy handed the contrap to Melissa.

"If that's true, you can call them out. Tyler, you can bring them back!"

One of Sova's guards rushed into the tent, breathless.

"A ghost patrol just passed the camp. I'm pretty sure they saw us."

The girls exchanged glances.

"We're running out of time," said Melissa. "The army could be here any minute."

"Do you remember the words?" Lucy asked Tyler.

Tyler thought for a moment.

"Yes, I know what to do."

"Then do it!" shouted Lucy and Melissa in unison. They followed Tyler outside where she set the contrap to the *Brimstone Chasm*, turning the lever full-circle until it clicked back into its original position.

"Vorago expositus."

The flipped the contrap over to watch the crystal as the *Chasm* opened, emitting a hot, sulphurous glow. She glanced at Melissa and Lucy waiting expectantly at her side. They nodded.

"Do it!"

"Phasmatis licentia, Albert Goodwin."

A peal of thunder rolled from the sky as heavy clouds quickened to swirl and flash with light. Tyler gripped the contrap with both hands as it trembled. The trembling mounted to a frantic shake and with a rushing wind from the crystal, a storm erupted. Lightning crackled from the *Chasm* into the night as the tower relinquished Albert with an overbearing stench of burning brimstone. He coalesced in front of the girls, looking astonished amid steam where lightning had struck the ground. He saw the tents and the darkness of the ice sheet and finally his gaze settled upon the girls, weary, dazed and frowning.

"Wotcher."

Sluggish snow began falling.

"Albert! You're back!" said Tyler, astonished but glad beyond belief.

"Yeah, looks like I am. Listen. You got t' bring them others back, too. There's 'undreds of 'em!"

"What do you mean?"

"I got the Ghost Squad and 'undreds o' ghosts down there in the tower, all just awaitin' to come out and fight. There's an 'ole army!"

"I don't understand. Who are they?"

"They're the sleepers, o'course. From Sheol."

Tyler gawked at him, the beginnings of a wry grin invading her face. Her questions could wait until later.

"Phasmatis licentia, Zebedee Lieberman." Lightning cracked and ice hissed. Zebedee appeared next to Albert, smoke rising from his top hat as brimstone clouded the air. Zebedee blinked at his new surroundings and lit his pipe as a new wind blustered the camp.

"Phasmatis licentia, Izabella Kremensky." The storm burst again from the glowing crystal and the icy gale rose to howl across the ridge. Tyler steadied herself and continued, battered by hail and sleet. "Phasmatis licentia, Kylie Marsh. Phasmatis licentia, Marcus. Phasmatis licentia, Kinga. Phasmatis licentia, Danuta." With each new ghost the sleet fell harder and the sky cracked with lightning as an electrical storm swelled overhead. She called out Wulfric the Saxon, John the infantryman, Isla the Dickensian girl from the poorhouse, the Jews, Judith and Leon, the Welsh girl Bronwyn and Yakudu the

African slave. Tyler babbled until she ran out of names.

"Don't forget Claudia!" shouted Albert, above peals of thunder. "I told ya', I found 'em all!"

"Phasmatis licentia, Claudia."

As the smoke and steam cleared she viewed the Ghost Squad who mostly gazed back in shock and wonder. They all started talking at once and it was a while before Tyler could call order and hear what Albert was trying to tell her.

"There's 'undreds, an' you don't know their names. The only way this is going to work is if I give you the name of the next ghost and that ghost passes you the next name once he's out. Do you see? Everyone in there knows at least one other ghost by name."

Tyler nodded, emphatically.

"Give me a name."

"Molly Goodwin," said Albert, without pause.

Tyler began work, using the command to bring through ghost after ghost from the *Chasm*. The number of those gathered on the ice around the tents grew with each passing moment as ghosts shot like lightning onto the ice.

Through the tempest a drone flew into camp and hovered, scanning the scene with two red eyes and roving light.

"Take it down, Mojo." said Tyler. The machine swivelled to focus on her and flew closer.

Lucy drew her gun and peppered the spy drone with bullets until it crashed, hissing, to the ground. Steam rose from its ruined shell.

Tyler stood back to take in the spectacle of newly arrived ghosts. They stretched out deep into the darkness of the ice sheet, their figures softly iridescent. Albert was right. He had brought her an entire army and there were still more to come. Urgently, she summoned out more ghosts as Sova armed himself, ready to fight. Izabella appeared in Tyler's face.

"Enough, girl! Don't you see? The contrap draws its power from the ghosts within. It weakens with every ghost you release!"

Tyler stopped to examine the glow from the contrap's crystal. It was dimming.

A guard, hugging his coat tightly against the storm, ran in from the outskirts of the camp to shout.

"They're coming!" He stopped, panting before them. "Hundreds of ghosts, approaching the rise!"

"Let's hope we have enough ghosts!" Tyler ran to a sleigh, barking orders.

"Arm the ghosts. Distribute every blade you can find!" She and her team dashed among the ghosts, handing out blades until they ran out. She noticed Sova and his handful of men preparing for battle, loading guns and checking ammunition, and approached them.

"Let my team and Albert's army handle the ghosts. When we've cut a path to the lab, come running. There'll be armed men to deal with."

Sova nodded curtly and snapped shut the barrel of his bear gun.

Lucy found Tyler in the crowd to report.

"Only a handful of our ghosts have weapons."

"There's nothing we can do about that. We'll just have to win more as we go. Every ghost we slay will leave a blade behind for us to claim." Tyler turned to Albert. "Organise your army. Get everyone with a blade to the frontline. Spread the word. Everyone will get a blade but we have to win them first. I have to get to the front. The contrap is our best hope."

She found Kylie among the Ghost Squad nearby.

"Kylie, with me." Tyler led her to the back of a sleigh and yanked down the heavy lead box of Mordecai chains. She unlocked the numerical padlock and opened the lid. The chains glimmered brightly. "Have the strongest members of the Ghost Squad take a chain each. Use them on any problem ghosts. If we encounter gloves, be ready."

"Consider it done." Kylie shoved her glasses higher onto the bridge of her nose and turned to organise the squad.

A second spy drone descended to hover, staring at Tyler. She drew her gun and blasted it to the ice. As it lay buzzing like an injured insect, a smaller, darker object floated into view over the ridge. Klaus and the others raised their guns. It drifted nearer, a two way radio carried by a *cloaked* ghost. Tyler threw up her hand.

"No, wait!"

The radio approached and dropped at her feet. A moment later, Angel's voice issued from it.

"It's all right, Fräulein May. You can pick it up. I can promise you it is just a regular radio."

Tyler snatched it from the snow and hit the talk button.

"This has to stop. You're outgunned. I have the contrap. Why not end it now and save further needless bloodshed?"

"Deliver the contrap to me and we have a deal."

"We've been here before and you know I can't do that."

Laughter crackled from the radio's compact speaker.

"Fräulein May, I applaud you. You are a bulldog with a bone. You simply will not roll over and die, will you?"

"Not while there's breath in my body."

"Before the night is out I will personally suck it from your lungs. Though, I believe I have found your weakness: You will not kill my precious gloves. You cannot kill the innocents with whom they abide. You would no longer be the brave defender of the weak, but would become a mindless murderer, your heart blackened to tar. Tell me, Fräulein, how many of those around you share your heady morals? How many of your *English* countrymen would rather fold and say *kill them, they are casualties of war*? It's time to embrace your destiny. It's time to kill or be killed. Auf Wiedersehen, Fräulein."

Tyler dropped the radio and crushed it under her boot with one heartfelt stamp. She crested the ridge as, behind, Albert's army formed in lines. On the far side of the slope Angel's legion faced her, marching in rank, their grey coats blowing in the wind.

Angel's distant voice rose behind the legion.

"KILL THEM! KILL THEM ALL!"

Tyler brandished the contrap, the fiery glow of the *Chasm* catching in the eyes of her opponents' closest ranks. Screaming the command, she dropped to one knee and swept the contrap across the frontline as the grey coats charged.

"Phasmatis licentia!"

They morphed into light, dropping their blades and cascading into the crystal with a tumultuous roar of wind.

Tyler balanced the contrap as the crystal brightened.

"Compenso pondera."

A great swathe of the grey coats *cloaked*. Others dropped their blades to flee. Tyler waved Albert's army forward to harvest fallen weapons, and she strode through to reap more of the legion. She glanced ahead at the laboratory, now only a few hundred metres from her position. Through the ranks of ghost soldiers she saw the unmistakable blue glow of gloves in the shadows of the giant stilts. She gritted her teeth as freezing rain smashed against her face.

I'm coming for you, Angel.

*

Albert led his troops into battle.

"For the hope bringer! For Tyler and the sleepers of Sheol! CHARGE!" The army raced for the frontline where blades peppered the snow. Alongside his armed men, he fought back grey coats as they pressed in from the flanks, while his unarmed ghosts gathered weapons. Before him, Tyler brought the contrap around in a slow arc, sucking grey coats into the *Chasm* like dust into a vacuum. They screamed and shrieked as they realised their fate. They tried to turn, to outrun the draw, but nothing could stop the *Chasm's* greedy power. It grabbed with an unquenchable thirst, drinking them from the ice and air, dragging them, wheeling through the haze, as they dissolved into neon light. Again she uttered the balancing command.

Albert watched a further clutch of grey coats succumb to the will of the *Chasm*. He waved his troops forward to keep pace with Tyler.

"ONWARDS!"

*

Tyler pressed into the enemy, collecting those who failed to quickly flee and forcing others to the edges of the battle. A broad, empty arc of ice surrounded her. She had no plan as such, only a gut full of conviction that this had to be done. The glimpse of the gloves spawned a deep seated rage, and she fixed her eyes on the stilted laboratory. *That* was her goal and she was going to take it or die trying.

To her sides, her team fanned out, armed with the last remnants of ammunition shared from Sova' sleighs. They walked with Tyler, picking off any living souls who dared to approach among the legion. Freddy trudged with a dogged determination, hardened by his recent battles, a bear gun at the ready, his pockets full of shells, and an ice pick in his belt. Klaus stomped on, a blade in one hand, his C7 in the other. To their sides, the Ghost Squad marched; the Saxon Wulfric, the slave Mufa, Zebedee and Kylie, each weighted with the heavy, glowing chains.

Barely aware of those around her, Tyler pushed forwards. She gathered every grey coat within reach into the *Chasm* as fighting intensified in the wings where the two sides met.

The clash of iron arose as the contrap drew power from each new ghost it collected.

Control

The Ghost Squad cast their chains to bind the strongest of the grey coats. Once captured, they were easily dispatched with gallows blades, leaving the chains for reuse. Other soldiers saw the glimmering chains and retreated, fear widening their eyes.

Melissa's voice broke through the frenzied battle noise.

"Tyler, reveries! There aren't many, but *someone* must have summoned them. I think Heydrich is here!"

Tyler fumbled in her pocket for the plastic bag labelled *Reinhard Heydrich*. She took out the bone and clamped it to the contrap with her bandaged fingers. As though in response the chopper beyond the laboratory fired into life. Three figures with glowing blue heads and hands fled to the craft and boarded.

Tyler sprinted into the legion, screaming.

"Phasmatis licentia!"

Grey coats scattered. The slower ghosts morphed into light as they were sucked into the *Chasm*. She dashed for the chopper but halving the distance between them she knew she was too late. The chopper lifted from the ground, billowing snow onto the edge of the battlefield.

She drew close enough to glimpse a bluish face at the passenger window. Angel flashed Mengele's unnerving smile back at her as the chopper ascended. He was content enough to have escaped. He had lost little and would create more ghosts for his legion and build more machines.

With Angel's retreat the remaining legion weakened, its venom ebbing. Many grey coats *cloaked* and abandoned their blades, leaving their comrades to face Albert's army, the contrap and the chains of the Ghost Squad.

To one side of the laboratory, Sova and his men drove in on their sleighs to snipe at the remaining enemy agents.

Tyler reached the laboratory, furious to have allowed Angel and Heydrich to escape. She placed a grenade on the doorstep and retreated before its detonation. Climbing the steel stairs amid the clearing smoke, she entered through the wrecked doorway. At the far end of the room a line of gloves guarded a bulky metal machine the size of a minibus. They opened fire, spraying holes in the end wall around her as she leapt back to shelter in the doorway.

Melissa and Lucy ran up the stairs to aid her.

"Gloves. Half a dozen or so," Tyler reported.

"They're trapped in there," said Lucy. "Use the chains and the *Chasm*!"

"Okay. Take cover."

Tyler followed the other girls back down the steps and hid beneath the laboratory as the Ghost Squad arrived. She quickly explained the situation.

"We don't have enough chains to take them all," said Zebedee.

"Does anyone have a Taser?" asked Tyler. "I lost mine with the rest of our kit."

"I do," said Melissa, taking her Taser from her holster.

"Lucy?"

"Uh-uh." Lucy shook her head.

Tyler switched to the *Present Eye* and focused through the flooring into the laboratory above.

"There are seven including Beast."

"Seven of them against six chains," said Kylie.

"Dual attack," said Lucy. "Send the ghosts up through the floor with the chains while we distract from the doorway. I'll take the Taser." She glanced at Melissa. "Unless *you'd* rather?"

"Be my guest." Melissa passed her Taser and spare cartridges to Lucy.

"Make sure you chain Beast," added Tyler, as Freddy arrived to join them. "Go." She watched the Ghost Squad glide to the other end of the laboratory and rise up to pass through the floor, holding their chains at the ready.

"Good luck."

*

Gunshots exploded from within. Lucy ran up the stairs to distract with gunfire, taking care to avoid hitting the gloves. Dipping her head around the doorway, she glimpsed two gloves on the floor already bound in chains. She ducked back and fired off a burst from her C7 into the opposing wall. A second glance showed her a third fallen glove and another wrestling Wulfric for possession of his chain.

Lucy ducked back again, waiting for the right moment to strike.

A shape filled the doorway as Beast thundered into her, smashing the Taser from her hand. She toppled from the side of the stairs to the snow below. Beast bounded down the steps and paused at the base to sweep bullets across the battlefield. From the shelter of the block, Melissa ran at him. He turned as her shoulder drove into his midriff, knocking him sideways and dashing the gun from his hands. He straightened and in two strides towered over her. He looked down at her deciding whether to crush her with his boot or his bare hands.

Behind Beast, Freddy stepped out from beneath the stairs, checking the magazine of his P99 and finding it empty.

He dropped the gun and tugged the ice pick from his belt. Beast raised a fist the size of a sledgehammer, ready to strike Melissa. Freddy dived and, hitting the ice, swung his pick to wallop it through Beast's foot. Beast rolled, howling, to the ground.

Tyler closed in, showing him the contrap.

"Didn't your *Führer* tell you? This is something you gloves should fear. "Get back Freddy." She aimed the contrap's crystal as Freddy hurried aside. "Phasmatis licentia."

Beast scrambled for his gun but his spirit hissed from his body like steam. For the briefest of moments it formed in his likeness before swirling into the *Chasm* with a rush. His vacant body slumped to the ground, changing in an instant. A moment later a blond teenage boy lay in his place, swamped within Beast's huge clothes, screaming and rocking in the snow, grasping his pierced foot.

Tyler stepped closer to look down at the boy's pain-twisted face and patted him on the shoulder.

"Sorry about your foot."

Six gloves remained inside, at least three of them bound. Lucy scrambled to reclaim the Taser and ran back up to the doorway as another glove, this one a stout woman with the hard look of a prison guard, approached in an effort to escape. Lucy shot a Taser dart into her neck before she could raise her gun. She fell to the ground stunned and Lucy grabbed her collar and dragged her down the icy steps. She stood back to allow Tyler to use the contrap. A blond girl awoke from the woman's altering figure to look up, pale and shaking. The woman's clothes hung from her like rags. Tyler tore off her coat and threw it to the girl.

Kylie reached Tyler to report.

"Four gloves chained. One remaining. The room is now clear of our ghosts."

Tyler turned to Lucy.

"Shall we?"

Lucy fitted a new Taser cartridge and nodded.

"Let's finish this."

They approached the entrance together and Lucy glanced into the room. She whipped the Taser around the door jamb and pulled the trigger. Instantly, the jolt of electricity dropped the glove to the floor. Tyler stepped in and one after the other collected the gloved ghosts into the *Chasm.* Five semi-naked, bewildered, pale-faced teenagers peered back at her in shock.

Outside, the din of battle ceased as the last of the

legion fled. Sova hobbled over to the steps where the others gathered, his bicep bleeding from a bullet wound.

"Casualties?"

"I don't know," said Tyler, looking around and trying to ascertain if any faces were missing. She found Albert and breathed a sigh of relief.

"The Ghost Squad are all here," said Kylie.

"You?" Tyler asked Sova.

"Four men dead. The rest wounded." He dabbed at his bleeding arm and winced.

"There could be others inside. Soldiers or prisoners."

Tyler switched the contrap back to the *Present Eye* and trained it through walls and into the further chambers of the laboratory block. The first was empty, the second occupied by laboratory equipment. She paused on the third when she focused on three prisoners sat, shackled to the walls.

"Klaus, see if you can find a radio to get help. I'm going in."

She hurried up the steps, through the bullet-riddled GAUNT machine chamber and on through to a third room. She burst through the door and stood wide-eyed before the prisoners.

From the wall opposite, almost unrecognisable, Chapman peered back at her. Unkempt hair shadowed his drawn, bearded face. His glasses were missing and, from what showed through his dirt-soiled clothes, his lean figure was painfully malnourished. Below his left eye a deep, purple bruise coloured his cheek. He tried to stand but collapsed back to the floor. The other prisoners were in no better shape. Chapman dropped his gaze as his shoulders shook, a broken reflection of his former self.

Tyler ran to him.

*

The storm subdued and the wait for rescue seemed to last forever. The living rallied to the aid of the prisoners, the de-gloved teenagers and those wounded from the battle, gathering in the laboratory block to shelter from the cold winds. They shared clothes around until everyone had something warm to wear, even if it was grossly ill-fitting.

In the absence of any keys, Tyler smashed Chapman's shackles free with the butt of her C7. She remained with him as he ate a ration pack from Sova's dwindling stores. He watched her with a concern bordering on distrust, as though she might vanish like a mirage at any moment.

"Thank you." The effort of talking was costly. He winced and touched his lip where a fresh welt swelled around a bleeding split. She noticed more bruising across his jaw and figured it might be broken.

"You don't need to say anything. Just rest and get better. It's over. They're sending a plane. We're going home."

"How did you-?"

"Find you? Long story."

"This place, it's his, the man they call the Sceloporus. It's Eichmann's glove."

"We figured as much. I'm sorry but he escaped with the others on the helicopter."

Chapman nodded, his mouth twitching into a fleeting, grim smile.

Not bothering to use the door, Albert walked in to find Tyler.

"Weaver was with us in the *Chasm*."

Tyler looked up. Lucy crossed to join them.

"What? You saw Weaver?"

"Yeah. He's dead. I didn't know if you knew."

Lucy's gaze bored into him.

"We knew. If he was with you in the *Chasm* where is he now?"

"He chose to stay behind."

"WHAT?"

"You don't understand. There's others down there, other ghosts trapped in the *Chasm*. When I told 'em I was sure you'd see us through the crystal, a team elected to stay to 'elp rescue the others from them death camps. When they's all free and in the tower, Tyler can call 'em out, and Weaver with 'em."

"But he could get stuck in there forever! Why didn't you bring him out with you?"

"He wanted to stay. It were nought to do with me. I'm sorry, Lucy Loo."

Lucy sat on a chair and buried her nose in her hands.

"Listen, 'e was an 'ero in there. You seen the ghosts who came out. They wouldn't be 'ere now if weren't for Weaver. 'E'll be all right. I know 'e will."

Tyler left Lucy wrestling with Albert's news, and searched for Izabella outside the block where Sova was busy feeding the dogs. She found her hovering among the multitude of ghosts.

"We need to talk."

"Then talk."

"There's something wrong with the contrap. It keeps switching itself to the *Ghost Portal*, sometimes at the worst moments, like it's broken."

"Oh, dear." Izabella's clouded eyes shifted, without focus, to the horizon.

"What do you mean, *oh dear*? Do you know what's going on with it?"

"Not really, but it can't be anything good. The balance is shifting. We're losing the battle."

"We just *won* the battle. What battle are *you* talking about?"

"The greater battle. The contrap is evil, was created by evil. You've not forgotten that, have you?"

"No."

"No one will be safe until it is destroyed."

"I want to destroy it. It's just that–"

"Right now it's too useful? Oh, dear. Well, it won't be useful when you no longer control it. It will be a curse. The enemy will turn it against you. It will seek to thwart you at every opportunity."

"So someone else is controlling it? Someone else is switching it?"

"Tell me, girl, when it switches by itself, does it help or hinder?"

"It hinders. It nearly killed Lucy."

"Oh, dear."

"Stop saying that!"

Dark Matters

Melissa poured tea. Tyler straightened a picture on her kitchen wall and eyed the spot where the teaspoon used to reside. Today it remained obediently in the cutlery drawer. She reminded herself one more time.

Bates is gone for good.

The workmen had made a good job of fitting new doors, locks and deadbolts, and the house felt safe. She finished making Lucy's coffee and the girls carried their drinks into the lounge to sit in the warmth of the sunlight cascading through the bay windows.

"What are we going to do about Yash?" asked Lucy.

"We need more evidence before we can make any accusations," explained Melissa. "He has something going on with a staff sergeant named Abigail Dodd. I wouldn't be suspicious but they only ever meet up when they think no one's watching, usually late at night, and she's nothing to do with our division." She confessed to Lucy about her surveillance of the office.

"You sure they're not *doing it*?" asked Lucy.

"It's strictly platonic so far, though I still have a backlog of footage to check from the camera in his office. How's Chapman? We need him up and about before we make any allegations."

"He'll be on his feet in a day or two. No lasting damage." Tyler sipped tea.

"What about the book," asked Lucy. "You find anything of use?"

Melissa placed Streicher's book on the coffee table and opened it to an illustrated page.

"I haven't got the ring working yet, if that's what you mean, but there are some pretty weird things in here." She flipped through pages to show them. "All these strange drawings, snakes or dragons forming rings like the ouroboros, surreal landscapes with caverns, towers, ruined trees, forests and rivers."

Tyler took the book to examine a page depicting a landscape of writhing serpents, the ground drawn with rolling plumes of substance rising from it.

"It's the *Chasm*. Look, this stuff here is the fire-fog I told you about. The place isn't crawling with snakes like in the picture, but the ground itself moves like a bed of snakes. It's like the artist was trying to describe the nature of the place but wasn't sure how to explain it."

"That's the *Chasm*, all right," said Albert, appearing at her shoulder between Zebedee and Izabella.

Tyler turned the pages to see skeletons, diagrams of flasks and urns, boxes, unrecognisable beasts and winged creatures.

"I think the guy who created this book knew something of the *Chasm*. Maybe he'd even been there."

"The skeletons could be the grave or Sheol," suggested Albert. "The urns an' boxes could be to do with that too, so it ain't just the *Chasm*."

"Why would Streicher and the NVF want to know more about the *Chasm* and Sheol?" asked Lucy.

"I wish I knew," Tyler admitted. "I guess they're planning something."

Melissa cleared her throat.

"Oh, they're definitely planning something. I've searched the files you copied from NECRO 904. It makes for interesting reading, *if* you're a scientist researching the utilisation of cryogenic germanium."

"What?"

"Exactly. You'd need a degree in quantum physics to even begin to understand this stuff, but I did some research."

"Here we go," muttered Lucy.

"Basically there only seems to be one reason why someone would be experimenting with germanium at sub-zero temperatures. To attempt the detection and study of particles of dark matter."

"Again, what?"

"You don't know about dark matter?" Melissa asked Lucy.

"No. I have a life."

"Okay, I'll make this simple for you. A few years ago scientists discovered huge discrepancies in the calculated mass of solar systems and stratospheres in space. Subsequent studies suggested the miscalculations could only have resulted because of one reason: The planets, stars, dust, ice and gases out in space were not made up of only what could be seen. There had to be other stuff, invisible stuff that passed right through the visible matter without being noticed. They called it dark matter and they've been searching for it ever since. Apparently it's pretty hard to find."

"So the NVF are trying to detect dark matter. Why? Why does Angel want to know about dark matter?"

"The plural curtain," said Zebedee, knowingly.

The others turned to stare at him. He blinked, surprised by their sudden attention, and took a long suck on his pipe.

"What?" he asked.

"What do you mean?" asked Tyler.

"You know, the plural curtain. The inter-zonal stratums between the realms." The girls gawped and he glanced at each of them in turn. "Don't you remember the tear between the realm of the *Ghost Portal* and the *Chasm*? I'm merely proposing the theory that what separates the realms might be dark matter. No ghost I've ever met knows of what they are made."

"'E wants to tear a rift between the under-realms into the realm of the living," said Albert, suddenly. "That's 'is plan. That's why 'e wants to know about this dark matter and the plural curtain. 'E wants to join the realms."

"But that would be catastrophic," murmured Izabella. The others turned to her waiting for an explanation.

"Imagine the evil of the *Chasm*. The contrapassi, the liliths and God knows what else, the punishment, death and torture, all of it spilling unabated into the world. It would creep from nation to nation like an unstoppable cancer, until every inch was plagued. He would rule. A demon king, over-lording his reign of terror. Humanity across the globe would be plunged into an unimaginable Hell. The mortal nature of your realm would endure.

The second death of the *Chasm* would cease to be and in its place would remain only death."

"He can't make that happen, can he?" Melissa paled.

Izabella set her jaw determinedly and met Melissa's pleading gaze.

"*Not* if we stop him."

*

Melissa finished reviewing the data from the surveillance camera in Yash's office. The dirt on Yash had run disappointingly dry. *So what if he delayed governmental acceptance of Chapman's proposal? As acting section chief he was well within his rights to do so. The affront is personal but not academic. Perhaps he is not the enemy after all. Perhaps he is only doing his best under challenging circumstances and had more important things on his mind.*

She replayed the footage of Dodd and steeled herself for a final day of surveillance. She packed up her laptop and left the apartment. There was one lead remaining and she needed to eliminate that before dropping the entire thing and giving Yash the benefit of doubt.

Staff Sergeant Abigail Dodd.

Melissa drove to HQ and loitered nervously outside, waiting for a glimpse of Dodd within the building's portico with its elegant arch and four iron-crossed standing lamps. Street surveillance was really not her thing. Three hours of killing time on her iPhone finally paid off. Dodd left the building. She turned left towards Lambeth Bridge and crossed the road to walk alongside the black railings by the Thames sluggish flow. Dodd paused to dig in her purse for sunglasses and put them on before turning onto the bridge.

Melissa followed, carefully angling the hidden

camera sewn into the side of her shoulder bag. For an hour she tracked Dodd on the other side of the bridge. Dodd met a younger brunette woman in a sharp grey suit for lunch at Sirena's, an Italian restaurant.

Melissa captured an image of the brunette on her phone and ran a background check. All clear. Melissa watched another lead evaporate. Despondently, she tailed Dodd back across the bridge. Once inside Thames House, Dodd was a more challenging target. Melissa followed her through the doorways and corridors until Dodd passed a security check and entered a meeting. Melissa groaned inwardly.

What a pointless exercise.

*

It was not until late in the evening that Melissa thought again about Yash and Dodd. She had spent the remainder of the day bent over Abraham's book of Astral Theorem, fruitlessly attempting to learn something of use about the ring of gallows iron she wore upon the middle finger of her left hand. Still numb and moody from Weaver's death, Lucy had withdrawn to bed, leaving Melissa alone with an uninspired TV program. Yash resurfaced in the subsequent void of her mind.

Was I really that wrong about him? It irked her that she had so chronically misjudged a situation. *That just isn't like me.* On a whim she switched off the TV, booted her laptop, and opened the digital footage from her bag-cam, scrutinising Dodd's every move.

Halfway through the footage of Dodd crossing the bridge, Melissa paused the video and rewound several seconds to replay. She watched those few seconds five times, frame by frame.

"Lucy, get in here now. You need to see this."

*

Tyler's mobile vibrated, its screen illuminating the ceiling of her bedroom with sudden brightness. She roused enough to grab it from her bedside table and clumsily tap the green button on the touch screen, trying to shake off the rigors of sleep. Chapman's voice hit her like a bucket of iced water.

"Wake up and put the coffee on," he ordered. "We'll be there in thirty."

"Mr Chapman?"

"Just do it, Ghost!" Chapman hung up.

Tyler checked the time display on her phone before dropping it onto the bed with a groan.

Five past three? What now?

She threw on some clothes and dragged her unwilling body down the stairs to put the kettle on.

Of course the section chief of the Joint Intelligence Committee wants to drop in for coffee and cake at three in the morning. Why not?

The doorbell rang and Tyler peered through the spy hole of her new front door to check. Melissa waited with Lucy, her laptop case in one hand. Tyler unlocked and opened the door. The girls entered and helped themselves to seats in the lounge. Tyler followed to stand in the doorway, hands on hips.

"Would somebody like to tell me what's going on?"

"Chapman told us to wait for him," said Melissa, unclasping her case and setting up her laptop as a second car pulled up the driveway outside. Headlights flashed across the curtains.

"That'll be him," said Lucy.

"Great. You let him in. I'll fetch the coffee." Tyler brought a tray laden with milk, mugs and a pot of coffee, and placed it on the coffee table as Chapman took off his coat and slung it over the back of the couch. He sank into the couch looking thin but strong and much recovered.

"Play the data," he told Melissa.

Melissa replayed the few seconds of pertinent footage. Tyler watched.

"Staff Sergeant Abigail Dodd of Section B. Melissa tells me she's been meeting secretly with Yash. Watch her closely as she passes this man on the bridge." Chapman indicated an Iranian in a black bomber jacket walking towards the camera.

"When was this taken?" asked Tyler.

"This afternoon with one of Melissa's clandestine cameras."

On the screen Dodd continued to walk, passing the man without breaking stride. His gaze briefly settled on her. Melissa stopped the video.

"Did you see it?" asked Chapman.

"See what?"

"The nod."

Tyler shook her head.

"Play it again," said Chapman.

Melissa replayed the footage. Tyler watched again and saw Dodd give the subtlest of nods as the man glanced her way.

"Okay. You think it means something? Who is he?"

"His name is Abdul Atef. He's a terrorist known to MI6. He's already under surveillance and we plan to take him when the time is right. The department tracking his movements flagged Melissa's actions up to me two hours ago with a warning to back off before we blow their operation. But the point is they unaware of any connection to Dodd. In short, Melissa just linked Yash to a wanted terrorist through Dodd. We don't know what that nod meant but we're guessing something's going down and Dodd just gave the go-ahead.

"Melissa also brought me up to speed with Yash's blatant disregard for my directive regarding the new department. I'm taking back control as of tonight. *Denby, Watts and May* is now a verified department of the MI6. Consider this your first assignment. In a few moments you'll need to brief your ghosts. First thing in the morning we're taking down Yash and Dodd."

Smoke on the Water

The girls waited with their reinstated section chief as he sat behind his desk. The Director of MI6, a silver haired man in his fifties, sat next to him.

Yash entered, closed the office door behind him, acknowledged the Director and approached the desk.

"You called for me, Sir."

"Sit. You're in it up to your neck." Chapman closed a file on his desk as Yash pulled up a chair and Tyler and Melissa sat each side to hedge him in. Lucy remained standing, her hands in the pockets of her leather jacket, an index finger gently resting against the trigger of her P99.

"If you have an accusation to make, fire away," said Yash. Behind his back Lucy smirked.

"Side arm and ID on the desk. Slowly," the Director instructed.

A glimmer of fear flashed in Yash's eyes. He reached

into his jacket, carefully removed his gun, unloaded it, checked the chamber and placed it before Chapman with his ID.

"What's this about?" he asked, as Chapman dropped the weapon, magazine and ID into a desk drawer.

"I'm investigating you for treason. Yesterday, an associate of yours was observed passing information to a known terrorist." He swivelled the laptop on his desk to show Yash the footage.

"Dodd," said Yash. The video clip looped. "Is that it? A colleague nods to a stranger and I'm a threat to national security?"

"This is London, Yash. No one makes eye contact in the street. No one nods to a perfect stranger without reason. And nodding to a known terrorist? That's one hell of a coincidence." Chapman glared.

Yash glowed back at him and the Director across the desk.

"It's confession time, Yash. If you have anything to say, say it now. You have been observed meeting secretly with Dodd on numerous occasions, and she just gave a terrorist the okay for a move of some kind. Either you have an Iranian terrorist working for you as a plant or *you* are working for him. Which is it?"

"No. You're wrong."

"Talk."

"I met Dodd to propose a joint mission. Her department has sleepers placed with people in the black market. They could help locate and obtain artefacts we strongly desire, artefacts once belonging to Adolf Hitler, to be precise. Ask Dodd. She'll corroborate my story. The man in the street is nothing more than an unhappy coincidence."

Chapman raised an eyebrow as the Director stood.

"At this moment, Dodd is being taken into custody for questioning. The two of you will remain our guests for the duration of the investigation, all authority revoked."

"That's fine. I've nothing to hide," said Yash.

Chapman leaned forward on his desk, revealing a pair of handcuffs.

"Your hands, please."

Yash stood to offer his wrists. Chapman rose to cuff him. As the cuffs neared, Yash lashed out, his fist catching Chapman on his bruised jaw. Chapman recoiled, his head thwacking against the wall behind. The Director made a grab for Yash but received a punch, splintering his nose. He dropped, blood streaking his shirt.

Startled, Lucy yanked out her gun but he was ready for her. Her shot passed his ear as he knocked her gun aside and the bullet ploughed into the wall. Yash shouldered her to the ground, running for the door. Lucy twisted on the floor to fire off two further shots. The first tore through Yash's left calf. The second thumped into the door. Tyler reached it the moment it clicked shut while Melissa drew her gun.

"Call Blithe!"

Chapman recovered enough to speed-dial security.

"CODE BLACK. KILL THE LIFTS. KILL ALL THE LIFTS, NOW!"

Tyler bolted after Yash as Lucy joined her. They glimpsed him turning at the end of the passage and followed, shooting. Albert *uncloaked* ahead of her, sprinting after Yash. At the turning, Tyler and Lucy retreated as bullets blasted the opposite wall. Albert continued and they quickly lost sight of him.

"He has a gun! Where did that come from?" asked Tyler, her back to the corner of the wall.

"We never checked him. He could've carried it on his ankle. Albert's on him."

"But Albert doesn't even have a blade. All he can do is follow."

They heard the lift doors opening and turned the corner to see Yash slip in. Lucy took a shot as he ducked safely behind the lift's side wall. The polished steel doors closed. Albert *cloaked*. Tyler ran to a wall console.

"Take the stairs," she told Lucy. She scanned her thumb to open the biometric lock on the console and pressed the alert button to speak through the facility's audio system. Hidden speakers around the building relayed and amplified her voice as Lucy hit the stairs.

"Suspect loose and armed. Locate and contain Yash Baines." A repetitive alarm droned loudly. She sprinted to the lift. Melissa turned the corner as Tyler hammered the lift button with her fist.

"He's heading down," said Tyler. "Lucy's taking the stairs but she'll never outrun the lift."

Tyler leapt down the stairs three at a time. At the end of the second flight she turned into an empty lift atrium. The lift was dead, its number display unlit. The level appeared deserted. She bounded down steps to the next floor and found Lucy training her gun on the closed lift doors.

Lucy glanced at her, keeping the gun trained on the lift.

"Either he got off on three or he's trapped between floors."

"Level three's a ghost town. I think we have him."

Security officers in flak jackets and SWAT gear flooded into the surrounding area, guns trained on the lift. Chapman arrived, gun in hand.

"Where is he?"

"We think he's trapped between levels two and three. He shot out the cameras." Tyler jutted her chin towards the stairs. "Get a team up to level three and tell security to repower the lifts."

A tense moment passed, drowned by the droning alarm. The lift lights blinked on and its deep, hydraulic rumble resumed. Tyler used the *Present Eye* to search for Yash but before she could focus in on the lift, it arrived and the mechanical doors opened.

Lucy made a quick sweep of the inner space.

"Empty. He's gone."

"Check the ceiling," said Tyler. Security men battered ceiling panelling aside with the muzzles of their guns and hoisted up an officer to check the shaft vault.

"All clear," he reported.

"Damn it, where's he gone?" said another of the officers.

A voice issued from an officer's radio.

"Lift atrium all clear on level three. Repeat, all clear on level three."

Zebedee appeared beside Tyler.

"They've missed him. He *is* on level three, heading deeper in. Albert's following."

"We're in lockdown," said Lucy. There's nowhere he can go."

Tyler took a radio from an officer and headed back up the stairs, gun poised and the bad feeling in her gut expanding.

Something's wrong.

Kylie met her at the top of the stairs.

"This way." She waved Tyler on down the corridor, leading the way. They passed several doorways to wind their way through more corridors and junctions, until Kylie stopped by a door signed *Data* and pointed.

"He went in there."

Droplets of fresh blood marked the floor. Tyler rapped on the door with the butt of her P99.

"Come out, Yash!" She listened to silence and glanced inside through the *Present Eye* but found the room utterly dark except for several blinking red LEDs. "Albert, are you in there?"

She put two shots through the wood of the door and listened. Still no sound from within. Two officers joined her at the door, guns poised. She nodded and reached for the door. Lucy rounded the corner to shout.

"Wait! Who knows what resources he has tucked away? The door could be booby-trapped."

"We can't hang around. Kylie saw him go in there."

"Then let me do it. This is all my fault. I should have stopped him. Get back."

Tyler grabbed Lucy to drag her away from the door. "It's not your fault, Lucy! Wait!"

Melissa arrived as Lucy fought free.

"What's going on?"

"We think the room could be booby-trapped."

"Then wait for bomb disposal."

"Yash is still free." Lucy grabbed the door handle as Albert drifted through the wall to shout.

"NO!"

His cry was obliterated by a blast that erupted from the doorway and rocked the building. The outer wall blew apart in a thunderous ball of flames taking Lucy with it while Tyler and Melissa, sheltered by the wall, staggered back from the heat. Smoke and dust rose from the gaping hole. Below, shrapnel rippled the surface of the Thames for hundreds of metres as smoke drifted over the water.

Melissa screamed.

"LUCY!"

Tyler stared, unwilling to comprehend what she had seen.

Lucy's dead. Lucy's gone.

She felt a panic rising in her chest but was unable to subdue it. Her heart pounded as though it might rip a hole in her rib cage. Her breathing hastened until she hyperventilated, the rapid, unstoppable breaths incapacitating.

"Lucy," she murmured between gasps.

Melissa stooped over her, pale as the moon, and Tyler's world dimmed. Gasping for air, she passed out.

*

Tyler remained unconscious for six minutes before her breathing returned to normal and she surfaced to the red and blue flashing lights of emergency services, and Melissa, watching over her. Dazed and wishing she had not woken, she allowed the paramedics to test her responses.

Lucy was dead and everything had changed forever.

The Reverie

The service was brief and sterile. Chapman walked stiffly to the podium and, for a moment that felt like eternity, viewed the congregation. Every seat of the conference hall was occupied. He let his gaze brush over Mr and Mrs Denby in the front row, unable to meet their eyes. He cleared his throat, polished his glasses and set them on his nose before grabbing the podium for support.

"Lucy Denby was an officer of outstanding quality.

"In life she was hardworking and highly gifted in physical ability. She was a sharp-shooter and a skilled officer. She was brave, honest and resolute, and her commitment to the Service was second to none. Her dedication and no-nonsense attitude will forever be remembered." He paused, appearing to want to say more, but left the podium.

At the end of the service the reverend closed with a bible reading.

"John, chapter five, verse thirteen. Greater love has no one than this: to lay down one's life for one's friends."

*

Nothing of Lucy's body was recovered from the waters of the Thames, though Mr and Mrs Denby requested a proper burial to provide a place and a headstone to visit. Lucy's casket contained only the shredded remains of her leather jacket as the bearers lowered it into the ground in a graveyard reserved for servicemen and women. When the short ceremony attended by close friends and family ended, Tyler looked for Chapman. She spied him under verbal attack near the hearse and rushed to weave through the scatter of mourners.

"...worthless promises and reassurances. You said she would be working under the protection of the best, that she would receive the finest training available, that she would have prospects of a long and fulfilling career." Mrs Denby stepped closer, her heavily-lipsticked mouth inches from Chapman's face. "You said you would personally watch over her. What happened?"

Mr Denby attempted to draw his wife away apologetically but failed.

"I did everything poss–"

Tyler pushed her way between Chapman and Mrs Denby to interrupt.

"He did everything within his power to protect Lucy, to protect us all. He always has. Lucy chose to sacrifice herself to save those around her. It was *Lucy's* choice, *not* his. *This* man nearly died working to make our country, *your* country, a safer place. You owe him your gratitude. We all do."

Tyler stared Mrs Denby out until she walked. Chapman watched Mrs Denby go before turning to Tyler, dour faced.

"That's the second time you've saved me this week."

"And it's the last, Sir." She handed him a white envelope bearing his name in her careful handwriting. "I'm resigning. I've thought long and hard about it and I don't want to do this anymore. I *can't* do this anymore, not without Lucy."

He frowned, irritation registering in his eyes.

"Resignation denied. You're needed, now more than ever."

"But, Sir..."

"No. Put it out of your head, Tyler. In case you haven't noticed, there's a war on and I've just lost two more agents. I can't afford to lose another."

"I know. I'm sorry. It's just that I can't function without the team and without Lucy there *is* no team. It's over."

Chapman threw her a measuring look and exhaled.

"Listen, I knew a talented, young school girl once. Amazing what she could do with nothing but a bag of smoke bombs and her own God-given courage."

"Now I know you're biased. I had the contrap even then."

"That maybe so, but the point's the same. It was your courage that shone through. Back then you had an uncommon valour and it's still in you. Tyler, I'm not superstitious but I believe the contrap came to you for a reason. I don't think it's your time to quit. Take some leave. See how you feel in a few days."

Tyler gazed across the graveyard at Melissa staring at Lucy's open grave. She felt his hand rest on her shoulder.

"I'm very sorry about Lucy. I know it's no consolation but Yash will never see the light of day again."

Tyler knew Yash had survived the blast but would be horrifically scarred for life from burns to his upper body and face. He was already in a high security prison.

"Did you know there's a reason she wore black?"

Tyler shook her head.

"It was in the background check we ran on her before we took you girls on for training. At the age of nine she lost a younger brother, Jonathan, to meningitis. She self-harmed for a few years after that until her second year of secondary school. At twelve she stopped self-harming but she never stopped wearing black, never stopped mourning him. I suppose she felt guilty in a way because his life was taken and hers was not. And by the way, her grandparents on her mother's side were Jewish survivors the Sobibor Nazi death camp."

Chapman left her as Albert appeared at her side, slipping his cap from his head.

"Cheer up, Missy. We're all on a journey an' we got a long way to go before we reaches the end."

*

Melissa glared red-eyed at Lucy's belongings, her clothes tossed over the foot of her bed, her CDs, books and magazines. Grimly, she began packing everything into boxes for return to Mr and Mrs Denby. Six boxes later she opened a drawer and stopped, staring at a padded envelope. She read Lucy's handwriting on the front.

For Mel, in the event of my death.

*

Tyler took out the contrap and switched to the *Tower of Doom*. For three days she had viewed it only to find a half-ruined tower. Several times when she squinted and strained her eye, she glimpsed a lone ghost sitting on the top of the rubble wall and once she saw several tiny figures moving there. None had waved.

Now she blinked at the miniature amber scene. Hundreds of ghosts lined the walls and one wiry figure she fancied was Weaver stood higher than all the rest, with his hands at his sides, simply gazing back at her.

This is it! They're ready to come out of the *Chasm*. Weaver's done it!

*

Tyler busied herself in her house, cleaning and perfecting the positioning of her few ornaments and arranging her furniture. She felt safer knowing Albert was there. Each waking moment of the nights since her return from Greenland she had looked up from her bed to see him standing sentry at her window, his narrow figure framed against the moonlight on her curtains.

Zebedee and the rest of the Ghost Squad never seemed far away. She had only to call and they would appear before her. Two days remained before Klaus was to visit. She smiled at the prospect of spending time with him in her home, away from any mission.

She played CDs, vacuumed carpets and polished cutlery obsessively, anything to avoid dwelling on Lucy's death. She sat in the lounge and drafted list after list of challenges, trying to outline on one small page the monumental tasks ahead of her. One after the other she screwed the lists up and tossed them into the waste bin, the enormity of it all too great.

At twenty past two that afternoon her mobile rang, its shrill tone cutting through *Winter Song* playing on her stereo. Abandoning her lists she crossed the room to answer it.

"Hello."

"Hi, Tyler. How's you?"

"Not great. You?"

"Same. I've spent all day studying the book. I was just trying to keep busy but I think I've found something. Do you fancy coming over."

*

Melissa opened the door, her makeup smudged and blurred around her eyes.

"Hi," said Tyler. Melissa bit her lip to fight back her brimming emotions and tilted her head.

Come on in.

Tyler entered to stare at the apartment where Lucy's possessions were meticulously boxed and labelled.

"Maybe we should have met at mine."

"No, it's okay, really. Life goes on. I packed her stuff."

"So I see. I bet that's the most organised she's ever been."

"I also found this." Melissa held up a mobile phone and tapped the screen. "She left it for me, a duplicate of her phone with automatic backup. You want to know why?"

"Why?"

"Because she knew she was going to die one of these days and she didn't want all her work to be wasted."

"What work?"

"I checked the phone last night. TAAN now has over six thousand members. That's six thousand street warriors ready to fight our cause, six thousand, each contactable with a simple text from *Mojo*."

"Wow. I had no idea she'd reached that many."

Their eyes fell upon Abraham Eleazar's strange manuscript, open on the coffee table.

"What about the book?"

"I found the answer to the ring, I think."

"You mean how to summon reveries?"

Melissa nodded.

"I haven't tried it. I don't *want* to try it. When I realised it was time, I called you."

"I s'pose it's not every day one commands reveries, is it?"

"Exactly. I thought it would be better to wait until you were here, just in case anything goes wrong."

"What could possibly go wrong? So we're going to summon a reverie, right now. All of a sudden that sounds crazy."

"It *is* crazy. Maybe we shouldn't."

"But if we have the power to control the reveries it could change everything. Think of all the times Heydrich set them on us, all the times we could have fought back or just sent them away."

"I know, but now it comes to it, I really don't want to do it."

"But you know we have to, right?"

Again Melissa nodded, her eyes flitting from Tyler to the book and to the ring of gallows iron on her own finger.

"Show me what you found."

They sat on the couch and Melissa pointed to a section on an open page.

"This list caught my eye. It's the same list of archaic names as inscribed on the ring. An obvious connection, so I began translating the surrounding texts. It's written in an odd style that's hard to understand but I think I have the gist of it now." She indicated an illustration of an ouroboros on the opposite page. Within it nestled a second smaller ring. "See this? It's not just an image representing the gallows ring. It's a circle, an empty circle, to be precise. The smaller ouroboros inside represents the gallows ring, a ring within a ring."

"I'm not sure I follow."

"No, neither did I at first. The question was, empty of what?"

"So what's the answer?"

"Gallows iron."

"What else?"

"Yes, it kind of makes sense in a weird way. There's also a measurement noted. It meant nothing to me until I realised it is a radius, given in cubits. To operate the ring you must be standing in a circle with a radius of three cubits, free of gallows iron, except for the ring, of course. That's a circle of around two and a half metres." She pulled a length of chalk from her pocket to show Tyler.

"Ready?"

"I don't know. This gives me the creeps. It's witchcraft, isn't it?"

Melissa levelled her gaze at Tyler.

"And what do you think the contrap is? What are you doing each time you use that thing?"

"Yeah, but I'm not drawing circles on the ground and all that hocus pocus."

"What's the difference?"

Tyler stared at Melissa for a moment.

390

"Sometimes you have to fight fire with fire," said Melissa.

"But if you play with fire you get burned."

"Look, we can sit here all day waring in clichés or we can get on with it. Didn't we fight to get the book in the first place so that we could learn how to use the ring?"

"Okay, we'll do it, but only to help us fight the oppressor. Only until we've won and he is gone, then we destroy the ring, the contrap and every gallows blade in existence. Agreed?"

"Agreed!"

They stood.

"Give me a hand," said Melissa grasping an end of the coffee table. Tyler took the other and they carried the table to the side of the room leaving an area free of obstructions. Melissa measured, chalked a circled and stood at its centre. "Oh!" She pulled a gallows blade from the inside of her boot and handed it to Tyler. "Take this and stand over there."

Tyler stood away from the chalk line while Melissa hesitantly read the list of names from the book.

"Namtar, Anzu, Pazuzu, Ninurta, Asag..." She enunciated each name with careful precision until the last of the seven names was uttered and waited, the only sound the ticking of the lounge wall-clock. Two minutes passed. When nothing happened she looked at Tyler.

"Oh well, we gave it a shot."

"Wait," said Tyler. "I feel something. Someone's coming! A ghost is closing in!"

A sudden movement by the window startled them. They watched a reverie pass through the wall. Unshaven and wearing tattered clothes and a grimy leather cap, the vagrant ghost stood, gawping. It released a low, zombie-like moan.

Melissa backed away, staring at the ghost tramp, a mixture of fear and wonder distorting her features as afternoon light cascaded through his miasma to pool on the floor.

"Test it out, Mel! Give it some orders."

"Sit down," commanded Melissa. Slowly, the reverie sat cross-legged on the floor.

"Stand."

He stood gawking and awaiting further instruction.

"It works, Tyler. It works!"

"Yes, I see that. Mel, there are more coming. I feel them. Do something! Order them away."

Melissa stared in panic at the iron ring on her finger.

"Now, Mel, or this place will be swarming with reveries!"

Melissa shook herself.

"Return to your haunts." She pointed to the wall where the ghost had entered. With a further groan, the reverie turned and ambled back out, passing through the wall. Melissa flashed a crazed smile at Tyler. She prised the ring from her finger and stepped out of the circle, glancing fearfully at the apartment walls.

Tyler smiled her first tentative smile in days.

"Return to your haunts?"

"It was the only thing I could think of to say. Hey, it worked didn't it?"

"Melissa Watts, Lord of the Reveries."

"*Lady*, no, *Queen* of the Reveries, if you don't mind!"

"You did it! You can command them! Do you realise what this means?"

392

"Yeah. We're gonna give Heydrich a run for his money." Melissa stared at the wall. "I wish Lucy had been here to see that."

Epilogue

Tyler switched to the *Tower of Doom*. She wanted to check no rescued sleepers remained trapped in the tower and she wondered how the tower would rank her current situation. She had the Ghost Squad back, an experienced crack team of phantom spies under her command. She had Albert, watching over her twenty-four hours a day and, through him, the support of an entire army of rescued sleepers. She had the contrap and all its accompanying powers and Melissa could summon and command reveries through the gallows ring.

Surely the dodgy old tower should be high if not almost complete.

She blinked at the scene beyond the lens. The tower had somehow managed to dilapidate further since her last viewing.

How can that be?

A flicker in the crystal truncated her moment of disappointment as she found herself suddenly staring into the *Ghost Portal*. She glanced up to make sure no one was messing with the contrap. Albert stood watching the night through her bedroom window but she was otherwise alone.

So who made the switch to Ghost Portal*?*

She swallowed and peered back into the crystal to see the huge, dark planet of the portal's sky had descended and drawn nearer, pressing through eddies of grey memory mist.

"The Black Sun."

As she watched, it swivelled like an enormous, featureless, roving eye before coming to a brisk halt, as though locking into place. Tyler stared in terror as the oppressor's wry laughter echoed in her mind.

It *was* an enormous eye. And the enormous eye was looking at *her*.

*

The following day Tyler and Melissa met to visit Lucy's grave. Melissa drove and Tyler talked most of the way aware that any silence would result in an unwelcome focus. Neither wanted to talk about the possibility of Lucy's ghost making an appearance, although they both knew it was possible and that it was the reason for their visit so soon after the funeral. Independently they had reached the same unspoken conclusion.

No body to bury, no proper burial, which means she might roam. And where do the newly dead like to hang out if not at their gravesides?

Tyler's phone rang. She took it from her pocket and answered a call from an unrecognised number.

"Who is this?"

"As welcoming as ever, Tyler."

She knew the voice immediately and turned to Melissa.

"It's Sova.

"How's the investigation going, Sova, if that's your real name."

Laughter sounded on the other end of the line.

"Are you with the girls? I have news."

"I'm with Mel." Tyler left it at that. Explanations could wait for another time. "Wait, I'll put you on speaker. There, we're listening."

"I thought you would like to know, we found Řezník Barak. He's beaten up but safe. We tracked him down to a prison cell in a remote Austrian castle. My people are investigating the entire place. It's been running as a centre for the NVF."

"Can you keep us informed of further developments? Any intelligence regarding the NVF could be useful, Special Agent Sova."

"Of course, of course, but that's Commander, if you don't mind. I've just been promoted for my efforts in the case."

"Congratulations, Commander. Well done."

"Thank you."

"Look after yourself. Goodbye."

Sova hung up and Tyler pocketed her phone as the cemetery came into view.

Melissa turned the car into the car park and Tyler reached into the back seat for the black flowers ordered especially with Lucy in mind. They entered the grounds through the scrolling iron gates, the only breathing visitors. Walking to Lucy's grave they passed a hundred other headstones and stone crosses. A scatter of larger monuments sprang tall and pale, tranquil angels with praying hands and folded wings, embellished arches and obelisks.

Lucy's gravestone was not yet erected but a colourful bed of wreathes and bouquets, left by mourners, rose from the settling soil. Tyler and Melissa added their black offerings of dahlias, hellebores, lilies and night tulips.

"She would have liked these," said Melissa, arranging her bouquet among the others.

Tyler searched for Lucy's ghost. She scanned the far reaches of the cemetery and sensed several harmless reveries, but Lucy was not among them. A few moments of silent disappointment passed.

"Mel, could you give me a few minutes alone. I've a few things I want to say."

"Sure." Melissa left the graveside.

Tyler waited until Melissa was beyond earshot before beginning. She stared at the soil heap.

"I'm sorry. It was a brave and selfless thing you did. I'm grateful. Everybody's grateful. I guess you proved what kind of a person you really were in the end. We'll miss you, Mojo. We'll miss your overbearing negativity and your big, stomping boots because, in a weird way, you made us smile and you helped us get through. I've never met anyone else quite like you and there'll never be another.

"Anyway, I don't want to get all sappy but I had to say, thank you. You saved my life more times than I remember and I wish I could have done the same for you.

"But I have to say, your timing *really sucks*! I can't believe you chose to leave us right now, *right now* when we need you the most! You swore a pact, Lucy. The three of us promised to free the gloved kids. Did you forget that?"

*

Melissa drove and Tyler remained quiet until the silence swelled to an unbearable peak.

"I don't know why but I had to get a few things off my chest. Lucy was–"

"A royal pain in the–"

"Yes!" Tyler laughed through tears. "But she was great with it. It felt weird taking to an empty grave, though."

"Yeah. I really thought she might be there, but I guess *no body* means she'll never be a reverie hanging round her grave because it's not a real grave."

Tyler thought for a moment.

"Not *her* grave... Mel, turn the car around. Wrong cemetery!"

The Tyler May series so far

The Haunting of Tyler May
(book one)

The Thieves of Antiquity
(book two)

The Brimstone Chasm
(book three)

Gallows Iron
(book four)

Ghosts of Redemption
(book five)

Follow the Tyler May series
www.tylermay.co.uk

Acknowledgements

Ghosts of Redemption was edited by Edward Field.

Cover Artwork
Photographic images provided by Winternetmedia.
Image of Prague's astronomical clock courtesy of Charles Sibthorpe.
Concept and graphic design by The Dream Loft.
Featured models: Oriana Weids, Dainelle Grant and Joyy Tamsett.